CW01624632

AUTOMAN

Slowly the vapour was taking on the form of a man with the proportions and bearing of a Greek god. Bright rays of light radiated from him like a shining white aura. He was tall. Six foot four at least. But what was startling was that while his face, perfect in every detail, was real enough, his body was luminously translucent, as though he were clad in a shining blue gridlike armour, similar to the VDU's graphic display. Through it there seemed to be a kind of Milky Way of twinkling stars which were impossible to look at for long without turning away, for every star had the brilliance of a laser.

The rays of light began to spin and all at once the Adonis came to life. He turned to Walter and regarded him with penetrating blue eyes.

'Hello, Automan,' Walter said sheepishly.

By the same author

PRIVATE SCHULZ (with Jack Pulman)
BULLSHOT
BLOODBATH AT THE HOUSE OF DEATH

AUTOMAN

Novelisation by
Martin Noble
based on the original teleplay by
Glen A. Larson

A TARGET BOOK
published by
the Paperback Division of
W. H. ALLEN & Co. PLC

A Target Book
Published in 1984
by the Paperback Division of
W. H. Allen & Co. PLC
44 Hill Street, London W1X 8LB

Copyright © 1984 Twentieth Century Fox Film Corporation

Printed in Great Britain by
Anchor Brendon Ltd, Tiptree, Essex

ISBN 0 426 19975 8

This book is sold subject to the condition that it shall not, by way of trade or otherwise, be lent, re-sold, hired out or otherwise circulated without the publisher's prior consent in any form of binding or cover other than that in which it is published and without a similar condition including this condition being imposed on upon the subsequent purchaser.

Prologue

SUBJECT: WALTER NEBICHER
DESCRIPTION: MILD MANNERED COMPUTER WHIZZKID WITH DELUSIONS OF BECOMING A CRIMEFIGHTER
LOCATION: COMPUTER SECTION, LOS ANGELES POLICE DEPARTMENT (LAPD)
KNOWN ASSOCIATES: LT JACK CURTIS, ROXANNE CALDWELL, LAPD
KNOWN ENEMIES: CAPTAIN E. G. BOYD, CHIEF OF DEPARTMENT, LAPD
SPECIAL PECULIARITIES: AUTOMAN

I'd better start by saying that I'm just an old-fashioned street cop with the kind of name that's easy to remember, easy to forget – Jack Curtis. Not like Wally Nebicher – no one could ever quite forget a name like that, but then again no one could ever quite remember it either. He was a walking disaster but when he sat down at that console of his, well, then you weren't just dealing with Wally, you were dealing with the eighth wonder of the world . . .

There's some things you should know about Walter. Like when he was a lonely, spotty, skinny thirteen year old with a body like a stick of celery he was already a budding professor. Maybe he couldn't talk to people but his keyboard was learning how to tap out some neat chunks of dialogue. Soon he was dreaming up all these arcade games with names like Mousetron and Guzzlemat. He wasn't doing it for money, fame or glory – most of these games were too far out in any case to be commercial. But they were clever, you'd have to say that. It was like he was experimenting, stretching himself.

But that wasn't Wally's hangup. See, he developed this obsession. It all began when he teamed up with another oddball, name of Ralph Donetti but known as Donut. It seems they'd got this shared interest – or fantasy – picturing themselves as crimefighters: Starsky and Hutch, Batman and Robin, something like that.

The trouble was, Nature had decided different. Nobody ever saw Donut run in his life. As for Wally, well, you'd be doing him a big favour calling him uncoordinated, physically that is. Adolescence kind of landed on Wally like a giant pimple and stuck around a dozen years for the laughs. Parts of him grew too quickly and then gave up. Other parts didn't get the message and carried on growing. Like his arms and feet.

Wally was not someone you would want to hang around with in a car if he was doing the driving. But if you put him in front of a computer and let his fingers do the walking, that was another matter. Maybe he was a genius, but for some reason none of his computer stuff ever got off the ground until he created Automan. There – you see? I wasn't going to mention *him* but you just never know when or where he's going to turn up.

Back to Walter. As you might expect, his parents wanted that their only son should be a credit to them – maybe even be a doctor like his father. But Wally had other plans. He wanted to go and join the Los Angeles Police Department as a street cop, fighting for truth, justice and the American Way. Before Ma Nebicher died from hysterics a compromise was reached. Wally would forget cops and robbers, the Nebichers would forget doctors and nurses. Instead he landed a scholarship to Berkeley, majoring in never phoning home and specialising in giving his mother heartache. Somehow he also graduated in electronics and went on to MIT on some fancy research fellowship.

Now comes the interesting part. You would think after ten years that Wally would have grown out of his adolescent dreams of crime-busting. But suddenly here's the wonderboy back in LA, and that was when I first met him – in the new computer section of the LAPD. The cat came back. This time he'd got Washington and millions of dollars behind him because he was apparently heading a team of analysts who, Captain Boyd told us (the poor guy looked like he was having a seizure as he said it), were supposed to be dragging our antiquated police methods into the 1980s.

Boyd (he runs the department if you haven't guessed) hated Wally's guts before he had even set foot in the squad room. Me, I reserved my judgment. We've all got a job to do. Well, it turned out that the team of analysts consisted of Wally Nebicher and his computer – but the kid was all right. He was keen. And apart from all these crazy ideas of his and the way he started to follow me round the office like a lost sheep, I figured I might even get to learn something from him.

So now you have it. There was me, Lt Jack Curtis, a member of the old school. Walter Nebicher, a member of the new school. And then there was Automan.

I'd sure as hell like to know what school *he* came out of.

1

'Hey, come on honey . . . I'm only going to be gone a week . . . and it could change our whole lives.'

Joanne Wills fought back the tears.

'But a week is such a long time,' she sobbed.

'You can always give Paul a ring.'

Paul worked with Martin Wills at Globalcom where they were both top computer engineers. But maybe not for too much longer. If Marty got this job it would be goodbye LA and hello London. She tried to smile. She knew her husband was right but the house would seem so empty without him. Maybe she *would* give Paul a ring. She began to smile.

'Hey, that's better,' Wills murmured, wiping her eyes solicitously.

Joanne nodded.

'Let me do it,' she said with mild exasperation. 'You'll make a mess.'

A grating whine came over the PA.

'This is the final boarding call for Transglobal Flight No. 525 non-stop to London –'

Wills bent down to kiss his two young daughters.

'Now you two'll take good care of Mommy, won't you.'

'We will,' said Karen.

'No, we won't,' said Jane confidently. 'Uncle Paul will do that. I heard him say so.'

'Kids!' Wills said affectionately.

'Don't forget to buy our dollies in London,' said Karen, picking her nose.

'Would Daddy forget your dollies?'

'Uncle Paul says –'

The roar of a departing Boeing 747 drowned the rest of the shattering revelation. Martin released his daughters, gave Joanne a final hug and bent to pick up his leather attache case.

'One week,' he repeated, waving goodbye.

Joanne and the two little girls waved back. She grew pensive as she walked them out of the departure area, thinking of Paul. Suddenly a week seemed very short.

Two clean-cut men in executive suits had been observing the touching scene. As one moved hurriedly towards the boarding tube, the other spoke into a tiny airport walkie-talkie.

'We're ready,' said Peterson, a bland, silken-voiced New Englander with strong chin and weak eyes.

Two stewardesses were checking boarding passes at the door of the tube.

'Oh, Mr Wills,' called out Peterson, hurrying up to him, as Martin turned to look. 'Thank goodness we caught you in time.'

'In time for what? I was just about to catch a plane.'

Collins nodded understandingly. 'Mr Davis would like you to phone him before you board.'

Wills glanced apprehensively at his watch, darting an anxious look at the passengers boarding the plane. As if to reassure him, Peterson opened his wallet and showed it to him.

'Security,' Martin read. 'Well, if the boss wants me to call . . .' he cast a searching eye over both men – they looked like it was serious '. . . I guess I call.'

'I certainly would,' Collins murmured, with all the sympathy and deference of a well-groomed barracuda.

*

'I can't believe this,' said Willis grinning broadly as he stepped out a phone booth five minutes later. 'How many engineers get to fly the corporate jet?'

'You must be pretty important to your company,' said Peterson as the two men escorted him towards the escalator.

Martin coughed modestly. 'I don't guarantee this'll change my mind about taking that job with the competition.'

'We really wouldn't know anything about that,' laughed Collins. For an instant his eyes met those of Peterson.

Fifteen minutes later a black limousine pulled up next to a large private jet in a sparsely occupied area of the airport's private terminal.

'Well,' said Wills as he climbed out of the limo and looked up at the massive plane, 'they do know how to impress a guy.' He stared at the advanced lines of the Gulfstream SMA-3 multi-mission executive jet and whistled.

Peterson and Collins smiled as they gestured to him to board the plane. At the top of the steps stood a dazzling young stewardess.

'I can't believe this whole thing is for me,' Martin gushed, staring at the stewardess.

'Right this way, Mr Wills,' she said. He followed her into the super-plush interior and installed himself in one of the few seats, gazing at the lavish bar, the subdued lighting.

'I mean . . . this is class.' He smiled happily up at Collins who loomed above him.

'You'll never be the same,' Collins replied, joining Peterson in a seat behind him.

'Here you are sir,' said the stewardess, pouring him a drink.

‘Thank *you*,’ said Wills, lifting his glass and turning round to Peterson who grinned back at him.

Collins was not smiling. A veiled, menacing look had transformed his sharp Celtic features, as he reached inside his jacket for a revolver which he quietly loaded.

The Gulfstream SMA-3 roared down the runway, lifted up and streaked off into the night. Flames shot backwards out of the high-speed Rolls-Royce fanjets. Within moments it had disappeared into the murky unknown of a dark night . . .

2

Armageddon was drawing to a terrifying climax somewhere in deep Deep Space. In seconds galaxies were born and died. Stars exploded in brilliant supernova cascades, instantly degenerating into white dwarfs. From the cockpit of a vast and powerful supersonic flying machine multicoloured lasers were being fired and from other starships lasers flew back across the screen from every angle. Some actually shot *through* the screen with a piercing, ear-shattering whine.

In the far distance a blue starship appeared, heading directly towards the cockpit.

A pair of eyes, intent, dedicated, assured, spotted it instantly. Fingers ruthlessly pulled the trigger.

Zooooom . . . . wheeeeee . . . . kerponggg! Boom, boom, boom!

Walter Nebicher, star pilot of the universe, had sealed his enemy's fate.

A pink space-fighter sneaked across the horizon. Nebicher zapped it in microseconds. It exploded into a myriad of tiny fragments.

'*Enemy destroyed*!' came a low-pitched computer-synthesised voice.

P. J. Hawkins was impressed – terrified would be more accurate. He was perspiring freely.

'Awright!' he wheezed breathlessly. All this was really out of his league.

'We're not out of danger yet,' said Walter quickly.

A klaxon sounded and a second synthesised voice, this time vaguely female by the register and intonation: '*Danger, danger, danger . . . Alien vessel coming in fast and locked on target*!'

Out of nowhere there appeared another alien ship, gargantuan and menacing, and coming in too fast to stop. It fired and smoke rose up *in front of* the cockpit; it actually seemed to Hawkins that smoke and flames were dancing around him. The star pilots were doomed.

'*Abandon ship, abandon ship, abandon ship . . . we are destroyed*!'

P. J. Hawkins stared at Walter in amazement.

'What happened?'

'Nobody's perfect.' Wally shrugged.

They were seated in Walter's crude basement workshop. Debris from many months of late-night sessions – Coke tins, the shattered carcases of VDUs and a chicken (supplied by Dolly Nebicher on her first and last visit to Wally's Hollywood apartment), electronics magazines and candy wrappers – had occupied all available floor space like squatters. The flames engulfing them were being projected from a Cineramic screen. Walter flicked a switch and the flames disappeared. The screen went blank. Starfighter 3-D had run its course.

Hawkins exhaled.

'Those flames are so real I hurt.'

Walter clambered out of his cockpit seat. There was a loud screech, followed by a bloodcurdling wail, a terrifying hiss, a pitiful mew and the pounding of retreating paws.

'That's the beauty of 3-D,' he said enthusiastically, after he'd given up trying to entice the cat out of its hiding place inside a disused washing machine. 'It puts you *in* the game. So . . . what do you think?'

'You want the truth?' said Hawkins, back in his role

of aggressive hustler as he climbed out of the cockpit and blew his nose, looking distastefully at a mouldy pizza.

'Sure,' said Walter nervously.

'Agent to client?'

'Of course.'

'You're too late. I had fifteen hundred orders lined up when you first told me about it.' He joined Walter who was standing by the computer reading a printout. 'Now . . . I got less than fifty. Other people are out with 3-D, faster and better.'

Walter dragged his attention away from the printout.

'Not better,' he said indignantly.

'Maybe,' Hawkins conceded grudgingly. 'But I really came to tell you to pull the plug on this one.'

Walter blinked nervously and pulled himself up to his full five foot five inches.

'Mr Hawkins . . . I've invested a lot of money in this game. Practically everything I earned off Space Monkey.'

The middleman sighed. 'What can I tell you . . . You took too long.'

He instantly regretted saying it. The poor nebish looked like he was going to cry. (Wrong – Wally was having problems with his new 3-D contact lenses.)

'You got anything else?' said Hawkins gruffly.

Walter hesitated, then turned away, moving to a dark corner of the basement where there was some kind of large rectangular object obscured by a black drape. Hawkins may have imagined it but, for a moment, as Walter put out a reverential hand towards it, a low hum and a vibration akin to that of a miniature earthquake seemed to be emitted.

Walter shook his head. 'It isn't ready.'

Hawkins shook his head as well. 'Kid . . . if I were a

betting man, I'd say . . . it never will be. You're a dreamer. I think you oughta stick to the little home-video stuff.'

Walter sighed. Explaining it to Hawkins was going to be like teaching relativity to a baboon.

'No one's going to touch me on this one for years, Mr Hawkins . . . It's . . . scary.'

Hawkins nodded knowingly. 'Scary . . . like in a horror game? They already got those in 3-D. Apes coming at you . . . cobras . . . guys with spears. . . .'

'I mean scary as in too real,' said Walter.

Hawkins stared at him. 'I don't think I follow . . .'

'You ever heard of a hologram?'

'A what?'

'It's a three-dimensional image that can be created without the use of a screen.'

Hawkins was well out of his depth.

'So . . . ?' he said, wiping the sweat off his forehead. The workshop was at the correct low temperature but he glowed even in frost.

'I'm on the verge of perfecting it,' Walter explained. 'I just need access to more power.'

'Uh, huh,' Hawkins muttered dubiously.

This was too much for Walter. 'All right,' he declared. 'You think you're on the frontier of software in games . . . Hold on to your hat, Mr Hawkins.'

With a touch of ostentation he whipped back the black drape to unveil not a sophisticated piece of video arcadery but an old floor safe which had probably been manufactured in the early 1900s. Bending down he started to work on the combination.

Hawkins scratched his armpit.

'A little melodramatic, isn't it?'

'You won't say that when you see it,' said Walter, removing a small cartridge from the safe.

Hawkins tried to peer over his shoulder. 'What is that? A home game? I thought we were talking arcade.'

Walter ignored him. Going over to the computer he fed in the cartridge and began to punch up a program. Graphics appeared on the VDU, at first in grid form, but quickly developing into the clear profile of a human male which began to rotate first horizontally then vertically. At each rotation, the figure sharpened in detail.

'I call it Automan . . . He's a crime fighter,' said Walter modestly.

Hawkins looked at his watch. 'That thing's a crime fighter? I don't know if that has any real snap for a kid . . . You know?'

'No, that's just a graphic display,' said Walter, stepping back from the console. There was a pause.

'Something supposed to happen?' said Hawkins, clearly getting bored.

'It's calling up the next phase of the program,' Walter replied distractedly, checking the readout with the recent printout.

'Uh, huh? What's it do now, find itself a mugger?'

Walter did not reply. Suddenly there was a slight rumble. Then the whole workshop seemed to judder. Flakes of old paint and pieces of plaster came down from the ceiling. A Seven-up bottle began to dance around on a rickety table and the primitive ceiling light started to swing. Hawkins was sweating again; his fingers groped for a table.

'Hey, what is this?' he said, looking round the room in alarm.

'Shhh . . .'

The next moment the low-pitched rumble began to rise in tempo and pitch until it was oscillating at an incredible rate. The Seven-up bottle shattered and, almost simultaneously, a dazzlingly bright octagonal sphere burst into mid-air, glowing, dancing, spinning . . .

3

'What the hell is *that*?' gasped Hawkins, his eyes on stalks. 'It looks like a high-voltage Tinkerbell!'

Walter turned and looked about to find P. J. Hawkins standing on the stairs leading out of the basement. He looked like he was back in Starfighter 3-D and had just been sucked into a black hole. The sphere continued to dance around him.

'In a way, you're close. It's a cursor.'

'You're darn right it's a curse,' wheezed Hawkins.

'No, curs*or*. Like on a computer. It sort of points the way to what's coming next.'

Hawkins eyed him suspiciously. 'There's a *next*?'

Even as he said it, a vapour began to appear in the room. As it swirled around it started to take shape. Hawkins backed further up the stairs.

Slowly the vapour was taking on the form of a man with the proportions and bearing of a Greek god. Bright rays of light radiated from him like a shining white aura. He was tall. Six foot four at least. But what was startling was that while his face, perfect in every detail, was real enough, his body was luminously translucent, as though he were clad in a shining blue gridlike armour, similar to the VDU's graphic display. Through it there seemed to be a kind of Milky Way of twinkling stars which were impossible to look at for long without turning away, for every star had the brilliance of a laser.

One look was enough for Hawkins. He disappeared.

The rays of light began to spin and all at once the Adonis came to life. He turned to Walter and regarded him with penetrating blue eyes.

'Hello, Automan . . . welcome,' Walter said sheepishly.

Automan spoke.

'Thank you, Walter. It's a pleasure to see you.'

The voice was exquisitely modulated, assured, rich, with the faintest echo.

'I must say, Walter, you're very good,' Automan said, examining himself with meticulous care and admiration. 'I look . . . wonderful.'

'If you do say so yourself,' Walter giggled nervously.

Automan looked concerned. 'Well, you programmed me to be honest,' he protested and then paused. 'Tell me, why did you call me Automan?'

'It means that you're the world's first truly automatic man,' said Walter. 'You can do anything because –' he eyed Automan uneasily, '– you're not real.'

'Oh, but I am,' replied Automan firmly. 'I'm as real as you are – just different. And, thanks to you, perfect.'

'Nobody's perfect, Automan.'

'That's not true, Walter. You've programmed me to observe other people and do whatever they can do as well as they can do it.'

Walter looked bashful and tried to think of a suitable reply.

'On a scale of one to ten,' went on Automan, 'think of me as an eleven.' He smiled at Walter complacently.

Walter smiled back feebly. 'I've created a monster,' he muttered under his breath.

Out of the corner of his eye, Walter could see the cursor buzzing around a photograph of a stunning-looking woman which he had pinned to the wall.

'Cursor – what are you doing?'

Cursor was growing exceedingly amorous.

'Yes, yes, I know Roxanne is beautiful. You'll have to

forgive Cursor,' Automan added for Walter's benefit. 'He seems to have your eye for the ladies.'

Walter couldn't blame the cursor. Roxanne Caldwell was a peach and she also happened to work for Captain Boyd down at police headquarters which was how he came to be working with her eight hours a day at the LAPD and dreaming of her at nights. He had still not plucked up enough courage to ask her for a date but he was working on it. So was Cursor.

'Sometimes a programmer gets a little too personally involved in a program,' said Walter. 'Your image is getting much sharper and well-defined, Automan.'

'Yes,' Automan agreed. 'However . . . I must warn you . . . that even the new circuits are drawing far too much amperage for us to be able to . . . Oh, oh . . . Walter!'

Automan was flashing on and off, and sparks were flying from a fuse box in the corner of the basement. Walter rushed over to the computer and shut it off. Immediately the cursor vanished; Automan slowly faded away after it.

'Damn!' said Walter. 'It happened again. I was hoping the new chipboards would reduce his power needs.'

Trembling, Hawkins emerged from the steps where he had been cowering. 'What in the name of heaven was that?'

Walter looked unconcerned. 'Nothing,' he replied.

'What do you mean, nothing? I just saw . . . a something . . . and it *talked*!'

'That was Automan,' Walter said diffidently.

'Automan!' Hawkins was inspired, as if he had created it himself. 'My God, we're rich. No one's working on this.'

Walter shook his head. 'They are . . . but they're way

behind me.'

'Then why are you sitting here looking so depressed? How soon can I have it?'

'I can't work on it here,' sighed Walter, gesturing around the shoddy workshop. 'I haven't enough power. I've tried to work on the computer down at police headquarters, but that isn't real easy. They don't like moonlighting.'

'Kid . . . You get this right, you'll never have to moonlight again.'

'That's not the point,' said Walter, knocking over a mug of cocoa. 'I like police work. I just can't get anybody to take me seriously. They're all afraid of computers. Well, almost all of them,' he added, thinking of his only two allies, Roxanne and Lt Jack Curtis, though even they seemed to regard him merely as an eccentric fixture.

Before Hawkins could reply, the phone began to ring. Hastily, Walter scrambled over to a cluttered corner and picked up the receiver. A pile of dishes crashed to the floor . . .

'Nebicher? This is Jack Curtis,' came the world-weary street-wise voice of Wally's idol.

By reflex Walter sprang to attention. 'Lieutenant –'

'Are you OK, kid?' said Curtis with mild concern, shifting his feet on the desk and idly removing his gun from his shoulder holster. Opening the cartridge case he purged three expended shells, tossing them in the wastebasket. Outside his cubicle uniformed police and plainclothed detectives milled around the squad room. It was as familiar a sight to Curtis as the back of his gun. He often imagined he'd been born in that cubicle.

'Sure, I'm . . . fine,' replied Wally, making a space for himself among the garbage.

'I'm sorry to bother you at home, kid. I got something. It could be important . . . Any chance of you slipping in here tonight?'

'Yes, sir. You bet . . . I'm as good as there.'

The line went dead. Lt Curtis looked at the phone in his hand and smiled for a moment, then his face resumed its normal deadly solemn expression as he quietly reloaded his gun.

'This is exactly what I'm talking about, kid,' shouted Hawkins, gesticulating furiously to catch Walter's attention as Wally hurriedly donned a jacket that said ARCADE on the back. 'You either want to be in the game business or you don't.'

'I've got to earn a living, Mr Hawkins,' said Walter as he hunted for his car keys. 'The royalty on Space Monkey hardly even covers parts on the 3-D game you already said is obsolete.'

He picked the keys out of a bowl of cat food and started for the door.

'Because you took too long,' said Hawkins following in his wake. 'It coulda' been the hottest thing in the country.'

The agent was still trying to talk to Walter as he descended the stairs of his apartment out into the street where Wally's dilapidated and much abused Plymouth blotted the run-down street of brownstone houses.

'How soon?' shouted Hawkins as Walter climbed into the car.

'How soon what?'

'How soon can I have it?'

Wally shrugged. 'When I get time to finish it.'

He fired up the Plymouth and immediately backed into the Lincoln behind and the Mercedes in front, then reversed back into the Lincoln and finally, miraculously, pulled out into the traffic, almost causing two cars to crash into each other.

As Lieutenant Curtis had pointed out on more than one occasion, Walter was not a skilled driver.

4

Walter Nebicher raced across the squad room to the glass-enclosed computer section. Curtis, looking harried and worn, was already waiting for him.

'All ready for you, Jack,' said Wally as he moved to a control keyboard. 'What've you got?'

Curtis pulled out of his pocket an odd collection of small bits of paper, matchbox covers, notes on tickets, and threw them on the desktop.

'I don't know,' he sighed. 'Just bits and pieces, but I got the feeling it's all there. I just can't put it together.'

He stared at Walter like he wasn't there: he was looking through him into infinity.

'Something wrong, Jack?' said Walter in alarm.

'Yeah . . . everything,' Curtis replied, lighting a Lucky. 'Me, the job, the world.'

'That doesn't sound like you. You're the best detective on the force.'

Curtis slid the scattering of notes under Wally's nose. Walter looked at them curiously as the lieutenant sauntered over to the window and looked out over Los Angeles.

'It's all moving past me, kid,' he sighed wearily. 'Crime used to be simple – good guys and bad guys.' He turned to see what progress Walter was making, clearly none at all. 'Just copy down the names, numbers, anything you find on those scraps. I'm working on a hunch they've got something to do with this rash of kidnappings. Another scientist disappeared last week. OK, so it's all bits and pieces but –'

'What are we looking for?' said Walter, transferring the notes to a grubby wallet.

'Oh, I don't know, some kind of pattern . . . I've got names of companies, countries, people. There's got to be a connection between them.' Curtis rubbed his hands over his eyes. He looked as though he hadn't slept for a month. 'Now look, you said this machine could talk to other machines, right?'

Walter's eyes lit up. 'Interface with other computers – right!'

'Uh, huh, I want you to do that. Corporations, cars . . . flight numbers. Get your machine to talk to other computers that might have any of these names or companies, or anything. I mean, if a guy took a flight some place, find out who else was on the flight, who –'

'Paid for the ticket,' Walter jumped in.

'Right,' said Jack encouragingly.

'Who else on the flight might have worked for any of the companies listed,' Walter went on like a good pupil. 'In other words, you want every name in this pile cross-referenced against every other.'

Curtis smiled with amusement. 'There you go, there you are you see, cross-referencing. See, they didn't even have that word when I got started. Cross-referencing. Well, now that should scare the *hell* out of the crooks out there.'

For a brief moment, Wally wondered if the lieutenant was taking a rise out of him, but one look at his face convinced Walter that Curtis was genuinely impressed.

'Sure,' Walter agreed.

'But it doesn't,' Jack went on. 'You know why? Because those crooks have got computers as smart as yours.'

Lt Curtis didn't underestimate computers but neither did he underestimate the criminal mind. And it didn't do to underestimate Lt Curtis.

The phone rang and Walter answered it: the call was for Curtis.

'Jack? I think we've got them.'

It was Tanya Du Boise, Interpol's top agent in Los Angeles.

'Another young engineer flying to London, this time for Supertech, has been diverted from his boarding gate by two men.'

'When?' asked Curtis.

'Just now. He's making a phone call verifying their credentials and then they're taking him to the other side of the airport to the private air terminal. It has to be the same MO they used last week.'

'Right, stay put. I'll be right down.'

He hung up quickly and turned to leave. 'I'll be calling in,' he muttered over his shoulder.

'I may not be having anything for a couple of days,' Walter called after the lieutenant.

'OK, Walter, but I need a promise,' said Curtis, picking up his coat and turning back to face him.

'Sure.'

'Don't show anyone in the Department what you come up with, OK? *Anyone*.'

Walter laughed nervously. 'You're about the only one who . . . talks to me anyway.'

Curtis grinned. 'Thanks kid.'

Only after he'd gone did his words strike Walter as ominous.

5

A pair of headlights approached through the swirling LA fog and came to a stop on an airport apron at the private terminal. Lt Jack Curtis switched off his lights, lit a Lucky and waited.

Presently another pair of lights appeared, blinking twice. Curtis returned the signal. Again he waited.

A svelte young woman in her mid-thirties wearing a chic black trench coat climbed swiftly out of the other car and made her way over to a chain-link fence. Curtis got out of his car and went to meet her. They embraced with the intimacy and respect of old lovers, good friends and battle-worn colleagues.

'Jack, I'm worried,' said Tanya.

'*You're* worried? I'm the one who's gonna walk out there.' He pulled out his gun.

'I'll be here. I'm armed,' she pointed out.

'Fat chance. They see you, they'll start shooting, we both know that.' As he spoke he loaded the gun and replaced it in his pocket.

'Then what chance do you have of stopping them?'

He smiled. 'It's called chutzpah.'

'Chutzpah –?'

'It's Jewish for . . . stupid.'

This time Tanya smiled. 'You aren't Jewish,' she said, leaning over to kiss him.

'But I am a little stupid, right?'

'If you go alone – yes.'

A car was coming down the apron, its headlights projecting shafts of light ahead of it as it moved up to a private jet. Curtis's expression set hard as he flipped the Lucky out into the night.

'Better get to it,' he said grimly.

'Just like that,' she murmured.

'Piece of cake.'

'What's the signal?' Tanya asked.

'Gunfire . . . it'll mean I blew it.'

'Don't say that,' she said softly.

'I wouldn't if I meant it.'

He kissed her lightly on the lips one more time and headed off into danger.

The Gulfstream SMA-3 executive jet stood idling on an apron in the airport's private terminal. Next to it a black limousine illuminated the tarmac. Chuck Wilson, senior engineer with Supertech, shook hands with the two clean-cut security personnel and glanced at the delicious stewardess who awaited him at the base of the plane's boarding steps.

'I can't tell you how much I appreciate this royal treatment,' said Wilson.

Peterson smiled. 'From now on it'll all be like this. You're a very important man to our firm.'

'What firm was that?' came a terse voice through the fog.

Startled, the three men turned to look. Lt Curtis walked leisurely towards them, pulling his wallet from his pocket.

'Who are you?' said Peterson suspiciously.

Curtis flashed his wallet. 'Immigration.'

'I don't think I understand,' said Peterson. 'We've never been questioned before.'

'And we won't bother you now,' said Curtis in an even tone. 'We're just being hassled about not paying closer attention to private planes going in and out of here. What is your destination?'

'London.'

Curtis's eyes narrowed. 'May I see some identification on you three?'

Peterson assumed his best PR manner.

'Look, Mr Wilson is already late,' he smiled disarmingly.

'That's right,' added Wilson. 'I was scheduled to go out on Pan Am when the company decided to send me on their own plane, and –'

'Show the man your identification,' Collins broke in. 'He's just doing his job.'

They took out their wallets and passports, and Curtis examined them.

'Global Guard. You both work for them? And you work for Supertech?'

Wilson looked puzzled, turning to Collins and Peterson. 'I thought *you* were with Supertech.'

'We contract all security work for them,' replied Peterson calmly. 'That's why the special interest in you since you became such a valuable man. Officer,' he added in a less unctuous tone of voice, 'unless you have some specific problem with this departure, I must insist you allow this plane to take off.'

Curtis handed back the documents and replied without expression: 'No, no . . . everything seems to be in order. Thank you very much. Have a nice flight.' He smiled – barely – and walked away.

'Right this way please, Mr Wilson,' said Collins cordially enough, as the engineer mounted the steps, then quietly added to Peterson, 'He can connect Wilson to the plane.'

Peterson nodded and pulled out his revolver, taking aim as Curtis continued to move away.

'What are you doing?' shouted Wilson from the

steps, and tried to deflect the gun. But he was just too late. The bullet tore into Curtis's right arm: he fell writhing in agony on the tarmac as Peterson shoved the gun into Wilson's gut.

'Onto the plane,' he snapped. 'Right now! Don't look back!'

Collins meanwhile ran up beside the immobile form of Jack Curtis. As he started to feel for a pulse, Curtis suddenly sprang to life, spinning over and raising his own gun. But with lightning speed it was kicked out of his hand by the chauffeur of the limousine who got back into the car as Collins dragged Curtis aboard the jet.

Just before they were inside, Curtis looked round to hear the sound of running feet. Collins had spotted Tanya at the same moment.

'Get her! Now!' he shouted at the chauffeur as Tanya ran across the tarmac, her gun aimed in front of her.

'Run, Tanya, run!' Curtis yelled, then Collins pushed him into the plane, whose doors were now sealed closed.

The limousine began to turn and head towards Tanya, bearing down on her as she stood, frozen in place, her gun lifted and aimed at the driver. She fired, but the car kept coming. At the last moment she dived out of the way. Turning, she could see the tail-lights racing off into the darkness. In the other direction she was just able to make out the jet's flashing lights as it disappeared into the foggy night.

She began to sob. At first the tears came lightly then she broke down in grief and frustration.

6

PRIORITY CODE:
AUTOMAN
WHAT IS YOUR CLEARANCE?
CRIME FIGHTER

Walter Nebicher punched in the code and waited. He knew he was taking a risk working on this at police headquarters, but he had drawn a complete blank on the information Lt Curtis had given him. This would be a chance to find out just what Automan was made of.

He was so engrossed that he didn't notice Roxanne Caldwell enter the glassed-in computer section. She watched with intrigued amusement as he frantically typed from what seemed to be a stream of consciousness. Suddenly she went pale and stared in alarm.

The neon lighting, diffused above wide ceiling plates, began to dim, and the room started to rumble. A glass on top of a filing cabinet next to her began to vibrate and a small high-pitched note emanated from it. A framed Van Gogh print fell from the wall; files and papers followed.

The information on the VDU suddenly disappeared to be replaced by a bright hexagon which burst out of the screen. Then, between Walter's computer terminal and the wall of equipment, a strange white haze began to appear. Roxanne gazed at it, spellbound, as the vapour gradually took on the definite shape of a man. The water inside the glass above the filing cabinet began to simmer. Roxanne gasped.

Automan had materialised.

A moment later, everything went haywire: a dial marked CIRCUIT OVERLOAD swung into the red segment; the glass of steaming, bubbling water exploded; a printer burst into flames. Before the whole lab blew up, Walter hastily switched off the master power switch, turning round to see Roxanne standing, petrified, behind him. Automan vanished. The lights returned to normal.

Walter rushed over to the printer and tried to dowse the flames with a stack of fan-folded printout paper.

'What the hell is going on here?'

Captain E. G. Boyd, the Department chief, had burst into the room, livid with rage.

Walter raced to another cabinet from which smoke was wafting. Hastily he opened the electronic component drawer and flipped a switch, turning off the entire section. Before he replied he darted a beseeching look at Roxanne.

'You trying to set fire to the whole place?'

'No, sir,' Walter replied nervously. 'It was an accident.'

'I did it,' Roxanne blurted out.

'You did it,' Boyd replied with the deepest scepticism.

'I knocked over a glass of water into this . . .' she gestured towards the cabinet '. . . whatever it is.'

'It's a keyboard –' Walter volunteered apologetically.

'And *I* thought it was just a typewriter,' snarled the chief. 'What are you doing in here anyway?' he added to Roxanne.

'I had to check over these requisitions with Wally,' she replied hurriedly.

'Never mind about that now. Just phone my wife and tell her I have to meet with the Commissioner tonight 'bout these damned kidnappings. I'll be home . . .

when I get home.' He turned back to Walter and wagged an angry finger at him. 'Make sure the Feds pay for this. I don't want to see it appearing on one of those cost-sharing accounts.'

'No sir,' said Walter, wondering how he was going to explain Automan to the US government.

Detective Ted Smithers had observed the whole episode through the glass partition. Casually, he edged up to Boyd as the chief stormed out of the computer room.

'You tell him off?' His buddy-buddy manner was lost on Boyd who was too tired – and thick-skinned – to notice.

'I tell him off, Washington cuts us off,' the chief replied wearily.

'So what? Who needs a roomful of machines? We need more men.'

Boyd yawned. 'Half the new men I put on are coming out of funds earmarked for that computer program in there. So grin and bear it . . . He goes without any help and you got four extra detectives.'

Smithers looked sour. 'It's a crime we gotta let Washington run our department.'

'Smithers, if I had my way, I'd trade the whole mess in there for one good coffee machine, but then we wouldn't get the money. It's all a big game. Learn to play it.'

The captain turned into his office, leaving Smithers standing there with the glimmer of a smirk on his face.

'I'm sorry I got you in trouble,' Walter was saying to Roxanne back in the computer room.

She shook her head and her honey-blonde hair rippled gently, reminding Walter that he should begin programming Autowoman. 'That's all right . . . But . . .'

'I can't talk about it right now . . .'

'You're going to have to,' she insisted, 'or I won't sleep.'

The thought of Roxanne not sleeping was oddly stimulating, but Walter put it to the back of his mind. 'Roxanne,' he began. 'I had no business using the police computer for my personal projects.'

'Is that what all that was –'

'It's just a game,' he broke in hastily.

Roxanne fixed her astonishing green eyes on him knowingly. 'That wasn't a game. That was a person.'

Walter couldn't resist a proud grin. 'You really think it looked like someone?'

'It *was* someone.'

'It was a hologram,' he said confidentially.

'A what?'

It sometimes seemed to Wally that he was surrounded by a wall of terrible, almost medieval, ignorance. 'An electronic simulation in three dimensions,' he explained patiently. 'You see, you take photographs of someone . . .'

Checking that Boyd wasn't hovering beyond the glass partition, he quickly opened his briefcase and showed her an album of head-on, side and top views of Robert Redford, Paul Newman, Arnold Schwartzenegger and Tarzan.

'This is four people,' Roxanne pointed out.

'It *started* out as four – then I added some more.' He flipped over the pages to reveal similar pictures of Burt Reynolds, Christopher Reeve, Richard Gere, Lee Majors, Tom Sellick . . . 'Now they're all in there together . . . They're becoming one.'

'Becoming . . .' she whistled. 'You sound like your

machine is about to give birth.'

'That's an interesting way to put it.'

'What's it going to do for a brain? Whose thoughts is it going to have?'

'Everyone's. I programmed in all kinds of good stuff for super sleuthing from Sherlock Holmes to James Bond.'

Roxanne stared at him for a moment. Was this all for real? 'Do you mind if I sit down?' she said weakly.

'No, not at all,' Walter replied, moving over to the computer and switching on the power. 'It might be better this way.'

Roxanne was surprised and perturbed. 'You're serious . . . You're going to show me your new game?'

'It started out as a game – Automan. Now it's real. Here, I'll show you.'

'No!' she exclaimed and then, in resignation. 'Yes.'

He restarted the program, punching up various keys.

PRIORITY CODE:
AUTOMAN
WHAT IS YOUR CLEARANCE?
CRIME FIGHTER

They waited. And waited. Roxanne looked at him with a trace of pity. 'What happened to Automan?' she asked softly.

Walter stared at the VDU. There was no sign of Cursor.

'Damn,' he muttered.

'It isn't working?'

'It either isn't getting enough power . . .'

'Or?'

'Or he just isn't ready to come out.'

Roxanne began seriously to wonder if Walter wasn't

suffering from the strain of overwork. Or maybe Captain Boyd was finally getting to him.

'Isn't ready?' she echoed. 'Wally, this isn't Broadway. What's to be ready? It's a *game*!'

'It's a computerised program that has all the functions of a real person,' he insisted. 'If the computer is still assimilating the facts . . . it won't appear unless it's ready . . . that's the way computers work.' He wasn't sure if he really believed this himself. After all, hadn't Automan turned up in his basement for Hawkins' benefit? No, that was crazy. But then, for whose benefit was it?

Roxanne felt like she wanted to cry. 'Wally,' she said gently. 'Why are you doing this?'

Walter felt like he wanted to cry. 'You think I'm crazy,' he said edgily. 'That's why you won't go out with me.'

'I don't think you're crazy. And you haven't asked me to go out with you, but –'

Walter held his breath. Was this the moment of truth?

'– you are a little strange sometimes. I mean, the way you keep to yourself and all.'

'What choice do I have?' Walter complained miserably. 'The Captain won't let anybody talk to me. He doesn't believe in computers.'

Roxanne was loyal. 'You have to understand – he's an old-fashioned cop. He doesn't trust change.'

'But he's wrong . . . Lieutenant Curtis trusts me. He just gave me a whole investigation to run.'

'Wally,' she said, getting back to the immediate point. 'Why did the power dim?'

'It . . . takes a lot of power. It draws it from the whole building.'

She sighed. 'Wally, you can't be doing things that'll

get you suspended. You know the Captain's just waiting for an excuse.'

'I know.'

'I just thought I'd warn you.'

'Why?' he asked curiously, as she turned to go.

She hesitated, one hand on the doorknob. 'Maybe Lieutenant Curtis isn't the only one in the department who's on your side.'

7

Sometimes it was hard to recall what his wife looked like. Sometimes it was even harder to recall if this was good or bad.

One thing was for sure. This was one of those days Captain Boyd would rather forget. Some radical pinko reporter from the *Trib* was raking up all that stuff about bribery and corruption on the force. Then that schmuck Nebicher had practically destroyed the computer section – though maybe that *would* have solved his problems.

He'd only told Smithers half the story. Washington was leaning on him to get results – the usual spiel about cost-effectiveness or they'd cut off the funds, and he was already three-quarter-way into next year's budget. On the other hand he had to handle Nebicher with kid gloves – that part of what he'd told Smithers was quite true.

The story he'd been fed was that some big-time moneybags lawyer called Donetti owed his life to Doc Nebicher, the whizzkid's father. It seemed this guy's son – a fatso – used to hang around with the genius at high-school. The lawyer had high hopes for him until tragedy struck: the kid was killed in an auto accident, seemed he was running to catch a bus but was too slow. Now the old man was retired and donating his millions to computer research in memory of the son – anonymous patronage. The long and short of it was that half the Washington funds were tied up in the Donetti trust fund.

He couldn't touch Nebicher but he could make sure he wasn't let out on the streets. As long as Boyd was in charge the genius would stay in his cage.

But he had other problems on his mind. They were getting no further solving the kidnappings and the meet with the Commissioner had been acutely embarrassing. And now this. He pushed his way through the mill of TV reporters, police and forensic teams and shouted across at Smithers.

'What happened?'

Smithers made his way through the herd of bystanders that littered the downtown garage where the shooting had taken place.

'The parking lot personnel reported hearing gunshots,' he shouted back over the wail of police sirens. 'When they arrived on the scene they found Lieutenant Curtis's weapon, and bloodstains behind his car which match his type.'

Boyd ran his fingers through his thinning hair and replaced his hat. 'What was Jack doing prowling around a garage in downtown LA?'

'Captain, I told you I wasn't getting any cooperation from Curtis,' Smithers replied vehemently. 'He's a hotshot. He wants all the glory so he doesn't share his evidence.' He pointed distastefully at the scene. 'This is what it got him.'

Boyd stared at him. 'You think the kidnappers got him?'

'I don't know too many cops who leave their car and gun behind if everything's OK.'

The logic of this was conclusive. 'All right,' said Boyd

hopelessly. 'Add Curtis to the list . . . That makes eleven.'

'Twelve. We just got a call from the Supertech Corporation. Their top engineer disappeared before his flight to London.'

This was the last straw for Captain E. G. Boyd.

'Their top engineer? What *is* this? What kind of loonies are behind it?'

The roar of the Gulfstream SMA-3 broke through the stillness of a delightful morning in the Swiss Alps. As it landed a blue Volvo 245 GLT estate car drove up followed by an ambulance. While Lt Jack Curtis, his right arm in a sling, was escorted by a medical team accompanied by armed guards into the ambulance, Chuck Wilson, the Supertech engineer, was bundled into the Volvo by Peterson and Collins. They drove quickly in tandem through the Alpine roads until they arrived at what appeared to be a luxury hotel, nestling in the mountains, and overlooking a sparkling lake.

But this was no vacation resort. As the vehicles arrived at a security gate two men, in quasi-military uniforms like those of Ski Patrolmen and carrying Uzi submachine guns, stood at either side as the gates opened automatically and allowed the vehicles to pass through into the complex of buildings that formed the Alpine Institute of Technology.

'Drink in the freshness of the Alps, Lieutenant,' said Lydell Hamilton in a rich, deep purr. 'This will be your home for some time.' He drew open the curtains and window of the ultra-modern rest-room and turned to view his latest arrival lying pale and haggard in the hospital bed.

'I get enough snow any LA winter,' replied Jack

Curtis bleakly, taking in the immaculately cut Savile Row tailoring, the odour of expensive cologne and cigars, the general air of a well-fed cat. He looked as though he'd stepped out of a London gentleman's club. If anyone had to get their hands dirty, it wasn't going to be Hamilton. Maybe that was where the male nurse who stood by Curtis's bed came in.

'Oh, there's much more than snow here,' said Hamilton suavely. 'People save for a lifetime to come to these mountains.'

'What's my price?' said Curtis, anxious to get to the point.

'I suppose you could say your freedom. But if you make the right adjustments, you can live a life here that would fulfil anyone's dreams.'

The lieutenant smiled wanly. 'Like it or not.'

Hamilton grinned. 'Everything is a trade-off. I just want you to know that we'll be interrogating you as soon as you're a little stronger. By then I hope you'll realise that our best interests are your best interests.'

'And if I don't?'

'Well,' Hamilton eyed the male nurse for a moment, 'I suppose the alternative to a good life is a good death . . . and degenerating from there for a really hard case. We might arrange . . . a very bad death.' He started to move towards the door. 'I must leave this picturesque paradise for a few days . . . but think about it. We need only know the extent of your penetration into our organisation. By that I mean anyone at all to whom you may have given any information about our work – anyone. However insignificant they may have seemed to you. Goodbye.'

As Hamilton departed, an image arose, unbidden, into Curtis's mind. It was of Nebicher standing by the coffee machine talking animatedly to him about integrated circuits, demonstrating with a paper cup while hot black coffee trickled from the machine and splashed all over his shoes.

8

Several small leaning towers of Pisa were stacked around Walter Nebicher in the computer room. Some were built out of discarded coffee cups and empty coke cans; others were made out of piles of printouts. In the next few weeks the towers continued to grow higher and to lean more dangerously as day and night he worked feverishly at the computer, programming every bit of information he could find and calling up different programs. Sometimes he worked at his note pad, figuring out more complex programs.

Around him the computer room was quickly deteriorating as wastebaskets filled to overflowing and the carpet began to disappear under piles of printout, newspapers, telephone directories, and half-eaten salt beef sandwiches. The view through the glass partition was occasionally decorated by the lovely face of Roxanne Caldwell gazing in with increasing concern and, at one point, by Captain Boyd glowering angrily.

The chaos of the computer room was nothing to the squalor of Walter's basement workshop where the work continued. Now haggard and unshaven, Walter tapped out the familiar program and for the umpteenth time waited.

PRIORITY CODE:
AUTOMAN
CROSS REFERENCING
RE: LT. JACK CURTIS
SEARCHING

'What happened to you Jack?' he sighed. 'You've got to help me find out. I've run everything you gave me and it still doesn't mean a thing to me.'

He punched a few more buttons.

'Come on, Automan. Do something. Where are you?'

'Stop it!'

Walter wheeled round in surprise. Roxanne was standing at the top of the stairs.

'It's been three weeks,' she said angrily. 'You're going to lose your job . . . your mind . . . everything.'

He opened his mouth to object, but Roxanne was determined to have her say. 'Wally, you're never going to see Jack again. Something terrible has happened and he's not coming back.'

Walter stood up and began to pace the room – a hazardous procedure because there was little spare floor that wasn't occupied by the horrendous mess. 'You're wrong, Roxanne,' he insisted, 'and it's not just Jack. Something has happened to a lot of people. That's what Jack was having me check out the night he die – disappeared.'

'Then how can wasting your time down here possibly help find Jack?' she said more gently, seating herself on the edge of a table.

'What happened to Jack was in my computer. I just couldn't reach it. Automan – ' he gestured towards the console '– can change that. I've programmed him to be everything I ever dreamed of being as a policeman.'

She went over to him. 'Wally, please,' she implored, 'I'm your friend. Give it up. You can't see what's happening. It's turning into more than a super game: it's becoming an obsession.'

'No,' he said, waving his hands about as his voice rose a tone in pitch, 'it's become a reality. I've already created him and I've fed every case Jack ever worked on into Automan's memory bank.'

'There!' she cried triumphantly. 'You see, Automan is just another name for your friend Jack.'

'No . . . He's much more than that. I figured why stop with Jack's experience? Why not add in the experience of the whole darned department?' He smiled at her.

'Sure, as long as you're building this super cop, let's go all the way. When do I get to see him?'

Walter blushed. 'I . . . I don't think he's coming.'

'Why not?'

'He hasn't got anything to report.'

He knew this sounded ridiculous and was prepared for her reply.

'It's getting worse and worse,' Roxanne said in a low voice.

'No, it's getting better and better,' he said, some of his enthusiasm returning. 'I'm learning to understand him . . . and his limitations.'

She chuckled. 'I'm glad he has some.'

'Oh, sure. He has a lot of them, just like the rest of us, only different. He's just a great big grown-up game.'

Roxanne looked at him for a moment, considering.

'Wally,' she said at last. 'If he isn't coming, do you think we could go get a cup of coffee and a sandwich? You don't look like you've eaten in days.'

He relaxed. 'That'd be swell. Give me a minute and I'll even shave.'

'Great,' she said, moving towards the stairs, then hesitated. 'Maybe you'd better turn off your machine.'

'No, it's all right,' Walter assured her as he followed her out. 'Automan may decide to show up when he sorts out some of the facts I sent him.'

She shook her head. It was hopeless. It was only then that she noticed the lovingly mounted and framed photograph of herself, taken at least year's Squad Room Xmas party, staring at her from the wall. He saw that she'd seen and they both blushed, pretending that she hadn't.

'Wally!' Roxanne shrieked as he revved up the Plymouth. It crashed into the bruised Lincoln behind and the battered Merc in front. 'Somebody's going to call the police!'

'I *am* the police,' he reminded her as he tore into the traffic, causing a pickup truck to swerve.

STANDBY FOR CROSS REFERENCE
SEARCH RESULT:
GLOBAL GUARD SECURITY
755 MULBERRY STREET
STANDBY FOR AUTOMAN

For a few moments all was still. Then the basement workshop began to rumble, the light started to sway. The garbage on the floor seemed to ripple and, like an urban sand dune, garbage on higher surfaces dropped down to level out the mess. It was almost as if this moment had been chosen to prove incontrovertibly the existence of the Second Principle of Thermodynamics under correct laboratory conditions.

Suddenly the room was filled with the pulsating sound and appearance of a tiny orb, a dancing cursor, suspended in mid air, which burst out of the VDU and moved about the room, up and down, from side to side, in and out. Its presence marked the imminent materialisation of another life form. Like an advance scout, a standard-bearer, a form of electronic escort, the cursor appeared, circling the room once and then standing by. Moments later the host form made its transformation.

Swirling vapour appeared beyond Walter's desktop computer, crystallising at once into an electronic Mr Universe. Automan was back and growing more real by the second. It was as if he were rapidly working through all the dimensions – now three-dimensional and then again becoming four-dimensional, the last belonging to the world of energy and time. There was an aura around him, a mysterious glow, as if he were charged with electromagnetic forces that were only potential but unmanifest in the world as we know it.

'Walter, Walter!' He spoke in a controlled, resonant voice. 'Walter, I've urgent news! Walter!'

Cursor suddenly remembered Roxanne's picture and buzzed around it for a second. Then it homed in on the poster of a nude pinup and traced a laserlike heart around it delightedly, emitting its high-pitched beeps.

'Yes,' agreed Automan, 'she is really something, but we have more important work to do. We must find Walter!'

Walking as if several inches above the floor – which was in fact the case – Automan moved to the stairs and ascended, the cursor moving with him.

9

With an excruciating grinding of gears, Wally crashed the Plymouth into the back of a police car parked in front of the diner. The doors opened and two irate uniformed policemen hurried out.

'Hey pal –' one began.

'It's all right, I'm a cop,' said Wally, flashing his badge. 'Special Section.'

'Since when do they look like that at Special Sections?' growled the other cop, staring at Roxanne.

'Special undercover assignment,' she jumped in. 'I'm a cop, too.'

She flashed her badge and followed Walter into the diner, passing several massive Harleys that were also parked in front of the restaurant, leaving the two officers to inspect the damage to their car.

Walter and Roxanne made their way through the motley collection of freaks, junkies, winos and oddballs who frequented the place, including the leather-jacketed members of a West Coast motorbike gang who stared at Roxanne with crude and undisguised interest.

She ignored them, turning to Wally. 'We've got to get some food in you,' she whispered. 'You're driving like you can't see.'

Wally looked puzzled. 'I can see fine. I always drive like that – poor muscular control.' A country rock band was playing on the jukebox. Walter's eyes lit up. 'I've been taking dancing lessons to try and improve my coordination. Want to get down.'

Before she could react, Wally leapt from the bar stool and was flailing his arms and legs around in a ludicrous attempt at some down and dirty dance moves. Roxanne couldn't bear to look, but several of the diner's clientele began to watch with amusement.

'Now that guy's weird,' said a biker.

Eventually, to Roxanne's relief, Wally gave up, re-joining her at the bar.

'You know you're in trouble, Wally, when weird people start finding you weird,' she whispered.

'Do you find me weird?' he asked anxiously.

'Not usually,' she replied. 'Up until Lieutenant Curtis disappeared I just thought you were misunderstood.'

'And now . . .'

'Well, you have to admit, you couldn't show me Automan.'

Wally sighed. 'I told you . . . He only appears when he's ready.'

As he spoke the room started to tremble and shake. He paled visibly. Then he realised. It was just the subway.

'It was just the subway,' he said to Roxanne.

She looked at him in surprise. 'What did you think it was?'

'Well, for a minute . . .' He shook his head. 'Nothing. You wouldn't understand.'

'But I'm trying to. Please explain why you couldn't make Automan appear.'

'He wasn't ready. That is, his program wasn't ready.'

She looked at him curiously. 'Wally, you talk about him as if he were human.'

'He is. I mean his energy is real . . . like a spirit, yours and mine . . . but he doesn't have a tangible body.'

'Nor will *you* if you don't start eating,' she said, pointing at the untouched plate of sandwiches they had ordered: he grinned and ate. Then it hit her what he had really been saying. 'That's why I could see it . . . HIM!'

'Sure,' said Wally between munches. 'He's just like an image on a television set. Although Automan looks more real because he's holographic . . . three dimensional.'

'Wally, would you consider coming home with me after we eat?'

His heart skipped a beat, and he nearly choked on his pastrami. 'What for?' he gulped.

She hesitated. 'I don't want you living in that house all alone . . . At least not for a while.'

Walter couldn't believe what she'd just said. With dry throat and thumping heart, he moved over to kiss her. Gently she took his head and pressed it against her chest. The room seemed to shake and tremble.

Another subway train had passed by below them.

Softly she raised his head and moved slightly away. 'We don't have that kind of relationship, Wally. I just want to mother you.'

He swallowed and looked down. 'It's better than nothing. If you knew how long I've stared at you from that computer room.'

As he was talking, one of the bikers looked over at him, and noticed Roxanne for the first time.

'Hey, Du Ron,' he said hoarsely, turning to another biker with a sallow, pockmarked face, long greasy hair tied in a pony tail, gold rings pierced in his ears and a hook nose: he looked like a diseased pirate. 'Check this action. Now how does a little guy like him get on so good with a chick like her?'

Du Ron turned to look. His eyes focused on her with

manic lechery compounded by Southern Comfort and amphetamines.

'Awright!' he rasped. 'Now we're talkin'!'

'Maybe he's a delivery service,' another biker suggested flippantly.

'Yeah, for us,' said the first biker, a red-faced pig with thick ginger beard.

'What "us"?' growled Du Ron. '*I* am the deliver-ee. Hey . . . honey . . . honey!' He rose from his table and ambled over, looming over Roxanne.

Walter eyed him uneasily. 'Were you speaking to us?' he said nervously.

'Ignore them, Wally,' Roxanne whispered.

'But we're cops,' he whispered back.

'*They* won't care,' she replied in a louder voice.

Du Ron laughed. 'Yes, I do. I do care, sweetheart.' He stooped even closer to her. 'In fact, I've got great news.' He paused theatrically. 'I'm in love.'

'I'm warning you for your own good,' Walter said. 'You don't know who I am.'

Du Ron bared his teeth. 'So?' he growled. 'Is that supposed to make a difference?'

The other bikers had formed a tight little circle around them, so that they could enjoy Walter's humiliation – and maybe death.

'Wally, please,' Roxanne cautioned him.

'Stay out of this, Roxanne,' he said. 'I'll handle it.'

He didn't say it smugly. In fact he was very frightened but determined to handle the situation gracefully. He stood up.

'Now you guys hold it right there,' he shouted.

As he did so, Cursor suddenly popped up behind him. The gang of bikers stared in bewilderment and confusion, as the room began to shake. This time it was no subway train.

'You take one step further,' Wally went on, 'and you're going to have to answer to me.'

The cursor had spotted Roxanne and was making a literal beeline for her, then moved down into her glass and sneaked for a second into her cleavage, popping out again and settling for a vase of roses. She let out a plaintive cry, and jumped up to squeeze Walter's arm.

'Wally,' she screamed.

But Walter still didn't look back. Unaware of the cursor's arrival he simply took her arm, still facing the storm troopers.

'You see, Roxanne,' he said with satisfaction, 'you just have to be firm.'

Du Ron had had enough of this. He wasn't going to lose face merely because of some spooky little conjuring trick.

'OK, wise guy,' he shouted above the rumbling that was increasing every second, 'I don't like tricks.'

With that he broke his beer bottle in half and took another step towards Walter. The juddering accelerated, stopping everyone, including Du Ron and Walter, in their tracks. The bikers looked terrified.

'What . . . ?' Walter gasped, noticing for the first time that the lights were dimming and flashing. 'It *is* him. But he couldn't . . .'

'Oh, my God,' whispered Roxanne. 'You don't mean –'

The vapour that had appeared in the middle of the diner quickly metamorphosed into the stunning, shimmering form of Automan.

Roxanne was riveted; the quasi-Hell's Angels were speechless; Wally was furious.

'Who told you you could leave the basement?' he demanded.

Automan was about to reply when the porky biker

jumped out of his chair.

'What is it?' he said, staring in terror at the luminous vision.

'I dunno,' another biker replied helpfully.

'Just some kind of photograph,' growled Du Ron with a sneer. 'It ain't real.'

'Good evening, gentlemen,' Automan said cordially.

'It talks,' gasped Porky.

'Come, Walter,' said Automan, making his way towards them, 'it's time. We've some very evil men to eradicate.'

'That's it for me,' said a biker in shades.

'She's all yours, pal,' Du Ron said to Wally generously, as he edged out of the diner. 'All yours.'

He dropped his bottle, turned and half-trampled the dirty group behind him. The other bikers trailed after him.

Porky was last in line. 'Er, we gotta go,' he mumbled, slinking out of the door. Seconds later, the Harleys could be heard revving up and roaring away.

'It's time?' Walter asked, dimly realising that his life-long fantasy of crime-fighting was about to be put to the acid test out on the streets, even if computer-aided. 'Now? At this very minute?'

'Yes!' replied Automan firmly.

'I have to go, Roxanne,' Walter said apologetically. 'Say something.'

Too stunned to speak, she sank into the arms of a middle-aged customer seated behind her.

'Roxanne will be fine,' said Automan evenly. 'Hurry. We must be back before morning.'

'You heard him, Roxanne,' Wally said hastily. 'I have to go. I'll never forget this evening. Thank you. I'll call you.'

He headed for the door, opened it and walked out.

Automan, too, headed for the door – and walked through it.

10

'I don't know whether I'm thrilled to see you – or disappointed.' Wally said as they walked away from the diner. Cursor hovered a few feet behind. All the motorcycles had gone.

'We now have the necessary facts assimilated to find Jack,' said Automan as he strode ahead, his luminous body blazing a trail, as it were, through the night.

'What?' Wally said in astonishment. 'Why didn't you say so?'

'I just did.'

'How do we find him?'

'A step-by-step process based on the facts you programmed.'

Walter shook his head. 'They were Jack's facts. I just refined them. Where do we go? Is Jack alive?'

'We won't know until we are further along.'

They had arrived at Wally's Plymouth. He was about to get in but Automan stopped him.

'What's the matter?' Wally asked.

'We haven't time to ride in that.'

'You haven't seen me drive,' Wally said indignantly. 'In fact, you've never been out of the basement. How do you know how much time we have?'

'I know my own limitations,' Automan replied. 'The city's power requirements will treble at dawn. You must ride with me.'

Wally stared at him uneasily. 'In what?'

'Cursor,' he called out to the sphere.

The cursor darted out into the street and in a flash

began to etch out the structure of a highly advanced and incredibly futuristic car. Like a holograph light pen it ran and reran across the length and breadth of the car, each time tracing more and more elaborate details until the car seemed – almost – solid. Like Automan it was undeniably three-dimensional. Like Automan it seemed to shimmer and pulsate with energy, and like Automan it was not exactly solid, but translucent. Strangely this seemed to add to, rather than diminish, the sense of power emanating from it.

A man walking by with several poodles on a leash, gaped at the eerie phenomenon, as if witnessing the creation of the world, and became totally intertwined with his leashes as the shimmering subsided, revealing the most beautiful speed machine Walter had ever seen.

'Man,' he gasped. 'Do you have a set of wheels!'

'No, I don't,' replied Automan seriously. 'But Autocar does.'

'Autocar!' Walter repeated, still stunned that somehow he was responsible for this . . . miracle.

'Get in,' said Automan calmly.

Walter climbed awkwardly into the car. In an instant Autocar sped noiselessly down the road at a phenomenal speed, zipping in and out of traffic which seemed to move out of its way as if it were any other ordinary oncoming vehicle.

Some kids in a beat-up old Ford leaned their heads out to check out the car that had just flown past them.

'Hey, now, that's somethin' they ain't got in Santa Ana!' shouted one.

'Maybe they wanna drag!' yelled another.

The Ford roared after Walter and Automan.

Autocar was streaking towards the end of a block. Ahead of it was a T-junction, the traffic flowing heavily along the street that ran at right angles to it. Automan seemed oblivious to the cross street looming ahead. Walter, on the contrary, could think of nothing else as his eyes grew wide in panic.

'You drive worse than *I* do!' he screamed.

Automan reclined in his seat as though he were an extension of the car, or vice-versa. He said nothing.

Walter stared through the windshield and then screwed up his eyes. 'You'll never make the turn,' he groaned, covering his face in his hands.

Then an extraordinary thing happened.

Without slowing, sliding, skidding, without even rounding the corner in the usual arc, with no G-forces tearing at the car causing it to swerve, Autocar simply made a hard left turn on a deadly ninety-degree angle, in the same way that a cursor would in a computer game.

Far back along the street it had just turned, the Ford came to a stop.

'Even if they did wanta drag,' said the underage driver, 'I don't.'

'My God,' Wally wailed, 'that was a ninety-degree turn.' He was lying on the floor, legs up, having been pasted against the side window upside down. He dragged himself back into the passenger seat and stared once more in amazement at Automan, who was seated in exactly the same position as earlier as if he were somehow welded to the car.

'You programmed me to make a ninety-degree turn,' he remarked equably.

Walter snorted. 'That was for a game. All games make ninety-degree turns – Donkey Kong, Pac-man –'

'Yes. I know him quite well –'

'Wait a minute,' Wally broke in, dumbfounded.

'You know *who*, quite well?'

'Pac-man,' replied Automan with a cheerful smile. 'We're close friends. Now Donkey Kong on the other hand is an animal –'

'This is a bad dream. I'm making this up.'

'You did make this up . . . All of it. Remember?'

'Yes . . .' said Walter, trying to marshal his thoughts. Everything was moving too fast for him, and that included Autocar. 'But . . . this is a lot more real than I'd planned on.'

'Why? Did you imagine that yours was the only wavelength in the universe, the only dimension in space?'

At that moment the car did another ninety-degree turn again slapping Walter against the window. Once more he ricocheted onto the floor.

A drunk coming out of a bar at the corner was in time to see what appeared to be a low-flying UFO streaking past. He blinked, stared, blinked again and turned back into the bar.

'I don't suppose you'd mind signalling next time,' said Walter, but the sarcasm was lost on Automan.

'It's unnecessary, in as much as nothing can touch us, and we cannot impact on anything else.'

This Walter found impossible to believe, as he cranked himself back up into a sitting position and rubbed himself down.

'There is no need to look for bruises because you have none,' said Automan. 'Your physical reactions are entirely based on your normal expectations of living in a material world.'

Walter examined himself in astonishment. 'You're right! But how –'

'Mine is a world of space and energy. Not substance.'

'Then how do you explain that I'm riding in your

car?' Walter said, even more baffled.

'You can explain it.'

Walter looked around him and gave up. 'No, I can't.'

'When you entered this force field, you entered into my world. You are now in my dimension.'

Wally felt himself. 'I feel the same.' He reached over and touched Automan. 'I can't feel anything – except a tickle.'

'Electrocharged space.' Automan explained. 'Put your hand on the wheel.'

Tentatively, Walter allowed his hand to approach the wheel. His hand went through it.

'Now put your hand on top of mine.'

Again Walter obeyed. 'Aghh!' he screamed. 'My hand is gone!' Unaccountably it seemed to have merged into Automan's — or rather, it had disappeared, ending at the wrist, while Automan's had replaced it, becoming an extension of his own. He pulled it back and it re-appeared.

'Now put it back *and* try the wheel,' Automan commanded.

He did so and suddenly the car turned ninety degrees. Once again he was plunged against the far window.

'Did I do that?' he said weakly.

'*We* did.'

Autocar sped up to a large office building and without decelerating instantly stopped, hurling Walter into the front window.

'I *wish* you wouldn't do that!' he groaned.

'Sorry,' Automan said. 'I keep forgetting. But this is the building.' As he spoke, he climbed out of the car and Walter noticed once more that he did not bother to open the door – he simply walked through it. Walter did the same – the climbing-out bit, that is.

Automan began striding across the road, and Walter ran breathlessly behind. He was quickly discovering how hard it was to keep up with a four-dimensional smartass. Suddenly a taxi bore down on them, jerking to a stop seconds before it would have hit them – or at least Walter.

'Hey, look where you're going,' shouted the driver angrily. 'Who do you think you are?'

Automan turned and smiled at him. 'I'm very sorry,' he replied courteously. 'But I'm quite new to this world. Forgive me.'

The cab-driver gaped at him, unhooking his mike without taking his eyes off the shimmering pedestrian. 'Dispatch. This is Unit Fourteen,' he said hastily. 'I want to report seeing a . . .' The words got stuck in his throat as he turned his attention from Automan to Autocar.

The cursor was, with almost lightning speed, 'de-rezzing' the car – in other words unmaking it, employing the same lightpen method in reverse which it had used earlier to construct it. In seconds the car had vanished.

'Go ahead, Unit Fourteen,' said Dispatch. 'You want to report seeing a what?'

The cursor zipped from the space where the Autocar had been moments earlier. It hovered just in front of the cab, talking to the driver in cursor talk.

The driver's face had turned a deathly white. 'Never mind,' he muttered. 'I'm taking the rest of the night off.'

The cab tore away.

11

'What building?' said Walter, looking up at the office blocks that towered above them. 'I don't know what you're talking about.'

'The facts you programmed into my systems were looking for a common denominator. This is it . . . Global Guard.' Automan was looking distinctly pleased with himself.

'The private security company?'

'Hired by each of the companies involved with an employee disappearance.'

'What for?' Wally asked.

'To safeguard its employees against kidnapping and extortion.'

Wally was confused. 'Yet, they were responsible for each guy that disappeared. That's pretty sloppy work.'

'That's what I thought.'

'Thought?' Wally echoed, staring at his creation. 'You reasoned this all out?'

Automan was nonplussed. 'You programmed me to use deductive logic.'

'Then what's the logic coming here at this time of night?'

'I require more information to begin tracking Jack. Are not these later hours best for breaking and entering?'

'Breaking and entering?' Wally repeated in astonishment. Wasn't he supposed to be a cop?

'A police term used in countless records programmed into my systems by –'

'Me, I know, I know,' sighed Wally wearily. 'Yeah, this is the best time. How do you propose –'

'I can only show you,' said Automan, holding out his translucent hand. 'Come, enter my dimension.'

Wally grinned. 'You're kidding.'

'I'm not programmed to kid,' replied Automan seriously. 'Move into my form.'

Walter eyed his form with growing unease and then moved cautiously over until, as his hand had earlier, his body merged into that of Automan's. He had completely disappeared and he felt different . . . super-charged.

Automan's mouth opened to speak. 'Hey, I'm you!' came Wally's voice.

'You can never be me,' replied Automan – same mouth, different voice. 'You are still you.'

'Then how can I be talking with your body?'

'You're talking *through* my body,' Automan explained calmly.

'Have it your way,' came Wally's voice, 'but this is bizarre . . . Woooioe!'

Automan appeared to be dancing around like Michael Jackson.

'Get down . . . get down,' Walter began rapping.

'If you're going to toy with my form –' Automan said in an offended tone.

'Hey, lighten up, Automan,' came Walter's voice. 'It isn't every day that a guy like me grows a foot.'

'You'll be serious enough when you learn what I've learned,' Automan warned. 'Cursor!' he called.

The cursor streaked across and moved to the entrance of the building. Automan/Walter followed, trying the doors and finding them, not surprisingly, locked.

'So how're we going to get in there?' Walter said

sceptically.

'The molecular structure of this building is like a sieve to me,' replied Automan.

'Meaning what? You can see through the walls?'

'See through them?' said Automan. 'I can *walk* through them.'

As he spoke, the cursor moved up against one of the doors – and vanished through it to the other side. Automan was then able to do likewise.

'Wow!' came Walter's voice, instantly fading as Automan disappeared into the reception hall of Global Guard . . .

'. . . The next target will then be moved tomorrow night,' said Lydell Hamilton crisply. The oily cordiality with which he had addressed Lt Curtis had gone completely, to be replaced by an almost military precision in his speech and bearing.

The men seated around the boardroom table of Global Guard's LA head office also bore the marks of recent military or intelligence service – carefully pressed clothing, close-cropped hair, a posture at the table that spoke of their strict obedience and close attention. In the centre of the table was a large globe with a massive bronze hand cupping it, augmented by a few bolts of lightning and assorted weapons of death and destruction over a motto that read: 'TO SAFEGUARD YOUR WORLD'.

'Peterson, Collins, you will anchor the team as usual,' Hamilton continued. 'Are there any questions?'

Peterson raised his hand and Hamilton nodded for him to speak. 'The subject in question, one Don Cramer, is known to have purchased a handgun this week –'

Hamilton interrupted him impatiently. 'The one

place they don't expect trouble is on a commercial airline where they know people can't be armed, including them. They're not foolish enough to try to carry weapons through Federal Security checks. Next item . . .'

12

'Why do I feel like it's a little risky breaking into a place that specialises in security?' came Walter's voice out of Automan's mouth as Cursor led the way through the elevator door that opened onto the executive floor.

'Probably because we're not alone,' said Automan as he moved confidently down the thick blue carpeted floor.

'What?' said Walter, his voice an octave higher.

'Look, I can see eight life forms seated in a room at the end of this corridor,' said Automan.

Walter looked through the superhologram's X-ray eyes and marvelled. Although the door was closed he could still see the meeting that was going on behind it.

'So can I,' he said excitedly, then realised what this meant. 'We're not alone!' he hissed. 'And here comes one of them now.'

The boardroom door opened and a tall, attractive secretary emerged. Automan vanished into the wall: Cursor hung poised. As the young woman moved down an adjacent corridor, the cursor suddenly turned itself into a thumping valentine-like heart and streaked after her. Smitten, it vanished down the corridor.

'The cursor will give us away,' came Walter's voice as Automan reappeared out of the wall.

'No, he won't,' said Automan, pointing down the corridor. 'Cursor!' he snapped in a low voice. The cursor popped back to hover once more at his shoulder. 'Now you stay with us,' he added. The cursor bobbed up and down, chastened.

'We must get there before the meeting breaks up,' Automan said to Walter. 'We may get vital information.'

With the cursor floating obediently near his shoulder, Automan walked through another wall, across an office, through yet another wall until he was standing outside the conference room.

Within Automan's form, Walter was able to observe, through a veil-like substance which he guessed was the molecular structure of the wall, the meeting which was drawing to a close.

'Our last item of business,' Hamilton was saying, 'involves the unexpected abduction of police officer Lieutenant Jack Curtis.'

'Auto –' Walter began.

'Shhh!' hissed Automan.

'The Interpol agent working with Lieutenant Curtis managed to escape and still has not been located,' Hamilton went on.

'The limo driver thought it better to evacuate the scene rather than risk identification and capture,' put in Peterson.

'I know what the driver thought,' Hamilton snapped. 'However, in the light of what we now know about Tanya Du Boise's relationship to Officer Curtis, it seems obligatory that she be marked for a priority removal. Any dissenting votes?'

Peterson hesitated before speaking. 'Consider it more of a question,' he said, 'isn't tampering with an international police officer risky, considering she hasn't come forward with any information against us?'

Hamilton opened his attache case and inserted a thin folder. 'Proof and suspicion are poles apart in the world of policemen,' he said firmly. 'She wouldn't have been at the loneliest part of the airport that night if she did not have suspicions. I suspect that what she is working on now is proof.' He looked at his watch, and added briskly, 'Find her and remove her in time for your scheduled flight tomorrow night.'

'Yes, sir,' said Peterson.

Hamilton glanced quickly at each of them. 'If there is no further business,' he concluded, 'we will adjourn.'

The men started to file out of the boardroom.

'Come on,' Wally whispered, 'we've got to get out of here.'

'I need all the information we can digest,' Automan said, refusing to budge, 'and we haven't gone through their files.'

'Forget the files,' Walter hissed impatiently. 'We have something more important to take care of.'

Reluctantly Automan turned and began to walk into the wall. But halfway through, he seemed to become stuck.

'What's the matter?' whispered Walter nervously.

'My power grows weaker . . .' Automan pushed through the wall just as the door opened behind them and Collins and Peterson entered the corridor.

'Did you hear anything?' said Peterson, looking around suspiciously.

Collins listened. 'No,' he replied with a shrug.

Satisfied, they walked on down the corridor.

Automan was about to walk through the next wall when, inside him, Walter registered a definite lowering of power. The next moment Automan had passed through and vanished, but with a noisy thud, Walter bounced off the wall, landing on the floor. He climbed to his feet groggily as Automan reappeared again.

'What happened?' said Walter, rubbing his head in a daze.

Automan looked apologetic. 'I'm afraid my batteries

need charging.' He walked over to an electric wall socket.

'Now I know I heard something,' said Peterson, stopping in his tracks and listening. They were still out in the corridor.

'What?' said Collins.

'Voices . . . From in there.'

'Impossible!' Collins fired back. 'That's the file room.'

Suddenly the lights began to dim. Collins was convinced.

'Something's going on,' he snapped, reaching inside his jacket and hurriedly fumbling for a key . . .

13

'Ahhhh!' sighed Automan as a jagged arc of blue-white electricity raced into his palm. His hand was all but plugged into the wall socket and there was a look of deep satisfaction on his face.

'Aahhhh!'

'Auto!' whispered Walter nervously. 'Someone's trying the door.'

Automan closed his fist and the power arc ceased as, replenished, he pulled Walter to him in one swift movement and raced for the wall. A second later Collins and Peterson rushed in, their guns drawn, but the room was empty. They looked around in bewilderment.

There was the whoosh of an elevator door opening.

'Down the hall,' shouted Peterson. 'The elevator!'

As they rounded the corner they were in time to see Automan stepping in to the elevator.

'Stop, or I'll shoot!' Collins called out.

Automan stopped but the elevator doors didn't. They started to close just as Collins fired a hail of bullets which, impossibly, passed through him. A second later the elevator started to descend.

'You missed!' said Peterson derisively.

'How *could* I?' said Collins, examining his gun. 'He was only ten yards away.'

'The question is . . . who is he? And what's he doing here?'

Another elevator arrived and they jumped into it.

'Those bullets,' said Walter, still inside Automan as

he/they raced out of the elevator and into the basement car park, 'how did he miss?'

'He didn't,' said Automan.

'That's what I was afraid of,' said Walter gloomily. He looked round the parking lot. 'We went down too far.'

'No matter,' replied Automan, gesturing to Cursor, who once again conjured up the Autocar. He/they jumped behind the wheel and the car sped off.

Peterson and Collins sprinted out of the elevator in time to see a luminous car flash past.

'There they go!' shouted Peterson.

They tore over to where their black limousine was parked.

Walter was beginning to feel more cheerful. At least he was still alive.

'I gotta say,' he chattered, 'this is the only way to go.'

'Thank you, Walter,' replied Automan, 'I enjoy your world as well.'

In the distance and rushing towards them was the parking machine and the crossbar that blocked the garage exit.

'Hey,' shouted Walter excitedly, 'if we can go through walls, do we have to stop for that crossbar?'

'Of course not,' said Automan, 'if you're within my force field.'

'And if I'm not?'

Automan raised an eyebrow. 'Try it and see.'

Just before Automan reached the crossbar Walter slid out from Automan, and over into the passenger seat.

As the sleek vision approached the garage attendant, he stared out from his booth.

'Hey, what're you doing?' he yelled out. 'Slow down,

slow –'

The machine raced by without slowing and passed right through the crossbar without touching it.

Walter meanwhile was draped over the top bar, his feet dangling over one side and his arms the other. But a few seconds later Autocar stopped abruptly, shot backwards through the crossbar and over Walter, enveloping him. The car raced forward again, this time with Walter inside.

The attendant dropped his ticket and change, his arms and mouth sagging as he stared at the crossbar which had not even a scratch – let alone Walter – on it. But the screeching of tyres brought him quickly back to reality. He spun round to see the black limo bearing down on him. He just had time to jump out of the way as the limousine barreled through the crossbar, shattering it into a thousand toothpicks and continued on out of the garage.

The attendant gazed vacantly at the retreating limo, spat, and returned to his booth to watch the rest of *Knight Rider*.

'It's some kind of sports car,' Collins shouted despairingly. 'We'll never catch it.'

Peterson gave a grim chuckle. 'He can't do any better than we can in traffic.'

Collins nodded, and cocked his gun.

In the distance they could see the gleaming car approaching an intersection.

'Now's our chance,' said Peterson, accelerating.

To both men's astonishment the autocar flashed round the corner, turning ninety degrees without slowing.

Collins looked at Peterson uneasily. 'We've all been working too hard,' he said, but it only seemed to make his partner even more determined.

'If he could make that corner,' Peterson snarled, '*I* can make it.'

The limousine ploughed round the corner and for a moment it almost seemed that it would make it. But not quite. It crashed through a drugstore window, shattering the glass front and smashing into fifty thousand dollars worth of merchandise before it came to a tumultuous stop. For a moment there was an unnatural silence: then a shrill burglar alarm began to wail.

Peterson and Collins stumbled out of the car, surveying the neatly demolished store and the wreck of twisted metal that had minutes earlier been a limousine.

'How're we going to explain this to Mr Hamilton?' Collins said hoarsely.

Peterson scratched his head.

'Very carefully. *Very* carefully.'

14

The Autocar zoomed up the road in which Walter lived and came to a dead stop outside the brownstone tenement building. Like a speeded-up training film on advanced driving it reversed, shot forward again and neatly locked itself into an immaculate parking position.

'Not bad!' said Wally, complimenting himself as he moved out of Automan's form and slid over into the passenger seat.

'Considering it was unnecessary to park it at all,' Automan added with a new, uncharacteristic note of irony in his resonant voice. Walter wasn't the only one who had been educated by tonight's little joyride.

They climbed out and almost immediately the Autocar began to glow and swirl around in a maelstrom of electronic light until it had vanished, leaving the cursor hovering above Automan's head.

'The girl they were talking about,' said Wally as they climbed up the steps, 'she called the department . . . it was on my phone list. I didn't think anything of it . . . She didn't mention Interpol or Jack.'

'That would be consistent with Lieutenant Curtis's secrecy,' said Automan after a microsecond's consideration. 'He was obviously afraid to share his information with the Police Department for some reason.'

'Yeah, I wondered about that.'

As they walked through the downstairs corridor, a door opened and Mrs McGorry peered out. The landlady had evidently been about to go to bed – or just got out of it.

'Hey, keep it down, Nebish,' she muttered, hastily fastening her dressing gown.

'Nebicher,' Wally corrected her. 'It's from the Aramaic for –'

'I don't care if it's from the Holy Grail,' she broke in. 'I don't want –'

At that moment she had seen Cursor. Quickly it darted away, while Mrs McGorry took off her glasses, rubbing her eyes. She put them on again which was when she took in Automan, all six foot four of him. She began to preen herself, patting her hair and straightening her robe.

'Well, if he ain't the cutie,' she giggled coyly. 'Thinking of taking a room-mate, kid?'

Wally blushed a beetroot colour, picturing Roxanne installed in his apartment. 'Uhhh, well,' he stammered, 'maybe . . . kinda . . . I don't know.'

She frowned. 'Normally I'd have to charge you more –' her eyes switched to Automan and her face softened '– but in his case . . .' She fluttered her eyes.

'I'll . . . let you know,' Wally muttered in embarrassment.

'You do that,' Mrs McGorry said, smiling at Automan in what was clearly intended to be a fetching manner.

To Wally's astonishment, Automan gave her a broad, suggestive wink. 'Thank you Moneypenny,' he said, 'I'd like to think of you as my own little Octopussy.'

She sighed deliriously and retreated behind her door.

'Why'd you do that?' Walter hissed at Automan as they ascended to his apartment.

Automan was unflappable. 'You programmed me to.'

Wally looked perplexed.

'James Bond, remember?' Automan reminded him.

Walter sighed. 'No matter how you're programmed,

we're still going to have trouble explaining you.'

'Not at all,' said Automan airily. 'I won't be around that often.'

'What?'

'Walter, there's never going to be enough power available during the day when everyone else is up and using my sources.'

They had reached the door of Wally's apartment. 'Auto,' he implored, 'we've got hot leads. We've got to work on them.'

They entered the apartment by their separate routes.

'Walter, you can work on them,' said Automan. 'You're a policeman.'

'I'm a computer-room expert,' Wally pointed out. 'I don't go out in the field.'

'Why not?' Automan asked in puzzlement.

'Well . . . it just isn't done,' Wally said a little sheepishly.

'It's going to have to be, if you're going to find out what's become of your friend.'

The cursor was beginning to dance around as it grew dimmer.

'I know, Cursor,' Automan said to it.

'You're dimming,' Walter said anxiously.

'Right now, at this moment, I can feel three million toasters, waffle irons, and television sets turning on,' said Automan, his voice becoming fainter as he became more ethereal. 'There go the electric razors, toothbrushes and heaters.' He was almost invisible now. 'I'm sorry, Walter. Keep me programmed. I'll be there when the facts warrant my presence.'

Almost simultaneously Automan and Cursor snapped out of Walter's dimension. In desperation, he rushed over to where the hologram had been and felt it. An empty, useless gesture.

'God,' he groaned. 'What have I done? I thought I felt helpless before.'

A sound came from the basement. He broke into a grin and rushed downstairs. 'Auto, you're back,' he called out hopefully.

His mouth dropped. The room was empty. But the noise he had heard was real enough and it came from the printer. Intrigued, he moved over to it.

INTERPOL
ADDRESS: 9255 SUNSET BLVD
AGENT: T. DU BOISE

'Thanks, Auto,' Wally said, tearing off the printout. 'I guess it's the best you can do during business hours.'

15

'Yes . . . This is Walter Nebicher of the LAPD. Nebicher . . . N.E.B.I.C.H.E.R. Well, look it doesn't really matter, I'm returning a call from a T. Du Boise . . . Thank you very much.'

The door to the computer section opened and Roxanne walked in. She still looked dazed from her encounter with Automan and it was clear she wanted to talk about it. She looked beautiful when she was shocked.

'Wally –'

'Shhhh,' he said, cupping his hand over the mouth-piece. 'Hello? . . . Who is this?'

'This is Tanya Du Boise,' came the husky Parisien accent of Interpol's chief LA agent.

'Tanya!' Wally repeated, surprised. He'd assumed 'T.' was male. He cleared his throat. 'Well . . . I'm returning your call.'

'It's been several days,' she said with an evident mixture of anxiety and relief. 'I left many messages.'

'I'm sorry,' Wally said shamefaced. 'I just didn't recognise the name and with my busy caseload –' He ran his hand over his empty in-and-out trays.

'Can we meet?' said Tanya.

'When?'

'Tonight. 7.30. Broadway and Hill Street.'

'That's Chinatown,' said Wally.

'You must come alone. Tell no one of this rendez-vous. Not even other officers.' She was deadly serious.

'Rendezvous,' Wally chuckled to hide his excitement. 'Good name for it. Right. No problem. Oh, I'll be coming in a plainclothes car . . . old Plymouth. No one'll ever believe I'm a cop.' He hung up.

'Well,' he grinned nervously, 'the plot thickens. I'm going to a rendezvous.'

'Wally,' Roxanne pleaded, 'we've got to talk about last night.'

But Wally was already praying to the Holy Trinity – Philip Marlowe, Sam Spade and Charlie Chan. 'You don't understand,' he said loftily. 'I've got a rendezvous – in Chinatown.'

'Walter,' Roxanne groaned. 'You're not a detective. You could get killed!'

Walter was indignant. 'You saw my friend!' he said pointedly.

'That's what I want to talk to you about it. That was an illusion. It was very good, I'll admit that, but it wasn't real.'

Walter couldn't believe what he was hearing. 'Roxanne,' he said, 'I'm going to solve the biggest case on the books. Eighteen disappearances of key personnel from over a dozen corporations.'

Roxanne rolled her eyes. 'We have a task force of fifty men on that case and *you're* going to solve it.'

'Me *and* my *friend*,' he reminded her.

'Wally,' she sighed, 'don't even mention him again.'

'OK, but he's going to be very angry.'

Roxanne headed for the door. 'He can't be angry,' she threw at him defiantly, 'because he doesn't exist.'

The room started to tremble, and she stared around in alarm.

'I'm sorry . . . I'm sorry,' she said, close to tears, but if Wally had asked her to whom she was apologising she would have been unable to answer. In any case it was too late because she had run out into the squad room, avoiding the stares that were being aimed at her from all directions.

Wally glared at the computer sternly. 'When did I program a temper?' he muttered. Gradually the trembling stopped.

Chinatown, on the north side of downtown LA, might have been created for a rendezvous such as this one, thought Wally as he pulled up his Plymouth behind a large truck. The lanterns and neon of Gin Ling Way lit up the evening sky, the smell of Cantonese and Mandarin cooking lent a keen edge to an appetite freshly whetted not so much for food as for danger. He felt that any moment something extraordinary could happen. He was hungry for experience and here was where it would start.

There was an almighty crash as his Plymouth collided with the truck and his bumper fell off. Without further thought, he got out of the car and headed for Broadway and Hill Street.

It was after only a couple of minutes that it occurred to Wally, with a kind of sixth sense that seemed to have been awakened in him during the past twenty-four hours, that he was being followed. He looked round surreptitiously but saw nothing and no one out of the ordinary. He carried on walking, making his way past the massage parlours, porno shops, strip joints, gambling dens, nightclubs, restaurants and oriental shops and supermarkets, their windows jammed with merchandise from China, Taiwan and Japan. This must be where the big drug deals were made; where cold-blooded, callous, sadistic ritual murders took place in murky back rooms; where big money changed hands over a game of Russian roulette which could only end with a bullet in the brain and a one-way trip to the morgue. He could almost taste the dark excitement, the aura of crime. It was here on the sidewalk and he was a part of it – that is, he was part of the fight against it. He'd have to remember it all just as it was so that he could feed it into Automan's databanks.

Then he heard it: the sound of footsteps walking in time with his. He speeded up and the footsteps accelerated behind him. He slowed down; uncannily the footsteps remained synchronised with his. He swung round – again there was no one. He walked on for a minute and then slipped into the doorway of a Korean restaurant. This was how Charlie Chan would have flushed out the enemy. He waited and listened, his senses attuned and alert in a way he couldn't remember before, except perhaps when he'd created and piloted Space Monkey and Starfighter 3-D – and, of course, Automan.

But this was different: this was reality. He remembered what Roxanne had said about Automan: *That was an illusion. It was very good . . . but it wasn't real.* Of course, he knew different, Automan *was* real. But this was real in another way. The computer had been switched off. He was alone out on the streets, frightened and exhilarated at the same time.

Now there could be no mistaking the footsteps. They were mere yards away. His heart began to beat fast, his mind raced. What would Jack have done? he wondered desperately. He'd have faced his opponent squarely; he'd have known the right time to move and when to go for the jugular. If necessary he'd have slugged it out with guts and skill. Now Automan on the other hand would have checked through his programming and made the most reasonable evaluation of the possibilities and logical consequences, using all the data at his disposal and then, if in doubt, walked through the wall.

Deep in his heart he suspected he was not a fighter, and knew he wasn't a hologram. He was Wally Nebicher from Santa Clara and scared as hell. He slipped further back into the doorway.

'Don't go inside, Officer Nebicher,' came a voice from the sidewalk . . .

16

Wally froze, and then relaxed as he recalled the accent. He was minutely disappointed and infinitely relieved.

'How did you recognise me?' he said sheepishly, moving out of the shadows.

'You were right,' said Tanya Du Boise, a flicker of amusement on her lips. 'You don't look anything like a cop. That and the Plymouth . . . What's left of it.'

He gazed at the Interpol agent, trying hard to conceal his sudden excitement. She was the embodiment of his fantasies: glamorous, mysterious, foreign, sophisticated – the older, mature, exotic woman prepared to deal with him on equal terms and, above all, this was a genuine twenty-four-carat rendezvous.

'OK,' he swallowed, 'I'm game . . . Where to?'

'You're not frightened,' Tanya remarked. 'I like that.'

'Why should I be? You're a friend of Jack's.'

'How do you know that?' asked Tanya, colouring.

Wally grinned. 'You pronounced my name right.'

Tanya became businesslike. 'Start up the street. We can't stay in any one place.'

'Why?'

'They're looking for me,' she replied grimly. 'Walk.'

'*Who's* looking for you?' said Wally as they made their way up the street.

'The people who have Jack,' Tanya replied simply.

'Who are they?'

'I was hoping you could tell me.'

'What's your connection to Jack, and what makes

you think I could help?'

Tanya hesitated. 'We were working together. He from the Los Angeles end . . . and I from Switzerland.'

Wally was intrigued. 'He never mentioned that.'

'What *did* he mention?'

'A lot of names, dates . . . companies. He wanted to find a correlation between them.'

'And did you find any?' Tanya asked.

'Yes . . . My friend –' Wally blushed '– that is my computer found that each of the companies had a tie-in with Global Guard.'

'Global Guard,' Tanya repeated in surprise. 'But they'd be the last people in the world who'd want to see those people disappear . . . Or would they?' She stopped, and stared at him in horror. 'My God . . . if they're involved – '

'Right,' Wally completed. 'No one's safe. They practically control all the investigations.'

'Why would they do it?'

'When we find Jack,' Wally replied confidently. 'we'll know.'

'If he's alive,' she said in a low voice.

They had reached a dark alleyway and Walter began to feel the nausea building up in the pit of his stomach.

'Don't say that,' he said desperately.

She looked at him for a moment, her face softening. 'You like him very much, don't you,' she said gently. 'He liked you.'

'Did he say that?'

'Often.'

Walter gave a rueful grin. 'He's practically the only one in the department who paid any attention to me.'

'You may have been the only one he trusted,' Tanya said seriously.

'Why?' he asked curiously, remembering suddenly

Jack's last words to him: *Don't show anyone in the department what you come up with. Anyone.*

'He suspected a leak on the task force to solve these kidnappings,' said Tanya.

He whistled. 'That's hard to believe.'

'Jack was grabbed at the airport's private jet terminal . . . not the city garage as reported.'

'What can I do?' he asked gravely as the implications sank in.

'You've already done it. I never would have dreamed of zeroing in on Global Guard . . . They're so respected . . . so above suspicion.'

'Then that's their strength,' he said.

'Yes . . .' Tanya seemed all at once to be somewhere else. Then her manner became brisk. 'Thank you, Walter,' she said quickly. 'I can take it from here. You've been a great help.' She leaned towards him and kissed him full on the mouth.

Walter was devastated. He had never been kissed quite like this before. It was as thrilling as crime-fighting. He drew his arms around her for a second helping but, rather like Automan doing one of his vanishing tricks, she literally melted out of his arms and hurried off down the street. He caressed the air for a moment, looking after her longingly.

'If I can be of any *more* help,' he called out, knowing as he did so that she was already too far away to hear, and she was not looking back.

Perhaps it would have been better for her if she had. The black limousine seemed to come from nowhere. It was practically identical to the one that still graced the downtown drugstore like some advanced experiment in destructive art. With a terrible screech the limo skidded to a stop inches behind her.

Tanya wheeled round but she was too late. Collins

and Peterson, looking considerably more alert than they had the previous night, raced from the car, grabbing her as she screamed at them and hurling her into the back seat. In seconds the car was speeding south towards downtown LA.

At first Walter was too shocked to move. Then he was running up the street screaming her name. He reached his now-bumperless Plymouth at the same moment the tail lights of the limo disappeared round the corner. Jumping into the car, he sped off into the mid-evening traffic already aware that the situation was hopeless. There was nothing to give even a hint of which way the limousine had gone.

'Damn,' he muttered, hitting the steering wheel in frustration. 'Where are you when I need you, Automan?'

Suddenly the car began to shudder and tremble.

'It's . . . it's . . . you,' Wally gasped. 'You're coming!'

The Plymouth juddered to a halt. The trembling ceased. No cursor appeared, no vapour except a cloud of black exhaust, but that was usual. Wally leaned his head out of the window in puzzlement and then despondently noticed it – a very flat tyre.

'It isn't you,' he mumbled.

17

'Wally!'

He tore his attention away from the computer into which he was programming new data.

'Oh – hi, Roxanne,' he replied abstractedly.

She closed the door of the computer section and sat down beside him at the console.

'What are you doing?'

'You wouldn't understand,' he muttered, as he continued to punch the keys.

'Try me,' Roxanne said quietly. 'I'm trying to save your job.'

His fingers arrested in mid-type, he turned and stared at her. 'I didn't know I was going to lose it.'

'What do you think I'm doing here so late?' she said. 'The Captain is fed up with you running in and out without telling anyone what's going on.'

'But the Captain can't understand what I'm saying anyway,' Wally said with a shrug. 'And I don't blame him. After all, this terminal's patched into the most sophisticated information banks in the world.'

'Why don't you share what you have with him?'

Wally frowned. 'I can't.'

'Why not?' said Roxanne, perplexed.

'I can't tell you that,' said Wally feeling wretched. 'You work for him.'

Roxanne wanted to scream. '*You* work for him,' she reminded him angrily.

'No . . . maybe Nebich is still working for Lieutenant Curtis,' came a gruff voice.

Wally and Roxanne both shot their heads round to see Captain Boyd standing, red-faced, by the door.

'I'd better get back to my desk,' Roxanne said quickly.

'You do that, Officer,' said Boyd with more than a hint of sarcasm.

'Well,' said the captain, closing on Wally menacingly, 'you want to explain this to me?'

'What's that, sir?' Wally stammered.

'You put out an all-points on a limousine, licence number AJA 611. Do not apprehend . . . Notify Special Sections, Officer Nebicher.'

'Uhhh –'

'Don't fence with me, boy!' the chief stormed. 'By now you've checked out the registration on the car and know who owns it. Who is it and what's it all about?'

'The car is on a corporate lease,' Wally said nervously. 'Probably a dummy holding company for someone else.'

'So why are you checking it out? You like the colour? The wire wheels? You left your hat in it?'

Wally steeled himself. 'It was involved with a kidnapping I happened to witness,' he blurted out.

'When? Where?'

'Chinatown . . . About two hours ago.'

Boyd looked bewildered. 'I haven't seen any reports of a kidnapping in Chinatown,' he muttered.

'It won't be reported. I was the only witness.'

It was like pressing a button marked 'Aggravate'. The chief was livid. 'Nebicher!' he bawled. 'I'm not going to wring it out of you one drop of blood at a time. I'm going right for the juggler. Tell me what you're up to or you're suspended.'

'I'm simply following up on some data given me by Lieutenant Curtis before he disappeared.' Walter was beginning to wish that *he* could disappear into the computer.

'You're following up!' Boyd repeated with a smile: then his face contorted with rage. 'YOU'RE following up!' he screamed. 'Who in the hell do you think you are?'

Police in the squad room were beginning to stare through the glass partition.

'Well,' Wally stammered. 'The lieutenant did come to me to –'

'You're nothing but a glorified typist,' the captain snarled, 'with all your overpriced machinery that's about as good as a broken refrigerator.' He turned to go. 'Now I want everything you've got and I want it now.'

The computer lights started to flash angrily. Wally wheeled round in panic.

'No,' he hissed.

'What's going on?' said Boyd.

'Oh, the resistors are just oscillating,' Wally said quickly. 'It happens that way sometimes.' He shook his head. 'Some of this equipment's old-fashioned. We should phase it out.'

'I'll phase *you* out!' the captain barked, though he had started to calm down a little.

Walter glared at the computer: the lights returned to normal, and he handed some printouts to the chief.

'And don't give me that backwash,' Boyd grumbled. 'I want bottom lines . . . what's it all add up to?'

Wally gulped. 'Global Guard, sir.'

'Global Guard?' Boyd repeated in astonishment. 'What're you saying? They're the biggest independent security organisation in the world . . . What've they got to do with anything?'

'They're mixed up in the kidnappings,' said Wally. 'I don't know how.'

The chief stared around at the computers, shaking his head. The world was growing crazier every minute. 'Nebicher,' he said quietly. 'I don't want what you just told me to go outside this room, do you understand me?'

'Sir, the facts –' Walter began.

'Don't talk, listen,' Boyd hissed. 'If you turn this department into the laughing stock of the country, I'll personally send you and your travelling circus right out of the window – understand?'

'Yes, sir,' Wally mumbled.

Captain Boyd turned and stormed out. Wally watched him go, feeling hurt and humiliated as he walked back to the keyboard. He ran his hands over the keys as if stroking a pet.

'He doesn't mean it,' he muttered. 'He just doesn't know any better . . . but he's right about one thing. We can't tell anybody about this. We're up against some powerful enemies. I just don't know what to do next . . .'

Suddenly something Tanya had said came back to him. *Jack was grabbed at the airport's private jet terminal . . . not the city garage as reported.*

'Wait a minute!' he whispered to himself. 'Maybe I do!'

He thought for a moment and then sat down at the keyboard. 'Jack disappeared from the charter jet terminal where corporate jets are going out all the time . . . If they grabbed Tanya, chances are they're going to move her out quickly. Come on Automan . . .'

PRIORITY CODE:
AUTOMAN
WHAT IS YOUR CLEARANCE?
CRIME FIGHTER

'Let's plug into the airport flight plan,' he muttered

as he typed in the request, 'and see whose little birdies are going bye bye tonight . . . and who amongst them is tied to Global Guard.'

The mainframe's ten and a half inch tape reels began to whirr . . .

18

'You OK?' said Smithers, walking into Captain Boyd's office.

The captain was standing with his back to him, staring morosely out of the window. He looked terrible.

'Ahh . . . this kidnapping is getting under my skin,' he growled, putting on his jacket and lighting a Winston. 'Everybody's becoming an expert, trying to get in on the act.'

'Like who?' Smithers asked suspiciously.

'Like the Chief . . . the Commissioner. Even Nebich has decided we aren't doing the job so he's out filing kidnapping reports from Chinatown.'

'Chinatown?' Smithers stiffened slightly.

Boyd shrugged it off with a wave of the hand: the smoke blew into Smithers's eyes. 'Don't worry about it. He has delusions of being a real cop.' He glanced at Smithers. 'What've you got?'

'Nothing new,' Smithers sighed. 'We've run down every possible terrorist lead, both domestic and abroad . . . zip.'

Boyd gave a puzzled frown. 'Odd . . . By now you'd usually have ten groups taking credit.'

'Well . . . this case is kind of unusual. The companies have been cooperating in keeping these disappearances pretty quiet.'

'For their own good,' Boyd nodded. 'It can't help in recruiting personnel when you have to tell a prospect that the last two guys in the same job were kidnapped.'

'No, sir.'

'OK,' said Boyd, picking up his hat and walking to the door, 'well, let's call it a night. I guess we'll go back to work on Monday. At least they haven't grabbed anyone today.'

A strange look crept into the detective's eyes. 'No, sir,' he muttered.

'Coming?' said Captain Boyd, walking across to the elevator and pushing the button. A car arrived almost immediately.

Smithers shook his head. 'I gotta grab a couple of things from my office. See ya Monday.'

Boyd nodded and disappeared behind the closing elevator doors. Smithers watched him go, the smile fading from his face, to be replaced by a look that was menacing and lethal. He turned his attention at once on the glass partition that divided the computer section from the main squad room . . .

Walter stared hopelessly at the numbers and readouts racing by on the VDU. This was going to take forever.

'Come on, Auto,' he pleaded, 'what's happened to you? It shouldn't take you this long. All this is, is a routine search. Come on, man. Where are you?'

'Right here.'

He spun round to find Smithers looking down at him coldly. The detective grimaced and Wally assumed it to be some kind of a smile.

'I hear you've been holding back.' There was something in his tone which struck Wally as not entirely friendly.

'What?' he said nervously.

'Another kidnapping in Chinatown,' Smithers growled. 'I didn't hear nothin' about it.'

Walter laughed uneasily. 'Hey . . . I don't know what to say about it. The Captain thought I was seeing things.'

The detective started acting confidential. 'Tell me what you think you saw.'

'A girl was grabbed by two guys in a limo.'

'You get a licence number?'

'Yeah . . . It checks out a leased car.' He gestured towards the computer. 'I'm trying to verify ownership.'

Smithers nodded. 'I'd appreciate you calling me if you come up with anything. You know . . . ' he laid a hand on Walter's shoulder ' . . . Jack was a friend of mine, too. We worked very close . . . We didn't keep secrets.'

Wally glanced uneasily at his shoulder. 'Yeah . . . Well, that's good to know.'

Smithers nodded and returned to the squad room, moving down the line of desks to a phone which he picked up. Wally watched him with a growing sense of panic.

19

The limousine turned into the tarmac of the private air terminal just as the Gulfstream SMA-3 jet was being pulled out of the hangar by a tow mule. It parked beside another limo, Peterson climbing out of the first car and Collins emerging from the second.

'Mr Peterson will take you out to the plane, Mr Cramer,' Collins said to the businessman seated in the first limousine. 'I have one more guest to get who'll be travelling with you.'

'Oh . . . From our company?' said Don Cramer with good-humoured curiosity. He had not been expecting star treatment.

'No, not exactly,' said Collins. 'But I'm sure you'll find her company just as agreeable.'

He smiled as Peterson and Cramer walked off to board the plane out on the ramp, then he climbed into the second limousine. Inside, a heavy-set chauffeur was keeping a loose eye on the woman sitting shackled in the back.

Tanya Du Boise was beginning to think that her only hope of rescue was Walter Nebicher – and it was not such a comforting thought as she would have liked. Walter was very sweet, and obviously devoted to Jack. He was also enthusiastic and from what she had heard, amazingly clever, but their meeting had convinced her that she had more chance of being rescued by the Tupamaros.

The limousine's phone buzzed and Collins picked it up.

'Global,' he snapped.

'Got room for one more?' Detective Smithers asked tersely at the other end.

'What's happened now?' Collins sighed.

'Someone spotted you in Chinatown.'

'We'll dump the car – ' Collins began impatiently.

'You'd better dump a little cop I'm going to bring you, too,' said Smithers caustically. 'He was there.'

'Who?'

'A friend of Lieutenant Curtis's who happened to be with Tanya.'

'Pretty big coincidence,' Collins chuckled drily. 'What's he know?'

'That's what we'd better find out,' said Smithers.

'You need help?'

'With this guy?' The detective snorted. 'My mother could take him.'

'If you can't get here in forty minutes, we lose our flight clearance,' Collins reminded him. 'Hamilton won't like that.'

'We'll be there.'

Smithers hung up and looked through the partition. That little shmuck Nebicher was still pacing around his fitted kitchen trying to get the chicken to roast. Smithers decided to do a little roasting himself.

'Come on, Auto,' Wally was saying as Smithers opened the door. 'How long can it take to see if any of the corporations who're using Global Guard have jets out tonight?'

'Why don't we go on out to the airport and see for ourselves?'

For the second time that night, Wally spun round to find Smithers towering above him. This time he wasn't the slightest bit friendly.

'I was just talking out loud,' Wally explained.

Smithers nodded understandingly, pulling his service revolver out of its holster. 'Bad habit,' he agreed. 'Let's go.'

There was no way out, Wally realised, looking longingly back at the computer. But Automan was resting wherever the world's first truly automatic men take their vacation. Probably some Fourth Dimension Miami.

'That ain't gonna help ya,' Smithers growled. 'Move it.'

Wally moved towards the door, raising his hands like they did in the Cagney movies.

'Keep your hands at your side,' Smithers hissed. 'Look normal.'

He shoved his gun inside his overcoat pocket and the two officers boarded the elevator.

'Jack was right,' Wally said as they waited for the doors to close. 'He thought there was an inside man.'

'Jack was stupid,' the detective sneered. 'If *he'd* played along he could have been rich.'

'Where is he?' Wally said.

'We're going to take you to him.'

'Please indicate your desired floor and step to the rear of the car,' came the synthesised elevator voice.

It seemed there was no way out but down.

As the doors closed behind them a light began to flicker on the reception desk in the squad room which all at once started to rumble. Inside the elevator the overhead light fixture seemed to dim slightly. Wally noticed it at once and clenched his fists tightly to control his excitement. The elevator car itself seemed to be slowing down as well – at least by the sound of it – and the car started to shake. Beneath their feet they could feel a powerful vibration as though –

'My God! An earthquake!' Smithers gasped.

The moment of inattention was all Wally needed. He grabbed Smithers's gun hand and pinned it inside the detective's trench coat. For the next minute the two men struggled for possession of the gun but here it must be said that Walter's basic knowledge of physical combat had mostly been confined to practice sessions of Karate Joe versus the Interplanetary Maniacs, and his experience in the field was negligible.

With speedy efficiency Smithers kneed Wally in the stomach and finished him off with a couple of effectively placed judo chops. Walter was hanging on, but only just, when a bright dancing light appeared suddenly in the car. Smithers rubbed his eyes and then stood rigid, paralysed with fear, as Cursor orbited around him.

'Aaahhhh! What is it? . . . What is it?' he whispered.

'It's kind of like an honour guard for a friend of mine,' Wally volunteered informatively from the floor.

'Get it away! . . . Get it away!' the bent detective babbled hysterically.

The cursor swooped directly towards Smithers who just had time to duck out of the way.

'I really don't have any control over it,' Wally said apologetically. 'But you might ask *him*.'

In small jerks, like a robot, Smithers turned his head to look behind him.

'Hi Smithers,' said Automan genially.

The detective seemed to wither as he lost consciousness, sinking to his knees in the corner of the elevator.

20

'You took your time getting here,' said Walter as he knelt down and, taking Smithers's gun, shoved it into his belt.

'You have any idea how many flights a day corporations have out of Los Angeles?' said Automan, his professional pride ruffled.

'What about tonight?'

'Three possibilities,' Automan replied calmly.

The elevator car was about to reach the basement.

'I can narrow it down the rest of the way,' Wally said impatiently. 'They're waiting for me. If I'm right, a certain limousine will be there too.'

'Parking level one,' said the elevator synthetically. 'Have a nice evening and drive carefully.'

'Thank you,' Automan replied with evident pleasure.

Wally make a note to himself to modify the response-to-pre-recorded-vocal-synthesised-programs program. You just don't go around talking to elevators. 'What'll we do with him?' he said, referring to Smithers.

'These elevator cars are computer-operated,' said Automan. 'See if you can shackle him to the railing of the car.'

'You got it,' said Wally, using the detective's handcuffs, 'but what are you going to –'

'Car three computer control, this is Automan. Would you mind –'

'Automan, you can't talk to –' Wally tried to stop him, but Automan had taken charge.

'– taking this car out of service and running it up and

down until further notice?'

'Automan!' Wally tried again.

'It would be my pleasure, Automan,' said the elevator cordially.

'Automan, how – ?'

'You forget, Walter,' he said. 'My computer can talk to other computers.'

With Cursor hovering overhead, they rushed out of the underground parking area.

'We're in a hurry, Cursor,' said Automan.

The cursor streaked across to the driveway and began spinning, glowing brightly. In moments the advanced, futuristic lines of Autocar began to appear like a graphic light display, shimmering in the darkness.

'Walter, do you know how to *use* that gun?' said Automan solicitously.

Wally glanced at the revolver, shamefaced. 'Oh, well –' he cleared his throat. 'No.'

'Then we won't need it.'

Reluctantly he drew it out, unloaded it and threw it in a trashcan. The cursor meanwhile had finished its job. Flashing, it dissolved away in shimmering light, leaving Autocar in its place. They climbed in and at once sped off into the night.

'The flights are all within the next hour,' said Automan as they shot through the heart of Los Angeles.

'We'll never make it in this traffic,' Wally wailed.

'No problem,' Automan replied nonchalantly. 'I happen to know –'

'– the traffic light computer quite well,' Wally joined in. 'I know, I know,' he said, rolling his eyes.

As the Autocar raced up the street it wove its way miraculously through the long queues of traffic, and each red light turned to green for it.

'The Captain says we have to be rolling within the next few minutes or refile our flight plan,' said Peterson as Collins, escorting a tired, reluctant and handcuffed Tanya Du Boise, joined him on the steps leading up to the plane. 'I don't have to tell you how dangerous that is, with certain people liable to be reported missing at any moment.'

Collins looked around nervously. 'He said he'd be here with the cop,' he muttered.

'What is this?' said Cramer in alarm as Peterson moved Tanya along the passenger gangway and deposited her in one of the luxurious seats close to the businessman.

'A security breach,' Peterson replied sharply. 'Don't worry, she won't give us any trouble.'

Cramer eyed his beautiful new travelling companion speculatively, then noticed her handcuffs.

'I *would* worry, if I were you,' she said to him dourly. 'We're both being kidnapped.'

Cramer darted a terrified look at Peterson.

'You're quite safe, Mr Cramer,' he replied calmly. 'In fact, you're in for the time of your life.'

'Keep your seat belt on,' warned Peterson, pulling out his gun as Cramer, panicking, tried to climb out of his seat, 'or you could get hurt.'

Cramer sank back into his chair, realising for the first time the gravity and hopelessness of his situation.

21

'There!'

As Autocar zipped onto the approach road to the apron, Automan pointed to where the private jet stood idling.

Wally stared in dismay as the SMA-3's steps were pulled up, the cabin sealed. The plane was beginning to taxi. It was only then that he noticed Collins eyeing the Autocar warily, and putting his hand under his coat.

'I'm starting to wish I'd kept that gun,' he said under his breath.

'There's a better way,' said Automan.

Wally threw him a questioning glance but, without saying a word, Automan reached out his hand, merging with Walter who moved over to complete the merger.

As the Autocar shot towards Collins, the security man drew out his gun and fired.

'He's shooting at us,' Automan remarked in a matter of fact sort of way as a hail of bullets passed straight through the Autocar. One of them seemed – though Walter may have been imagining it – to whizz through his head. It reminded him of Starfighter 3-D.

'Why do I get the feeling we're right about that plane being the one we're after?' he spoke out of Automan's mouth.

'Aim right for him,' Automan instructed.

'We want him alive –' Wally began.

'We won't hurt him,' Automan assured him.

The Autocar bore down on Collins. Seeing no way out, he emptied his gun and dived to the tarmac. The car screeched to a halt by his feet.

To Collins's astonishment a huge figure, with a body that twinkled like a planetarium, jumped out of the car which he had chased the previous night. Then to his terror, Automan picked him up and held him in the air.

But that was nothing to what followed. The apparition began to talk to him in an excited, high-pitched voice.

'Naughty boy,' it said.

Collins waved his legs about in the air like a floppy doll.

'Put me down!' he moaned. 'Don't hurt me!'

'Ahhh!' said Walter, with relish. 'I just may want to break you in half.'

'What are you?' Collins wailed. 'Where are you from?'

Walter/Automan shook him about a little. 'Don't tell him,' a deep, resonant voice came out of Automan's mouth.

'I won't,' Automan nodded to himself in a higher register.

Collins stared down in amazement.

'If you'll let me bend him a little,' Wally pleaded.

Automan's expression changed magically from childlike anticipation to magisterial denial. 'No,' he seemed to say to himself in a calm, assured voice. 'We have work to do. Where is that plane going?' he said to the petrified criminal.

'I don't know,' Collins piped.

Automan rattled him about a couple of times and then turned him upside down.

'Switzerland,' Collins blabbered. 'I don't know where.'

'Perhaps if you contact the tower . . .' Automan suggested.

'Me? They won't listen to me,' Collins groaned.

'I wasn't talking to you,' Automan rebuked him sternly. 'Wally?' he added.

'They have no way to stop an international flight on my say-so,' a frenetic voice came out of Automan's mouth. 'I haven't got any proof or anything.'

'Then we have only one choice,' Automan said. 'Cursor,' he commanded.

The Autocar suddenly began to glow brighter and brighter until it seemed as if massive energy forms were being exchanged.

'We must take flight, Cursor,' Automan said.

Instantly a high-pitched series of tones was emitted. The Autocar was evolving into a new pattern, changing pitch and direction until the machine had been transformed into something of an entirely different order. The entire structure began to glow and glisten, then its lines became clear and distinct. Instead of the sleek automobile there stood a ravishingly elegant supersonic jet plane technically at least two centuries ahead of anything in existence.

'Fantastic!' Wally exclaimed.

Collins moaned. 'I don't feel so good . . .'

'You will,' Wally assured him. 'Climb in! How does he climb in, Auto?' he appeared to ask himself.

'I'll show you,' replied Automan.

An instant later, with Collins in his/their arms Automan/Walter had shifted in time and space: they were now inside the cockpit.

Automan nodded.

'Very nice,' Wally agreed, still merged within his creation. 'If you'll just buckle in back there, fella.'

Automan/Walter tossed Collins onto a back seat of what he could now see as he looked around in a daze was an advanced four-passenger fighterplane.

'Who are you, man . . . er . . . guys?' he asked in a patently ludicrous attempt to regain his self-composure and be pally. 'What's coming down, man – men?'

'Just be good and you won't get hurt,' said Wally doing his Bogart imitation.

'I think I'd better drive, Walter,' Automan said discreetly. 'There's no immediate danger to you.'

Collins's eyes nearly popped out of his head as a skinny young guy appeared to climb out of the big guy's sequinned see-through body, and moved over into the co-pilot's seat.

'I think you're right,' said Wally, sighing with relief. 'And I could use a little rest. That guy's heavy.'

Collins hid his face in his hands.

'I'm dead and I'm being punished,' he groaned.

'Hang on, Wally,' Automan warned. 'You're going to be pulling a few Gs.'

Walter turned white. 'I just hope you don't fly like you drive,' he cracked.

From a standing start the plane suddenly – with absolutely no acceleration – streaked off into the sky like a Sidewinder air-to-air missile, flying at a thousand miles per hour and sucking Wally and the security man back against their seats.

'You *do*!' Wally managed to gasp.

'Preliminaries are not necessary in an energised vehicle,' Automan explained, as he sat in peaceful harmony with the airborne jet.

'OK,' said Wally when he had got his breath back. 'What's the plan? We're here and they're there.'

'We simply follow them to their destination,' Automan replied.

Wally leaned over to him, mindful of Collins's presence, and whispered: 'Automan, I know your energy field is able to protect me against bodily harm, and I'm grateful for that, but what do we do if we land in the middle of a gang of terrorists? I don't have any way of attacking them or freeing Jack . . . I'm not even armed.'

Automan paused, applying the full power of his massive logic systems, and taking advantage of access to the world's most sophisticated databanks.

'That's something we'll have to prepare,' he announced finally.

Wally smiled nervously. 'Oh, good . . .' he whispered. 'I'm glad this is well thought out.'

22

Lydell Hamilton climbed out of the blue Volvo estate car which had pulled up to meet the Gulfstream jet as it taxied to a stop on the runway of the near-deserted airport.

'Welcome, Mr Cramer,' he called out genially as the executive was led down the stairs of the boarding ramp. 'My name is Lydell Hamilton . . . I'm your host.' He glanced briefly at Tanya Du Boise as Peterson removed her shackles and pushed her down the boarding ramp.

'What are you going to do to me?' said Cramer, evidently very frightened.

Hamilton smiled. 'Nothing but make your stay here as pleasant and comfortable as any man has ever enjoyed on the face of this planet.'

Cramer stared at him in bewilderment. 'I don't get it,' he said.

'You will . . . come.'

An armed guard led Cramer to the Volvo while Hamilton turned his attention to Tanya.

'I'm sorry you made it necessary to bring you here,' he said sternly 'But as is the case with all our guests, the pursuit of excellence in any profession has its price.'

Tanya's eyes blazed with hostility. 'Where's Jack Curtis?' she demanded.

'You'll see him soon enough,' Hamilton replied coldly.

He gestured towards the Volvo and Tanya climbed in. Behind them the crew closed up the plane and jumped into another car. Soon the two vehicles were speeding through the mountain roads on their way to the Alpine Institute of Technology.

Autoplane streaked through the Swiss countryside, sometimes grazing icecapped mountain peaks, sometimes skating above glorious blue lakes, its flight path computer controlled for maximum efficiency.

'It isn't a very populous area,' commented Automan, looking through the cockpit as the plane approached a field and touched down for a perfect landing. 'That's bad.'

'That's good,' said Wally. 'It should be easy to find their stronghold.'

'No,' Automan contradicted him with a shake of the head. 'It's bad, they don't appear to have a very large power supply.'

Wally paled, remembering the last time. 'Auto, I don't like the sound of that. As a matter of fact, I don't like the look of it. You aren't dimming on me?'

Automan nodded apologetically. 'I don't know how to tell you this, but . . . until it grows dark and we can draw on the entire power supply of the area –'

'Auto,' Walter groaned. 'NO!'

'I'm going to have to be leaving you.' He was rapidly dimming as Walter looked around in panic.

'Auto,' he whimpered. 'You can't bring me here to these mountains, with all these criminals and then just leave me here, naked, stripped of my best tricks.'

As Automan vanished so did Autoplane. Walter and the dozing security man suddenly fell to the ground. Fortunately the jet had touched down so that both landed in reasonable working order – only Collins's spirit had been crushed. He rose groggily to his feet, staring about him.

'What happened?' he gasped. 'Where are we?' He

eyed Wally dubiously.

If Walter could no longer hide inside a hologram he could still cloak himself in Automan's mystique.

'Easy pal,' he warned. 'Or I'll give you more of the same.'

But Collins was looking around, scanning the empty field.

'Where's that other guy?' he said, baffled.

'Where I can call him when I need him,' Wally replied with admirable bluster, though inside he was feeling as wet and hollow as soap bubbles. 'On your feet,' he commanded.

Collins may have been confused, but he was sure of one thing. He wasn't going to mess with a guy who'd just put him through the worst nightmare of his life.

'Move it!' Wally snapped.

'Where?'

'You know where – march!'

Torn between terror and a sense of the utter absurdity of having literally been held up by a schizophrenic ghost, Collins led the way towards the Institute.

23

The two estate cars drove through the entrance gates of the Alpine Institute of Technology and drew up next to the administration building. Tanya and Cramer climbed out and were led inside.

It was a fantasy of modern architecture and interior decor – glass stairways, subdued lighting, exotic plants and the latest electronic surveillance equipment. The people who wandered about may have been dressed as though for a ski resort, the bar may have served the most exquisite tropical cocktails, the restaurant may have employed the services of the world's most skilled Cordon Bleu master chefs – but video cameras and TV monitors were rigged up at every corner.

'I don't get it,' said Cramer testily. 'What is all this?'

'A prison,' Tanya replied gloomily, 'if I were to judge by the guards and fortifications.'

Cramer stared and licked his lips as two shapely bikini-clad, bronze-skinned girls sauntered past them. 'Does this look like a prison?' he said sceptically.

'Can we leave?' she pointed out.

'Where would you go?' Hamilton chuckled. 'This is about all there is in this part of the Alps.'

'Please . . .' Cramer turned to face Hamilton. 'What am I doing here?'

'Exactly what you do back home,' came a familiar voice from behind him.

Cramer swung round. 'Chuck!' he exclaimed in surprise. 'And Marty!'

Martin Wills and Chuck Wilson looked remarkably

healthy and (Wilson at least, happy, considering they had now been imprisoned at the Institute for three weeks. Both were dressed in ski clothes, which seemed to be the preferred dress among the 'guests'.

'Don,' said Wills quietly. 'They told me you were coming. I'd hoped against hope they were wrong!'

'Marty!' Cramer repeated. 'For God's sakes . . . you're alive!'

'Joanne –' Wills asked anxiously. 'How is she?'

'How is she?' Cramer replied. 'She is worried, Marty. Damned worried. We'd all but given up –'

'Come, Miss Du Boise,' Hamilton interrupted. 'We have a debriefing session scheduled for you. But first . . .'

His words became inaudible as he led her away.

'What is all this?' Cramer asked the two engineers. 'What's going on?'

'Just what I said,' replied Wilson calmly. 'We're working same as we always did.'

'Not *quite* the same,' Wills corrected him, gesturing around the admin building.

'It's simple,' Wilson went on. 'They give us everything we could want. And in return we do our jobs.'

'I wouldn't exactly call it everything,' Wills reminded him. 'We're prisoners here.' Clearly Martin Wills was missing his family more than Chuck Wilson was missing his goldfish.

'But surely we can get out?' said Cramer. 'After we've finished our different projects.'

Wills looked grave. 'I've talked to a lot of people here,' he sighed. 'They've never heard of anyone leaving . . . not alive,' he added ominously.

'Come on, Marty,' said Wilson heartily, gesturing towards the bar. 'If you have to be a prisoner, this is a mighty fine prison to be in.'

Cramer raised an eyebrow. 'You sound as though you *like* it,' he said disbelievingly.

As they had been talking a phenomenally attractive redhead at the bar had been giving Wilson more than a passing degree of attention. She climbed off the bar stool and walked over to him. Wilson wrapped his arms around her, kissing her fondly and turning back to Cramer.

'Back home I was alone,' he said, 'no family, no one to care about. Here . . . well, there are times when I *do* like it . . . a lot.'

'Sure,' Wills said bitterly. 'You don't mind when you look up and see one of *those* watching.'

He indicated a monitoring camera immediately above them.

'But I *have* a family and so does Marty,' Cramer added.

Wilson merely shrugged, moving off with the woman to have a drink at the bar.

'Haven't you tried to escape?' Cramer asked Wills.

'I've been trying since I got here,' Martin replied grimly. 'And it's because of them that I'll never rest till I get out of this place!' Suddenly he looked desperate. 'Somehow, I'll find a way to be with my wife and my little girls again.'

24

Jack Curtis sat on the quay, looking out at the lake. The sky was a brilliant blue, the lake sparkled and, like an addict needing a fix, he craved the LA smog. This place was getting to him: even his instincts as a detective seemed to have taken a vacation. He looked with only mild interest – at least untainted by any kind of pleasure – at the patrol boat motoring past and carrying several guards. The sound of footsteps behind him produced nothing more than a frown. Indifferently he turned and then did a double take.

'Oh, Jack,' cried Tanya Du Boise, 'you're alive . . .'

He gazed at her, profoundly moved, but with mixed emotions. 'I wish I could say I was happy to see you,' he said, taking her in his arms, 'but you were our last hope.'

'I'll leave you to get reacquainted,' said Lydell Hamilton, turning to go.

'You don't expect us to talk for your guards?' Curtis threw at him.

'Am I that naive?' Hamilton smiled. 'No . . . her session is scheduled one hour from now. How long it lasts will be up to Miss Du Boise – and her answers.' He walked off, leaving the two of them – relatively – alone.

'Is it as bad as it looks?' she said quietly.

He laughed drily. 'Actually, I thought it *looked* pretty good. It's *being* here that's a throwback to the Dark Ages.'

'What's going on here, Jack?' she asked him as they wandered across to the bar in the main building. 'This looks like a *resort*.'

'It was once,' he replied. 'But now this place is the home of nothing less than slavery in the twentieth century.'

'Slavery? But why?'

'See these people?' he said, pointing to the various groups of abducted personnel, many of whom seemed to have become adjusted to their enforced stay. 'They all made the mistake of becoming invaluable to their respective companies. At that point a price was put on their heads to protect them.'

'Protected by Global Guard?' said Tanya, beginning to catch on.

'That's right. And as a result this hotel is populated by brilliant young scientists and engineers who sit in their neat little offices and donate their genius to the company store. For which a high fee is paid to Global.'

'By whom?'

'The companies they were working for before they were kidnapped,' said Jack.

Tanya stared at him. 'But that's bizarre. Corporations can't condone slavery!'

He smiled. 'Most of them don't. But these particular multinationals feel no allegiance to any one country or any one *person* for that matter.'

'How can they justify such a thing?'

'You haven't heard the lecture,' he chuckled. 'It's the corporations who are the abused parties . . . They pump millions of dollars into developing young talents only to have them show their gratitude by leaving to go to work for competitors.'

Tanya caught the drift. 'So the minute they threaten to go to work for someone else, Global Guard is brought in.'

'Correct, and the young men no longer run out on

their responsibilities. They sit here . . . they work . . . and they are treated to every luxury in life.'

He led her outside to where a spa and swimming pool looked over a spectacular view of the lake and mountains. But even here it was impossible to ignore the cameras and electronic eyes.

'Skiing, swimming . . . the ladies,' he said. 'What more could a man want?'

'You're not telling me they don't want to leave?' she said incredulously.

'Hardly,' he replied. 'What man accepts bondage as a price for anything? They try to swim, buy, ski their way out – there's no place to go. They're prisoners in a Winter Wonderland.'

'And what about us?' she said softly.

'Our hosts will ask you everything you knew about them before you were captured. Tell them the truth. If your story doesn't mesh with mine . . . we're probably both dead.'

She stared at him, but before she could reply, Peterson suddenly appeared with a guard.

'Miss Du Boise?' he said brusquely. 'We're ready for you.'

In spite of his own words, Jack Curtis acted unthinkingly, placing himself protectively in front of her, but the guard's Uzi was aimed directly at his brain.

'Jack, don't!' Tanya screamed.

Regretting the move instantly, he backed off, saying simply. 'Tanya, I'm so sorry you got into this.'

She smiled bravely. 'It'll be all right, you'll see. "Chutzpah" – remember?'

As Peterson led her away. Curtis could only watch with impotent fury, praying that she would not say or do anything that might endanger her life.

25

Two figures trudged along the Alpine road. One was tall, broad and powerful looking – and obviously scared out of his wits. Behind him walked a short, young, skinny little fellow and he too – though less obviously – was scared out of his wits. But Walter Nebicher knew that his life, and the lives of his friend Jack Curtis and Tanya Du Boise, together with those of dozens of engineers and computer experts, present and future, depended at that moment on his ability to act tough and only the hope that Automan would return kept him from turning round and running back down the road.

As they neared a bend in the road, an approaching vehicle could be heard. Without another moment's thought, Wally dived at the security man's calves, bringing him crashing down in the bank of foliage beside the road in a crude tackle. The Institute Volvo breezed by as they fell down the gently sloping ravine, falling on top of each other at the bottom.

'What'd you do that for?' Collins growled, as he picked himself up stiffly, convinced even more than ever that Wally was a highly dangerous, volatile and irrational party who should not be messed with.

'I don't want anyone to see us,' Wally replied truthfully enough as they climbed up the slope.

'Yeah? Then what're you gonna do about the gate up ahead?' said Collins, puffing from the exercise.

Wally cursed to himself. 'OK,' he said.' How do we get around that?'

'We don't,' Collins replied morosely. 'The guards are

all armed with submachine guns.'

'Nice – do they know you?'

'Sure, but –'

'OK,' Wally announced. 'For the moment I want you to forget all the superhuman powers you've seen me possess.'

'Look,' Collins gloomily reminded him, 'they'd just as soon shoot me as anybody . . . These guys are ruthless.'

Wally knew that he desperately needed to keep a hold on the situation and that meant keeping a hold on Collins.

'Hey,' he snapped. 'You've seen me in action. What am I – a squad of girl scouts? It's time to choose sides.'

Collins swallowed. 'You'll see that I get a break if I help you,' he pleaded.

'You can depend on it,' Wally said magnanimously.

'OK, I'll walk behind you . . . like you're my prisoner. You put your hands in the air.'

'Right,' Wally agreed. 'But no funny business. Just remember, I could have dropped you out of that fancy plane of mine at thirty thousand feet, instead of a few yards.'

Collins shivered. 'I won't forget what happened to me last night . . . Not ever.'

'Halt!' shouted the bearded guard at the security gates as he heard footsteps approaching.

Wally was the first to appear around the corner, his hands in the air. Collins was right behind him, his overcoat draped over his hand. It was clear to the guard that he had Walter covered.

'Ahh . . . Mr Collins,' said the guard as he recognised the Global man. 'How did you miss the car?' His accent was German.

'This one tried to make a run for it a few hundred yards up the road!' said Collins. 'They dropped me off to fetch him.'

The guard nodded, pushing a button to allow the gates to swing open and Collins marched Wally inside. After they had passed through he picked up a phone.

'This is the main gate,' he said. 'Alert the chief of security that Mr Collins found the escapee . . . That's right, they just entered the camp.'

'That was very good,' Wally said approvingly when they were out of the guard's earshot.

Collins was growing increasingly puzzled by his behaviour. 'Why are you going to all this trouble when bullets don't seem to bother you?' he asked.

'Well,' Wally laughed nervously. 'I may be indestructible but my friends in there aren't. I don't want them to wind up as hostages . . . OK?'

Collins eyed him uneasily for a second. 'OK,' he replied satisfied. 'What now?'

'Where's your main power supply?'

'In the far corner of the compound. Why?'

'We need to gain control of it,' said Wally.

'It's guarded,' said Collins, then added with a mixture of respect and fear, 'but I guess that won't bother you.'

'Like I said,' said Wally, 'I use my personal weapons of death and destruction very sparingly.'

The alert came just as Hamilton was concluding the interrogation of the Interpol agent, Tanya Du Boise. If Du Boise was lying then she was exceptionally skilful. It would appear however that the initiative had come from Curtis. They had no solid evidence: it was all inspired guesswork. Even so, it would probably be wise to phase down the LA operation for the time being and allow any leads the police may have gathered to cool down.

As usual Hamilton had employed what he liked to think was a subtle mixture of courtesy and ruthlessness to wear the subject down, but she had stood up to this first session remarkably well. The next two should determine whether she had anything to hide. Of course there was no question now of letting her go, but he was assuring her that she could prove very useful to the Institute as an operative when the news of an escapee's recapture obliged him to leave her in the guards' capable hands.

He raced out of the compound with two armed guards and Peterson, and jumped into a waiting jeep which tore through the main compound. How anyone could have even attempted an escape was a mystery but he would personally ensure that it did not happen again.

'How do we get to the generator without being observed?' Wally asked.

'It'll be tough in broad daylight,' was all Collins could say.

'OK – where can we hide until it gets dark?'

'That may not be necessary,' said Collins, noticing the jeep as it came roaring out of the compound. 'You'd better destroy them before they destroy us.'

'There's plenty of time,' Wally said casually. Inside, needless to say, he was turning into tapioca.

The jeep ground to a halt. The two guards jumped out, rushing up to grab Wally by the arms and began to frisk him.

'He's unarmed,' announced Peterson.

Wally managed to catch Collins's eye and gave him a wink.

Hamilton was livid. 'Where in the name of heaven did you drop in from, Collins?'

The security man was stuck for an answer.

'It's OK,' Walter whispered, 'tell him.'

'A plane . . .' Collins whispered. 'Well, kind of.'

'What plane?' Hamilton thundered. 'No plane was cleared for landing. Where is it? Who was flying it? This man?'

'Yes . . . no . . . well . . .' Collins stuttered.

Hamilton was fast running out of patience. 'Come on . . . This wind is biting into me, and apparently into your brain as well. I want to know exactly who this is and how you both got here. This is a serious breach of security.'

The two men were loaded into the back of the jeep and Peterson stole a look at Collins.

'What's the matter with you?' he whispered.

'Nothing,' he whispered back. 'Nothing at all.' He turned his back on his erstwhile partner and whispered desperately to Wally: 'When are you going to do something?'

Walter shrugged as the jeep drove off towards the detention centre. 'Patience,' he replied miserably. 'Plenty of time. Plenty of time.'

26

They were led along a narrow white corridor. Unlike the rest of the complex, the detention centre was crudely, almost ostentatiously, Gestapo-like in its primitive austerity. Naked light bulbs hung from the ceiling and on either side of the corridor the long row of small cells were fitted with iron doors and slender barred windows.

As Wally and Collins were marched through by Hamilton and Peterson, with two armed guards covering them from behind, moans and whimpers could be heard within the cells.

'Guard . . . please, help me,' a tortured voice floated from an adjacent cell, 'I'm willing to do anything, ughh –'

One of the guards had quickly stepped forward and smashed the arm that reached out from the cell window with the butt of his Uzi. There was an anguished howl and the protest ceased.

Wally paled but the escort moved on.

'What's going on here?' he whispered, leaning towards Collins. 'What's the matter with that guy?'

Collins shrugged. 'He refused to work.'

'At what?'

'At whatever he did before he was abducted,' Collins muttered. 'Except here, he does it for free. Or he ends up like these guys.'

'What happens to them?' Wally asked.

The Global Guard security man looked grim.

'They're starved, or worse . . . as examples to the others.'

'But that can't be going on,' Wally whispered. 'This is the twentieth century . . . There are laws.'

'Not for these people. They're all presumed dead . . . or will be in time.'

Wally opened his mouth to speak but Hamilton broke into the muffled conversation.

'You might keep that in mind, when you're answering questions,' he said sternly, stopping at the last door in the corridor. 'You too will be given a chance to work, or become an example to others.'

He snapped his fingers and one of the guards shoved Wally into the cell.

Collins turned to Peterson and the other guard who pressed the nose of his rifle into the small of his back. 'Boy, are you in trouble,' the disgraced security man warned, already picturing Wally's electronic genie, his miraculous *deus ex machina*, exacting terrible retribution on these disbelievers.

Peterson said nothing but nodded to the guard, who nudged Collins with the Uzi, forcing him into the cell.

The night was endless, the interrogation getting nowhere. Sweat poured from the bodies of the guards, and of Collins, Peterson and Hamilton. The mental anguish, common to victims of long hours of torture and persecution was betrayed in their stained and dishevelled clothes, darkened eyes, pinched faces.

In the middle of the bleak white room sat Wally who, in striking contrast, looked bright-eyed, lively – even dapper.

'. . . then Automan . . . well, actually the cursor . . . turned Autocar into Autoplane and we followed you right back here –'

'What is this ridiculous drivel?' muttered Hamilton angrily, wiping his forehead with a red silk handkerchief. 'I told you to use truth drugs.'

'We did use truth drugs, sir. And this is what we got,' replied Peterson wearily gazing at the Sony reel-to-reel tape recorder which had been playing back for the third time Wally's testimony. The truth drugs were a total success and the results had turned the interrogation into a total fiasco.

'Enough,' Hamilton snapped, stopping the tape. 'This ludicrous story of his is so ingrained in him it could only be the work of his friends at Interpol.' He signalled to the guards. 'Send him back to his pals Curtis and Miss Du Boise.'

Wally looked startled but said nothing.

'. . . I suggest you talk it over and agree to cooperate,' Hamilton went on as the guards woke up from their dozing and dragged Wally towards the door.

'Hear my words,' Hamilton added in a snarl, shooting him a look of pure venom. 'I will have the truth from you before the night is out, Nebish.'

'Nebi*cher*,' Walter corrected him apologetically: the truth drug was still working.

'Remove him,' Hamilton sighed.

The guards hurried him out. Hamilton sat pondering for a few seconds and then turned towards Collins.

'It was all the truth,' the Global man confirmed weakly. It was obviously long past his bedtime.

'Get him out of here!' Hamilton sneered.

'Are you trying to commit suicide?' Peterson hissed at his partner when Hamilton had stormed out.

Collins eyed him blearily. 'It might be the best way out,' he groaned. 'But I'll settle for getting drunk.'

27

'I bet even Devil's Island could look beautiful by moonlight,' said Jack Curtis, gazing at the silvery lake through his bedroom window.

'At least they need the others,' Tanya replied dispiritedly. 'Once they're satisfied they know all we know . . . well . . .'

'Take it easy, baby,' said Curtis, taking her in his arms. 'You've got to have hope.'

Tanya decided it was time she told him. 'There *is* one hope,' she said. 'The young man you told me about . . . I'm almost certain he saw them abduct me.'

'The young man I –' He stared at her. 'You don't mean Wally?'

'That's the one,' she nodded. 'He'll be certain to tell someone, and he knows the connection between the kidnappers and Global Guard.'

Curtis smiled ruefully. 'I'm afraid Wally isn't the sort of person you put all your hopes in.'

Tanya felt bound to come to Wally's defence. There was something about him that seemed to arouse her maternal instincts. 'He struck me as very capable,' she lied.

Suddenly the door opened and Wally was standing there.

'Jack!' he cried excitedly, closing the door behind him.

'Wally?' Curtis said in amazement.

'He's even *more* capable than I thought,' said Tanya, smiling.

'Thank God you're all right,' said Wally, shaking Curtis by the hand, 'and Tanya – this is great. Now we can move.'

Curtis screwed up his eyes. The mountain air must have got to the kid. 'Move!' he laughed. 'Wally, we're prisoners!'

'Only temporarily,' said Walter. 'We've got to find a computer bank.'

'They must have quite an assortment with all these engineers they have working for them,' Jack pondered.

'What do you want with a computer?' asked Tanya.

'I need to feed a little data into my information bank back home . . .' said Wally, thinking hard.

'How can you do that?' asked Curtis.

'A telephone modem . . .' muttered Wally as he paced the room.

Tanya turned to Curtis. 'Is he delirious?' she asked in concern.

'I think so,' he replied – though he was never entirely sure with Wally.

'Not at all,' Wally declared confidently. 'We just may have to wait a short while for some help.'

'Who'd help us here?' said Jack, sceptically.

'Well, unless I'm very much mistaken,' replied Wally thinking of the petrified Global Guard security man dangling upside down in Automan's translucent arms, 'we have at least one believer –' He was interrupted by an odd noise outside the room.

'Shhh!' Tanya warned.

They stared at the doorknob which was slowly turning. Curtis was poised to spring.

Then the door opened and Collins wandered in, meandering in a wobbly, zigzag fashion towards them.

'Nebish . . .' he hiccupped and Wally could smell the Scotch on his breath.

'Close enough,' Wally replied, referring both to Collins's physical proximity and to the reasonably incorrect pronunciation.

'Now wait a minute,' said Curtis slowly. 'This is the guy who snatched me!'

He threw himself in fury at the drunken security man but Collins shied out of the way and Wally laid his hand on Jack's arm to calm him down.

'Jack . . . easy!' he begged. 'This is our *help*.'

'OK, I've done my part,' Collins mumbled. 'Now let's get the big guy and get out of here!'

Curtis and Tanya exchanged mystified glances.

'First you've got to get us to a computer room,' said Walter.

'Computer room,' Collins repeated groggily. Then something seemed to click in his befuddled brain. 'They're not in use at this hour,' he giggled.

In crocodile formation, led by Collins who tottered in a kind of commando-style crouch, Wally, Jack and Tanya made their way along the dark corridors that wove in a labyrinth to the computer room. Wally immediately seated himself at the console and examined the equipment.

'Looks good,' he remarked. 'This is really sophisticated stuff. All I've got to do is push this button and we're ready to make the connection.'

He pushed a button marked PHONE MODEM and began to type into the computer.

'Mind telling us what you're doing, Wally?' said Curtis anxiously, 'in as much as we could be running for our lives?'

'We don't want to run against guns,' he replied without looking up. 'I'm sending for help – by dialling my home phone number . . .'

'Home phone number? I don't understand,' said Tanya.

'Computers can talk to each other,' he explained. 'I'm reaching out for mine.'

Tanya still looked puzzled but Collins chipped in, 'Don't worry about it. I seen him work. This kid's good.'

Wally stopped typing and folded his arms.

'Now what?' said Tanya.

'Now we wait –' Wally began.

'That won't be necessary,' said Lydell Hamilton calmly as he walked into the computer room, followed by Peterson and two armed guards. 'I needed to know your most immediate source of rescue since you were foolish enough to walk in here so arrogantly.'

'I wouldn't get too cocky, Mr Hamilton,' said Collins belligerently. 'His help is like nothing you've ever seen.'

'His help is apparently a computer, six thousand miles away,' Hamilton sneered. 'Which you will be interested to know –' he smiled at Wally '– is being dismantled as we speak.'

'It'll be too late,' Collins insisted. 'The kid's good.'

'He's telling you the truth,' said Wally. 'So in the interest of not letting anyone get hurt –'

'*I* give the orders here, Mr Nebish,' Lydell Hamilton snapped. 'Kindly march. A nice midnight execution is so preferable to the noisy daylight variety which might unnerve our guests – don't you think?'

28

The guards pointed their guns, and Wally, Curtis, Collins and Tanya exchanged glances. Wally's reach just hadn't been long enough.

'Wally,' Tanya said angrily, 'what do you think you were accomplishing marching in here without telling anybody what you were up to? You left us no way out –'

'Ease up, Tanya,' Curtis broke in. 'We didn't do so hot either.'

'Hey, stop worrying, will you,' said Collins. 'The kid's good. I seen him work. Trust me.'

He clung to this phrase like an article of faith.

'Shut down all of the compound lights,' barked Hamilton as the prisoners filed out. 'I don't want any witnesses to what must be done.'

Peterson nodded and walked over to an electric panel. As lights began to dim or go out all over the compound the needle on a light board meter marked POWER AVAILABLE began to rise . . .

The four prisoners were being marched out into the courtyard and away from the main building.

'It's now or never,' Curtis muttered to Wally who was walking by his side. 'When I say go, we jump them.'

'No, wait . . . don't,' Wally shouted, but he was too late.

'Now!' Curtis yelled – and lunged at one of the guards behind him. The guard brought the barrel of his gun down on the back of his head, and Curtis collapsed to the ground.

'Jack, are you all right?' Tanya cried, as she bent down beside him and lifted his head tenderly.

Hamilton pulled her away from him. 'There's no need to worry, Miss Du Boise,' he snapped. 'You're not going to live long enough to feel any pain.'

She stared up at him hatefully but Hamilton was suddenly distracted by the sound and fury of a howling wind that turned at once into a hurricane: shutters throughout the compound slammed and crashed against walls and windows and those lights that were still switched on dimmed or were extinguished altogether.

Hamilton turned and looked up into the sky as gusts of wind blew through his hair, forcing him to squint.

'Damned gales,' shouted Peterson above the turmoil. 'The wind can be like ice –'

'Uh, uh,' went Collins, shaking his head numbly.

Hamilton had turned his head to peer, across a line of shaking trees, at the summit of a distant mountain. There was a faint glow, growing brighter and apparently coming towards them. He turned his head in the opposite direction.

'The generator is arching,' he yelled.

They all looked to where great tongues of lightning-like electrical power were licking the generator. The last of the lights instantly failed.

'Must be drawing too much power,' shouted Peterson.

Hamilton shook his head, mystified. 'With the field lights off we are drawing practically nothing,' he shouted.

A strange, mischievous smile had appeared upon Walter's face and Collins noticed it instantly.

'You're good!' he said with respectful admiration.

Now the whole environment seemed to be participating in a cosmic upheaval, an elemental dance fashioned out of wind, shutters, trash cans, shaking branches, flashing lights and petrified human beings.

The light made its entrance above the 'V' between two mountains, dazzling their eyes as it hovered motionlessly perhaps some three miles in the distance. The next moment it was yards away, swirling, dancing, shimmering.

'Cursor,' Wally called out, 'you made it.'

Peterson stared at the blazing hexagon, dumbfounded. Hamilton's mouth dropped. A vapour began to swirl around in their midst, quickly taking shape and size . . . and light.

Automan stood twinkling before them.

'You are good, Walter,' he said in a commanding, resonant voice.

Peterson went white, raised his gun and emptied it. Wally grinned, counting the shots quietly to himself as the bullets whizzed through the hologram and out the other side. It was like watching someone throw a losing die in snakes and ladders.

At the sound of gunfire, guards from all over the camp were running out of the various bungalows and from the main building.

Hamilton refused to be distracted by the hallucination. In one motion, he snatched away a guard's gun and grabbed Tanya who was, like the others, staring in disbelief.

'Who is that?' she gasped, hardly aware that she was now technically a hostage. '*What* is that?'

'All right . . . stay back, whatever you are,' Hamilton shouted, 'or she dies!'

Collins pulled a face, like he'd been cheated out of his favourite toy. 'Uh-oh,' he complained petulantly. 'And just when we were doing so well.'

Automan had, indeed, been forced to stop in his tracks, but Wally was quick to see a solution.

'I can't get to you, Auto,' he called out. 'You'll have to get to me.'

Automan looked at him and nodded; the next moment he had vanished, to reappear in Walter's place, behind Hamilton. The Institute's founder and organiser spun round in fury.

'I warned you,' he said threateningly, and then stared in terror, as Automan/Walter took a step towards him.

'You warned him, not me,' Wally spoke out of Automan's mouth.

Tanya gasped. 'Wally, Wally. Where did you go?'

'Right here, Tanya,' he said. 'Don't worry.'

'Take them,' Hamilton called out to the armed guards.

'Cursor,' said Automan.

At once the cursor began emitting a high-pitched beep and as it swirled around it traced in finer and finer detail the lines of a Mark XII battle tank. The guards stood rigid like toy soldiers transfixed by the sight as the tank's turret slowly turned until it was aiming directly at them. A moment later they dropped their weapons and ran for their lives.

'Come back, you cowards!' Hamilton shouted. 'It isn't real. It's an illusion.'

'Very good, Mr Hamilton,' said Walter out of Automan's mouth. 'But what *is* real . . . and what is illusion?'

The tank suddenly disappeared and the cursor reappeared, dancing around in circles and distracting Hamilton, mesmerising him like a snake.

'Where did it go?' he whispered in bewilderment, then pulled himself together as he noticed a jeep parked near the main building. 'Peterson!' he commanded.

'Fire up the jeep and bring it here.'

Peterson began to run towards the jeep but suddenly stopped in his tracks. 'Which jeep?' he asked sheepishly.

'That – ' Hamilton began, turning to point. He stared in amazement: there were now three jeeps.

'One of 'em gets mileage you wouldn't believe,' Wally said with a smile.

With Tanya still locked in his arms, Hamilton backed towards the jeeps and carefully felt one of them. To his relief it was solid. He climbed in the passenger seat and Peterson took the wheel, started it up and raced off.

29

'Cursor!' Automan called out as the jeep tore away into the Alps.

The white light dropped down, spun around and, as before, conjured up Autocar.

'We must beat them to the airport,' said Wally.

'Say no more,' Automan replied, running to the car and separating himself from Walter who ran after him, jumping into the passenger seat. In a millisecond the Autocar went from a standing stop to maximum speed.

'Hey!' Collins called out as the car virtually vanished from sight. 'Couldn't you whip up one with room for me?'

He stared after them helplessly.

'I've had it with you!' grumbled Wally as he picked himself up off the back seat where he had been deposited after the usual G forces had pasted him upside down against the back window.

Automan grinned.

Ahead of them the jeep roared along a deserted highway carved out of the Alps, but Autocar was steadily gaining on it. Reaching a hairpin bend it took the corner at full speed by turning at the car's characteristic ninety-degree angle.

'Careful, Auto,' Wally cautioned. 'If we get too close, they may hurt Tanya.'

'There's only one road to the airport,' Automan

pointed out.

'We've got to find a way to make them think they're getting away clean, so they'll leave her behind without hurting her.'

'Then we have to get to the airport ahead of them,' said Automan.

'Like you said, there's only one road,' Wally reminded him.

'Who needs roads?' Automan replied loftily. 'Cursor . . .'

'Oh, no,' cried Wally, shielding his head in his hands.

As the Autocar raced along the motorway, the cursor began suddenly to retrace its outline, converting it *in situ*, so to speak, into Autoplane.

'Hang on,' Automan warned.

'When you think it's necessary to warn me,' said Wally nervously, 'I hate to think what's coming.'

Suddenly the Autoplane made a violent lurch and streaked into the sky, propelling Walter out of the front seat and dumping him upside down once more in the back seat.

Autoplane swooped low over the valleys that nestled among the peaks and canyons of the Swiss Alps. Automan was most gratified.

'We should get to the airport well ahead of them,' he remarked.

'I haven't a doubt in my mind . . .' Wally groaned, once again clawing his way back to the front of the plane.

'What do you think we should do to make them feel like they've successfully escaped?' Automan pondered.

'I was thinking about that,' said Wally. 'Can Cursor duplicate *any* kind of vehicle?'

'Their own plane, for instance . . .?'

Wally smiled, pleased with his own ingenuity.

'Kidnapped by their own hand . . . You have a poetic mind, Walter. I like it.'

'Of course you do – I programmed you,' said Wally with a tinge of smugness. 'You're the perfect police partner . . . We think alike.'

A determined look came into Automan's perfect blue eyes. 'Let's get to work,' he said.

The plane rolled over and swooped down into the valley. 'Oh,' Wally gasped. 'I wish you wouldn't *do* that.'

The SMA-3 jet's engines were already whining as the jeep raced onto the runway and screeched to a halt. The three of them climbed out and Lydell Hamilton turned to Tanya Du Boise with a courteous bow.

'This is where we part company, my dear,' he said suavely.

'They'll find you,' she predicted.

'I think not,' he smiled. 'I have millions stashed away in Swiss accounts. A little plastic surgery . . . a few bribes in the right places, and I rather fancy that things are going to be splendid for the rest of my life.'

With Peterson at his side, Hamilton boarded the plane which, after the steps had been raised automatically, quickly began to taxi down the runway.

Tanya was standing alone on the tarmac, watching as the plane took off when she heard footsteps approaching. The next moment Walter and Automan were beside her.

'How did you two get here ahead of us and where is –' she began but then she noticed the strange look on Wally's face. It was identical to the expression on Automan's perfectly exquisite features, and it reminded her of the way her colleagues at Interpol looked when they had thrown out some peculiarly attractive bait and were about to reel in a particularly big and tricky fish

30

'Would you sit down and relax?' Hamilton said irritably as he sipped his brandy and stretched his legs comfortably in his seat. The evening's events had been bizarre to say the least and the last thing he needed now was for Peterson to lose his nerve. He should have ditched him months ago but then he was surrounded by incompetents and mediocrity. What he needed was someone of the calibre of Tanya Du Boise. Perhaps when the repercussions of this unfortunate incident had quietened down, he would put out feelers . . . She was obviously wasted at Interpol.

As for that . . . thing – what had Nebish called it? Automat? – he was now completely convinced that it was merely some form of mass hallucination. There were many such examples in recent history and even further back – look at Joan of Arc, her so-called visions were clearly symptomatic of schizophrenia and could be traced to ergotism. He really should have checked the rye but it was popular with the Swiss and one couldn't keep tabs on every little detail, for heaven's sake.

'I can't,' said Peterson as he paced about the gangway, popping beers.

'Can't what?'

'Relax.'

Hamilton sighed. 'Then go and tell the crew to turn up the heat . . . It's strangely cold in here for some reason.'

Peterson nodded and walked through to the door of the cockpit. He knocked – but there was no answer.

'There's no answer,' he said.

Hamilton looked up from a *Newsweek* article which he wasn't really taking in.

'I said –' Peterson began.

'I heard what you said,' Hamilton snapped. He picked up the phone whose keyboard was built in to the arm-rest and buzzed. Then he buzzed again.

'That's odd,' he muttered. 'They've never failed to respond to my page before . . .' A wild, horrific thought suddenly leapt into his mind, and he began to pale. 'Oh, no,' he gasped.

He threw off his lap blanket, dumped his brandy glass on the floor and ran to the cockpit door, pulling it open. And then his face contorted in horror.

Where there should have been a pilot and co-pilot, there were two empty seats – in a cabin that was not a cabin but a shimmering holographic image. He howled in terror.

It was the cabin of Autoplane.

31

'The sun's beginning to come up, Walter,' said Automan, his voice sounding a little faint. 'I feel the generator beginning to ebb . . .'

'I understand,' said Walter, this time without experiencing that sense of dread and alarm that had preceded Automan's previous vanishing tricks. 'But how will we get out of here?' He and Tanya gazed around at the deserted airport, and then Wally's eyes fell on the real corporate jet.

Automan was ahead of him. 'That jet should be adequate to begin an exodus . . .' he declared. 'Tanya and Interpol should be able to do the remaining cleanup work.'

Wally grinned. 'Thank you, Auto.'

'Thank *you*, Walter,' Automan replied graciously. 'Cursor, shall we . . . ?'

He was beginning to fade as the cursor emitted its high-pitched beep. Suddenly both snapped out of the material dimension.

Tanya tore her eyes away from the apparition – or, rather, disapparition – and turned to its creator.

'Wally, please, you've got to tell me what's going on!'

'I *can't*,' he said desperately.

'But –'

'It's . . . it's top secret,' he said feebly. 'Please Tanya, don't tell *anybody* what you saw.'

She was going to object but just then one of the Institute's Volvos drove into the airport, and Jack Curtis climbed out, followed by Collins, Wills, Wilson and Cramer. She rushed to Jack's side and they embraced, as Wally greeted them all and together they walked to the plane.

Walter Nebicher was back where he belonged: sitting at his keyboard in the LAPD computer room. Around him stood Jack Curtis, Roxanne Caldwell, Captain E. G. Boyd and the other officers from the squad room. Ceremoniously Captain Boyd raised a glass (of Pepsi) in salute.

Wally blushed modestly, looking down into his keyboard. He wasn't used to playing the hero.

'To Jack!' said Boyd, basking in the reflected glory of a detective. 'Fifty men on a task force, and it's Lieutenant Curtis who saves the day. *My* Lieutenant Curtis.' He slapped him on the back. 'Welcome back, Jack – we're proud of you.'

The other officers crowded round Curtis to congratulate him. Wally was entirely ignored. Except, that is, by Jack Curtis who turned to face him as he made his reply.

'Thanks, all of you,' he grinned.'But I've got to be straight with you. Most of the credit for this bust goes to –'

'To you, Lieutenant,' Wally said quickly. 'Oh, I know Tanya Du Boise was a big help. But it just goes to show – not even Interpol can do better than the good old LAPD.'

The other officers nodded and murmured in agreement but Boyd was frowning. 'That's because *most* of the officers in the LAPD pull their own weight, Nebicher,' he growled. 'Not like certain adding machine – excuse me – computer jockeys I know.' He turned to the rest of the men. 'Now let's get back to work. We've got a city full of cases to solve.'

He led the others out but Roxanne lingered for a moment. 'Don't let him get to you, Wally,' she said gently. 'Just keep plugging instead of playing those silly computer games, and you're sure to prove the Captain wrong.' She followed the rest of the men out of the computer room, leaving Jack and Wally on their own for the first time in many weeks.

'You didn't have to do that, Wally,' said the veteran. 'I want to give credit where credit's due.'

Wally shook his head. 'It's better this way, sir, believe me.'

Curtis considered this for a moment and nodded. He was about to leave, but something held him back.

'Wally?' he said casually.

'Yes, Lieutenant?'

'There *are* a few gaps in my report. Gaps that I thought you could explain.'

Wally was tempted for a moment. 'Lieutenant . . . Jack . . .' he began.

'Yes?' Curtis looked at him curiously.

He started to open his mouth when suddenly the computer's lights began to flash, the overhead lights dimmed and the room started to shake. He closed his mouth and the tremor gradually died down.

'I'm sorry, sir,' he said in resignation. 'I doubt if I *can* explain.' For a moment his hands rested on the keys. 'I doubt it very much.'

THE FLOATING ADMIRAL

The Floating Admiral is treasure trov
from the past, the very first pub
of Britain's famous D
Who killed Adm
him drifting
the Vicar's din
the Club const
knowing the s
were Agatha C
Sayers and Free
Then Anthony B
the case, provided a solution, tied up
every loose end. G.K. Chesterton's
mystifying prologue, in proper paradoxical Chestertonian fashion was
written last.

And *then*, as a bonus, comes an appendix giving the fascinatingly different solutions conceived by each author as he or she wrote a chapter.

CW01623443

A superbly entertaining puzzle
for all lovers of detection
stories, with contributions
by

DOROTHY L. SAYERS
G.K. CHESTERTON
VICTOR L. WHITECHURCH
G.D.H. and M. COLE
HENRY WADE
AGATHA CHRISTIE
JOHN RHODE
MILWARD KENNEDY
RONALD A. KNOX
FREEMAN WILLS CROFTS
EDGAR JEPSON
CLEMENCE DANE
ANTHONY BERKELEY

THE FLOATING ADMIRAL

by
Certain Members of
The Detection Club

MYSTERIOUS PRESS

Mysterious Press books (UK) are published
in association with
Arrow Books Limited
62–65 Chandos Place, London WC2N 4NW

An Imprint of Century Hutchinson Limited

London Melbourne Sydney Auckland
Johannesburg and agencies throughout
the world

First published in Great Britain 1931
Reissued 1981 by Macmillan London Ltd

Hamlyn Paperbacks edition 1983
Mysterious Press edition 1988

© The Detection Club 1931, 1981

This book is sold subject to the condition that it shall not, by way of trade or otherwise, be lent, resold, hired out, or otherwise circulated without the publisher's prior consent in any form of binding or cover other than that in which it is published and without a similar condition including this condition being imposed on the subsequent purchaser.

Printed and bound in Great Britain by
Hazell Watson & Viney Limited
Member of BPCC plc
Aylesbury Bucks

ISBN 0 09 955850 5

INTRODUCTION

By Dorothy L. Sayers

THE FLOATING ADMIRAL

When members of the official police force are invited to express an opinion about the great detectives of fiction, they usually say with a kindly smile: 'Well, of course, it's not the same for them as it is for us. The author knows beforehand who did the job, and the great detective has only to pick up the clues that are laid down for him. It's wonderful,' they indulgently add, 'the clever ideas these authors hit upon, but we don't think they would work very well in real life.'

There is probably much truth in these observations, and they are, in any case, difficult to confute. If Mr John Rhode, for example, could be induced to commit a real murder by one of the ingeniously simple methods he so easily invents in fiction, and if Mr Freeman Wills Crofts, say, would undertake to pursue him, Bradshaw in hand, from Stranraer to Saint Juan-les-Pins, then, indeed, we might put the matter to the test. But writers of detective fiction are, as a rule, not bloodthirsty people. They avoid physical violence, for two reasons: first, because their murderous feelings are so efficiently blown-off in print as to have little energy left for boiling up in action, and secondly, because they are so accustomed to the idea that murders are made to be detected that they feel a wholesome reluctance to put their criminal theories into practice. While, as for doing real detecting, the fact is that few of them have the time for it, being engaged in earning their bread and butter like reasonable citizens, unblessed with the ample leisure of a Wimsey or a Father Brown.

But the next best thing to a genuine contest is a good game, and *The Floating Admiral* is the detection game as played out on paper by certain members of the Detection Club among themselves. And here it may be asked: What is the Detection Club?

It is a private association of writers of detective fiction in Great Britain, existing chiefly for the purpose of eating dinners together at suitable intervals and of talking illimitable shop. It owes no allegiance to any publisher, nor, though willing to turn an honest

penny by offering the present venture to the public, is it primarily concerned with making money. It is not a committee of judges for recommending its own or other people's books, and indeed has no object but to amuse itself. Its membership is confined to those who have written genuine detective stories (not adventure tales or 'thrillers') and election is secured by a vote of the club on recommendation by two or more members, and involves the undertaking of an oath.

While wild horses would not drag from me any revelation of the solemn ritual of the Detection Club, a word as to the nature of the oath is, perhaps, permissible. Put briefly, it amounts to this: that the author pledges himself to play the game with the public and with his fellow-authors. His detectives must detect by their wits, without the help of accident or coincidence; he must not invent impossible death-rays and poisons to produce solutions which no living person could expect; he must write as good English as he can. He must preserve inviolable secrecy concerning his fellow-members' forthcoming plots and titles, and he must give any assistance in his power to members who need advice on technical points. If there is any serious aim behind the avowedly frivolous organisation of the Detection Club, it is to keep the detective story up to the highest standard that its nature permits, and to free it from the bad legacy of sensationalism, clap-trap and jargon with which it was unhappily burdened in the past.

Now, a word about the conditions under which *The Floating Admiral* was written. Here, the problem was made to approach as closely as possible to a problem of real detection. Except in the case of Mr Chesterton's picturesque Prologue, which was written last, each contributor tackled the mystery presented to him in the preceding chapters without having the slightest idea what solution or solutions the previous authors had in mind. Two rules only were imposed. Each writer must construct his instalment with a definite solution in view – that is, he must not introduce new complications merely 'to make it more difficult.' He must be ready, if called upon, to explain his own clues coherently and plausibly; and to make sure that he was playing fair in this respect, each writer was bound to deliver, together with the manuscript of his own chapter, his own proposed solution of the mystery. These solutions are printed at the end of the book for the benefit of the curious reader.

Secondly, each writer was bound to deal faithfully with *all* the difficulties left for his consideration by his predecessors. If Elma's attitude towards love and marriage appeared to fluctuate strangely, or if the boat was put into the boat-house wrong end

first, those facts must form part of his solution. He must not dismiss them as caprice or accident, or present an explanation inconsistent with them. Naturally, as the clues became in process of time more numerous, the suggested solutions grew more complicated and precise, while the general outlines of the plot gradually hardened and fixed themselves. But it is entertaining and instructive to note the surprising number of different interpretations which may be devised to account for the simplest actions. Where one writer may have laid down a clue, thinking that it could point only in one obvious direction, succeeding writers have managed to make it point in a direction exactly opposite. And it is here, perhaps, that the game approximates most closely to real life. We judge one another by our outward actions, but in the motive underlying those actions our judgment may be widely at fault. Preoccupied by our own private interpretation of the matter, we can see only the one possible motive behind the action, so that our solution may be quite plausible, quite coherent, and quite wrong. And here, possibly, we detective-writers may have succeeded in wholesomely surprising and confounding ourselves and one another. We are only too much accustomed to let the great detective say airily: 'Cannot you see, my dear Watson, that these facts admit of only one interpretation?' After our experience in the matter of *The Floating Admiral*, our great detectives may have to learn to express themselves more guardedly.

Whether the game thus played for our own amusement will succeed in amusing other people also is for the reader to judge. We can only assure him that the game was played honestly according to the rules, and with all the energy and enthusiasm which the players knew how to put into it. Speaking for myself, I may say that the helpless bewilderment into which I was plunged on receipt of Mr Milward Kennedy's little bunch of brain-teasers was, apparently, fully equalled by the hideous sensation of bafflement which overcame Father Ronald Knox when, having, as I fondly imagined, cleared up much that was obscure, I handed the problem on to him. That Mr Anthony Berkeley should so cheerfully have confounded our politics and frustrated out knavish trucks in the final solution, I must attribute partly to his native ingenuity and partly to the energetic interference of the other three intervening solvers, who discovered so many facts and motives that we earlier gropers in the dark knew nothing about. But none of us, I think, will bear any malice against our fellow-authors, any more than against the vagaries of the River Whyn, which, powerfully guided

by Mr Henry Wade and Mr John Rhode, twin luminaries of its tidal waters, bore so peacefully between its flowery banks the body of the Floating Admiral.

PROLOGUE

By G.K. Chesterton

'THE THREE PIPE DREAMS'

Three glimpses through the rolling smoke of opium, three stories that still hover about a squalid opium joint in Hong Kong, might very well at this distance of time be dismissed as pipe dreams. Yet they really happened; they were stages in the great misfortune of a man's life; although many who played their parts in the drama would have forgotten it by the morning. A large paper-lantern coarsely scrawled with a glaring crimson dragon hung over the black and almost subterranean entrance of the den; the moon was up and the little street was almost deserted.

We all talk of the mystery of Asia; and there is a sense in which we are all wrong. Asia has been hardened by the ages; it is old, so that its bones stick out; and in one sense there is less disguise and mystification about it than there is about the more living and moving problems of the West. The dope-peddlars and opium hags and harlots who made the dingy life of that place were fixed and recognised in their functions, in something almost like a social hierarchy; sometimes their vice was official and almost religious, as in the dancing-girls of the temples. But the English naval officer who strode at that instant past that door, and had occasion to pause there, was in reality much more of a mystery; for he was a mystery even to himself. There were bound up in his character, both national and individual, the most complex and contradictory things; codes and compromises about codes, and a conscience strangely fitful and illogical; sentimental instincts that recoiled from sentiment and religious feelings that had outlived religion; a patriotism that prided itself on being merely practical and professional; all the tangled traditions of a great Pagan and a great Christian past; the mystery of the West. It grew more and more mysterious, because he himself never thought about it.

Indeed there is only one part of it that anybody need think about for the purposes of this tale. Like every man of his type, he had a perfectly sincere hatred of individual oppression; which would not have saved him from taking part in impersonal or collective op-

pression, if the responsibility were spread to all his civilisation or his country or his class. He was the Captain of a battleship lying at that moment in the harbour of Hong Kong. He would have shelled Hong Kong to pieces and killed half the people in it, even if it had been in that shameful war by which Great Britain forced opium upon China. But when he happened to see one individual Chinese girl being dragged across the road by a greasy, yellow ruffian, and flung head-foremost into the opium-den, something sprang up quite spontaneously within him; an 'age' that is never really past; and certain romances that were not really burned by the Barber; something that does still deserve the glorious insult of being called quixotic. With two or three battering blows he sent the Chinaman spinning across the road, where he collapsed in a distant gutter. But the girl had already been flung down the steps of the dark entry, and he precipitated himself after her with the purely instinctive impetuosity of a charging bull. There was very little in his mind at that moment except rage and a very vague intention of delivering the captive from so uninviting a dungeon. But even over such a simple mood a wave of unconscious warning seemed to pass; the blood-red dragon-lantern seemed to leer down at him; and he had some such blind sensation as might have overwhelmed St George if, charging with a victorious lance, he had found himself swallowed by the dragon.

And yet the next scene revealed, in a rift of that visionary vapour, is not any such scene of doom or punishment as some sensationalists might legitimately expect. It will not be necessary to gratify the refined modern taste with scenes of torture; nor to avoid the vulgarity of a happy ending by killing the principal character in the first chapter. Nevertheless, the scene revealed was perhaps, in its ultimate effects, almost more tragic than a scene of death. The most tragic thing about it was that it was rather comic. The gleam of the tawdry lanterns in the dope-den revealed nothing but a huddle of drugged coolies, with faces like yellow stone, the sailors from a ship that had put into Hong Kong that morning, flying the Stars and Stripes; and the final feature of a tall English naval officer, wearing the uniform of the Captain of a British ship, behaving in a peculiar way and apparently under rather peculiar influences. It was believed by some that what he was performing was a horn-pipe, but that it was mingled with motions designed only to preserve equilibrium.

The crew looking on was American; that is to say, some of them were Swedish, several Polish, several more Slavs of nameless

nationality, and a large number of brown Lascars from the ends of the earth. But they all saw something that they very much wanted to see and had never seen before. They saw an English gentleman unbend. He unbent with luxuriant slowness and then suddenly bent double again and slid to the floor with a bang. He was understood to say:

'Dam' bad whisky but dam' good. Whad I meansay is,' he explained with laborious logic, 'whisky dam' bad, but dam' bad whisky dam' good thing.'

'He's had more than whisky,' said one of the Swedish sailors in Swedish American.

'He's had everything there is to have, I should think,' replied a Pole with a refined accent.

And then a little swarthy Jew, who was born in Budapest but had lived in Whitechapel, struck up in piping tones a song he had heard there: 'Every nice girl loves a sailor.' And in his song there was a sneer that was some day to be seen on the face of Trotsky, and to change the world.

The dawn gives us a third glimpse of the harbour of Hong Kong, where the battleship flying the Stars and Stripes lay with the other battleship flying the Union Jack; and on the latter ship there was turmoil and blank dismay. The First and Second Officers looked at each other with growing alertness and alarm, and one of them looked at a watch.

'Can you suggest anything, Mr Lutterell?' said one of them, with a sharp voice but a very vague eye.

'I think we shall have to send somebody ashore to find out,' replied Mr Lutterell.

At this point a third officer appeared hauling forward a heavy and reluctant seaman; who was supposed to have some information to give, but seemed to have some difficulty in giving it.

'Well, you see, sir, he's been found,' he said at last. 'The Captain's been found.'

Something in his tone moved the First Officer to sudden horror.

'What do you mean by found?' he cried. 'You talk as if he was dead!'

'Well, I don't think he's dead,' said the sailor with irritating slowness. 'But he looked dead-like.'

'I'm afraid, sir,' said the Second Officer in a low voice, 'that they're just bringing him in. I hope they'll be quick and keep it as quiet as they can.'

Under these circumstances did the First Officer look up and

behold his respected Captain returning to his beloved ship. He was being carried like a sack by two dirty-looking coolies, and the officers hastily closed round him and carried him to his cabin. Then Mr Lutterell turned sharply and sent for the ship's doctor.

'Hold these men for the moment,' he said, pointing to the coolies; 'we've got to know about this. Now then, Doctor, what's the matter with him?'

The doctor was a hard-headed, hatchet-faced man, having the not very popular character of a candid friend; and on this occasion he was very candid indeed.

'I can see and smell for myself,' he said, 'before I begin the examination. He's had opium and whisky as well as Heaven knows what else. I should say he's a bag of poisons.'

'Any wounds at all?' asked the frowning Lutterell.

'I should say he's knocked himself out,' said the candid doctor. 'Most likely knocked himself out of the Service.'

'You have no right to say that,' said the First Officer severely. 'This is for the authorities.'

'Yes,' said the other doggedly. 'Authorities of a Court Martial, I should say. No; there are no wounds.'

Thus do the first three stages of the story reach their conclusion; and it must be admitted with regret that so far there is no moral to the story.

1

By Canon Victor L. Whitechurch

CORPSE AHOY!

Everyone in Lingham knew old Neddy Ware, though he was not a native of the village, having only resided there for the last ten years; which, in the eyes of the older inhabitants who had spent the whole of their lives in that quiet spot, constituted him still a 'stranger.'

Not that they really knew very much about him, for the old man was of a retiring disposition and had few cronies. What they did know was that he was a retired petty officer of the Royal Navy, subsisting on his pension, that he was whole-heartedly devoted to the Waltonian craft, spending most of his time fishing in the River Whyn, and that, though he was of a peaceful disposition generally, he had a vocabulary of awful and blood-curdling swear-words if anyone upset him by interfering with his sport.

If you, being a fellow-fisherman, took up your position on the bank of the River Whyn in a spot which Neddy Ware considered to be too near his, he would let drive at you with alarming emphasis; if boys – his pet aversion – annoyed him in any way by chattering around him, his language became totally unfit for juvenile ears. Once young Harry Ayres, the village champion where fisticuffs were concerned, had the temerity to throw a stone at the old man's float; he slunk back home afterwards, white in face and utterly cowed with the torrent of Neddy Ware's lurid remarks.

He lived in a small cottage standing quite by itself on the outskirts of the village, and he lived there alone. Mrs Lambert, a widow, went to his cottage for a couple of hours every morning to tidy up and cook his midday meal. For the rest, Neddy Ware managed quite well.

He came out of his cottage one August morning as the church clock, some half a mile distant, was striking four. Those who knew his habits would have seen nothing unusual in his rising so early. The fisherman knows the value of those first morning hours; besides which, the little River Whyn, which was the scene of his favourite occupation, was tidal for some five or six miles from the

sea. For those five or six miles it meandered, first through a low valley, flanked by the open downs on one side and by wooded heights on the other, and then made its way, for the last four miles, through a flat, low-lying country till it finally entered the Channel at Whynmouth. Everyone knows Whynmouth as a favourite South Coast holiday resort, possessing a small harbour at the mouth of its river.

Twice a day the tide flowed up the Whyn, more or less rapidly according to whether it was 'spring' or 'neap.' And this fact had an important bearing on the times which were favourable for angling. On this particular morning Neddy Ware had planned to be on the river bank a little while after the incoming tide had begun to flow up the stream.

Behold him, then, as he came out of his cottage, halfway up the wooded slopes of 'Lingham Hangar,' crossed the high road, and made his way down to the level of the river. He was fairly on in years, but carried those years well, so much so that there was only just a sprinkling of grey in his coal-black hair. A sturdy-looking man, clean-shaven, but with a curious, old-fashioned twist of hair allowed to grow long on either side of his head just in front of his ears; brown, weatherbeaten, lined face, humorous mouth and keen, grey eyes. Dressed in an old navy blue serge suit, and wearing – as he invariably did – a black bowler hat. Carrying rods, landing net, and a capacious basket containing all kinds of the impedimenta of his craft.

He reached the grassy bank of the river, put his things on the ground, and very slowly filled a blackened clay pipe with twist tobacco – which he rubbed in his hands first – and proceeded to light it, glancing up and down the river as he did so.

Where he was standing the river took a curve, and he was on the outer side of this curve, on the right bank. Away to the left the stream bent itself between the heights on the one side and the open meadows on the other. To the right, bending away from him, was the flat country, the river's edges bordered with tall-growing reeds. From this direction the tide was flowing towards him, swirling round the bend.

His first task was to haul in three or four eel lines he had thrown out the evening before, the ends being tied to the gnarled roots of a small tree growing on the bank. Two of the lines brought to land a couple of fair-sized eels, and, very dexterously, he detached the slippery, twisting fish from the hooks, washing the slime off afterwards. Then, slowly, he commenced putting one of his rods together, arranging his tackle, baiting with worms, and casting into

the stream. For some little time he watched the float bobbing about in the swirl of the eddies, now and again striking when it suddenly disappeared beneath the surface, once landing a fish.

He glanced around. Suddenly his float lost interest. He was gazing down-stream, as far as he could see around the bend. Slowly a small rowing-boat was coming upstream. But there was something peculiar about her. No oars were in evidence. She appeared to be drifting.

The old sailor was quick to recognise the little craft.

'Ah,' he muttered, 'that's the Vicar's boat.'

Lingham Vicarage stood, with its adjacent church, quite apart from the village proper, about half a mile down the river. The grounds ran down to the water's edge, where there was a rough landing-stage. The Vicar, he knew, kept his boat at this stage, moored by her painter to a convenient post. There was a little creek running into the grounds, with a wooden boat-house, but, in the summer months, especially when the Vicar's two boys were home from school, the boat was generally kept on the river itself.

As it came nearer, Ware laid down his rod. He could see now that there was someone in the boat – not seated, but, apparently, lying in the bottom of her, astern.

The boat was only about fifty yards away now. The swirl of the tide was bringing her round the outer side of the bend in the river, but Neddy Ware, who knew every current, saw that she would pass beyond his reach. With the quick action of the sailor he did not waste an instant. Diving into his basket he produced one of the coiled up eel lines with its heavy, lead plummet. And then stood in readiness, uncoiling the line and throwing the slack on the grass.

On came the boat, about a dozen yards from the bank. Skilfully he threw the plummet into her bows, and then started walking along the bank up-stream, gently but steadily pulling on the line till, at length, he brought her close up to the bank and laid hold of the painter at her bows. The end of the painter was dragging in the water. As he pulled it out he glanced at it. It had been cut.

He made it fast to a tree-root. The boat swung round, stern up-stream, alongside the bank. And Ware got into her. The next moment he was on his knees, bending over the man who lay in the stern.

He lay there on his back, his knees slightly hunched up, his arms at his sides, quite still. A man of about sixty, with iron-grey hair, moustache and close-cropped, pointed beard, dark eyes open with fixed stare. He was clad in evening dress clothes and a brown overcoat, the latter open at the front and exposing a white shirt-

front stained with blood.

Sitting on one of the seats, Ware made a swift examination of the boat.

A pair of oars lay in her, the metal rowlocks were unshipped. Apparently the dead man was hatless – no – there *was* a hat in the boat, lying in the bows; a round, black, clerical hat, such as Mr Mount, the Vicar, usually wore.

Neddy Ware, having looked around, got out of the boat and glanced at his watch. Ten minutes to five. Then, leaving the little craft moored to the bank, he hurried off as fast as he could go, gained the high road, which was some hundred yards away from the river, and started in the direction of the village.

Police Constable Hempstead, just on the point of turning into bed after having been on duty all night, looked out of the window in answer to Ware's knock at the door.

'What is it, Mr Ware?' he asked.

'Something pretty bad, I'm afraid.'

Hempstead, wide awake now, slipped on his clothes again, came down and opened the door. Ware told him what had happened.

'I must get the Inspector out from Whynmouth – and a doctor,' said the constable, 'I'll phone to the station there.'

He came out again in two or three minutes.

'All right,' he said. 'They'll run over in a car at once. Now you come along with me and show me that boat and what's in it. You haven't been messing about with anything – moving the body and so on, I hope?'

'I shouldn't be such a fool,' replied Ware.

'That's all right. You haven't seen anyone else?'

'No one.'

The policeman went on asking questions from time to time as they hurried along. He was a smart man, this young constable, eager for his stripes, and wanted to make the most of the opportunity. As soon as they reached the river bank he took a glance at the boat and its contents, and exclaimed:

'*Hullo*! Don't you know who that is, Mr Ware?'

'Never saw him before that I know of. Who is he?'

'Why, it's Admiral Penistone. He lives at Rundel Croft – that big house the other side of the river just opposite the Vicarage. Leastways, he's been in residence there about a month. He only bought it last June. A new-comer.'

'Oh! Admiral Penistone, is he?' said Neddy Ware.

'That's the man, right enough. But, look here: are you sure this

is the Vicarage boat?'

'Certain.'

'Queer, eh? That seems to mean something happened *this* side of the river, for of course there's no bridge till you get to Fernton – three miles lower down. Ah, and the parson's hat, eh? Let's see; what time did you first see the boat coming along?'

'A little after half-past four, I should say.'

Hempstead had his note-book out and was making pencilled jottings in it. Then he said:

'Look here, Mr Ware, I want you, if you will, to go back to the road and stop Inspector Rudge when he comes along in his car.'

'Very well,' replied Ware; 'nothing more I can do?'

'Not yet, at any rate.'

Hempstead was an astute man. He waited until Neddy Ware was out of the way before he began a little examination of his own account. He knew very well that his superior officer would take the case fully in hand, but he was anxious to see what he could, without disturbing anything, in the meantime.

As he got into the boat, he noticed a folded newspaper, half sticking out of the dead man's overcoat pocket. He took it out, gingerly, looked at it, and replaced it.

'Ah,' he murmured, 'the *Evening Gazette*, last night's late London edition. He wouldn't get that here. The nearest place where it's sold is Whynmouth.'

He would very much have liked to examine the contents of all the pockets of the dead man's clothes, but felt he had better not. So he got out of the boat, sat down on the bank, and waited.

After a bit the sound of a car running along the main road was heard, and in a minute or two, four men came across the meadow; Neddy Ware, a police inspector in uniform, and two men in plain clothes, one of them a doctor, the other a detective-sergeant.

Inspector Rudge was a tall, thin man, with sallow, clean-shaven face. He came up to Hempstead.

'You haven't moved anything?' he asked curtly.

'No, sir.'

Rudge turned to the doctor.

'I won't do anything, Doctor Grice, till you have made your examination.'

Doctor Grice got into the boat and proceeded to examine the body. It was only a few minutes before he said:

'Stabbed to the heart, Inspector, with some narrow-bladed instrument – a thin knife or dagger. Death must have been instantaneous. There'll have to be a post-mortem, of course.'

'How long has he been dead?'

'Some hours. He probably died before midnight.'

'Nothing more?'

'Not at present, Inspector.'

'Very well. I'll have a look now.'

He turned the body over, shifting it slightly.

'No sign of blood under him,' he said, 'or anywhere else in the boat that I can see. Let's have a look in his pockets – ah, it wasn't robbery. Gold watch and chain – wallet full of notes – they were not after that. Evening paper here – last night's date. That must be noted. Now – we've got to be as quick as possible. Tell me, Hempstead, what do you know about him?'

'He's Admiral Penistone, sir. Retired. A new-comer hereabouts. Bought Rundel Croft, a big house on the other side of the river, a few months ago. Took up residence there lately. I believe he has a niece living with him. But it's not in my district, sir.'

'I know.'

The Inspector turned to Ware.

'You say the boat belongs to the Vicar here?'

'Yes.'

'How long would it take for the tide to bring it up from his place?'

'Forty to forty-five minutes,' replied Ware promptly, 'with the tide as it is today.'

'I see. Now, the question is how are we to move him? We might pull the boat back against the tide. Won't do, though. Those oars must be tested for finger-prints before they are handled. Let's see – Vicarage on the telephone, Hempstead?'

'Yes, sir.'

'All right. I'll go there now. I want to see the Vicar. We'll phone to Whynmouth for an ambulance. Have to run him to Rundel Croft round by Fernton Bridge. You remain here, Hempstead, and if anyone comes along don't let 'em touch anything. I shall want you, Sergeant – we'll have to put you across the river from the Vicarage if we can get a boat there; I want you to mount guard over the Admiral's boat and boat-house. Perhaps you won't mind coming too, Mr Ware. You may be useful. There! We'll get a move on. Come along, Doctor.'

In a very short time the Inspector was driving the car down the short bit of road leading from the highway to the Vicarage. The front door of the latter faced the river, a lawn stretching down to the bank. Opposite, about a hundred yards from the bank, stood a large, red-brick, Tudor mansion, with a broad sweep of lawn in

front and the boathouse. The Inspector, the Vicar's hat in his hand, got out of the car and rang the bell; the others followed. It was a few minutes before the maid, who evidently had only just come down, opened the door and said her master was not up yet.

'Will you kindly tell him that Inspector Rudge wants to see him at once. Say I'm sorry to disturb him, but it's most important.'

'I'll tell him, sir. Won't you come in?'

'Thank you, no. I'll wait here.'

'Hullo, I say, are you a policeman?'

He turned. Two boys had come across the lawn, aged, respectively, about sixteen and fourteen, dressed in flannel trousers and shirts open at the neck, and carrying bathing towels. They were regarding him eagerly.

'Yes,' he said, 'I am.'

'Good egg!' exclaimed the elder, 'just what we want, isn't he, Alec? Look here; some blighter has taken our boat – cut the painter. Perhaps you've heard about it, though? Is that what you've come about?'

The Inspector smiled grimly.

'Yes – that's what I've come about, young gentlemen,' he replied, dryly, 'but you needn't worry about your boat. It's been found.'

'Hooray!' exclaimed the other boy. 'Got the beggar who took it?'

'Not yet,' said Rudge, with another grim little smile, 'that may not be so easy. Have you got another boat handy?' he asked.

'Only our old punt – she's in the boat-house.'

'Well, do you two young gentlemen think you could manage to put my detective-sergeant here across the water in her? He wants to pay a call at Rundel Croft.'

'Rather!' Peter Mount looked with boyish admiration at the sergeant. 'Is there going to be a man-hunt? Cheerio! We'll help you. But you don't suspect old Admiral Penistone of sneaking our boat, do you? He crossed back in his own last night. He'd been dining here, you know.'

'Oh, had he!' said the Inspector. 'No, we don't suspect him. Now – will you do what I asked?'

'Come on,' said Alec to Sergeant Appleton, 'the tide's running pretty strong, but we'll put you across all right.'

They went down to the boat-house with the sergeant.

'Good morning, Inspector. Good morning, Doctor Grice – ah – it's you, Ware, I see. What's the meaning of this early morning deputation?'

The Vicar had come out of the house; a man of about fifty, of medium height, sturdily built, with clear-cut features and hair a little grey. He asked the question of the Inspector, who replied:

'I'll explain directly, Mr Mount. Is this your hat?'

The Vicar took it and looked at it.

'Yes; certainly it is.'

'Then would you mind telling me if you remember when you had it last?'

'That is quite simple. To be absolutely accurate, at twenty minutes past ten last evening.'

'And where?'

'You are very mysterious, Inspector. But I'll tell you. My neighbour who lives opposite was dining with us last evening, with his niece. They left just about ten. I went down to the river to see them off, and put my hat on. After the Admiral had crossed the stream in his boat with his niece I sat down in that little summer-house and smoked a pipe. I took off my hat and laid it on the seat beside me – and, absent-mindedly, I forgot to put it on again when I returned to the house. It was then that I set my watch by the clock in the hall – twenty minutes past ten. But will you tell me why you ask me this – and what you have all come about?'

'I will, sir. This hat was found in your boat early this morning. Your boat was drifting with the tide up-stream. And in her was the dead body of your opposite neighbour, Admiral Penistone – *murdered*, Mr Mount.'

2

By G.D.H. and M. Cole

BREAKING THE NEWS

'Murdered! Good God!' the Vicar said – and it was well known, the Inspector reflected, that the Vicar of Lingham had a ridiculously exaggerated respect for the Third Commandment. He had stepped back a pace at the shock of the news, and some of the colour was fading from his cheeks. 'But – *murdered* . . . How – what do you mean, Inspector?'

'I mean,' said Rudge, 'that Admiral Penistone was stabbed to

the heart some time before midnight last night – and his body placed in your boat.'

'But what – why . . . ? How could he have been?'

'And your hat,' the Inspector remorselessly amplified, 'was lying in the boat beside him. So you see,' he added, 'that the first thing I had to do was to make enquiries at your house.'

The Vicar turned on his heel abruptly. 'Come into my study,' he said. 'We can talk better there – I don't suppose you want my sons, at present?' The Inspector shook his head, and followed him into a quiet, brown room with wide sash windows, the very model of what a clerical study, owned by a none too tidy cleric, should be. As he led the way in, the Vicar stumbled over something, and with a little gasp caught hold of the table for support. 'You – you must excuse me,' he muttered, as he motioned the Inspector to a chair and sank into one himself. 'This is – a very great shock. Now, will you tell me what I can do for you?'

Rudge scanned him a minute before replying. Undoubtedly he had received a very great shock. He was pale; his hands were none too steady; and his breath was coming and going quickly. Whether the cause was merely the sudden impact of violent death on a sheltered clerical life, or whether there was some graver reason, the Inspector did not know enough to decide. At any rate, there was no sense in causing further alarm at the moment. So when he spoke it was in a gentle reassuring tone.

'What I want to find out immediately, Mr Mount, is exactly what happened last night, as far as you know it. Admiral Penistone, you say, came over to dine with his niece – what is the lady's name, by the way?'

'Fitzgerald – Miss Elma Fitzgerald. She is his sister's daugher, I understand.'

'About what age?'

'Oh – I should say a year or two over thirty.'

'Thank you. They arrived – when?'

'Just before seven-thirty. In their boat.'

'And left?'

'Slightly after ten. I can't fix it to the minute, I'm afraid; but they were just taking their leave when the church clock struck, and Admiral Penistone said, "Hurry up, I want to get back before midnight" – or something of that sort; and within a very few minutes they were gone.'

'And you saw them off?'

'Yes. I went down to the landing-stage with them, and Peter – that's my eldest son – helped them to start. It's sometimes a little

awkward getting off, if the current is running strongly.'

'Did you actually see them land?'

'Yes. It wasn't dark. I watched them take the boat into the Admiral's boat-house, and then, a little later, I saw them come out of the boat-house, and go up to the house.'

'I should have thought those trees at the back of the boat-house would have screened them from you,' said the Inspector, who had made good use of his eyes. 'Or do you mean they were crossing the lawn?'

The Vicar looked at him with respect. 'No, they were in the trees,' he said. 'But Miss Fitzgerald had on a white dress, and I saw it showing through them.'

'But Admiral Penistone hadn't a white dress?'

'No . . . I suppose,' the Vicar reflected, 'that now you mention it I couldn't say I saw the Admiral leave the boat-house – but seeing his niece I naturally concluded he was with her.'

'Very naturally,' Rudge concurred soothingly. 'And you yourself stayed out smoking until – ?'

'Twenty past ten.'

'And then?'

'I locked the house up and went to bed.'

'And you heard nothing more of your neighbour?'

'Nothing,' said the Vicar. 'Nothing at all,' he repeated more loudly.

'What about your sons? Or your servants? Would they have heard anything?'

'I don't think so. They had all gone to bed when I came in.'

'Thank you. Now, Mr Mount, can you tell me this? Did Admiral Penistone seem in his usual spirits during the evening?'

The question appeared to distress the Vicar. 'I – I don't think I can really answer that,' he said. 'You see, I haven't known the Admiral at all long. He has only recently come to the neighbourhood . . . I really hardly know him.'

'But still,' Rudge persisted, 'you might have noticed if he seemed distressed, or worried in any way. Did he?' And, seeing the Vicar still hesitated, he pressed his point. 'If you did notice anything, Mr Mount, I really think you should tell me. It's of the highest importance that we should find out everything we can about the poor gentleman's state of mind at the time – and I assure you I know how to be discreet.'

'Well,' said the Vicar, fidgeting a little. 'Well . . . it's nothing, probably. But I should say – yes – that the Admiral was perhaps a little worried. He was not as – as amiable as usual. And he was

generally a very pleasant man – not at all snappish.'

'He was snappish with Miss Fitzgerald, perhaps?' the Inspector suggested quickly; and the Vicar blinked.

'Oh no . . . hardly . . . I shouldn't say that at all.'

'But he acted as though there was something on his mind . . . I suppose you've no idea what it was?'

'I think – I don't know – it may have been his niece's marriage. He said something about it. Nothing much.'

'Oh, she's getting married, is she? Who to?'

'Somebody called Holland, Arthur Holland. From London, I think. I don't know him.'

'And Admiral Penistone didn't approve?'

'I don't mean that. I mean, I don't know. He didn't say. Only he seemed as though something might have gone a little wrong. Perhaps it was to do with her settlements; she has a good deal of money, as I understand, and the Admiral is – was her trustee. But I really don't know anything about it.'

'I see. Had you, yourself, known Admiral Penistone long?'

'Only since he came here, about a month ago. I called on him, you know; and we got acquainted.'

'And you saw each other fairly often?'

'Oh, two or three times in the week, perhaps. Not more.'

'Ever hear him speak of any enemies – anyone who'd have a reason for killing him?'

'Oh, no, no!' The Vicar looked shocked, but hastened to add, 'Of course, I really know nothing of his life before he came here.'

'Had he many friends? In the neighbourhood? Or outside? Where did he live before?'

'Somewhere in the West, I believe. I don't remember his ever telling me the district. I don't think he knew many people about here well. Sir Wilfred Denny, over at West End, saw most of him, I fancy. I believe he had old friends down to meet him, sometimes.'

'Ever meet any of them yourself?'

'Oh, no,' said the Vicar.

'I see. Well, I think I'd better be getting over to his place now,' the Inspector said. 'I'm very much obliged to you, Mr Mount. I'll want to have a word with your sons and your servants some time, just in case any of them noticed anything that might help us. But that can wait. By the way,' he turned at the door to add, 'can you tell me what sort of a young lady Miss Fitzgerald is? Liable to – to be very upset, I mean?'

The Vicar smiled a little, almost in spite of himself. 'I shouldn't

think so,' he said. 'I don't think Miss Fitzgerald is at all the fainting type.'

'Very devoted to her uncle, eh?'

'I couldn't say, particularly. About as much as most nieces are to their uncles, I imagine. Perhaps she is rather a reserved young woman – has interests of her own. But this is just gossip – you can see for yourself what you think, Inspector.'

'That's true enough. Well, I'll be going,' the Inspector said, and noted the expression of relief which overspread the Vicar's face. 'I know we aren't popular visitors,' he thought to himself, 'at the best of times. But need he show *quite* so plainly how glad he is to get rid of me? I wonder if there could be any other reason – if he knows anything more than he's said. But – the Vicar of Lingham, and a most respectable Vicar, from all I've ever heard of him! I must say it doesn't sound likely.' And, so thinking, he made his way back to the car, and drove rapidly the three miles or so which he had to cover to reach the house a hundred yards away.

It was close on eight o'clock by the time he reached his destination; but Rundel Croft obviously did not keep early hours. One or two of the windows facing him still had their blinds down; and the hall, when he was admitted to it, was obviously undergoing its matutinal clean-up. A rather down-at-heels butler, of the type which seems to have become a butler because its wife is a good cook and itself has no special ability of any kind, opened the door to him and blinked uneasily in his face. Rudge asked for Miss Fitzgerald, and was told that she was not yet about. Apparently she always breakfasted in bed. Rudge then asked for Admiral Penistone.

'He's in his room, still,' the butler said, looking faintly hostile, as though he did not approve of early morning visitors.

'No, he isn't,' Rudge said sharply. 'He's had an accident.' The butler goggled at him. 'Look here – what's your name?'

'Emery.'

'Look here, Emery, I'm Inspector Rudge from Whynmouth, and I must see Miss Fitzgerald at once. Admiral Penistone has met with a very serious accident – in fact, he's dead. Will you find Miss Fitzgerald's maid, if she has one, and tell her that I want to speak to Miss Fitzgerald as soon as she can possibly come down. And come back here when you've done it. I want a word with you.'

With no more than an inarticulate noise the butler shuffled off, and it was ten minutes or so before he returned, with the news that Miss Fitzgerald would be down in a quarter of an hour. The Inspector took him aside into a square, rather beautiful morning-

room, and began questioning him about his master's movements of the night before. But he got very little help from his interview. It seemed to him that the man must be either phenomenally stupid or else dazed with shock at his master's death; and yet the latter did not seem to be the case. Beyond a muttering or two of 'Dear, dear!' and the like, he hardly appeared to have taken in the news; and the Inspector felt some surprise that a retired naval officer should keep so incompetent-looking a servant. Yet the house appeared well cleaned, if it did rouse itself rather late in the day.

Admiral Penistone, the Inspector learned, had last been seen by his staff at about a quarter past seven on the previous evening, when he and his niece had gone down to the boat-house to row themselves over to the Vicarage. (He never allowed anyone to disturb him in the morning until he rang, which accounted for his absence being unknown.) As he was going to the boat-house, he had told Emery that he need not wait up, but was to lock the front of the house and go to bed, leaving the french window of the drawing-room, which led to the lawn and the river, unbolted. 'I was to lock it,' Emery said, 'but Admiral Penistone always had his own key.'

'Stop a moment. Was this window bolted when you came down this morning, or not?'

'No,' Emery said; but added that that didn't mean anything. Half the time the Admiral didn't bolt it. It was locked, and nobody was likely to come burgling from the riverside.

Then he hadn't seen the Admiral again? No. Or Miss Fitzgerald? Yes, so to speak. He meant that, as he and his wife were going up to bed, a bit after ten, might have been quarter-past, they'd seen Miss Fitzgerald coming up the path from the boat-house. At least, they'd seen her dress; they couldn't see her properly in the dark. The Admiral wasn't with her then; but they supposed he was behind, locking up the boat-house. No, he didn't know if the boat-house was locked now; he supposed it was, but it wasn't his work to go down to the boat-house. No, he couldn't say they'd actually seen Miss Fitzgerald come in; she might have, or she might have stopped on the lawn. He and his wife weren't particularly noticing; they were going to bed.

And that was all Emery had to say. Questioned about his late master's mood of the previous evening, he seemed to have no idea, and simply stared with a moon-faced imbecility. He 'supposed he was much as usual.' The Admiral was occasionally 'short' with his servants (the Inspector reflected that it would take a saint not to be short with Emery at least a dozen times a day); but

beyond that his butler had nothing to say. Masters, apparently, were phenomena that were occasionally short, like pastry; but one accepted the fact, and did not conjecture about the cause. At least, not if one were as limp and uninterested as Emery appeared. No, his wife and he had only been a month with the Admiral; they had applied for the post from an advertisement; they were last with a lady and gentleman in Hove, for a year and a half. At this point, somewhat to Rudge's relief, a much more intelligent-looking maidservant appeared, and announced that Miss Fitzgerald was awaiting him in the dining-room.

'She's ugly!' was the Inspector's immediate reaction on first beholding the niece of the late Admiral Penistone. And then: 'No, I'm not so sure that she would be, in some lights. But she'd take a good bit of making-up, I shouldn't wonder. And, jiminy! isn't she sulky-looking?'

Miss Elma Fitzgerald was very pale. But it was not the pallor of fear for a possible accident to her uncle, but that peculiar to a very thick, opaque skin. She was big and heavily-made, with long limbs and broad shoulders, and would have been better suited, obviously, by long trailing draperies than by the tweed skirt and jumper which she had rather carelessly put on. She had largish, strongly-marked, but roughly-designed features, with a wide jaw and full chin, and dark brows nearly meeting in her white face. Her hair was dark and coarse, done in flat plaits around her ears, and under her eyes, which were so little open that the Inspector could not at first glance determine their colour, were lines and dark pouches. She was, to him, distinctly unattractive; and 'a year or two over thirty' was, he thought, a generous description. Yet she was certainly a woman of personality, and in a kinder light and with artificial aids to lighten her skin and hide the disfiguring lines, she might even have been attractive.

'Yes?' she said in a voice that contrived to have a rasp and a drawl simultaneously. 'What do you want?' At any rate, the Inspector thought, she was not going to waste his time.

'I am sorry to have to tell you, Miss Fitzgerald,' said he, 'that Admiral Penistone has met with a serious accident.'

'Is he dead?' The tone was so matter-of-fact that the Inspector jumped slightly.

'I am afraid he is. But did you – were you expecting – ?'

'Oh, no.' Still she had not raised her eyes. 'But that's the way the police always break things to one, don't they? What happened?'

'I'm sorry to say,' said the Inspector, 'that the Admiral was murdered.'

'*Murdered*?' At that the eyes did open wide for a moment. They were grey, very dark grey. They would have been fine eyes, Rudge noted, if the lashes had been longer. 'But – *why*?'

As that was exactly what the Inspector wanted to know himself, he was momentarily brought to a stop.

'His body was found,' he said, 'at half-past four this morning, drifting in a boat up-stream and stabbed to the heart.' Miss Fitzgerald merely bowed her head in acquiescence, and seemed waiting for him to continue. 'Damn her!' the Inspector thought. 'Hasn't she got *any* natural feelings? You'd think I'd told her there was a cat on the lawn!' Aloud he said: 'I'm afraid this must come as a good deal of a shock to you, madam.'

'You need not consider my feelings, Inspector,' said Elma Fitzgerald, with a glance which said, more plainly than words: 'And it is a gross impertinence on your part to make any enquiries into them!' 'I suppose you have some idea why – this happened? Or who did it?'

'I am afraid I don't see it very clearly yet,' the Inspector said. 'I wondered – if you could . . . ?'

'I can't,' said Miss Fitzgerald with decision. 'I haven't any idea' – she spoke slowly – 'why anyone – anyone at all – should want to kill my uncle. I suppose – ' But the sentence stopped there. Whatever it was she supposed, the Inspector, wait as he might, was not to be privy to it. 'What do you want me to tell you?' she continued at length. ('I wish you'd be quick and go about your business,' her voice conveyed.)

'Just this, madam,' the Inspector said. 'When did you last see Admiral Penistone?'

'Last night. When we came back from dining at the Vicarage.'

'What time would that be?' The Inspector believed in getting his information confirmed from as many sources as possible.

'Oh . . . a little after ten, I think. It struck ten just before we left.'

'And you rowed across, and came up to the house with the Admiral?'

'No, he didn't come up to the house when I did. He was locking the boat-house, and he said he thought he'd like a cigar before he went to bed. So I said good night to him, and came straight up to the house.'

'Was there anyone about when you came in?'

'No; but Emery and his wife had only just gone to bed, I think. I saw the lights going on and off as I came up. They must have been shutting up the house.'

'And then – what did you do?'

'I came straight up, and went to bed myself.'

'You didn't hear Admiral Penistone come in?'

'No. But I wasn't listening particularly. He often stays up quite late, walking about,' said Miss Fitzgerald.

'I gather,' said the Inspector, 'that Admiral Penistone, last night, appeared rather worried and distressed?'

'I don't think so . . . No. Why should he have been?'

'You hadn't had a – a disagreement with him at all?'

'You mean,' said Miss Fitzgerald with disconcerting penetration, 'about my marriage. That – is – pure – gossip.' There was a considerable amount of contempt in her tone. 'My uncle was not in the least opposed to my marriage. He was a little worried, I believe, about the best way of arranging the money side of it – but that was only a question which would settle itself, in time. That was all.' But there must be a little more to it, the Inspector swiftly reflected, or she wouldn't have tumbled so quick to what I was talking about.

'Then you can't suggest at all what was worrying him?'

'I don't think for a moment there was anything,' said Miss Fitzgerald; and made a slight movement that at least suggested a gesture of dismissal.

'I see. Well . . . ' The Inspector would have liked to continue the interview, but did not see, at the moment, exactly what other information he could well demand. And it was perhaps hardly in the best of taste to sit there pestering a lady in her first grief – if she was grieved. There was a sudden twitch of a strong, rather large hand, that suggested more emotion than appeared on the surface, at any rate. 'Just one more thing, Miss Fitzgerald, and then I need not trouble you further. Can you give me the name of Admiral Penistone's lawyers?'

'Dakers and Dakers. They live somewhere in Lincoln's Inn, I think.'

'Thank you. And if I could see Admiral Penistone's papers now – and the servants – '

'I think all his papers are in the study. Emery will show you.' Miss Fitzgerald leaned across and touched the bell. 'Inspector,' she said, a little suddenly, 'will you tell me – what happens? Will they be bringing him – here?' It was the first trace of real emotion her voice had shown, and Rudge hastened to assure her that the body would be taken to the mortuary, and that every effort would be made to spare her as much as possible.

'Thank you,' she said, returning to indifference again; and at

that moment Emery shuffled in. 'Emery, take the Inspector to the Admiral's study, and let him see anything he wants to. And you'd better none of you go out of the house. The Inspector may want to speak to you.' She leaned back in the chair, and made no movement, as Rudge, looking, he hoped, not as puzzled as he felt, followed Emery out of the room.

The Admiral's study was a large and pleasant room on the first floor, looking out upon the lawn and the river. It was in fairly good order, though it had obviously not been cleaned this morning, and there were a few papers, dating probably from the previous evening, lying untidily upon the desk. Rudge took in the appearance of the room with a practised eye, and reflected that it ought not to take long to make it yield up any secrets it possessed. Then he dismissed the hovering Emery. 'And you're not to let anybody into the house for the present, please, wtihout asking me about it,' were his final instructions. Emery, with a muttered 'Very good,' shuffled off again.

The desk and a small filing cabinet which stood beside it were the only likely receptacles for papers in the room. The filing cabinet, when opened, disclosed nothing but newspaper cuttings neatly sorted. The desk was locked, but Rudge had prudently possessed himself of the dead man's keys, and he very soon had it open. The first thing which he found was a pistol, perfectly clean and fully loaded, lying all by itself in a little drawer. He formed his mouth into the shape of a soundless whistle, and proceeded to unearth writing-paper and envelopes, a drawer full of pipes, another with a few letters of recent date, another with bank-books, stub-ends of cheque-books, income-tax forms and other financial paraphernalia, and a fifth which contained only a large legal envelope inscribed Elma Fitzgerald. In view of what the Vicar had said, the Inspector conjectured that the contents of this envelope might possibly have some bearing upon his case, and he settled himself down to study them as a preliminary. The first item was the 'Last Will and Testament of John Martin Fitzgerald,' bulky and wordy beyond even the normal run of such documents; and the Inspector, whose mastery of legal jargon was not as thorough as he could have wished, found some trouble in disentangling its provisions. He had succeeded in making out that John Martin Fitzgerald was the Admiral's brother-in-law, and that his will devised his property, whatever that might be, in equal proportions to his son Walter Everett Fitzgerald, 'if he should be found to be alive at the date of my death,' and his daughter Elma Fitzgerald; and had noted that if the son turned out to be dead ('I

suppose he must have disappeared or something. It's a funny way to put it anyhow.') Elma Fitzgerald would get all the property on her marriage – when his attention was arrested by what sounded like an altercation below-stairs. For a moment or two he listened, and judged that, in spite of his orders, some visitor must be trying to force an entrance into the house. And as he strongly mistrusted Emery's power to oppose even a determined fly, he went down into the hall to see what it was all about, and found, as he had anticipated, a pink and perplexed butler feebly flapping at an enraged visitor who had already penetrated as far as the foot of the stairs.

' – the Inspector *said* – ' he was bleating.

'To hell with the Inspector!' the intruder retorted; and, glancing up, found himself looking straight into the eyes of the said Inspector – a contingency which disconcerted him not at all.

Nor need it have done so. Whoever he was, the intruder was easily capable of dealing with a dozen inspectors. He must have been six foot three at the very least, with the build and gait of an athlete, moreover, who specialised in events requiring exceptional strength. Above a pair of magnificently broad shoulders was set a handsome head with sunburned face and neck, a square chin, and short aquiline nose, brown hair cropped so close that it could hardly indulge its natural curls, and big, fiery, hazel eyes, which glared up at Rudge with all the righteous indignation of a supporter of Law and Justice resenting the interference of Law with his own avocations.

'I told Mr Holland,' Emery bleated, 'that you'd said nobody was to be let in without orders.'

'And I told him,' Mr Holland remarked, 'that I was coming in.'

'You're Mr Holland?' the Inspector said. 'Mr Arthur Holland?' Holland nodded. 'And you want to see – ?'

'I've come to see Miss Fitzgerald,' Arthur Holland said. 'And let me tell you I'm in a hurry, whoever you are. Here, Emery, go and tell Miss Fitzgerald I'm here, and be quick about it, will you?'

'Half a moment, sir,' the Inspector said, while a maid-servant came out of one of the rooms opening into the hall, and began to whisper to the butler. 'If you'll excuse me, I want a word or two with you myself, first. Did this man tell you that Admiral Penistone has – ?'

'Been killed? Yes,' the young man said. 'Is that any reason why I shouldn't see Miss Fitzgerald? She'll need someone – '

'Beg pardon, sir.' Emery approached deferentially. 'But Miss Fitzgerald's away.'

'*Away*!' The exclamation burst from both men simulataneously.
'Yes, sir. She's just had her bag packed, and driven off in her car, Merton says.' He indicated the maidservant in the hall 'Not ten minutes ago, sir.'
'Whew!' With an internal whistle the Inspector brooded on this new development.

3

By Henry Wade

BRIGHT THOUGHTS ON TIDES

Still frowning with annoyance at the escape of this important witness, Inspector Rudge turned to his companion.
'If you'll kindly step into the study, sir,' he said, 'there are some questions that I'd like to ask you.'
'They'll have to wait,' said Holland curtly, turning towards the front door. 'I'm going to find Miss Fitzgerald.'
'No, sir!' There was a ring of authority in the Inspector's voice that brought even the masterful Holland up with a round turn. Rudge was not going to lose two witnesses before he had done with them.
'I must ask you to attend to me first, sir, please. I shall not detain you longer than I can help.'
With a wry smile, Arthur Holland followed the Inspector into the study and, declining a chair, leant his back against the tall mantelpiece.
'Well, what is it?' he asked. 'Fire away.'
Rudge took out his note-book and made a show of preparing to take down vital information. He had often found this effective with recalcitrant witnesses.
'Your full name, sir, please?'
'Arthur Holland.'
'Age?'
'Thirty-three.'
'Address?'
'Lord Marshall Hotel, Whynmouth.'
Rudge looked up.

'That's not your permanent address, sir?'

'I hope not.'

'Then may I have it, sir, please?'

'I haven't got one.'

The Inspector's eyebrows lifted, and he opened his mouth as if to argue the point but, changing his mind, licked his pencil and wrote down, audibly:

'No permanent address.'

After a moment's thought he continued:

'Occupation?'

'I'm a trader.'

Rudge looked slightly puzzled.

'Commercial traveller, sir?'

'Good God, no! I trade in raw materials – rubber, jute, ivory – that sort of thing.'

'In London, sir?'

Holland writhed with impatience.

'They don't grow in London, man. I'm in England now, fixing up markets.'

'Ah!' The Inspector felt as if he were getting nearer the bone. 'Then will you tell me, sir, in what part of the world you get your raw material for the London market?'

'I didn't say the London market. I said I was in London to fix up markets – London's only a centre, the markets may be in any part of the world.'

The policeman's irritatingly stupid questions were drawing more information out of Arthur Holland than he had intended to give.

'Quite, sir; but you haven't answered my question. In what part of the world do you yourself get the material for which you are trying to find a market?'

'Oh, wherever I think the going's good at the moment,' replied Holland airily. 'Burma, Kenya, S.A., India – I move about.'

Holland hesitated.

'It won't be very difficult for me to find out, sir,' said Rudge quietly. 'Better for you to tell me.'

The reply came slowly – almost unwillingly:

'China.'

'I see, sir. And no particular or permanent address in China?'

'No.'

Inspector Rudge whisked over a page and started afresh.

'Now about last night, sir. Were you at the Lord Marshall last night?'

'Yes, I was.'

'You arrived at . . . ?'

'I got to Whynmouth just before nine.'

'Ah; by the express?'

'Yes.'

'From London?'

'Yes.'

'And you spent the evening . . . where?'

'In Whynmouth.'

'You didn't come out here to see your young lady?'

'I knew she was dining out. I stayed in Whynmouth.'

'Very patient of you, sir. You remained in the hotel?'

'I had a stroll by the sea after dinner. I went to bed early.'

'Perhaps there would be someone who would be able to confirm what you say about your movements, sir?'

The Inspector's voice was casual – too casual. Holland's eyes narrowed.

'Are you suspecting me of killing the Admiral?' he asked harshly.

'Oh, dear, no; oh, dear, no. Why, I didn't even know of your existence till an hour or so ago. Funny, isn't it? No; that's just routine. We like to know – and if possible to confirm – the whereabouts of everyone in any way connected with the deceased at the time of the crime. I just thought it possible you might know of someone who could confirm your statement.'

'How can anyone prove whether I was in bed or not? I happen to make a practice of sleeping alone. Funny, isn't it?' quoted Holland with a sneer.

'Ah, then you know the crime was committed after you went to bed?'

Holland stared.

'How the devil should I? I've only just heard of it.'

'Quite, sir; quite. Like me only just hearing of you. Now about Miss Fitzgerald. Have you any idea where she's gone?'

'Not the slightest.'

'But when you were dashing off to find her just now, you must have had some idea of where to look.'

'She might have gone to London.'

'And you might be able to find her in London?'

'I might.'

'Then perhaps it would be as well if you did, and asked her to return here without delay.'

Holland nodded.

'I'll tell her, but she's likely to please herself about that.'

'It'll be wise if she pleases herself by coming back, sir. You'll keep in touch with us, in any case, won't you, sir?'

Holland halted, with his hand on the door.

'Does that mean that I'm to be under observation or whatever you call it?'

'I shan't put a man on to watch you, sir, but I'd like you to keep in touch.'

With a grunt Miss Fitzgerald's 'young man' swung open the door and strode out of the room. There was a smile on Inspector Rudge's face as he pressed the bell.

'I'd like to see Miss Fitzgerald's maid – Merton, I think you said her name was – please, Emery.'

A minute later Merton was sitting on the edge of a chair, nervously eyeing the formidable Police Inspector. She was a fresh-looking English girl of about twenty-six, attractive without being actually pretty, and evidently intelligent. Inspector Rudge decided at once to put her at her ease – one of his favourite alternatives of examination.

' "Merton" they call you?' he said with a friendly smile. 'Sounds a bit formal to me. I expect you've got another name, eh?'

'Jennie's my Christian name, sir.'

'Ah, that's better. Well, Jennie, this is a sad affair and I don't want to upset you more than I can help, but I must just ask you a few questions about your employers. You see, I don't know anything of them; not been here long, have they?'

'No, sir; only about a month.'

'Were you with them before they came here?'

'Oh, no; I come from Whynmouth myself. I've only been here three weeks.'

'Ah, so Miss Fitzgerald didn't bring a maid with her when she came?'

'Oh, yes, she did – a French one – Mademoiselle Blanc she called herself, but Miss Fitzgerald called her Célie. She didn't stay long – told the other girls the place was like a mortuary – "dead-house" she called it – I don't know whether she meant Rundel Croft or Whynmouth, but I suppose she thought it was dull. Anyway she packed up and went off without waiting for her month, nor yet her wages, so the girls say. Miss Fitzgerald had to go to Marlow's Agency for another maid in a hurry and as they hadn't got one but they knew I'd been in a maid's situation but I'm living with mother now – she's not well – they asked me, and I consented to oblige.'

The last sentence, though rather involved, had the merit of explaining the situation. Inspector Rudge nodded.

'I see; so you don't really know Miss Fitzgerald very well.'

'Not so very, but I'm not blind.'

'I'm sure not. What did you see?'

'Just that they didn't look much like an uncle and niece to me.'

'Oh, they didn't? Why not?'

'The way she spoke to him – sharp and sarcastic – more like a wife, I should say. Not that I mean there was anything *wrong*.'

'But he was old enough to be her uncle – or her father, wasn't he?'

'Oh, yes – if you think that matters.'

'Did they seem fond of each other?'

'Not so as you'd notice it.'

'Rather the reverse in fact?'

'Well, of course, I really couldn't say. It's not my place to be with them – only with her.'

Jennie evidently felt that she had said too much already.

'Well, about her then. You knew that she was engaged to this Mr Holland, of course?'

'So she told me.'

'Did she seem to be in love with him?'

'I'm sure I couldn't say.'

'You didn't see them together much?'

'Not so much. But I never saw them kissing or holding hands.'

'Ah!' Here evidently was significance – a criterion.

'Now tell me, Jennie, did Miss Fitzgerald care about her appearance?'

Jennie stared.

'Funny your asking that, sir. It always puzzled me. Sometimes she didn't and sometimes she did. She'd be downright plain some days – like she was this morning – and then she'd take and do herself up till she looked real handsome.'

'And when did she do that? When her young man was coming?'

'I never could make out when she did or why she did – but it wasn't for him. Last night she was lovely – took over an hour to dress, when she usually flung her things off and on in five minutes. That white dress she wore was her favourite – it was chiffon with an overcoat of cream lace; she always wore a coloured flower – artificial – with it.'

'Ah! I'd like to have a look at that dress sometime,' said Rudge. 'I've heard it mentioned more than once.'

'Well now, that's another funny thing,' said Jennie, who was

now fully at her ease – as Rudge had intended. 'She's taken it with her! She only told me to pack sleeping things and a change of underclothes and stockings, but she must have packed that herself after I'd done.'

'But didn't you take it away – to brush, or whatever you do to it – when you called her this morning?' asked the Inspector, fumbling with half-guessed mysteries.

'Well now, there you are again! I didn't call her before you came – she likes to sleep late. But when I went to tell her you were here I went to pick up her dress and shoes and things to take away, but she snapped at me fierce and told me to go away, she wanted to get up. Of course, I went, but when she'd come down to see you, I went back to get them – and they were gone!'

'Gone! All the clothes she wore last night?'

'The dress and shoes and stockings were.'

'Didn't you look for them?'

'Of course I did. They weren't anywhere.'

'So that's why you think she took them with her?'

'Well, she must have. Where else could they be?'

Inspector Rudge looked thoughtfully at the girl, then nodded his head and drew out the notebook which had not previously appeared at this interview.

'I see, Jennie; thank you. I won't keep you longer now. Don't tell anyone else about that dress and things, but have a good hunt and, if you find them, let me know.'

When the girl had gone, Inspector Rudge sat back in his chair and pondered what he had just heard. The maid's judgment as to the relations existing between Elma Fitzgerald and her uncle, and again between her and her *fiancé*, might be a fault; the question of Miss Fitzgerald's spasmodic attention to her appearance was at present beyond him; but surely the disappearance of the dress and shoes which she had been wearing at the time of the tragedy – or at any rate on the evening of the tragedy – was significant? Could she be in some way connected with her uncle's death? She had appeared neither surprised nor distressed when she heard of it, but if she had been guilty – or even cognisant of it – would she not have feigned both? However, it was too early yet to indulge in surmise – let alone theories; there were many facts to be collected first.

To begin with, the newspaper. How had it come into the dead man's pocket? Rudge happened to know that the late London edition of the *Evening Gazette* did not reach Whynmouth till 8.50 – the express by which, incidentally, Arthur Holland had arrived.

No doubt a copy would be delivered at Rundel Croft, but that could not be till about 9 p.m. and the Admiral had left the house at 7.15 for his dinner at the Vicarage. Unless he had got a copy from the Vicarage, that seemed to imply that Penistone had returned to Rundel Croft after leaving the Vicarage at 10 p.m. – but then why was the paper in his overcoat pocket? Had he gone back to fetch it in order to read it out of doors – surely that was inconceivable? Or had he, on his way back to Rundel Croft, met someone who gave him the paper – not the delivery boy, it was too late for that. Someone, perhaps, who had brought the paper out with him – had brought it, perhaps, from London – Arthur Holland, for instance? Holland, who had spent the evening by the seashore and then gone early to bed – by himself. But here again was surmise – facts were what he wanted. Rudge rang the bell.

'Emery, did your master take in the late London *Evening Gazette*?'

'Yes, sir. Tolwhistle's boy brings it out of an evening – gets here about nine.'

'Did he get here last night?'

'Yes, sir,' said Emery, a faint look of surprise on his stodgy face.

'Where did you put it?'

'In the hall, sir.'

'Is it still there?'

'I couldn't say.'

'Go and have a look, and if it's not there, find out whether it's been tidied away.'

Looking more surprised than ever, Emery slouched out of the door. Rudge thought it would probably be ten minutes at least before the tortoise-like butler returned, so he reached for the telephone which stood upon the writing-table and put a call through to Tolwhistle's, the Whynmouth stationer. The number was engaged, and while he waited Rudge let his mind drift back to the missing dress. He remembered that when he sent Emery off to ask Miss Fitzgerald to come and see him it was ten minutes before the butler returned and then it was with the information that Miss Fitzgerald would be down in *a quarter of an hour*. There was, in fact, an interval of twenty-five minutes between despatching his message and the arrival of Miss Fitzgerald. Did her appearance – slovenly in the extreme – justify or explain such a long delay? Was it possible that the mysterious 'niece' had spent part of the time in hiding the clothes she had . . . ?

The telephone bell trilled.

'Tolwhistle's? I want to speak to Mr Tolwhistle, please. That

you, Mr Tolwhistle? Inspector Rudge here. I want some information; quite confidential. Sounds trivial, but isn't. Do you supply the Reverend Mount, Vicar of Lingham, with newspapers? You do. Does he have a late London *Evening Gazette*? Left it off at the end of last year? Said what? Oh, spoilt the morning's – yes, I see. Any chance of anyone else supplying him? No, you'd have heard of it, of course. Thank you, Mr Tolwhistle. Keep my questions to yourself. I'll explain them some day.'

That settled the question of whether the Admiral had got the paper from the Vicarage; there remained the two alternatives of his having come back to the house, fetched his own paper, and gone out again, or having met someone outside who had for some reason given him the paper.

Impatient at the long absence of Emery, Rudge went to look for him. There was no sign of the butler, but Police Constable Hempstead was standing in the hall.

'I came to report that the body has been taken to the undertaker's, sir. I formally handed it over and obtained a receipt.'

The Inspector blinked. Here was efficiency carried to full stretch.

'Right,' he said. 'This house isn't in your district, I think you said?'

'No, sir, but the corpse was found in it.'

'And you think it your duty to see that its presence is accounted for?'

'That's for you to say, sir.'

Rudge grinned. He knew that this keen-eyed young constable was itching to be 'in' the investigation.

'All right,' he said. 'Here's a job for you; go down to the boat-house and find out from Sergeant Appleton whether he's found anything significant. No. I'll come with you. If there's anything, I shall want to see it for myself and we mustn't keep our detective-sergeant there all day.'

And so, forgetting all about the newspaper, Inspector Rudge accompanied P.C. Hempstead across the park to the boat-house. As he went, he asked his subordinate whether anything particular had struck him about the case.

'One or two things, sir. In the first place, the body's clothes were almost dry – the back *quite* dry. But there was a heavy dew last night. If he had been lying about in grass, or even in the boat, since midnight (Doctor Grice fixed the time of death, you remember, sir, as before midnight) wouldn't the clothes have been wet?'

Inspector Rudge eyed his companion with interest.

'From which you infer . . . ?' he asked.

'That the Admiral was killed indoors and kept indoors – or at any rate under cover – for some time after he was killed.'

The Inspector was silent for so long that Hempstead began to fear that he had exceeded his duty. Just as they reached the boat-house, however, Rudge said:

'That's a neat point; we'll talk about it later. Ah, Appleton, sorry to keep you waiting. Found anything?'

Detective-Sergeant Appleton was a square, solemn-looking man, valuable as a detective rather for his persistence in following up small clues than for any brilliance in deducing theories from them.

'Only two suggestive points, sir. This boat's very clean and rather wet inside – looks as if it might have been swabbed out recently. That's one; the other is that its bow's facing inwards. The Vicar's sons tell me that the Admiral always used to go in stern first, so as to be facing the right way when the boat went out again.'

'Ah, Navy trick, eh? That's worth noting. Nothing else? No blood, signs of struggle, footmarks, fingerprints?'

'No to the first two, sir. There are one or two good footmarks I've covered with boards and there look to be plenty of finger-prints all over the boat and sculls.'

'We'll have to examine them later. Any theories, Appleton?'

'None, sir.'

Inspector Rudge sat down on the bank and motioned to his subordinates to join him.

'Light up,' he said, pulling a pipe out of his pocket. 'Think better smoking, and we must think now. The Vicar's hat, in the first place; why was it in the boat?'

'Put there by the guilty party to throw suspicion on the Vicar,' hazarded Sergeant Appleton.

'Improve on that, Hempstead?'

'The other alternative is that the Vicar left it there himself, sir, and forgot he had.'

'He stated positively that he had his hat on when he saw the Admiral off after dinner last night and that he left it on the seat in the summer-house.'

'But supposing he went out in the boat after that, sir?'

'Ah, you mean . . . well, never mind what you mean. Now, why was the painter cut?'

'Someone was in a hurry,' said Appleton.

'Someone wanted to suggest that the boat was stolen,' murmured Hempstead.

'And the rowlocks were unshipped,' the Inspector added his quota of surmise, 'either because the body was dumped into the Vicar's boat from another and the boat then cut adrift, or . . . to suggest that explanation, eh, Hempstead?'

'Possibly, sir.'

'Now, can anyone explain why the body was found where it was and when it was?' asked the Inspector, adding to himself, 'and if it was.'

Sergeant Appleton brightened.

'Yes, sir,' he said. 'I thought that out while I was waiting. If the murder was committed at midnight, as Doctor Grice says, and the boat cut adrift then, it would have gone right out to sea, because the tide was at full ebb then. My theory is that the murder was committed several miles up-stream and that before the boat reached Whynmouth the tide turned and floated back to where it was found.'

'What time did the tide turn?'

'According to Mr Ware, sir,' said Hempstead, 'it turned about 3.45 a.m.'

'Well, let's work this out. He told us, you remember, Hempstead, that it would have taken forty to forty-five minutes for the boat to get from the Vicarage to the spot where he was when it reached him; what time was that?'

'Just after 4.30 a.m., sir.'

'That means it left – or passed – the Vicarage at about 3.50 a.m. – only five minutes after the tide turned?'

'That's right, sir.'

'Then that means that if it was set adrift from here or from the Vicarage it must have been only just before 3.45 a.m. – otherwise it couldn't have got back to where Ware found it by the time it did. But it's nearly light by 3.45 – they wouldn't have left it as late as that. It looks as if Appleton's theory was the right one.'

Sergeant Appleton beamed, but P.C. Hempstead looked mulish. Rudge noticed the look.

'Out with it, Hempstead,' he said. 'You've got a theory, I can see.'

'Well, sir, if I might make the suggestion, you've overlooked slack tide. For an hour or so before the turn the tide's so slack that it's barely running. It's possible that a boat might fetch up against the bank for quite a time. My theory, as you know, sir, is that the body wasn't in the boat long enough for the dew to make the clothes wet. I think it was set adrift from here about 2.30 or 3 a.m. If the person who did it was a stranger to the place he might not

think of the river being tidal – he'd expect the boat to float straight out to sea. But what happened was that it floated a few hundred yards, and then, as the tide slackened, drifted into the bank; at 3.45, when the tide turned, it drifted off again and so floated up on the flow till it reached the spot where Neddy Ware found it at half past four.'

4

By Agatha Christie

MAINLY CONVERSATION

'That's a pretty good theory too,' said Rudge.

He always believed in being diplomatic with his inferiors. In this instance, nothing in his face showed which of the two theories struck him as being the right one.

He nodded his head once or twice and then rose to his feet. He looked behind him at the trees near the boathouse.

'There's one thing that strikes me,' he said. 'I wonder if there's anything in it?'

Appleton and Hempstead looked at him enquiringly.

'In my conversation with the Vicar, he mentioned that he had seen Miss Fitzgerald's white dress through the trees.'

'As she was going up to the house, sir – yes, I remember his saying that. Anything fishy about that, do you think, sir?'

'No, I imagine it's perfectly possible. Miss Fitzgerald was wearing a white chiffon dress with a cream lace coat. If the Vicar saw the dress, then clearly she was not wearing any coat or cloak over it. After all, why should she? It was quite a warm night.'

'Yes, sir.'

Appleton looked puzzled.

'On the other hand, the Admiral, when he was found, was wearing a thick brown overcoat. Anything strike you as odd about that?'

'Well – yes, I suppose it is a little queer – that the lady shouldn't have had anything warmer in the way of a wrap than a lace coat, and that the Admiral – yes, sir, I take your meaning.'

'I'm going to ask you, Sergeant, to take a boat across to the

Vicarage and ask there if the Admiral was wearing a coat last night.'

'Right, sir.'

When the sergeant had departed, the Inspector turned to Hempstead.

'Now,' he said with a twinkle; 'I'm going to ask you a question.'

'Yes, sir?'

'Who is the biggest talker in Whynmouth?'

P.C. Hempstead grinned in spite of himself.

'Mrs Davis, sir, who keeps the Lord Marshall. Nobody else can get a word in edgeways when she's about.'

'One of that kind, is she?'

'Yes, indeed, sir.'

'Well, that will just suit me. The Admiral was a newcomer to the place. There's always talk about a new-comer. For ninety-nine false rumours, there will be one true thing that somebody has noticed and observed. Attention has been focussed on Rundel Croft. I want to know just what has transpired in village gossip.'

'Then it's Mrs Davis you want, sir.'

'I want to go over to West End too, and see Sir Wilfrid Denny. He seems to be the only person in the neighbourhood who knows anything about the murdered man. He might possibly know whether the Admiral had any enemies.'

'You think he was in hiding, sir?'

'Not exactly in hiding. He came here openly, under his own name. It's not an unusual thing for a retired naval man to do. But the loaded revolver in the desk tells a tale. That's *not* so usual. I could do with knowing a little more about Admiral Penistone's career. Ah! here comes the sergeant back again.'

The sergeant, however, did not return alone. With him were the two boys from the Vicarage. Their eager, boyish faces were alight with curiosity.

'I say, Inspector,' cried Peter, 'can't we help in any way? Haven't you got a job for us of any kind? Fancy old Penistone, of all people, to get murdered!'

'Why do you say "of all people," young gentleman?' enquired the Inspector.

'Oh! I don't know.' The boy flushed. 'He was so very – well, correct and nautical. All present and shipshape! Sort of old fellow who'd look at you if you forgot to call him "sir" even once.'

'A martinet and a disciplinarian, eh?'

'I suppose that's what I mean. Years behind the times.'

'I don't think he was a bad old geezer,' said Alec tolerantly.

The Inspector turned to Appleton.

'What about the coat?'

'The Admiral, sir, was *not* wearing a coat when he came to dinner last night.'

'Rather not,' said Peter. 'Just nip across the river and there you are. Why should he wear a coat? The Fitzgerald hadn't got one either.'

'Wasn't she *sweet*?' minced Alec. 'All in white like a blushing bride. And old as the hills really.'

'Well,' said Rudge. 'I must be getting along.'

'Oh, but, Inspector, what about *us*?'

Rudge smiled indulgently.

'Suppose you two young gentlemen have a look for the weapon,' he suggested. 'It wasn't in the wound. Somewhere along the river bank maybe . . . '

He retreated, smiling to himself.

'That'll keep 'em busy,' he said to himself. 'And do no harm either. They might even come across it – stranger things have happened.'

As he got into his car and drove in the direction of Whynmouth, his brain worked busily. The evening paper was now accounted for. The Admiral must have returned to the house some time between ten o'clock and midnight, donned an overcoat and slipped the evening paper into his overcoat pocket. Then he had gone out again – where?

Had he taken the boat? Had he gone either up-stream or down-stream to keep some appointment? Had he walked to some house near by?

As yet, the whole thing was a mystery.

On arrival at Whynmouth, Rudge pulled up opposite the Lord Marshall Hotel.

The Lord Marshall prided itself on its old-world air. The hall was dark and narrow and an intending visitor was bewildered by finding no one to whom to apply. Usually, deceived by the general dimness, application was made to a guest who repulsed the newcomer frostily. On the walls were sporting prints of a humorous nature and several glass cases containing fish.

Rudge knew his way about the Lord Marshall well enough. He crossed the passage and tapped at a door marked 'Private.' The high-pitched voice of Mrs Davis bid him enter.

At sight of him the lady took a deep breath and began without wasting a minute:

'Inspector Rudge, isn't it? And it's well I know you by sight, as

indeed for the matter of that I know everybody in these parts. And not only by sight, too, for we've passed a remark now and again though I dare say you don't remember. But there, as I always say, to be well known to the police isn't what you might call a compliment and I'm just as well pleased that we haven't, as you might say, *really* met before. And I can tell you this, Inspector Rudge, you couldn't have done a wiser thing than come straight to me this morning! Seeing that you're a new-comer in the place – only been here two years, haven't you, or is it three? – I declare time does run away. That's what I'm always saying. No sooner is one meal over than it's time for another. And dinner I will have served to time. These new-fangled people arriving in cars, eight o'clock, nine o'clock, even, and wanting dinner. Cold supper, I can manage, I says, but dinner is served at seven o'clock, and then everyone's free to walk about and very pleasant it is around the harbour on a summer evening, and so the young people think – and even the older ones!'

Feeling the need of refilling her lungs, Mrs Davis paused for an infinitesimal moment. She was a jolly, good-humoured-looking woman of fifty, dressed in black silk. She wore a gold locket and several rings.

Without allowing Rudge a chance to speak, she swept straight on:

'You needn't tell me what you've come about. It's Admiral Penistone. Got the news half an hour ago, I did. And "Well," I said, "we're here to-day and gone tomorrow." But not gone this way, most of us – or so I devoutly hope. Stabbed to the heart with a narrow instrument, that's right, isn't it? And depend on it, that's a stiletto, that's what I said! One of those nasty, murdering Eyetalian stilettos. Wops they call them in New York – the Eyetalians, I mean, not the stilettos. And you mark my words, you'll find out that whoever murdered the Admiral had been in Italy. Naturally it couldn't have been an Eyetalian – he'd have been noticed. Used to sell ice cream, they did, in my young day. But now they have Walls and those others and much more wholesome stuff, I dare say. No – we don't have many foreigners in Whynmouth – except of course Americans – and they're not really what you'd call foreigners – just a kind of queer English, that's how *I* look upon them! And the stories those boatmen tell them – why you'd think they'd be afraid of a judgment – and the poor innocents lapping it up – but there, I'm getting away from the subject. And a sad subject it is.' She shook her head, but with no overdone air of melancholy. 'Not that you can say the Admiral

was one of us yet. Why, he'd only passed through Whynmouth half a dozen times. Barely knew him by sight, we did. And his niece! A most peculiar young lady, if you ask *me*, Mr Rudge! Very odd things I've heard about *her*. Her young gentleman's actually stopping in the house now. Came down last evening by the 8.30. And if you ask me, I say "No." '

'Eh!' said Rudge, completely bewildered by this sudden dramatic stop interrupting the flow of speech.

'I say "No," ' repeated Mrs Davis, nodding her head very violently.

'No to what?' asked the Inspector, still puzzled.

'I say, if you ask me if he's the murderer, I say "No!" '

'Oh! I see, but I never suggested anything of the kind.'

'Not in words, but it's what it comes to. Cut the cackle and come to the horses, as Mr Davis used to say. I'm never one for beating about the bush.'

'What I was going to ask you was – '

Mrs Davis interrupted serenely.

'I know, I know, Mr Rudge. Whether Mr Holland went out or not last night, I cannot tell you. Bit of a rush we had with the charabancs, and you can't notice everything. What I mean to say is you can't be in two places at once. And what with the gas being poor and one thing and another, I'm putting in the electricity this year. Old-world is old-world, but some things people won't stand. Hot water system last year and electricity this. But there, I'm wandering off the point again. I was just going to say – what was I going to say?'

The Inspector assured her that he had no idea.

'Admiral Penistone was a friend of Sir Wilfrid Denny, was he not?' he asked.

'Now there's a nice gentleman for you – Sir Wilfred Denny. Always a cheery word and a joke. A shame he should be so hard up, poor gentleman. Oh! yes, he and the Admiral were acquainted. They do say that's why the Admiral came down here to live. But I don't know about that. There's those who say that Sir Wilfred was none too pleased when he heard his friend was coming down here to live. But there, people will say anything, won't they? I'm never one to say a word myself. Too much harm done by gossiping. Keep a still tongue in your head and you can't go far wrong. That's my motto. And one thing I will say is a wicked shame. To take the Vicar's boat to do their dirty work in. Trying to drag him into it, poor gentleman. As if he hadn't had troubles enough in his life.'

'Had a bit of trouble, has he?'

'Well, it's a long time ago now. Six and four the little boys were, and how she could do it! Depend upon it, a woman who leaves her husband and her children – well, there's not much to be said for her – not when it's a good Christian husband like the Vicar. (There's some I could name as *deserve* to be left.) Leaving her little children, that's what I can't get over. And a pretty gentle lady too, by all accounts. I never saw her myself. It happened before Mr Mount came here. And who it was she went off with, I've forgotten. But a very handsome gentleman, I've always heard. Those handsome ones have a way with them, there's no denying it. Well, well, I wonder what's become of her? Dear, dear, life's a sad mix-up. And if I haven't gone right away from the subject again! Talking about Mr Holland we were – and he's a handsome fellow if you like. And yet they say Miss Fitzgerald doesn't seem to think so, for all they're engaged to be married.'

'So that's what they say?'

Mrs Davis nodded very significantly.

'And what the Admiral wanted to see Mr Holland about, I've no idea,' she went on. 'But it's crossed my mind that maybe the young lady wanted the engagement off, and sent her uncle to do the dirty work for her. Though why it couldn't have waited till the morning . . . I dare say that's exactly what the Admiral thought, and why he changed his mind and said he had a train to catch.'

Inspector Rudge made a valiant effort and interpreted this cryptic pronouncement.

'Do you mean,' he said, 'that Admiral Penistone called here last night?'

'Why, of course he did. Asked the Boots for Mr Holland. And then, just as the man was going off, called him back again, hemmed and hawed and looked at his watch, and said he had a train to catch, there wouldn't be time for him to see Mr Holland.'

'What time was this?'

'I couldn't say exactly. It was after eleven o'clock. I was in bed, and glad to be there. Such a day as we'd had. Really, these charabancs – they do take it out of one! There were a lot of people about still. These warm nights you can't get the people to bed.'

'A train to catch,' mused the Inspector.

'That would be the 11.25 I expect,' said Mrs Davis. 'The up train for London. Six in the morning it gets there. But he didn't go by it. What I mean is, he coudln't have gone by it, because if he had, he wouldn't have been lying murdered in the Vicar's boat.'

And she looked at Inspector Rudge triumphantly.

5

By John Rhode

INSPECTOR RUDGE BEGINS TO FORM A THEORY

Inspector Rudge assumed an expression of profound admiration. 'My word, Mrs Davis, it takes a woman like you to put two and two together like that!' he exclaimed. 'Of course the Admiral could not have caught the train, now I come to think of it!'

Mrs Davis chuckled good-humouredly. 'There, now you're laughing at me,' she said. 'I don't know how it is, but most of my visitors always seem to find a joke in something or other I say to them. Perhaps it's just as well, it keeps them cheerful and contented, and what I always say is: make your visitors happy as long as you're sure they have got enough money to pay their bills. Not that they often manage to hoodwink me – '

'I'm sure they don't,' interrupted the Inspector politely. 'It would take a clever man to do that, I'm certain. By the way, how was it you knew all about the murder of Admiral Penistone before I got here?'

'It isn't always those that get about the most that hears the most,' replied Mrs Davis roguishly. 'Here am I, not been outside the house this blessed morning, and I warrant I know more about it than anybody else in Whynmouth, barring the police, of course, Inspector. You see, it's this way: you came in by the hotel entrance, and you wouldn't have noticed it. But if you go up the side street there's another door that leads into the Shades. It's put there, apart from the house, so that it won't interfere with the hotel visitors. They get their drinks in the smoking-room, and pay more for them, too. It's the outside customers that use the Shades, fishermen and the like of that, such as the gentlemen who use the smoking-room wouldn't care to associate with. Not that there's anything amiss with them, bar that they're a bit free with their language sometimes. They're polite enough to me when I go in there in the mornings at opening time to see that all's right and comfortable.'

'Ah, so you heard about the murder in the Shades this morning, did you, Mrs Davis?' suggested the Inspector.

'Why! that's just what I was going to tell you about!' exclaimed Mrs Davis, in a slightly hurt tone. 'But you gentlemen in the police are all the same. You're so short with your questions that a body can hardly get a word in edgeways. As I was going to say, I was in there this morning when Billy the barman was taking down the shutters, and as soon as he unlocked the door in walked a couple of chaps with ambulance badges on. I asked them if there had been an accident, and they told me how Mr Ware of Lingham had found the Admiral's body in the Vicar's boat, which was floating about, with no one in sight.'

At this moment, as though in answer to Inspector Rudge's inward prayer, an agitated-looking cook appeared from the back regions and muttered something in Mrs Davis's ear. 'Why, there now! if it hadn't altogether slipped my memory,' she exclaimed. 'I've been so interested hearing you talk, Inspector, that I've never ordered the joint for lunch. You'll excuse me if I run off and see to it, won't you, Mr Rudge?'

The Inspector waited till Mrs Davis had disappeared, then, when he was satisfied that she was out of hearing, rang a bell marked 'Porter.' In a few minutes a bald-headed individual hustled into the entrance hall, still struggling with the short jacket which he had hastily thrust on over his rolled-up shirt sleeves. From his appearance he seemed to have been interrupted in the act of stoking the central heating system. He looked at Inspector Rudge enquiringly. 'Yessir,' he remarked.

'I'm Inspector Rudge, and I came here to make certain enquiries. You knew Admiral Penistone, I believe?'

The man scratched his head. 'Well, sir, I can't rightly say as I knew him,' he replied. 'I've only seen him once in my life, and that was last night. Came in here, he did, and asked for Mr Holland.'

The Inspector nodded. 'So I believe. Now, I'm particularly anxious to know how he was looking then. Did he seem worried, or anxious, or anything like that?'

'I couldn't very well say, sir. You see, it was gone eleven, and I was just going to shut up the house. Mrs Davis is always telling me to be careful of the gas, and there was only one light burning. The Admiral came just inside the door, and stood where you might be standing now, sir. "Is Mr Holland in?" he asks, sharp like. And almost before I had time to say he was in bed, he said that it didn't matter and that he couldn't wait, as he had a train to catch. He wasn't here no more than a few seconds, sir. He seemed in a hurry, but I couldn't properly see his face. I wouldn't have known who it

was if he hadn't told me.'

Again the Inspector nodded. 'You'd recognise him again if you saw him, I suppose?' he asked.

'Well, sir, I might and I mightn't. I never got a proper sight of him, as you might say.'

'Oh, well, it doesn't matter,' said the Inspector carelessly. 'Was Mr Holland in when Admiral Penistone called?'

'I'm pretty sure he was, sir, leastways, his boots was outside his door. I saw them when I went up to bed soon after. And he didn't come in later, I know that for a fact.'

'How can you be sure of that?'

'Why, sir, because I locked the door as I always do round about half-past eleven. If anybody wants to get in after that, they presses the bell, which rings in my room, and I comes down and lets them in. And the bell didn't ring last night, sir.'

'I see. And when is the door opened again?'

'I unbolts it first thing, when I comes down in the morning, sir, round about six, that is.'

'What do you do after you unlock the door?'

'Why, sir, I lights the kitchen fire and puts on the kettle for a cup of tea.'

'Did you happen to see Mr Holland this morning?'

'I was in the hall when he went out after breakfast, sir. About nine o'clock that would have been. And he hasn't come back since, at least not that I know of.'

The sound of Mrs Davis's voice, rapidly growing in intensity as she returned from the back regions, caused Rudge to beat a hasty retreat. He slipped out of the hotel, and began to walk towards the police station, reviewing the scraps of information which he had picked up at the Lord Marshall, and congratulating himself upon having had the idea of interviewing Mrs Davis. Gossip though she might be, her freely-expressed opinions of people were based upon a certain native shrewdness. The Inspector felt that he had already gained a valuable side-light upon Sir Wilfred Denny, and that even the revelation of that curious episode in the Vicar's past might prove instructive. As to Holland, Mrs Davis's conviction that he was not the murderer was certainly well-grounded if he had spent the night in the hotel.

But of course, the most interesting thing he had learnt was the alleged visit of Admiral Penistone shortly after eleven last night. Unfortunately it was impossible to decide whether the caller had been the Admiral or not. The porter's identification of him was obviously worthless. He did not know the Admiral by sight, he

could not even undertake to recognise the caller again. Where, in fact, had been the Admiral? He had last been seen shortly after ten, by the boat-house. That would have given him an hour to get to Whynmouth. Hardly time to have walked the distance, and yet he was hardly likely to have taken the car out. Had he done so, somebody would have been sure to have heard him. Could he have come down in his boat? Possibly, if the tide had been flowing the right way.

Inspector Rudge frowned. He was no seaman, and he had begun to regard the vagaries of this infernal River Whyn as a personal affront to him. His idea of a self-respecting river was a placid stream which knew its own mind and flowed always in the same direction, like, say, the Thames at Maidenhead. But the Whyn was mad, subject, like a lunatic, to the influence of the moon, and changing the direction of its flow in obedience to some law which was past the Inspector's comprehension. He decided that he would have to consult some expert on that point. For the present, he imagined that if the tide had been flowing down the river, there was no reason why the Admiral should not have called at the Lord Marshall at the time stated.

But on the other hand, his behaviour there had been quite contrary to what the Inspector had gathered of his character. He seemed to have been of a peremptory and determined nature. Rudge could not have imagined him walking into the place, with the intention of seeing Holland, and then suddenly changing his mind on the score that he had barely time to catch his train. It would have been more like him to have stamped about the hall till Holland had been dragged from his bed.

Unless – yes – that was a possibility. Suppose his visit to the hotel had been merely to assure himself that Holland had arrived? From the fact that the porter had offered to go and see if he was in, he would have known that he was staying in the house. Perhaps, having ascertained this, his object had been accomplished, and the excuse about the train had been trumped up on the spur of the moment, to account for his exit. He might not have wanted to see Holland just then.

On the other hand, if the visitor had not been the Admiral, why had he given his name? To make it appear that the Admiral had been in Whynmouth at that particular time? This opened up a wide field for speculation, in which one central fact was apparent. The visitor must have known something of Admiral Penistone's movements that evening. And therefore every effort must be made to trace him.

And what about Holland himself? The Inspector was not at all satisfied on the subject of that impulsive gentleman. Mrs Davis may have been right in her conjecture that Miss Fitzgerald was not eager to marry him, but he was by no means certain that she was equally right in her opinion that he was not the murderer. There was no means of verifying his statement that he had spent the night in the hotel. He could easily have slipped out during the confusion that appeared to have reigned before eleven, and returned just after six in the morning, when the door was unlocked and the porter was busy with the kitchen fire. Had he done so, and met the Admiral in Whynmouth or elsewhere? The more he considered the matter, the wider the field of speculation seemed to extend before Rudge's vision.

His original intention had been to drive out and see Sir Wilfrid Denny at West End, after he had finished with Mrs Davis. But the possible light which that loquacious lady had thrown upon the Admiral's movements decided him to defer the visit. He had formed the rudiments of a theory as to the time and place of the murder, but the possibility of this theory depended upon the tides in the River Whyn, and upon this subject he must seek expert advice. Why not have another chat with Neddy Ware? He knew the tides as no one else did, his hobby had rendered a study of them absolutely necessary to him. And besides, there was always the chance that he might have observed some detail which he had not recollected in the first excitement of his discovery.

Inspector Rudge turned his car towards Lingham once more, and very soon reached Ware's cottage. The old man was at home, smoking his pipe contemplatively after his midday meal. He greeted the Inspector hospitably, and the two sat down in a room decorated with models of ships and faded photographs of the vessels in which Ware had served.

'You want to know about the tides in the river?' he replied, in answer to the Inspector's explanation of the cause of his visit. 'Why, they're simple enough, so long as you remember that it's high water, Full and Change, at Whynmouth at seven o'clock.'

Rudge laughed. 'I haven't a doubt it's simple enough to you,' he said. 'Personally, I haven't the foggiest idea what you're talking about. What on earth do you mean by high water, Full and Change?'

'Why, merely that it's high water at Whynmouth at seven o'clock nearabouts, on the days when the moon is full or new,' replied Ware. 'Now, take this morning's tide, for instance. Today's Wednesday, the 10th. It was new moon on Monday,

that's to say it was high water at Whynmouth at seven on Monday evening. It would be about eight yesterday evening and half-past this morning. You can allow six hours between high and low water, making it low water at half-past two this morning. The tide up here begins to flow half to three-quarters of an hour after low water at Whynmouth, or say soon after three. And that's when I went out fishing.'

'After three!' exclaimed Rudge. 'But I thought you said the church clock struck four not long before you saw the boat?'

'The clock!' replied Ware, in a voice of supreme contempt. 'You don't expect the tide to fall in with the children's games you play with the clock in summer, do you? You play a game of make-believe with the time, just because you haven't the courage to face the prospects of getting up an hour earlier than usual. It may be all very well for landsmen, but it won't do for sailors. To them, time's time, and you can't alter it.'

'I see. Then, by summer-time the tide began to flow this morning up here, soon after four. From what you tell me, then, I gather that it began to ebb about ten last night?'

'That's right, ten or a little before,' agreed Ware. 'As I say, the moon was new two days ago, which means that it was pretty well the top of the springs last night. I reckon the ebb must have run down the river nigh on three knots for the first couple of hours or so. After that it would have slacked off a bit, as it always does.'

'So that a man leaving here between ten and eleven would have had no difficulty in getting to Whynmouth by boat?' suggested Inspector Rudge.

'He'd have drifted there and likely enough gone straight out to sea,' replied Ware. 'That is, if he didn't use his oars. If he did, he could have got to Whynmouth in under the hour, easy.'

The old sailor had glanced shrewdly at the Inspector as he spoke. Rudge saw what was in his mind, and smiled. 'You can guess what I'm getting at,' he said. 'I thought it possible that Admiral Penistone might have taken his boat down to Whynmouth last night. But if he did, the boat cannot have come back by itself. Somebody must have rowed it back and put it into the boat-house.'

He paused, half expecting some comment from Ware, but the old man merely nodded, and continued puffing at his pipe in silence. Rudge tried a new tack. 'Why was the painter of the Vicar's boat cut, and not untied, Ware?' he asked abruptly.

Ware smiled. 'Because it couldn't have been anything else, as the Vicar's boys could tell you, if you asked them,' he replied. 'It's

no business of mine, this murder, but naturally my mind's been on it all the morning.'

'I'd very much like to hear the conclusions you've come to,' said Inspector Rudge quietly. 'Why do you say that the painter of the Vicar's boat couldn't have been untied, for instance?'

'I haven't come to any conclusions,' replied Ware impassively. 'That is, I don't know who killed the Admiral, if that's what you mean. But it isn't difficult to understand how the boats came to be found as they were.'

'Not for you, perhaps,' remarked the Inspector, 'but it would be a great help to me if you'd explain.'

'Aye, that I will. Now take the Vicar's boat first. She's not kept in the boat-house while the boys are at home, but out in the stream, tied to a post. Sometimes the lads remember to take the oars and crutches out of her when they come ashore, mostly they don't. I've seen them left in her dozens of times.

'Now, suppose they'd been out in her yesterday evening, and tied her up when the tide was high, or well up, as it would have been any time between seven and ten. You'll find, in any tidal river, that the greater part of the rise happens during the first three hours of the flood, and the greater part of the fall during the first three hours of the ebb. Right. They come in when the tide's well up, and what do they do? One of them stands in the bow, and makes the painter fast to the post. They're both well-grown lads, and they'd naturally make fast about four or five feet above the water. Then they'd pole the stern round, till it touched the bank and they could jump ashore. Maybe they were afraid of being late for dinner, and forgot the oars and crutches in their hurry.'

Inspector Rudge nodded. This did not seem to take him any further than he had got already.

'Now, take the Admiral's boat,' continued Ware. 'From what I hear, she was seen either in, or alongside, the Rundel Croft boat-house soon after ten. Now this I'm pretty sure of. If anybody took her out between ten and one this morning, they didn't row far up the river. You don't make much headway with a heavy boat like that against a three-knot tide. You take it from me, if she went out at all, she went down-stream, and not up.

'After one this morning – I'm talking in shore time now, not real time – things would be different. There'd be only a gentle stream running down till four, perhaps a knot at the most. Anyone could row against that; it wouldn't take them more than a couple of hours to come up from Whynmouth, say, taking it easy. That's clear enough, isn't it?'

'Perfectly clear,' replied Rudge. 'It comes to this. If the Admiral was murdered in his own boat, it must have been somewhere below Rundel Croft, anywhere as far down as Whynmouth, in fact?'

'That's right. Now I suppose whoever murdered him brought the boat back with the body in it. Suppose they got back round about slack water. The chap, whoever he was, sees the Vicar's boat moored to the post in the stream, and hits upon the idea of putting the body in it. He goes alongside, lifts the body in, and then what does he do next? How is he going to cast off the Vicar's boat? Tell me that?'

'I don't exactly see the difficulty,' replied the Inspector. 'It wasn't made fast with a chain and padlock.'

'You didn't see what I was getting at just now,' said Ware, with a touch of impatience. 'Why, when he got back, it was dead low water, and the river had fallen three or four feet since the boat had been made fast. Don't you see? Unless he was a very tall man, he wouldn't be able to reach the knot unless he swarmed up the post. There was only one thing for him to do, and that was to cut the painter. And there's one thing about that you may not have noticed. That painter is a nearly new piece of inch-and-a-half manilla.'

'I noticed that it looked fairly new. But I can't see for the moment what that's got to do with it.'

'Ever tried to cut new manilla with an ordinary pocket knife? No, I suppose not. But you can take it from me that you'd find it a pretty tough job. And when you'd finished you'd have left a frayed edge. But this rope was cut clean through, like as though it had been cut with one stroke of a very sharp knife. Anyway, cut it was, and the boat left to drift.'

Ware tapped out his pipe, and began slowly to refill it. He drew from his pocket the end of a cake of tobacco, which he shaved carefully into the palm of his hand. 'This knife is pretty sharp,' he remarked. 'I keep it so on purpose to cut up my baccy. But I wouldn't reckon to cut through that painter with it at one stroke. No, it was a sharper and stronger knife than this that did the job, I'll be bound.'

While he proceeded to fill and light his pipe, Inspector Rudge's thoughts were busy. The possibility that Admiral Penistone had taken his boat out again and rowed down the river seemed to be greatly strengthened. In that case, he had probably been murdered somewhere near Whynmouth, and his body had reached the spot where it was found much as Ware had supposed.

But was there any way of verifying this?

In the first place, what time had he started? The doctor had given it as his opinion that he had been killed before midnight. Again, if he had indeed been the visitor to the Lord Marshall, he had reached Whynmouth soon after eleven. His departure from Rundel Croft could not have been very long deferred; his impatience to leave the Vicarage seemed to point to a desire to start as soon as possible. His excuse to his niece for not going up to the house with her, that he wished to smoke a cigar before going in, was probably mainly to get her out of the way. He had probably intended to start as soon as she was out of sight and hearing.

But if he had done so, how was it that the Vicar, who was in the summer-house till twenty minutes past ten, had not seen him? Suddenly Rudge remembered the Vicar's evident confusion when he had heard of the murder. Was it possible that he had actually seen the Admiral's departure on this mysterious journey, and had his own very good reasons for not disclosing the fact? It was at least possible.

The Inspector's reflections were interrupted by a remark from Ware, who had at last succeeded in getting his pipe to draw satisfactorily. 'Queer thing that I don't seem to recognise Admiral Penistone,' he said. 'There was only one of that name in the Navy List when I was serving, and I saw him more than once.'

'Did you? When was that?' asked Rudge eagerly.

'Why, on the China Station, twenty years ago and more. I was in the *Rutlandshire* then, one of the three-funnelled County class cruisers, she was, and the very devil to roll in a seaway. I remember once being caught in the edge of a typhoon, and she pretty nigh carried everything away, alow and aloft. That's her, over there.'

He pointed with the stem of his pipe to one of the photographs that adorned the room. 'Her sister ship was on the same station with us. *Huntingdonshire*, she was called, and you couldn't tell t'other from which, except by the bands on their funnels. Our six-inch guns for'ard was a bit higher above the deck, that was all. *Huntingdonshire's* skipper was a man called Penistone, and a better officer you couldn't meet. The *Huntingdonshires* swore by him. She was always a happy ship, all on board properly looked after. And smart too. Captain Penistone had been a gunnery expert before he was promoted, and he kept it up on his own ship. When he commanded her, *Huntingdonshire* had the best gunnery record in the Navy.'

'Was this the same man whose body you saw in the Vicar's boat

this morning?' asked Rudge.

'Well, if it was, he's changed a lot since I knew him. Not that the body I saw wasn't about the same height, and all that. But, if it was the same face, it has changed a lot in the last twenty years. It was the expression I go by mostly. The Captain Penistone I knew was a jovial sort of chap, with a cheery word for everybody, no matter whether he was just a stoker or the Admiral himself. And the chap I saw this morning, looked, with all due respect to him, an ill-tempered sort of devil.'

'I fancy he was, from what I've heard of him,' replied Rudge. 'Well, Ware, I'm much obliged to you for what you've told me. By the way, you'll have to give evidence at the inquest, you know. You'll get a summons to attend in due course. And I'll drop in for another yarn sometime, if I may?'

'Aye, you're always welcome,' said Ware cordially. 'And if you're a fisherman, I'll take you to a spot where there's some fine sport to be had. It's private by rights, like all the fishing here, but no one minds about me.'

Inspector Rudge left the old man's cottage, and started up his car. It was time to pay his deferred visit to Sir Wilfrid Denny. As he drove towards West End, his thoughts were busy with the problem of how to discover whether or not Admiral Penistone had rowed down-stream the previous night. If he had he was not likely to have been observed. The river ran out of sight of the road for the greater part of its course. Only at one point, Fernton Bridge, was it visible. There were certainly a few cottages close to its banks, but their inhabitants were pretty certain to have been in bed by ten o'clock. There was, therefore, only the faint possibility that someone had crossed Fernton Bridge at the moment that the Admiral had passed beneath it.

The fact that his journey was not likely to have been observed had another bearing on the matter. His murderer must either have known of his intention, or must have seen him by chance, either at Fernton Bridge or in Whynmouth. But if he had met him by chance, how did he happen to be provided with a suitable weapon? People didn't as a rule carry about with them daggers capable of inflicting such a wound. No, the casual meeting did not seem to fit in, somehow. The crime must have been premeditated. But until he could learn more of the Admiral's associates it was impossible to guess who could have known of his plans. There was always the likelihood, of course, that the murderer had arranged the rendezvous.

As he crossed Fernton Bridge, Rudge stopped the car and

looked over the parapet on either side. He found that he could see a few hundred yards, both up- and down-stream, before bends hid the river in either direction. On a clear night a boat would show up against the water for some distance. Having satisfied himself of this he continued his journey.

West End was a suburb of Whynmouth on the harbour side of the river, and consisted mainly of red-brick villas, each standing in its square of garden. But one older stone-built house remained hidden from its neighbours and the railway to the north by a high shrubbery. This, as Rudge had ascertained, was called Mardale, and was the residence of Sir Wilfrid Denny. The drive gate was open, and he drove in, to be struck at once by the neglected and overgrown appearance of the lawn that sloped down to the river, and the state of dilapidation into which the house had been allowed to fall. He remembered Mrs Davis's hint as to Sir Wilfrid's lack of means, which had apparently been fully justified.

There seemed to be nobody about as he rang the bell, but, after a long wait, an elderly and rather forbidding-looking dame appeared, and looked enquiringly at him.

'Is Sir Wilfrid Denny at home?' he asked.

'No, he ain't,' replied the woman. ' 'E was called to London hunexpectedly, and left by the first train this morning.'

6

By Milward Kennedy

INSPECTOR RUDGE THINKS BETTER OF IT

A tactful question or two elicited the facts that the 'call' had been a telephonic one, and that it was not Sir Wilfrid's habit to go often or regularly or, above all, early to London. He was not, it seemed, a city magnate, but a retired civil servant – 'one of those conciliar officers,' the woman explained. The Inspector began to understand the untidiness of the drive; for whilst your Business Man usually acquires his knighthood at the height of his prosperity and retires to affluence, your civil servant finds that a title is small compensation for the difference between salary and pension.

The news of Sir Wilfrid's absence was disconcerting, but on the

whole, and after a couple of seconds of quick thinking, not altogether unwelcome. Inspector Rudge was subconsciously aware that his enquiries were becoming unduly dispersed and that none of them by itself had so far earned the description of 'thorough.' As he thanked the woman, gave her a polite message for Sir Wilfrid asking him to get in touch with the police on his return, started up the car and drove back towards Lingham, his subconscious feelings took definite shape in his conscience, so definite that just before he reached the fork of the road he pulled in close to the hedge, stopped the car, lit his pipe, took out his notebook, and meditated.

He had been dashing about to and fro – from the Vicarage to Rundel Croft, from Rundel Croft to Whynmouth, from the Lord Marshall Hotel to Ware's cottage, from the cottage back to West End, and now he was going – well, where was he going now? Of course, he had wasted very little time, for the distances were all of them small; incidentally he wondered whether a little while ago he had been quite safe to assume that the Admiral could hardly have reached the Lord Marshall on foot by eleven o'clock, for now that he came to consider it the distance from Rundel Croft could not be much over two and a half miles at the outside. However, that was by the way; what the Inspector wanted at the moment was to plan out his campaign.

What had he learnt, in the first place, at Rundel Croft? By Jove, he had forgotten all about that newspaper. If Emery had discovered the 'regular' copy still in the hall, might not the explanation of the copy in the dead man's pocket be that he had indeed gone into Whynmouth? Well, it was idle to speculate; there, obviously, was one loose thread to be picked up. For the rest, his enquiries had been directed to two distinct pusposes – to find out something about the people involved, their history and characteristics and so on, and on the other hand, to discover what had happened after the dinner at the Vicarage on the previous evening. The more he considered it, the more annoyed he felt at Miss Fitzgerald's flight – he hoped to goodness that was too strong a word; and he wondered, doubtfully, whether he had not been a bit too generous in the liberty he had allowed to Holland. Still, neither of them, perhaps – unless his impressions were all wrong – was the best source for information about the Admiral. But what else had he to go upon? Practically nothing but the gossip of the Vicarage, the servants, old Ware and Mrs Davis, none of whom could boast more than a month's acquaintance with the dead man. The Vicar had suggested that the Admiral usually was

genial enough; his sons had implied rather the opposite. And old Ware – well, what reliance could be placed on his opinion? A petty officer could hardly have been intimate with the captain of a cruiser; and besides, twenty years was long enough to dim the vividness of his recollection. Of course, Sir Wilfrid Denny might have been able to help, but it was rather a leap in the dark. He might have known the Admiral no longer than had the Vicar; and if he had seen more of him in the past month it might simply be that the ex-gunnery expert had no particular penchant for clergymen; that would not be an unprecedented trait in a retired Admiral.

No, Rudge told himself, he must clearly get to work on less haphazard lines; there would be records at the Admiralty, there were the solicitors, there would be 'references' given to the house-agents when the lease of Rundel Croft was signed. And the thoughts of the solicitors reminded him of the will. He had not finished his study of it; its provisions might be of first-rate importance, as a guide to motive. He did not even know whether it was a copy of a proved will, though that obviously would make a vital difference.

There seemed to be plenty of enquiries to set on foot, and the first essentials seemed to be a telephone and a staff; it was not much use leaving both the sergeant and the constable to spend their day at the boat-house while he himself tried to be everywhere at once and to do three jobs at the same time. Still, he would not be in too much of a hurry; he was enjoying his pipe and he wanted to look all round the problem. What about last night's events? By Jove, there was a point which he seemed to have missed. Where was the key of the french window? Was the Admiral the only one who had a private key, or did his niece possess one also?

Rudge puffed away at his pipe and flicked over the pages of his notebook. The maid – yes, Jennie Merton: nice little thing, and quite intelligent. She had given him a pretty clear picture of Elma Fitzgerald and her uncle and the household as a whole. Had she, though? Had he not been a shade too ready to take her opinion as reliable? She had been there just three weeks; and yet when she had told him that Elma and the Admiral were 'sharp' with one another, and that Elma and Holland did not 'hold hands' much and that she could not understand the whys and wherefores of Elma's variability in getting herself up and putting on her best clothes – well, had not he been a bit too ready to think that there was something mysterious, almost sinister, in all of this? More likely the other maid, the one who had been so bored that she had left after a week of Rundel Croft, could have told him the inner

history of the Admiral's household: perhaps they were used to a gayer life . . . Anyhow, she must have been pretty thoroughly bored if she had chucked her wages in order to get away. He pulled himself up sharply; here he was, on the brink of labelling the vanished maid as a foreign adventuress – and all on the strength of a few words of Jennie Merton's.

And when he came to think about it, there was something, well, a little confusing about Jennie's account of the morning, and the disappearance of that white evening dress. Emery, apparently, had found Jennie, and Jennie had gone to wake up her mistress and to tell her she was wanted (the whole process taking no less than ten minutes). Then Jennie was told to clear out at once, as her mistress wished to get up. But at some stage she was told to pack a few things for the night. And when she started on the packing – and that, presumably, was while her mistress was being interviewed downstairs – the white frock had vanished and was nowhere to be found. Yet Jennie blandly assumed that the frock was *afterwards* packed in the bag by her mistress, as if that explained everything. It certainly seemed to suggest that her wits were not so wonderfully sharp after all. And what was more, he would have another word or two with her on the subject.

There was certainly a good job of work to be done at Rundel Croft. That was not to say there was nothing to do at the Vicarage. If the two boys had found no trace of the weapon, a proper search might need to be organised. And then the Vicar's hat: on the one hand he had been so quick to remember where he had absent-mindedly left it, which seemed a bit inconsistent; and on the other he had shown no perturbation when the subject was mentioned – at any rate infinitely less than at other points in the interview.

Inspector Rudge knocked out his pipe and started up the car. He was for Rundel Croft, and as he turned into the drive he found yet another reason for his decision – the traces in the boat and boat-house. He left the car in front of the house and hurried round and down in search of his two subordinates. They greeted him in a manner which suggested that they were bursting with news.

'Well, Sergeant?' he asked. 'Anything important? Found the weapon?'

'No, sir, but – '

'What, then? The footprints?'

'Er – no, sir.'

'H'm. Well, we'll hear about it in a minute.'

Then he realised that he was being rather needlessly abrupt and that Sergeant Appleton was now looking distinctly sullen.

'Sorry,' he said with a pleasant smile. 'The point is that we've a lot to get through and I want to get started at once on the jobs that are going to take the most time. Just set the wheels moving, you know. So if you haven't actually caught the murderer, or as good as done so – '

'Not quite that, sir,' the sergeant answered, his good humour restored.

'Then you, Sergeant, come up to the house with me. Hempstead, you'll stay on here. We'll be down again as soon as we can. Keep an eye on the opposite bank too.'

The two men hurried back to the house, and the Inspector led the way straight to the french window which was foremost in his thoughts; one thing was certain, the key was not on the outside. They hurried round to the front door and rang the bell; after an interval of at least three minutes, during which the Inspector fumed impatiently, Emery opened it and admitted them with the same air of incompetent reluctance which had been the Inspector's first impression of him.

'I want another word with you, Emery,' he began, sternly.

'Here it is,' said Emery.

'Here what is?' The man really seemed to be half-witted as well as painfully slow.

'*Evening Gazette*,' Emery explained, turning and pointing to a side table in the hall.

'The regular copy? The one which is delivered about nine? Where was it?'

'There.'

'But you told me you weren't sure. If it was lying there all the time – '

'No more I was,' Emery asserted, in weak indignation, 'and the minute I went to see and my back was turned, you skipped off.'

The Inspector snorted; he was unable to deny that the man had some reason on his side, but people who were as slow as the butler must expect all kinds of criticism.

'Had it been read?' was his next question. He saw at once that it was not calculated to produce a helpful answer, so he hastily amended it and extracted from Emery the opinion that the paper had not been touched since first it had been laid by him on the table.

The Inspector nodded; then picked up the paper and requested the butler to lead the way to the study. The sergeant was distinctly puzzled, particularly at the appropriation of the *Evening Gazette*, but followed in silence, and closed the study door behind them.

'Now, Emery,' the Inspector resumed, with difficulty restraining a tendency to shout, 'I want to know about the keys of the french window – the one you shut but did not bolt. First of all, were all the other doors locked and bolted when you went to bed last night? They were, eh? So that this was the only way by which the Admiral and Miss Fitzgerald could get in. I see. And now this window – how many keys are there?'

'I've got my key here on my ring,' the butler replied and quite briskly produced a fat bunch, selected the key and proffered it for inspection. The other took it, satisfied himself that it was the right key by unlocking the window, and handed back the bunch. He had wondered how the butler managed to remember not to leave the key in the lock inside; the bunch explained it.

'Right,' he said. 'How many others are there?'

'Only the one that I know of. The one the Admiral had himself.'

'Sure of that?'

'It's the only one I ever heard of.'

'Miss Fitzgerald hasn't got one?'

'No.'

'How d'you know?'

'Well, once or twice of an evening she's borrowed the key from the Admiral.'

'Oh, does she often go out in the evening?' The Inspector could not resist this deviation from the main channel of his questions.

'Now and again. With Mr Holland,' the butler told him, with an approach to a smirk.

'Walking out, eh?' Rudge suggested vulgarly; and the smirk became an accomplished fact. Rudge made a mental comparison of this with Jennie Merton's opinion; then, as if determined to keep Emery in his place, he asked sharply: 'What's happened to the second key – the Admiral's?'

'Well, I – I really couldn't say.'

'Where did the Admiral keep it? On a ring with other keys like you do, or separately?'

'By itself,' Emery told him. 'It used to lie on his table in the pen tray. It had a label.'

The Inspector strode sharply across the room.

'Well, it's not there now,' he announced. Several bright ideas sprang into his mind. The Admiral must have given the key to his niece when she walked up to the house ahead of him. She must either have come in and locked the door behind her – and so locked her uncle out: in which case how did he get the overcoat? Or else she must have left the window open, probably with the key

in the lock and her uncle must have come in, locking the door and pocketing the key – but there had been no odd key in his pockets, certainly none with a label.

Sergeant Appleton coughed.

'Maybe this is it, sir,' he said and held out a key to which was attached a small metal label with the word 'Window' engraved on it. He added, in answer to the Inspector's rather angry questioning look, 'We were going to tell you, sir, by the boat-house.'

'That's all for the present,' the Inspector said to Emery. 'I may want you again later, so you'll keep handy, see? Is there another telephone? Then this is an extention, I suppose?' (He pointed to one on a table at the far end of the study.) 'Just switch it through to here. And another thing: I shall want to see the maid – Merton – again in a few minutes.'

'Well, she's gone out,' the butler told him, with perhaps a tinge of malicious satisfaction.

'But I told you, didn't I – ' the other began, angrily.

'It's her mother. She's queer.'

The Inspector snorted again, and the butler hastily withdrew. It was useless to find fault with the poor creature; he could no more stop Jennie Merton going out than Mr Holland coming in, as Rudge observed to the sergeant.

'No harm done,' he added, in reference to the key; the sergeant rightly took this to be a veiled apology. 'Where did you find it?'

'In the boat – the Admiral's boat.'

'You haven't been messing about – '

'Oh no, sir. Not that there's any danger. Apart from the oars and rowlocks, she's as neat as a new pin.'

'H'm. What about the key for finger-prints?'

But it was easy to see that the rough surface of the label would not 'take' a finger-print.

'Someone took trouble with the boat,' said Rudge thoughtfully, 'so I wonder how the key came to be left there.'

'I don't think the state of the boat means much – necessarily,' the sergeant suggested. 'I had a word with the Vicar's boys. They say that Admiral Penistone always gave her a mop over, like, last thing after he'd finished with her for the day.'

The Inspector considered this. It seemed to fit in with the description of the Admiral as a precise martinet; and it might help to explain why, after hustling away from the Vicarage – directly after ten, because he must be in by midnight! – he had dawdled behind at the boat-house. But it was far from conclusive.

'Well, fire ahead,' he urged the sergeant.

'It just caught my eye, the edge of the label affair. Just sticking out from under the bottom boards of the boat. As if it had been dropped and had slipped down inside.'

'We'd better try it, just to make sure.'

He fitted it into the key-hole, and locked and unlocked the window.

'That's all right,' he agreed and stood silent for a few moments, tapping the key against the palm of his left hand and staring absent-mindedly about the room. Suddenly he emerged from his brown study and walked across to the mantelpiece. He took down a large, framed photograph of a naval officer in full-dress uniform.

'That's him all right, isn't it? Admiral Penistone?'

'Yes,' said Sergeant Appleton in some surprise; he was enlightened about the conversation with old Ware.

'It doesn't sound likely to me that he's not the real Admiral Penistone,' was his comment. 'If he isn't, he's pinched the whole outfit,' and he pointed to an engraved cup which also stood on the mantelpiece. A further scrutiny, moreover, revealed a 'group' of naval officers in the centre of which was a younger but unmistakably a likeness of the dead man. The names of the group were neatly printed below the photograph; and in the centre was the name of Captain Penistone.

'I don't think there's more than a shade of doubt,' the Inspector agreed. 'But we can't afford to take chances. That's one job I've got for you – to ring up the Admiralty.'

As he spoke, he took down a copy of *Who's Who* from a shelf full of reference books.

'Here we are,' he said. 'H'm. No address given, I see – just the outline of his career in the service. Gunnery, yes. China Squadron. Seems to have been a bit of a star-turn. Funny that he should have retired so young – I thought the axe was a modern invention. Anyway you ring up the Admiralty. If he's the right man, they can probably tell you a bit more about him, or suggest how we can find out. Go ahead, Sergeant, get on to the Admiralty.'

Sergeant Appleton took off the receiver. The line was dead; the lamentable Emery obviously had failed to switch the telephone through. The sergeant set off to remedy matters, and took the opportunity to give the butler a piece of his mind.

He returned to find the Inspector seated at the writing-desk, deep in a fresh attempt to translate legal language into common sense. It was not really as difficult as he had fancied, on his previous and hurried inspection of the will. The estate of Admiral

Penistone's brother-in-law apparently was divided equally (apart from one or two small legacies) between Elma Fitzgerald and her brother. Until her brother's death was established, she and her uncle were trustees for his share, the interest upon which, less a consideration to both of them, was to be put to the capital; on his death, the money went absolutely to her. As for her share, she did not receive the principal until she married, and until then her uncle and Mr Edwin Dakers, of Dakers and Dakers, were trustees. The only remarkable clause was a provision that if she married without the written approval of her uncle, she retained only a life interest in her share, the money on her death going to a series of charities. The Inspector was rather gratified to find that, as he had suspected, there was no question of the Admiral having been her sole trustee; his recollection of the law was that such a situation was hardly possible. The document of course was a copy; Dakers and Dakers probably would know if it was a copy of a proved will, and it might be necessary, for formal purposes, to inspect the original at Somerset House. The sergeant could talk to Mr Edwin Dakers . . .

But the sergeant did not seem to be getting on with his telephoning, the fact of the matter being that he was far from certain how exactly one 'rang up the Admiralty' and for whom one asked when one was in touch with that august department. The local exchange had not been particularly bright either, but was supposed to be making enquiries. The Inspector frowned, and glanced restlessly at the *Evening Gazette* which he had thrown down on the desk. He must have a careful look through the copy in the dead man's pocket. The way it was folded might be suggestive, or there might be a marked paragraph. The Admiral would surely not have bought an extra one, knowing that his own would be lying in the hall, unless there had been something of special importance in it. The 'news' did not look anything out of the usual: a 'London Flat Tragedy' occupied most of the front page, together with an account of fresh trouble in Manchuria (Moscow, as usual, was said to be giving liberal help to the latest unpronounceable War Lord) and a picture of the bridesmaids at a wedding at St Margaret's.

The telephone bell rang. The sergeant, still apprehensive, took up the receiver. His expression changed rapidly to one of surprise.

'Who? Yes. Hold on and I'll fetch – oh, very well. Who? Oh, yes, yes, just wait – ' he beckoned frantically to the Inspector, who came quickly across the room.

'Who is it?'

'Miss – yes – I'm listening – Miss Fitzgerald.'

'Give it to me,' the Inspector demanded. 'Come on, man.' The sergeant was scribbling illegible notes on the pad before him. At length and rather doubtfully he handed over the instrument. 'Miss Fitzgerald? This is Inspector Rudge. I'm glad you've rung up. I want to ask you – '

'Sorry,' he heard in Elma Fitzgerald's flattest tones, 'I can't wait now. I've sent you a message. And by the way, I'm *not* Miss Fitzgerald.'

There wasa click as she rang off. The Inspector swore, and joggled the lever furiously up and down.

'Trace that call, please,' he demanded of the exchange, and explained who he was.

'It's all right, sir,' said the sergeant. 'She was speaking from the Carlton, in London. She said so herself, and besides I heard the hotel exchange say so when the call came through.'

'What was the message? Wouldn't wait to speak to me, eh?'

'She said she understood you wanted to get in touch with her, and with Mr Holland. So you'd be interested to know that they were both staying at the Carlton and would be there for the next day or two, and then they would come back. She'd be out dancing tonight but would always be glad to see you by appointment. But would you remember to ask for Mrs Holland, as she was married by special license today.'

The Inspector digested – or began to digest – this news in silence. If Elma and Holland were man and wife, it made it difficult to . . . And then the will. If the Admiral was dead, the clause about his consent to his niece's marriage presumably fell to the ground . . . Elma's message certainly gave him something to think about.

'Well, Sergeant,' he decided, 'we'd better get on with it. Hurry up that call to the Admiralty, and after that I want you to get hold of Mr Edwin Dakers,' and he rapidly fired off a series of instructions, including one that he was to be told when Jennie Merton came back. 'I'm going down to the boat-house,' he ended and departed via the french window.

He found Hempstead patiently on guard.

'Any news?' he asked him.

'No, sir. No one been here.'

'No fresh discoveries?'

'No, sir. The sergeant told you about the key?'

'Yes. Good work. Anything happened opposite?'

'No, sir. The young gentlemen have been looking everywhere for the knife, but I don't think they've found anything. They said

they were going to have a bathe now.'

The sun was getting hot, and there was a note of envy in the constable's tones.

'Seen the Vicar?'

'Yes, sir. He's been watering the garden.'

'What, this morning? In the sun?'

'Yes, sir, with a hose. Worth watching, it was. He watered pretty well everything in sight – even the flowers now and again. But I shouldn't say he's done them much harm. I reckon he doesn't know an awful lot about gardening, and that's just what Bob Hawkins, who goes in twice a week, says.'

The Inspector surveyed the boat-house and its contents.

'We'll make casts of those footprints if we can,' he said, 'though they don't *look* very distinctive. And I think we'll take out the oars and rowlocks. We can't keep this place under observation for ever and if there *are* any finger-prints that'll tell us anything, we don't want them mucked up.'

He stepped into the boat and began cautiously to hand out the articles in question to Hempstead. Whilst he was so doing, the sound of voices on the opposite bank made him turn, rocking the boat rather perilously. The two boys, clad in bathing dresses, with towels in their hands, were coming down the rough, red-brick path from the summer-house. A sudden thought struck the Inspector.

'Hullo!' he called, as they reached the Vicarage landing-steps. 'I wonder whether you'd let me have the loan of your old punt for a while? It would save me going round by road every time.'

'Rather!' the elder of the two answered.

'If you could bring her across and swim back,' Rudge suggested.

'That's the idea,' the boy answered with a grin.

By the time the paraphernalia from the boat had been landed safely, the punt had arrived; the Inspector moored it to a ring in the Rundel Croft landing-stage.

'How many times a day do you bathe?' he asked pleasantly. 'Or has the search made you so hot?'

'It's all part of the search,' the younger replied, perhaps detecting a note of criticism in the question.

'We're going to try diving for the weapon,' the other added.

'Good,' said Rudge, 'though I'm afraid that what with the mud and the tide, and not knowing quite how big the weapon is likely to be, it won't be easy. I'd hoped you'd find it on the bank somewhere, but it seems you've drawn a blank.'

'All we've found is the Admiral's favourite pipe,' said Peter.

'Indeed! And where did you find that?'

'In father's study. He must have left it behind last night. He was smoking it after dinner.'

'Sure it's his?'

'Oh, yes. You'll see why when you see it. A dirty old meerschaum shaped like a nigger's head.'

'You haven't got it here, then?' As he asked, he realised that the question was a foolish one.

'It's up at the house.' Alec nobly refrained from a sarcastic comment, and stepped to the end of the punt, preparatory to diving into the river.

'I say, Alec, don't you think we ought to tell him – ?' his brother checked him.

'Tell him what? Oh, that. You are a fool, Peter. No, it's got nothing to do with it.'

'What's that?' the Inspector enquired.

'Oh, nothing,' was the airy answer. 'Something we lost, not something we found.'

'Better tell me, then,' Rudge suggested. 'Police job to find things, you know.'

'Then you can do the diving instead of us,' Alec suggested, brightly. 'Still, as Peter's said so much, I'd better tell you. But it's got nothing to do with your business. At least, I don't see why it should have. It's just that we – or at least Peter – left a knife in the summer-house yesterday afternoon, or he says he did, and it's not there now.'

'Is that so?' Hempstead too pricked up his ears. 'What sort of a knife? A pocket-knife, I suppose.'

'Well, no. It was a large-sized Norwegian knife. We'd used it to point a stake – you want a sharp knife for that. Anyway, it's lost; and the chances are that Peter never left it in the summer-house at all. He's as bad as father for not knowing where he's put things.'

And he plunged into the river, promptly followed by Peter, the Inspector getting somewhat splashed in consequence. But he was content to get this fresh news at the cost of a few drops of water, and with a smile on his face he watched the two lads swim across, scramble out on to the far bank and begin to dive valorously in search of the unknown weapon.

The smile slowly faded; evidence – or call it information – seemed to be piling up. He thought of the proverb about the difficulty of seeing the wood for the trees.

'Interesting, sir, wasn't it?' Hempstead's voice broke in on his thoughts. 'Things begin to take shape, as you might say.'

The latter phrase was as much a question as the former.

'Maybe,' the Inspector answered him, slowly, 'but there are plenty of puzzles yet. One thing, Hempstead, is that overcoat. Suppose the Admiral went out in his boat: well, I grant you he might take an overcoat with him, but it would need to be a very cold night before you or I'd put on a thick overcoat to row in. Other things apart, you want your arms free, don't you?'

The constable produced a throaty noise meant to convey assent without definitely committing him to it.

'And another thing,' Rudge went on, 'is that evening paper. Oh, lots of puzzles there are about that, as well as the cross-word. But the biggest is "where did he get it?" It must have come by the eight-thirty last night – there's no getting away from that.'

There was a pause; and then he added slowly and almost breathlessly, 'Unless it came down by road.'

And then he turned to Hempstead, just sharply enough to catch him smothering a yawn. He remembered that the unfortunate constable had been on night duty. That in turn suggested two things to him – first that he must get the oars and rowlocks up to the station, and that Hempstead could see to that and have himself 'relieved' at the same time; and secondly –

'You didn't notice anything particular in the way of cars in the neighbourhood, round about half-past ten, say, last night, did you, Hempstead?'

The constable considered the point.

'Well, now you come to mention it, sir,' he said at length, 'there was a car stopped in Lingham just about a quarter to eleven or thereabouts. I noticed it stop by the lamp in the Square. Closed car, it was, with a woman in it.'

'Alone?'

'That I couldn't say. I only know there was a woman because I saw her lean out of the window and speak to the chauffeur, or whoever was driving.'

'Would you know her again?'

'Can't say I should, sir. And I didn't notice the number of the car much, either –you see there was no occasion, then. I just happened to notice the car. It didn't stop above a couple of minutes and then drove on. Along the Whynmouth road.'

'And that, of course,' said Inspector Rudge, 'would take it past the Vicarage.'

7

By Dorothy L. Sayers

SHOCKS FOR THE INSPECTOR

Th Inspector ruminated for a few moments upon the fascinating possibilities suggested by this piece of information, and then, dismissing Hempstead with the advice to get a good meal and turn in, he walked slowly back towards the house.

'Yes, sonny, what is it?'

This was to Peter Mount, who had suddenly appeared at his elbow.

'A note for you from father, said the boy. 'I came across with it.'

'About the funeral, I expect,' said Rudge to himself. But the note ran:

Dear Inspector Rudge

I am anxious to run up to London this afternoon on an urgent matter connected with my clerical duties. I hope that there will be no objection to my doing so. I should not think of absenting myself if the case were not of great importance, since I know that you would prefer to have all your witnesses on the spot. However, I trust that I shall not be detained very long, and I shall, of course, make a point of being back in time to attend the inquest which, as I am informed by Mr Skipworth, will take place the day after to-morrow. I will keep you informed as to my movements, should you require to get in touch with me at any time, and should I be detained overnight, shall be staying at the Charing Cross Hotel.

Apologising for any inconvenience this request may cause you,

Yours very truly,
PHILIP MOUNT.

'Good lord! Another of them,' was the Inspector's mental comment. He stood for a few moments undecided, the note open in his hand.

He had to make up his mind. If he forbade the Vicar to go – well, he could scarcely do that wihtout committing himself to an accusation, for which step he was certainly not prepared. He could *ask* the Vicar not to go – but behind the courtesy of the expression the note seemed to carry a suggestion of mild determination. He had nothing definite against the Vicar, except that his hat and his coat had been found in a curious place, and that he was a bad gardener. He turned to Peter.

'I think I'd like to see your Dad if he can spare a few moments.'

'Right you are.'

'How did you get across, by the way?'

'Your new policeman brought the punt over for me – but he isn't very good at it.'

Rudge noted with satisfaction that Hempstead's deputy had arrived. That meant that he would be free to leave Rundel Croft if he wanted to. He spoke a word or two to the new arrival – a very stout man called Bancock – stepped into the punt and was poled across by Peter. On the way up to the Vicarage he noticed the drenched area round the summer-house. The hose had caught a clump of begonias at the edge of a garden-bed. One or two of the plants had been actually broken by the force of the stream, and on others the water-drops were standing like miniature burning-glasses under the bright sun. The Vicar would probably wonder, next day, why their foliage should be speckled with white heat-blisters.

The Vicar was in his study. He greeted Rudge cordially, but his face looked a little drawn. No doubt he had received a severe shock, thought Rudge. It was a strong face, though, and handsome in its rather set, ecclesiastical way. It looked honest, but you could never tell. According to local report the Vicar was a ritualist, and ritualists had odd ideas about the truth. They would, for instance, subscribe to the Thirty-nine Articles and then unblushingly invent ingenious ways to get round them. Rudge was rather well up in the different varieties of parsons, for his brother-in-law was people's warden at St Saviour's, Whynmouth.

'Well, Inspector, I hope you haven't come to tell me that I mustn't go to town.'

'Well, no, sir – not exactly. I shouldn't like to go so far as that, though I don't say but what I hadn't rather you stayed here. Still, as I understand you to say the business is urgent – '

He paused, to give the Vicar time to explain what the business was, but Mr Mount merely said:

'Oh, yes; it is very important. If it would have waited a couple of

days I should have tried to put it off, but I fear that is quite impossible.'

'I see, sir.' Rudge could not for the life of him see what clerical business could be so urgent as that, unless it was a summons from the Archbishop of Canterbury or an important conference, and if it were, why should not the Vicar say so? Mr Mount's face displayed, however, only the bland severity of one about to read the First Lesson.

'I take it that will be all right then, Inspector?'

'Oh, yes, sir. Provided, as you say, you keep in touch with us. And I'm very much obliged to you for letting me know of your intentions. It isn't everybody would be so considerate.'

'We both have our duty to do,' replied the Vicar. 'Besides,' he added, with a slight twinkle, 'if I had gone off without letting you know, you might have imagined I was running away from you, and that would never do.'

Rudge laughed dutifully.

'There's just one or two things I was going to ask you, sir,' he said, 'and I'm glad to have this opportunity. About the late Admiral Penistone. Should you say he was a quick walker?'

'No,' said the Vicar. 'Admiral Penistone never cared to walk much, owing to a wound he got in his foot during the War. A piece of shrapnel, I understand. He was not actually lame, but it tired him to walk very far or very fast. He always preferred to take the car or go by the river if possible.'

The Inspector nodded. This upset his recent calculations and left him where he was before. He went on to the next point.

'Do you sleep on the river side of the house, sir?'

'No. My sons and the servants sleep on that side, but my bedroom window is at the other side, overlooking the lane. Sometimes I get called up in the night to visit the sick or dying, and it is more convenient for them to be able to knock me up without disturbing the household. There is a side-door, you see, which opens on to the lane, with a bell which rings in my bedroom.'

'I see. Does your window command the high road?'

'Yes, in a sense. I mean, I can see the road, but it is, of course, a couple of hundred yards from the house.'

'Quite so. I suppose you did not happen to see a closed car pass along last night in the direction of Whynmouth?'

'That is rather a vague question. At what time do you mean?'

'At about a quarter to eleven. I thought perhaps you might have seen it when you were undressing.'

The Vicar shook his head.

'No,' he said at once, 'I am afraid I cannot help you. I came straight upstairs at ten-twenty, undressed and went to bed. I do not think I looked out of the window at all. But in any case, at the time you mention, I should be either in the bathroom along the passage, or' (he twinkled again) 'saying my prayers.'

'Just so,' said Rudge, embarrassed as every true Englishman is at the mention of private devotions. 'Well, it was just a chance, sir, but a very slight one. I couldn't really have expected you to notice. You'll be good enough to ring me up when you get to town, sir?'

'I certainly will,' said the Vicar. 'And thank you very much for your permission to elope. I promise you that I will not break my parole.'

'I'm quite sure of that, sir,' replied Rudge, with conviction, and took his leave.

He strolled slowly back through the Vicarage garden, his heavy boots squeaking loudly on the gravel in the hot hush of the August morning, Peter was still idling about the boat-house. Rudge looked at the post in the stream, with the end of rope still fastened to it by a couple of half-hitches. He wondered whether he had assumed too hastily that the body had been dumped into the Vicar's boat from another boat. He ought at least to take the precaution of examining the bank for footprints.

Search, however, revealed nothing very helpful. The grass edge was crumpled and broken in places, as it would naturally be if the Vicar's family were accustomed to board the boat from that point, but the grass itself was too short and dry to show definite footprints, and anything below high-water mark would naturally have been obliterated when the tide came up that morning.

Rudge sat down on the bank and stared at the river. The tide was just running down to the slack, and the ripples went clucking and clapping against the sides of the punt and the boat-house. On the other side lay the Admiral's boat, shivering slightly as the wash of the stream lifted her stern and dimmed the outlines of her mirrored shape in among the brown shadows. Between the bank and bank the sun blazed full on the water. Rudge found the tune running in his head:–

'Ol' man River, dat ol' man River.
He must know sumfin', he don' say nuffin' – '

That reminded him that he had promised to get his land-lady Paul Robeson's record of 'Swing low, sweet chariot.' And his wireless needed a new accumulator. Curse the river, with its perpetual

chuckle and its imbecile tidal vagaries. He knew the Ouse at Huntingdon – slow, solitary, regulated by pumps and weirs, and little used for boating because of its derelict and weed-grown locks. He had seen rivers in Scotland, tumbling and brawling and full of stones, useful for nothing but for fishing in – if you liked that kind of thing. He had even taken a holiday trip to Ireland and seen the majestic Shannon harnessed and set to churning out electricity. But this river was a secretive beast and no good to anybody. What was the sense of a river with three feet between its high and low tide twice a day?

He looked at the mooring-post again ('Swing low, sweet chariot') and measured with his eye the distance between the hitch of rope and the level of the river. Nearly eight feet. Neddy was right. Anybody on the river waiting to loose the boat at low tide would have to cut the painter. The boat would swing very low indeed ('coming for to carry me home'), and the painter would need to be a long one, if the boat was to ride in the water. Suddenly he got up, started out of his drowsy ruminations.

'I say, sonny,' he said aloud.

Peter emerged from the boat-house.

'How long should you say your painter was?'

'It's about three fathoms – eighteen feet, you know. It has to be pretty long, you see, to allow for the fall of the tide.'

'Yes, I thought it would be.' Rudge measured with his eye the end of rope as it trailed in the stream, then tried to remember the look of the end left on the Vicar's boat. Five feet or so at the most, he thought. But he couldn't be sure. Probably it was quite all right, but, just as a matter of routine, it wouldn't be a bad idea to fit the two cut ends together. He stared at the post again. He could see clearly in his mind's eye the Vicar's boat with the new manilla cut through and Neddy Ware demonstrating on his plug of tobacco the sharpness of the knife that had made the cut. The sun on the river was dazzling. Gazing at the post, Rudge's eyes swam with water. But it seemed to him that that end was cut less cleanly than the other.

'What is it?' asked Peter, staring first at the post and then at the Inspector.

'Nothing much,' said Rudge, 'just a little job I thought of, which I shall have to see to presently. I'll go across now, I think, if you are not wanting the punt.'

He poled himself across without disaster, and found P.C. Bancock stolidly reading a newspaper on the farther bank. Telling him to keep an eye on the house and to take any telephone

messages, Rudge hurriedly climbed into the police car and drove round across Fernton Bridge to Lingham. The Vicar's boat was there, having been carefully loaded on to a farm cart and locked up in the 'Dance Hall' of the local pub, where also lay, in charge of the local undertaker, the body of Admiral Penistone. On consideration Rudge had thought this the best arrangement, since the inquest would have to be held at Lingham, and it seemed better to leave the body there for the present, bringing it back, if necessary, to Rundel Croft for the funeral.

But the body did not interest Rudge for the moment. The boat with its painter was his object. On entering the 'Dance Hall' Rudge found the police photographer in possession. He appeared to have reaped a rich crop of finger-prints, and was now methodically exposing plates upon them. Rudge nodded to him to carry on, and then pulling out a folding tape-measure from his pocket he stretched it carefully along the painter. The precise measurement came out at four feet nine inches, from the cut end to the ring on the boat's nose.

He came out again, drove back, cursing the silly necessity of having to go three miles out of his way on every journey and, returning to Rundel Croft, got out the punt once more. Poling across to the mooring-post, he took his measurements.

From the bottom of the hitch to the end of the rope was eight feet, and, allowing for the rope used in surrounding the post and making the hitches, and for the spare end, you got another three feet. That brought the whole length of rope on the post to eleven feet. Add four feet nine inches, and you got a total of fifteen feet nine inches only. Two feet three inches of rope still remained unaccounted for.

Rudge, clinging affectionately with one arm to the post while he made his measurements, and digging his toes well in to prevent the punt from drifting off and leaving him like a monkey on a stick, shook his head at this. Then he took the cut end of the painter in his hand and considered it attentively. He had been right. This was no clean cut like the other. A sharp knife had been used, but the rope had parted gradually, and strands loosening out under the strain and one final strand having ravelled out beyond the rest.

He was left with his new puzzle. Why should anybody need a bit of rope only a couple of feet long? It could hardly have been used to tie anything up, for the thickness of the rope meant that nearly the whole of this length would be taken up in making the knot. Well – it was one more riddle.

He pushed off from the post and took up the punt-pole once

more. That piece of rope ought to be found if possible. But probably it had merely been thrown into the river, and if so, it would have gone out to sea by this time. Or (since the ridiculous Whyn flowed both ways) it might have gone up-stream after the Admiral. That did not seem to be a very promising line of research.

No message of any kind had been received at the house during his absence, and not quite knowing what to do, he wandered into the Admiral's study. There he found the sergeant, who, after considerable back-chat with the local exchange, had succeeded in getting through to the Admiralty and was trying to explain to a languid voice at the other end what department he wanted and whom he wished to speak to. The Inspector took over the instrument.

'This is the Whynmouth police,' he said, in a peremptory tone calculated to convey that, though the Navy might be a Senior Service, the Law was more important still. 'We want information about the career of Admiral Penistone, retired, late of the Chinese Squadron, and now living at Lingham. Will you kindly put me on to the proper person at once. The matter is urgent.'

'Oh!' said the voice. 'What do you want to know about him? I could look up his record for you, of course, I – '

'I don't want that,' said the Inspector. 'I want to speak confidentially to somebody in authority – and the quicker the better.'

'Oh!' said the voice again. 'Well, I don't know. You see, everybody's out at lunch, I think. One o'clock, you know. Look here. I think you'd better ring up again in an hour or two and ask for Extension fifty-five – they'll probably be able to tell you something there, don't you know. I'll send them a chit about it.'

'Thank you.' The Inspector slammed the receiver down and, after allowing the statutory thirty seconds, took it off again.

'Number please,' said the exchange.

'Look here, miss,' said Rudge. 'Have you got a London telephone directory? You have. Good. Would you look up the number of Messrs Dakers and Dakers for me? They're solicitors in – wait a moment – in Lincoln's Inn. Yes, I'll spell that. That's right, Dakers and Dakers. It's rather urgent.'

'I'll r-r-ring you,' said the exchange.

The remarks of the young man at the Admiralty had reminded Rudge that he had been on the job since six o'clock and had had no breakfast. He rang the bell and asked Emery if he could be given something to eat.

'Well,' said the retainer, dubiously, 'I don't know, I suppose so.'

He pondered, and then added: 'Me and Mrs Emery was just sitting down to gammon rashers. I dare say you could have a gammon rasher if you fancied it.'

The idea seemed good to the Inspector. He replied that he should fancy it very much indeed.

'Well, I'll tell her,' said Emery. He went out, and returned again in a few minutes.

'I suppose you would be wanting something to drink,' he suggested, reluctantly.

'Anything that's going,' said Rudge, pleasantly.

'Well, I dare say you could have a glass of beer,' said Emery. 'Me and Mrs Emery was just sitting down to a glass. Mrs Emery felt she needed a drop of something to raise her spirits.'

The Inspector readily accepted the offer of beer. Emery shambled slowly away, returning presently to enquire:

'If I was to bring it on a tray, would that do for you? We ain't never been accustomed to have the police about the place.'

The Inspector signified that whatever was most convenient to Mr and Mrs Emery would suit him. The man retired again, and after a considerable time returned to announce mournfully.

'Mrs Emery says you can have a gammon rasher if you want it. She says she hasn't made no sweet today, on account of being low in her spirits, but perhaps a piece of the Stilton would do for you.'

The Inspector replied that it would do admirably, and at that moment the telephone rang. On answering it Rudge found that he was through to Mr Daker's office. Mr Edwin Dakers and Mr Trubody were both out. Could the speaker do anything?

The Inspector explained that he wanted to speak urgently to Mr Edwin Dakers on business connected with Admiral Penistone. No, he was not speaking for the Admiral. The Admiral, in fact, was dead.

'Indeed? Mr Dakers will be very sorry to hear that.'

'In fact,' said the Inspector, 'he has died under very mysterious circumstances. I represent the police.'

'Indeed? Mr Dakers will be greatly distressed. If you will give me your number, I will ask him to ring you as soon as he comes in.'

The Inspector thanked the speaker and then remembered that Sergeant Appleton was still somewhere about, and unfed. He rang the bell again. Emery shuffled in and began at once with a reproachful expression.

'Now it ain't no good you ringing. Nobody can't hurry a gammon rasher. They wants a good deal of cooking if they ain't to give you bile.'

'Quite so,' said Rudge, 'but I was thinking about my sergeant. Do you think you could manage a meal for him too?'

'The sergeant,' said Emery, 'is taking a bite in the kitchen along of me and Mrs Emery. No offence, I hope.'

'Certainly not, no,' said Rudge, 'I'm very glad he should.' Emery withdrew again, while the Inspector pondered on Sergeant Appleton's superior enterprise and resourcefulness.

The gammon rasher – cut thick and well fried up – was brought in by Mrs Emery, a little bird-like woman with snapping eyes and a masterfulness of manner which explained to some extent her husband's crushed and wilted appearance. A single glance at the perfectly-cooked rasher with its accompanying green peas and chips explained another riddle. Evidently, Emery's feeble-mindedness was the price the Admiral paid for Mrs Emery's culinary skill.

Rudge expressed his appreciation.

'And how I could bring myself to do it I'm sure I don't know,' said Mrs Emery, 'with the poor master gone so sudden and Miss Elma away and the whole place in a uproar. Even the very smell of the meat seems almost 'eartless, as you might say. But there! that Emery is a man and man must 'ave 'is meat, if the 'ole world was to be swallowed up in Noah's flood.'

'True,' said the Inspector, 'we are a callous sex, I'm afraid, Mrs Emery. It's a great upset to you naturally. And with Miss Fitzgerald going away unexpectedly it's all left on your shoulders.'

'Ah!' said Mrs Emery. 'And when isn't it left on my shoulders, I should like to know? A lot Miss Elma troubled herself about the house. Might be a man for all the help she was. Now the poor Admiral, he liked to have things pleasant about him, and for all he was sharp in his ways, it was a pleasure to serve him. Many's the time I've had to speak sharp to Emery, for I could see as his shiftless ways was a hard trial to the master – but there! Emery's but a poor creature, though he is my husband. The Admiral, he gave him notice to leave at the end of the month but there! I didn't pay no attention. I just cooked him a nice dinner, such as he had a fancy for, and he said to me, "Mrs Emery, tell that blistering swab of a husband of yours that he can stay on and here's half a guinea for you to buy a bit o' ribbon.' He was a good master, and I'd say so if I was on my death-bed.'

'I'm sure of it,' said Rudge, sympathetically. He felt that he had unaccountably neglected Mrs Emery. If you want the truth about a man's character, he had always maintained, ask the servants. He now had two testimonies in the Admiral's favour and he felt they

were to be relied upon. Neddy Ware had echoed the opinion of the Admiral's own crew – and a crew is seldom mistaken about its captain. And Mrs Emery's evidence agreed with theirs.

'I suppose,' he said, 'that Admiral Penistone was a bit short-tempered at times, eh?'

'I don't think none the worse of him for that,' retorted Mrs Emery. 'I'd rather a man was short-tempered than poor-spirited any day. And the master had a lot to put up with. What with Miss Elma treating him so bad, and his worries and one thing and another – '

'What worries were those?'

'Well, now, Inspector, I don't know as I could rightly say what worries. But I did hear as he hadn't been treated proper by the Admiralty when he was a young man, and he never rightly got over it. Something to do with foreign parts, it was, and he'd say that he'd get himself set right yet, if it took him a lifetime. But Miss Elma, she hadn't no more sympathy with him than a man hasn't when you're fratcheted to death with babies.' Without pausing to explain this obscure comparison, Mrs Emery went on still more rapidly. 'She wouldn't listen to a word, Miss Elma wouldn't, just sat there looking as sulky as a cow and wouldn't so much as put her hand to a duster or put up a vase of flowers to make the place look homelike. And sorry I'm sure I am for Mr Holland, and him such a nice gentleman, if he marries our young lady, though what he could see in her I don't know. It's a miracle to me, with all these decent, sensible girls about that a man will always pick on the wrong sort, and as to being good-looking, I never could see it.'

'Well,' said Rudge, 'it's past praying for now. They were married this morning.'

'Well, I never,' said Mrs Emery. '*That's* what your sergeant was looking so sly about! "There's a surprise in store for you, ma'am," he says, "but I'll not tell you," he says, "for you'll be hearing it soon enough." Fancy! But if that isn't just like Miss Elma, before her poor uncle's cold as you might say, the 'eartless 'ussy! And surprised I am at Mr Holland doing such a thing, but there! Anything she said he followed like a lamb with a blue ribbon round its neck, but them big fellows is often the meekest when it comes to a woman.'

'You think Mr Holland is very fond of Miss Fitzgerald, then?' suggested Rudge. Would he ever get to the bottom of the relations between this pair? No two people seemed to agree about them.

'Fond he was,' said Mrs Emery, 'and is, I've no doubt, though how long it lasts is another matter. She took it cool enough, but

that's her way. Herself and her fancies, that's all that young lady ever was in love with, if you ask me, and he'll soon find out. Things look different when you're married. Artful she was, too, leading him on and putting him off as the fancy took her. But as to caring for him, no, the master knew that as well as anybody. If he'd been alive they wouldn't have got married so easy, and that's a fact, but to go right off and join their 'ands over his dead body, as you might say, is what I shouldn't hardly have thought Mr Holland capable of.'

'H'm!' said the Inspector. He was trying to remember how long it took to get a special license. He seemed to remember dimly that it required at least a day's notice. 'Maybe they had planned to get married today in any case.'

'Then they ought to have altered their plan,' replied Mrs Emery. 'Disgusting, I call it. But I shouldn't wonder if they had, come to think of it. Maybe that's what Mr Holland was so anxious to see the Admiral about last night.'

'Oh, yes. He rang up from Whynmouth, didn't he?'

'He did. I took the message myself. Wanted to see the master very urgent. I said as him and Miss Elma was over at the Vicarage and wouldn't be back till late – for I expected they'd stop to eleven o'clock or such, playing cards or something of that. The Vicar don't mind playing cards for all he's such a man for services and saints' days, but that's only to be expected, for fancy dress and candles is not what you could call religion, don't you think so yourself? Well, I said to him, they won't be back till eleven, I said, saying what I thought right at the time, which I couldn't be expected to know they would be early that night of all nights. One can but act for the best. So I said, why not go over to the Vicarage, but Mr Holland says, "no, he'll leave it and perhaps he might come up later." '

'And did he?'

'Not that I know of, but there, I'm a sound sleeper, thank God, and need to be, the work there is in this house. Emery, he's supposed to do the cleaning, but half the time I has to do it after him, and as for Jennie, she's a good girl but run off her feet by Miss Elma as won't do step or stitch for herself. Cooking is what I was engaged to do and with Miss Elma breakfasting in bed and getting up at all hours, I've only got one pair of hands.'

'Quite so,' said Rudge, 'and very capable ones I'm sure they are, Mrs Emery.'

'I'm sure I said when I come here as I ought to have a kitchen-maid under me, with all these brick floors. That's the worst of

these old-fashioned houses. But I've no complaint of the Admiral, for a rich man he was not, not but what she might have done something to help him if she had liked, for she's got plenty, so I'm told. And what she did with her allowance it's difficult to say, not that it's any of my business, for it's not, but nobody can't help their thoughts. And spend it on dress she did not, nobody could say that against her, barring an evening frock now and again, or a handsome coat. But them's not the things as takes the money, as you'll know well enough if you're a married man. It's the shoes and gloves and bags and stockings and jumpers. And I'm sure Miss Elma bothered as little about them as a young lady could do. That French maid she had, she used to complain dreadful of the shabby way Miss Elma went about.'

'Ah, yes – the French girl. What was she like?'

'Girl?' said Mrs Emery. 'They calls 'em all girls nowadays. But if ever she sees forty again, I'll be surprised. A nice little thing enough, to speak to, and spoke English beautiful. But I don't like a maid as is too intimate with her mistress. I've seen Miss Elma catch that woman's eye sometimes, when the master happened to be a bit put out and looks pass between them which did not ought to pass between persons in their stations of life. Let servants stick together and masters stick together – that's my motto, but for young ladies to be taking their maids into their confidences about the master of the house is unbecoming, to my way of thinking. It's my belief there was some trouble about it, or why did Ma'amselle go off so quick without her wages? There's the front door bell, who'll that be, I wonder? I hope Emery is answering it, as it's his place to do, but he's that flustered with all this. You'll have noticed, I dare say, as his head's not very strong. Now, I'm different. I'm one of the noticing sort. I may have been only a month with the Admiral, but a woman that's experienced – and I've been in many places in my time – don't take long putting two and two together. Oh, I could size up Miss Elma all right. Emery *has* remembered his duty for once, I'm glad to say.'

The door opened and Emery poked in his melancholy head.

'Here's two newspaper gentlemen waiting to see the Inspector.'

Rudge was about to consign the newspaper gentlemen to a warm spot, when it occurred to him that all God's creatures have their uses. He glanced at the card held out to him, and observed that it bore the magic words, *Evening Gazette*.

'I'll see them,' he said, shortly.

The two newspaper gentlemen were ushered in – a breezy man with a cropped head and horn-rimmed spectacles, the upper por-

tion of whose face appeared to have been darkened by some ineffectual form of sunburn application ('all handsome men are slightly sunburned'), and a morose man with a camera.

'Now,' said Rudge, 'how did you boys get on to this?'

Cropped-head grinned.

'Information received, eh, Inspector? "If it's not in the *Gazette* then it hasn't happened yet." We had it on the streets in the twelve-thirty. Do your best for us, won't you?'

'Well,' said Rudge. He thought for a moment and then gave them as much information as he thought was bound to come out in any case.

'*That's* O.K.,' said Cropped-head. 'Now, as regards yourself, Inspector. Our readers will want to know all about you. Perhaps you would be good enough to come and be photographed in the boat-house? Adds interest to the picture, you know. Well, that's awfully good of you. It won't take a minute. Is that the Admiral's boat? Just point carelessly towards it. That's fine. Make a good picture, eh, Tom?'

Rudge, in spite of himself, felt rather flattered.

'We shall say, of course, that you have the case well in hand and that there's obviously no need to call in Scotland Yard. Just so. Now, how about this niece? Could we get a word with her at all?'

'No,' said Rudge. 'As a matter of fact,' he added handsomely, 'I don't mind telling you something about her.'

The reporter was eagerly attentive.

'She went off to London this morning,' said the Inspector impressively, 'and got married – to a man called Arhur Holland, a trader, from China.'

'Did she? Quick work. That'll make a good story. Why the haste?'

'I can't tell you that yet. But look here. If I let you have that story exclusively, will you do something for me?'

'Sure thing.'

'I want to find out about Admiral Penistone's past career. Why he sent in his papers at forty-three, and why he rejoined the Navy afterwards and all about it.'

'Oh! I can tell you something about that,' the reporter laughed. 'I got that out of a man I know in the Chinese Embassy. The old boy got into trouble in Hong Kong in 1911. Some private matter. Something to do with a woman. One of the things that aren't done by naval officers. He was requested to send in his papers. No public scandal – you know the sort of thing. My man didn't know all the details, but he promised to get them for me. I'll let you have

anything I get hold of. I dare say we shan't print it all, because some of the parties may be alive, but I'll send you the dope on the whole thing. And, I say – if there's anything coming along that you feel you can let us have straight from the gee-gee's mouth, you will, won't you? That's a bargain.'

Rudge agreed readily enough. This was a great deal more hopeful than unwinding red tape from the Admiralty. Trouble in Hong Kong in 1911? That explained matters. No doubt as Penistone was a smart officer they were glad enough to let him rejoin in 1914. But it would have made a difference to him, naturally. Soured the old boy's temper a bit, no doubt. Was it possible that the murder was the aftermath of that old affair? It seemed a long time to keep up resentment, but where Chinks were concerned you never knew. And, by the way, Holland had lately come from China. What was that Mrs Emery had said about Holland? He had said he might walk over to Rundel Croft after eleven. Suppose he had done so?

Obviously Holland and Elma must be got hold of. They would have to be subpoenaed for the inquest in any case. He must tackle the coroner about that. A little job for Sergeant Appleton. He returned to the house and despatched his subordinate with a note. Hardly had he done so when the telephone rang.

Mr Edwin Dakers was on the line. He was indeed grieved and horrified to hear of the Admiral's death. He thought he had better come down to Rundel Croft at once. As Miss Fitzgerald's trustee and representative, it would be necessary for him to see her without delay. Doubtless she was greatly upset by this melancholy occurrence.

'I haven't noticed it,' replied Rudge, with a sort of grim satisfaction. 'In fact, no sooner did Miss Fitzgerald hear of her uncle's death than she went up to town and got married to a Mr Holland. I should be glad, sir – '

'*What*!' said Mr Dakers, in a tone so aghast that it seemed to shake the instrument.

Rudge repeated his information.

'God bless my soul!' said Mr Dakers, and paused for such a long time that Rudge began to think he had fallen dead with horror. Then he said: 'This is very unfortunate indeed, Inspector. I am more than shocked. I am horrified.'

'It certainly looks a bit unfeeling,' said Rudge.

'Unfeeling?' said Mr Dakers. 'It may be most gravely prejudicial to her monetary interests. Can you tell me where to find her?'

'They were staying at the Carlton, she said,' replied Rudge. 'Miss Fitzgerald – that is, Mrs Holland – ' (Mr Dakers groaned faintly) 'mentioned that they were going to a dance this evening. I should be glad, sir – '

'A dance at the Carlton?' interrupted the lawyer. 'She must be out of her senses. T'chk, t'chk, t'chk. Most distressing. I am not quite clear upon the point of law involved, but if I remember right, the Master of the Rolls held in the case of – dear me! I think I shall have to take Counsel's opinion. In the meanwhile I thank you very much for apprising me of these events. I shall go and see my client immediately, and – '

'I hope you will, sir, and I should be very glad if you could persuade her to come back at once. Mr and Mrs Holland will be subpoenaed, of course, but in the meantime it would be desirable – '

'Of course, of course,' replied Mr Dakers, 'most unfortunate and unbecoming. I shall make a point of advising her to return home without delay.'

'Thank you, sir, and I should be very glad, if I might have a word with you at some time myself. There are one or two little matters which I should like to have cleared up, in connection with a document we have here.'

'Oh!' said Mr Dakers. 'Yes?'

'In connection,' pursued Rudge, 'with a copy of a will, sir, made by John Martin Fitzgerald in 1915.'

'Ah!' said Mr Dakers. His voice sounded cautious. 'Yes. Yes, I see. In what way precisely, are you interested in that will?'

Rudge coughed.

'Well, sir, in a general way, as you might say. There's a brother mentioned in it, for example, and one or two other points that might be of interest.'

'Yes, I see. Well, Inspector, I think the best way will be for me to see you myself. I will endeavour to bring Miss Fitz – that is, Mrs Holland, down with me, but in any case, I shall arrive at Lingham tonight. Where shall I find you?'

'I shall be at Rundel Croft, sir.'

'Very well. I will telephone you when to expect me. When are you holding the inquest?'

'I should think the day after tomorrow, sir.'

'Yes. I shall be there, of course, to represent Mrs Holland. I think I should have been notified of this matter earlier. How is it that you did not ring me up until one o'clock?'

The Inspector would have liked to say that it was not his

business to notify the solicitors of suspected or suspicious persons, but he replied meekly that he had been busy and had only just had time to digest the contents of the will.

'It is unfortunate,' he added, 'that Mrs Holland did not herself acquaint you with the state of affairs.'

'It is; very,' replied the lawyer, dryly. 'Very well, Inspector, we will leave it like that.'

He rang off.

'And that's that,' thought Rudge, discontentedly. 'Nothing for it I suppose but to wait for the old blighter. Still, if he brings the Hollands back, that's something to the good. It's a pity there seems to be so little one can get on with. Hollands gone to town, Denny gone to town. Well, what about those cuttings?' He had not yet looked through the file of newspaper cuttings. They might perhaps suggest something in connection with Penistone's mysterious past. Or there might be other papers of interest.

The cuttings, as he had rather expected, seemed mostly to have to do with China, though a section of them seemed to be concerned with naval affairs. They dated from two years before the War and were neatly numbered and docketed to correspond with an alphabetical index in the Admiral's handwriting. Rudge noted a small bunch of cuttings collected under the heading, 'Denny, W.' These he turned over eagerly. They told him that Sir Wilfrid Denny had been for many years in the Hong Kong customs, retiring in 1921 with a title and pension. Apparently Denny had only come to Whynmouth in 1925, having previously lived in Hertfordshire. He was a widower of sixty-four, his wife having died fifteen years previously, in China. He had no surviving children, his only son had been killed in the War.

This was interesting. Sir Wilfrid, then, had also been connected with China. No doubt his friendship with the Admiral had dated from the latter's period of service on the Chinese station. Rudge returned the cuttings to their folder and was about to replace them in their file, when he noticed an endorsement on the folder 'See H 5 and X 57.'

What this cryptic reference might mean he could not think. He tried number five in the H file and found that it referred to a single cutting about an Able Seaman named Hendry who had been killed in a brawl in Hong Kong some years previously. This looked hopeful, but in turning to file X, he found no entries under that awkward letter. And indeed fifty-seven entries under X would, he thought, be unusual. 'X' must refer to something different. To what?

He turned to the alphabetical list, and under the letter F his eye was arrested by another entry. 'Fitzgerald, W.E.' The missing brother of Elma! Surely this would be of interest. Eagerly he turned up the file.

The folder marked 'Fitzgerald, W.E.' contained nothing but a slip of paper on which was scribbled in pencil, 'See X.'

'Damn X!' thought Rudge, 'where the devil has "X" gone to? Perhaps it was particularly private. The old boy may have hidden it in some safer place.'

Filled with excitement he began a thorough and careful search of the cabinet and the desk. The cabinet yielded nothing, nor, on a superficial examination, did the desk. At length, however, after lifting a mass of receipts and old cheque-books out of the well of the desk, Rudge came to a sliding bottom. He pushed this back and disclosed a key-hole. A little search of the Admiral's key-ring revealed a key of suitable size. He fitted it in. It turned easily. The door slid back and disclosed a folder similar to those in the cabinet and marked "X."

Before he had lifted it out, Rudge knew that he was to be disappointed. The folder lay flat as a visiting-card, and was, in fact, perfectly empty.

He was still gazing at it in chagrin, when the door opened to admit Jennie with a tea-tray.

'So you're back, Jennie,' said Rudge, pleasantly. 'It's very kind of you to bring me tea. Is your mother better?'

'Well, she's none so good, Mr Rudge, thank you. Doctor, he says it's her back. He's been down to her twice today and she's a bit easier now, but she's still very low.'

Rudge expressed his sympathy and noted that the sick mother seemed to be genuine enough. When he had eaten his tea, he continued his search for the missing contents of the folder, but without success. Three telephone calls came to break the monotony: one from the coroner, asking Rudge to come and see him first thing next morning; the next from Mr Dakers to say that he was still trying to get in touch with the Hollands and would be down on the eight-fifty; the third, much later, from the Vicar.

'I am speaking from the Charing Cross Hotel,' said the crisp Oxford voice. 'I find I shall be obliged to spend the night in town. I will ring you up again in the morning.'

Rudge thanked him, and rang off. Then after a minute or two he took an obvious precaution. He rang up the Charing Cross Hotel.

'Have you a Mr Mount – Rev Philip Mount – staying in the hotel?'

A slight pause; then: 'Yes, sir.'

'Is Mr Mount in the hotel?'

'I will enquire; will you hold the line, sir?'

A subdued babel; then the metallic clack of advancing footsteps and the rattle of the receiver.

'Hullo, yes: who is it, please?'

'That's him all right,' thought Rudge. Aloud he said, 'I just remembered something I wanted to ask you, sir,' and repeated his question about the length of the painter.

The Vicar confirmed Peter's statement and Rudge thanked him and rang off.

'All O.K. so far. I didn't like him going off like that, but he seems straight enough. Hope he is, because of these kids. But that rope's a teaser and no mistake.'

The eight-fifty arrived at Whynmouth in due course, and presently a taxi drew up at Rundel Croft. Rudge heard it turn up the drive and stop. His hopes rose, then sank again as he heard the door-bell.

'Mrs Holland would have walked in,' he muttered, disappointed. 'But no!' He cheered up again. 'The door's locked, of course, because of possible intruders.'

Emery's steps shuffled through the hall. The study door opened and a tall, thin, grey-headed man was shown in – alone.

'Mr Dakers?' said Rudge, rising and executing something between a salute and a bow.

'Yes,' said the lawyer, 'and you, I take it, are Inspector Rudge. Quite so. Well now, Inspector, I am sorry to say I have failed to see either Mr or Mrs Holland. They are certainly staying at the Carlton, and were expected back to dinner. I have left a note for Mrs Holland expressed in such terms that I think she can scarcely fail to pay attention to it. I need not say again how shocked and grieved I am at the whole occurrence.'

'I quite see your point of view, sir,' said Rudge, 'and I may add that the absence of Mr and Mrs Holland is making my own task none the easier. By the way, sir, I am in a somewhat peculiar positon in this house, with Admiral Penistone dead and nobody else in charge, so to speak, but I dare say I shan't be out of order in asking you if you have dined, before we go on to business.'

'Thank you, Inspector, thank you – but I require nothing. I am obliged to you. I should like to hear at once all the details of this sad affair.'

Rudge rapidly outlined the circumstances of the Admiral's death and the departure of his niece, while Mr Dakers contributed

a running commentary of 'Tuts' and 'Dear, dears.'

'There seems to be no doubt then, that Admiral Penistone was murdered.'

'None at all, I am afraid, sir.'

'He could not, I suppose, have – er – made away with himself and thrown the weapon into the river.'

This solution had not presented itself to Rudge, but he replied that judging by the position of the body and the general circumstances, he thought it almost outside the bounds or probability.

Mr Dakers nodded mournfully.

'I take it,' he said, with the air of a man taking a ferocious bull by the horns, 'that there is – er – no suspicion attaching to my ward or her husband?'

'Well,' said Rudge, cautiously, 'I couldn't say that suspicion attaches to any particular person so far. And other things being equal, the crime is certainly not the kind that we would suspect a young lady of. We know very little as yet about Mr Holland. Possibly you can help us there, sir?'

Mr Dakers shook his head.

'I know very little about him, beyond his name, and the fact that he was, in a manner, engaged to my ward.'

'Did the engagement have Admiral Penistone's consent, sir?'

The lawyer looked very shrewdly at him.

'I see what is in your mind, Inspector. Well, I suppose that is only to be expected, and it is quite useless for me to attempt to disguise the facts. So far as I know, Admiral Penistone, while reluctant as yet to give his consent to the marriage, had not definitely forbidden it. That is as much as I can tell you.'

'I see, sir. Now about this will of John Martin Fitzgerald; I presume that Mr Fitzgerald is dead, since you and the late Admiral were acting as trustees for Mrs Holland. Is this the copy of the actual will that was proved at the time of death?'

'It is. My friend John Fitzgerald was a solicitor; he died in 1916, and this was his latest will. I cannot say that it was a will I should have cared to draw up for him myself, nor was it, I think, a will he would willingly have drawn for one of his clients, but you know, Inspector, solicitors are notorious for making bad disposals of their own property.'

'What was the will proved at?'

'At about £50,000. That,' said Mr Dakers, 'did not represent the rewards of the law; the greater part of the money was inherited. But I had better begin from the beginning. John Fitzgerald married in 1888 Mary Penistone, the sister of the late Admiral. She

died in 1911, and left two surviving children: Walter Everett, born in 1889, and Elma Mary, born nine years later, in 1898. When Walter was twenty, he got into some kind of trouble at home. I think it had to do with a young woman who was attached to the family in a dependent position – in fact, the governess. His father was extremely angry and there was a terrible quarrel. Young Walter ran away from home and disappeared, and for some time his name was not allowed to be mentioned. You know the kind of thing. Elma, of course, was too young to be told what the trouble was about, but Mrs Fitzgerald always considered that her husband was too hard upon the boy.

'She died, as I say, in 1911, and I really think the worry about Walter helped to break up her health – in fact, as we used to say, it broke her heart. I know John Fitzgerald thought so, and it had a very softening effect upon him. He made efforts to find Walter, though without success, and he executed a will, dividing his property between Walter and Elma.

'Nothing was heard of Walter till the early part of 1915, when he sent his father a letter written from "Somewhere in France." He expressed himself as sorry for his previous bad behaviour and six years of neglect, hoped he was forgiven, and said that he was now endeavouring to turn over a new leaf and do his duty to his country. No word about where he had been in the interval. At the same time he enclosed "in case of accident" a will drawn in favour of his sister Elma. His father and sister wrote back at once telling him to come home as soon as he got leave, and that all would be forgiven and forgotten. He never did come home, though he wrote from time to time, and after the disastrous battle of Loos his name appeared in the lists of "missing, believed killed." His father was at that time a very sick man. He was suffering from Bright's disease, and had not very much longer to live. He absolutely refused to believe that Walter was dead. He had turned up before, he said, and would turn up again. Having in the meantime come into a large property, he re-drafted his will of 1911, leaving the disposition of his estate the same as before, but with certain additional clauses.

'I must now say a word about his brother-in-law, Admiral Penistone. He – you may know something about his history?'

'I have heard that there was some sort of interruption to his career in 1911.'

'Oh, you know about that? Yes, a disgraceful business. I need not go into details, but the affair was one which made it extremely unsuitable that he should be appointed as guardian of the young

girl. Understand me, I express no opinion as to whether Captain Penistone (as he was then) was actually to blame in the matter. But the mere fact that his name had been connected with such an unsavoury business should have been sufficient. However, John Fitzgerald, who never would believe ill of anybody – '

'An unusual trait in a lawyer,' Rudge could not help remarking.

'My good man, a lawyer in his private capacity and in his professional capacity may be two very different people,' retorted Mr Dakers with some asperity. 'John Fitzgerald could not think ill of his wife's brother. He maintained that Penistone had been unfairly treated, and by way of showing the world what he thought about it, he made him Elma's trustee, and inserted that preposterous clause about her marraige.'

'You yourself,' suggested Rudge, 'accepted co-trusteeship with Admiral Penistone.'

'And if I had not,' said Mr Dakers, 'he might have appointed some other black sheep who needed whitewashing. No. I made the best of a bad job, out of consideration for my poor friend's daughter. And I must say, in justice to Admiral Penistone, that I have had no cause to complain of his management of his ward's affairs. Although his manner was abrupt and at times disagreeable, I believe him to have been a perfectly honest man as regards money, nor was there anything unbecoming about the household he set up for his niece. Had there been, I should, of course, have interfered.'

'By whose wish was it that Miss Fitzgerald went to live with her uncle?'

'By her father's. I thought it unsuitable, but I could produce no valid grounds of opposition. Elma's share of the money was invested, by my advice, in sound securities, and the payments made to her quarterly by the trustees.'

'A very nice little income,' remarked Rudge.

'About £1,500 a year.'

'It surprises me a little,' sid Rudge, 'that the Admiral did not keep up a more elaborate establishment for his niece. This house is pleasant enough, but it is very remote, and they did not see much company, or so I understand.'

'That is true,' admitted Mr Dakers, 'but it was not altogether Admiral Penistone's fault. He himself naturally shrank from going much into society, and from 1914 to 1918 he was, of course, on active service, but he put no restrictions upon his niece. She was given a good education and had the advantage of two London seasons under the chaperonage of a very suitable lady, but I fancy

that society life was distasteful to her.'

'Odd that she should not have got married earlier,' said Rudge. 'A young lady with £25,000 or so should have had plenty of offers.'

The lawyer shrugged his shoulders.

'I fancy that Elma was – a little difficult,' he said. 'She is perhaps not – attractive, in what I may call the marrying sense. There were some – needy persons, of course, but they were not encouraged. Admiral Penistone would not have dreamed of consenting to a marriage except with a man of independent means. And then, unfortunately, there was the scandal about Walter.'

'What was that?'

'Why, that happened in 1920. Obviously the first thing that seemed advisable was to obtain from the Courts leave to presume Walter's death. We could not do anything till 1919, after the release of the British prisoners of war in Germany. His name was in none of the lists, and we expected to encounter no difficulty. Curiously enough, however, a man turned up who had been in Walter's unit in 1915, and this man stated that he had seen Walter alive in Buda-Pesth after the cessation of hostilities. He said he had not spoken to him, but that he had no doubt whatever of his identity. Walter was, I believe, a strikingly handsome man – he certainly was handsome as a boy. He was very like his mother, who was a most beautiful woman, much better-looking than her brother the Admiral, though there was a strong family resemblance.

'Well, of course, that meant further delay and more enquiries. We could get no news of Walter at all, but in view of the evidence of the soldier, the Court refused to presume death – naturally. Meanwhile, the affair had a very unfortunate sequel. As soon as it became known that Walter had probably not been killed during the War, we got the news that there was a warrant out for his arrest in Shanghai for forgery, if you please.'

'In Shanghai?'

'Yes. The warrant dated from 1914. Apparently Walter, when he left the country in 1909, had entered the employment of the Anglo-Asiatic Tobacco Company. He was in Hong Kong at first and in 1913 was transferred to Shanghai. He got into some sort of financial difficulties, I suppose. Anyway, he forged a signature of a client of the Company to a large cheque and ran away. The War broke out just about that time, and I suppose that in the general confusion the matter was held up or overlooked, till the news that Walter was supposed to have been killed in 1915 put an end to it. However, when it appeared likely that Walter had survived after all, up it all came again. The Admiral was very greatly distressed.

This further scandal, cropping up just when his own old trouble seemed to have been forgotten, soured his temper completely.'

'I take it Admiral Penistone had rejoined the Navy during the War.'

'Yes. He was a fine officer, and they were glad to get him. He did good service and finally retired for the second time at the end of the War with the rank of Rear-Admiral. But if other people had forgotten his previous troubles, he hadn't. They preyed on his mind, and this business about Walter finished him altogether. One man who had been semi-engaged to Elma withdrew rather pointedly when he heard about the brother, and Admiral Penistone said that he would not have his niece subjected to insult. He packed up bag and baggage and took her away with him to live in Cornwall. And there they stayed until a month ago. All this happened in 1920. Nothing has been heard of Walter since. So you see that the situation is rather a peculiar one.'

'Yes,' said Rudge thoughtfully. 'Walter seems to be awkwardly placed. If he comes forward and shows himself, he probably goes to penal servitude. If he doesn't come forward, he can't get his money.'

'That is the situation precisely. On the other hand, if he is dead, his share of the money goes to Elma under his will of 1914. Provided, of course, that is, that the witness was correct in stating that he was actually still alive after his father's death. If not, it still goes to her as residuary legatee under her father's will.'

'In that case Walter's death would be to his sister's financial advantage. I see. But now, Mr Dakers, how do things stand with reference to Mrs Holland's own share of her father's money? I presume that, the Admiral being now dead, the clause about the consent to the marriage becomes void.'

'That is exactly the difficulty,' replied Mr Dakers uneasily. 'The point of view taken by the Court in such cases is that the testator cannot have required the beneficiary to perform impossibilities. Thus it has been held, over and over again, that in the case of the condition becoming impossible of fulfilment, through Act of God, the gift remains.'

'Act of God?' queried Rudge.

'Yes. In the case of consent being required to a marriage, for instance, if the person whose consent is required dies before the marriage, then the condition is impossible of fulfilment, and the gift stands.'

'Quite so,' said Rudge, 'but what does Act of God mean precisely?'

'Well,' said the lawyer, a little reluctantly Rudge thought, 'that means – well, practically speaking, it means, under conditions which the beneficiary could not have prevented.'

'Let us speak quite plainly,' said Rudge. 'If Elma Holland should be found to have been concerned in Admiral Penistone's murder – '

'Of course, in *that* case,' said Mr Dakers, 'there would be no question of her inheriting. The law expressly forbids a criminal to profit by the fruits of the crime. But surely that does not arise.'

'I should hope not,' said Rudge. 'Then so far as I can see, Mrs Holland is now entitled to her inheritance?'

'Ye-es,' said the lawyer. 'I hope the Court will look upon it from that point of view. The difficulty lies in the extreme haste with which the marriage followed upon the death. I will be frank with you, Mr Rudge. I think it would be possible to contest the case, and I think that, if that occurred, we should have to take one of two lines about it. We could, of course, say that she intended to ask the necessary consent before the marriage and that, but for the death, she would have had time to ask for it. Now, of course, she did ask for it – several times.'

'With any reasonable expectation of ever getting it?' asked Rudge. 'Mr Dakers,' he added, as the lawyer appeared to hesitate, 'I will go so far as to tell you that I have witnesses here who are prepared to say that the Admiral appeared not to approve of the marriage.'

'Precisely,' said Mr Dakers; 'I must admit that there was – an appearance at any rate of objection. And that being the case, I do not quite know what the Court would think of a marriage so hastily concluded. It might be inferred that the Admiral was violently opposed to the marriage, and that, therefore, the marriage was undertaken with a definite intention of frustrating the object of the testator. The indecent haste attending the ceremony affords, you see, in itself a presumption that the death of the Admiral removed the only obstacle to the marriage.'

'And that being so,' said Rudge, 'an allegation might be made that the Admiral's death was not altogether – shall we say, by Act of God.'

'If such a monstrous allegation were made,' replied Mr Dakers, 'it would have to be refuted; in which case, the mere fact that the hastiness of the marriage might jeopardise the absolute right to the estate would constitute a very good answer to the charge.'

'Yes,' said Rudge, seizing on the weak point of the argument, 'provided the beneficiary was aware how the law stood.' He con-

sidered for a moment, and then said:

'And your second line of defence would be?'

'To show that the ceremony was not arranged until after death had made it impossible to obtain consent. If it were so – though I do not see how a licence could have been taken out in the time – it would be a complete answer to the contesting party. It has frequently so been held. For instance, in *Collett v. Collett,* the mother, whose consent was required, died in 1856. In 1865 the daughter married. The Master of the Rolls held that the gift over (that is, to the person who was to get the money in case the condition was not fulfilled, you understand) will not take effect, if the performance of the condition has become impossible through the Act of God and no default of the person who had to perform it.' (Mr Dakers, reading these words from a note-book, glanced over his pince-nez at Rudge, who said nothing. He resumed.) ' "Here it is reasonably certain that the mother, if she had lived, would have given her consent to this marriage, one eligible in all respects." There, you see, Inspector, is our difficulty. The Court seems to have based its decision to some extent on what the mother might reasonably have been expected to do.'

'I see,' said Rudge. 'And in this case the Admiral's consent could not very well be presumed with any certainty.'

'There again,' said the lawyer, 'who is to say? If the eligibility of the marriage, as such, is a factor to be taken into consideration, there seems to be no reason why Admiral Penistone should not have consented. Holland, so far as I know anything about him, seems to be a respectable man of suitable age and standing and with sufficient money of his own to take him out of the class of mere fortune-hunters. It is a very pretty case, Mr Rudge, and if I were not personally concerned it would give me great pleasure to see it thrashed out.'

Rudge was about to reply, when the sound of an approaching car was heard. A slight commotion followed at the front door. Voices and footsteps sounded and a minute after, the study door was thrown open.

'Inspector,' said Arthur Holland as he followed his wife into the room, 'we owe you an apology for running off like this, but we were in a hurry and were afraid you might delay us. Is this Mr Dakers? How do you do, sir? My wife and I received your note, and thought we had better come and set your mind at rest.'

'Thank you,' said Mr Dakers, rather dryly. 'Well, Elma, you have married in very great haste. I trust you will not have to repent it at leisure.'

Elma laughed. There was a faint flush of colour in her usually pale cheeks and she looked, Rudge thought, rather a prey to some consuming excitement than radiant with the happiness of a newly married woman.

'You have made a mistake, Mr Dakers,' she said. 'I haven't jeopardised anything or compromised anything. Look at that.'

She handed him a sheet of paper. Mr Dakers settled his glasses more firmly on his nose, read it with a 'Tut-tut' or two of astonishment, and handed it over to Rudge.

'That solves our problems, I think, Inspector.'

Rudge looked at the paper. It was typewritten, with the exception of the signature, and ran –

> *'I willingly give my consent to the marriage of my niece, Elma Mary Fitzgerald, with Arthur Holland.*
>
> *(Signed)* H.L. PENISTONE.'

It was dated the 9th August.

Inspector Rudge looked at Holland.

'When did this come into your possession, sir?'

'My wife gave it to me this morning,' he said. 'She had it last night from the Admiral.'

'At what time was that, ma'am?' enquired the Inspector.

'Just after midnight,' replied the girl, in a curious flat tone which reminded Rudge of his interview with her earlier in the day.

'After midnight? Did you see your uncle alive after midnight?'

'Why, of course,' interrupted Holland. 'I saw him myself. Yes, I know, Inspector! I didn't want to tell you about that because I was afraid you might stop us from going to town. But I'll come clean now. I saw the Admiral alive here in his study at a quarter past twelve last night.'

8

By Ronald A. Knox

THIRTY-NINE ARTICLES OF DOUBT

In the nature of the case, a policeman's life is bound up with surprises. A considerable part of the community is only too ready to set playful booby-traps for him, stretching wires across garden-paths or waiting in dark alleys with half a brick concealed in the foot of a stocking. Rudge had not risen to his inspectorship without some experiences of the kind, and he had come near to achieving that unwondering attitude which is (the old poet assures us) part of the stuff of happiness. But this sudden admission almost caught him off his guard. Grice's statement that the body had been a corpse since some time before midnight had seemed so evident a point of departure; all the other features of the case had grouped themselves round it so obligingly – the possibility of a journey into Whynmouth and foul play down-stream, the visit of the strange car, the darkness, the loneliness, the set of the tides. (By the way, why had he been so certain about the tides? Oh, yes, Neddy Ware; odd that Neddy should have been so positive about it.) Too late he realised that no single piece of evidence, except the misleading infallibility of the expert, had excluded the possibility of a murder well after midnight. And this, it seemed now, was what must have happened. Of course, Holland might be lying, but it was difficult to see his motive; why abandon a first-class alibi at the Lord Marshall for the honour of being the last man who saw deceased alive? It would be a fool's game, and Holland did not look like a fool.

In a moment, habit reasserted itself; he had drawn out the inevitable note-book, and was turning over the pages to a blank, remembering not to moisten his finger as he did so. 'I think I ought to tell you, sir,' he explained, 'that you are not bound to make any statement. You know well enough that you will have to be called at the inquest; and if you prefer to reserve – '

'My defence?' interrupted Holland, with heavy raillery. 'It is too kind of you. But, you see, here I am, all ready binged up with a cock-and-bull story carefully prepared to mislead you; it would be

a pity not to get it off my chest while I'm word-perfect. You would like to get me in jug first, wouldn't you, and take down my statement with no witnesses, so that you could cook it afterwards? I prefer the present occasion, if you don't mind.'

Rudge just checked himself in time from reminding the unseasonable jester that he wouldn't do himself any good by this kind of thing. After all, Holland evidently belonged to the opulent classes, who get the benefit of the doubt. 'Certainly, sir,' he amended, with some frigidity of manner. 'But I think perhaps if Mrs Holland – '

'You mean you want to be certain that we both pitch the same yarn? Well, it's bad luck, for a man on his honeymoon. But perhaps, Elma, if you wouldn't mind – ' A rapid look passed between them; on his side, it registered adoring confidence; on hers, was it a frown over his reckless demeanour? Or was there not, after all, a faint suspicion of disgust? Mr Dakers saved the situation, by indicating that nothing would suit him better than a turn in the garden with – in short, with Mrs Holland; there was much that needed discussion, he felt. And Rudge was left alone with his chief witness.

'Now, sir,' he opened briskly, 'when we last met you told a tale which was, you will admit, in contradiction with what you said just now?'

'These giant intellects! Yes, I told you I was in bed at Whynmouth. Actually I was here. A discrepancy.'

'Excuse me, sir, but what I'm getting at is this – was it *all* untrue, what you told me? For instance, I have it down here that you were not seen by anybody after eleven o'clock. Do you still stick to that? It doesn't seem quite so likely, does it? Perhaps you would try to remember anybody you passed on your way out here – you will have walked, I suppose? Or did you come by the omnibus?'

'The last 'bus, my dear Rudge, as you and I know very well, leaves at half-past ten. No, I walked; and I passed some of the gentlemen who had recently left the Lord Marshall, but they did not look as if they were likely to preserve a clear memory of their impressions. There were some lovers about, but I am afraid I cannot swear to their features, and I doubt if they could to mine. I had no speech with anybody.'

'Didn't you meet one of our men, for example?'

There was a fraction of a pause, almost as if a ready invention were suddenly at fault.

'No, I think not,' was the answer given. 'Once I looked up a

side-street, and thought I saw a policeman's lantern being flashed, but it might have been somebody lighting a bicycle lamp. I can't remember which street it was, now.'

'And you would be coming straight along the main road?'

'All the way.'

'Now, then, sir, let's get at this, if you don't mind. Were you meaning to pay this rather late visit all the time? Or were you delayed on the road? Or did the idea just come to you suddenly, when it was already closing-time or close on it?'

'My dear Inspector, you are a little elementary. I have no doubt the Boots told you that he saw my shoes out in the passage. And therefore the story I have decided to tell you is that I was already in process of going to bed when an accident made me alter my purpose. Looking out from my window, I saw a man turning away from the front door whom I seemed to recognise by the set of his shoulders. Then I told myself I was a fool; something about the hat convinced me that he was a clergyman. Then reflection told me that clergymen are not thrown out of pubs at closing-time. And I felt convinced, I don't know how, that it was poor old Penistone. I wanted to see him, as you know; I threw on the rest of my clothes hastily and went out into the street. There was no sign of him then, of course, but I hurried down the road I supposed he would be taking; and in the end – well, in the end I came all the way here.'

'On the off-chance of finding him still awake, late at night like that?'

'Inspector, I do not know whether you are a married man, or whether your bosom has always been impervious to the softer emotions. But if you will ask anyone who had been violently in love, he will tell you that a lover thinks nothing of walking a mile or two merely to stand outside a window and sentimentalise among the rhododendrons. That is all I would have done, if I had not found the lights going strong in the poor old Admiral's study.'

'You saw them as you came along?'

'Do you know, you would get much more information if you didn't try to catch a fellow out all the time. Of course, I didn't see them from the road. I had come round into the lawn, and saw them from there. I went up and knocked, and the Admiral let me in through the french window. He told me I had come just in time, "quite dramatic," he said – he was in the act of making out for his niece the document we had been waiting for these weeks past, his consent to our marriage. And, sure enough, it was on the table when we came into the drawing-room.'

'That would be – about a quarter past twelve, you say?'

'I didn't notice the time exactly. But I had started from the Lord Marshall soon after eleven, which is closing-time. I walked slowly after I had got out of Whynmouth, so I can't have been here till twelve or so; that's how I worked it out.'

'Yes, I see. Now, was it your impression that Admiral Penistone was just meaning to turn in when you came? Was he in his dressing-gown, for example? Was he smoking, or drinking a whisky and soda or anything? You see what I mean, sir – I want to find out if he went outside after you had left, and if so, why.'

'Well, I can't help you much there. He had a pipe in his mouth part of the time, to be sure. The only thing which made me feel he had not thought of bed-time yet was the litter on that desk; papers lying there, you know, taken out of their pigeon-holes. The Admiral wasn't the kind of man to go to bed without putting his papers to bed first.'

'Ah, that's very interesting. And you haven't any idea, I suppose, what papers?'

'Not the least, I'm afraid. I dare say in your job you sometimes have to look over a man's shoulder to see what he is reading, but we have a stricter code in the jute trade.'

Rudge felt the offensiveness of the reflection, but he achieved a passable smile. 'You didn't stay long, then? Just thanked him, maybe, and said you'd be getting back to Whynmouth?'

'Hardly more than that. He let me out at the french window again, and I went back to the Lord Marshall in that frame of mind in which a man finds himself, my dear Inspector, when he realises that the greatest dream of his life has come true. That is to say, walking on air, and not noticing much that went on round me.'

'Not even how you unlocked the front door of the hotel?'

'Why, I am afraid I had taken my precautions about that. I knew that Boots is fond of going to bed as early as he can, and does not like to have his sleep disturbed. So I was careful to leave the back-yard door on the latch – you will find that it had no bolts on it – and Mrs Davis, I am afraid, was none the wiser. I thought best not; she talks.'

'You're right there, sir. All the same, I wish you had been a little less quiet in your comings and goings; they'll put you through it properly at the inquest. But, of course, you'd leave your boots outside the door, so we'll have evidence that you were in before the front door was opened?'

'My dear Inspector, you think of everything. You want me to say that I was wearing, at a quarter-past eleven on the way to Rundel Croft, the same pair of boots which were outside my door

at half-past. Believe me, your technique is improving. But the sad truth is that when I got up and followed my phantom Admiral, I put on another pair – suède shoes, which one does not have cleaned, if one is wise, at the Lord Marshall.'

'Ah, that explains it. I suppose you did not by any chance bring a copy of the *Evening Gazette* with you to Rundel Croft?'

'I never read it. Its politics nauseate me.'

Rudge held his note-book at arm's length, as if studying an artistic effect.

'Well, that gives a clear account of your movements, Mr Holland. Now, there are one or two questions I would like to ask; but, as they don't bear directly on what happened last night, I shan't be surprised if you won't tell me. The first is just this: Why was it that Admiral Penistone at first didn't want to see you marry his niece, and then changed his mind?'

'I think you must be very busy looking for mysteries if you make a mystery out of that. If you come to think of it, I have only known the family a matter of three or four weeks. I first met my wife, since you are kind enough to be so interested in our private affairs, at Sir Wilfrid Denny's, just after she came here; and it was love at first sight with both of us. The Admiral – well, he was a man of circumspection, and he wanted to see more of me, I suppose. When his niece wrote telling me to come down to Whynmouth again, because she had good news for me, I only just dared to hope it was this. (That was when I got the licence.) But it seems my respectability was more self-evident to him than it is to you.'

'Oh, come now, no offence taken, I hope. And then there's this second question, which sounds impolite, but I must ask it. Why were you in such a hurry to get married, Mr Holland?'

Holland paused this time quite unmistakably; but his face did not suggest guilt or duplicity; he looked more like an honest man who knows more than he is at liberty to tell, and is not quite sure how much he can tell without a breach of trust. That, at least, is how Rudge read his expression for the moment or two while the embarrassment lasted. Then: 'Inspector,' said Holland, with a more serious note in his voice, 'you mustn't ask me to be responsible for a woman's fancies. I know you think it was very shocking to go and get married like that; very quietly owing to mourning in the bride's family, funeral bakemeats scarcely cold, and so on. But, well, I think the truth is Elma is far more nervous than her self-command lets you see. I think she was altogether rattled by what happened here that night, and she felt she was in danger here; who could tell she would not be the next victim of this

mysterious vendetta, or whatever it was? She wanted to get away from the place, and she wanted to have a man close to her, now that her uncle was gone, who would have a natural right to be her protector. There's that about me, you see; I may not be worthy of Elma, but I've got the right *format* for a chucker-out. And I suppose that's how she looked at it.'

'Yes, I see that. Now, may I ask you this? – did Admiral Penistone himself, when you last saw him, give you any idea of what had made him change his mind? Did he explain at all?'

'If you'd known him, you'd know that he wasn't a man for explaining things. He was short and sharp in conversation – hated to waste a word. And that night, why, he hardly said more than "Good evening," and "Come this way, I've something to show you," and "There, will that make you any happier?" Otherwise he just puffed at his pipe; that was his idea of conversation.'

'Ah, he was a great smoker, was he? Always the same pipe, I'll be bound; your true smoker never uses more than one.'

'He wasn't, then. Why, you can see for yourself how they're scattered over the mantelpice. If one wouldn't draw, he'd take to another.'

'I wonder – do you think it possible that he had anything on his mind, and that was why he said so little? Of course, I'm anxious to find out whether the unfortunate gentleman knew at all what was coming to him. Did he look worried or tired, for example, when you saw him?'

'Not that I noticed. No, not that I noticed. Of course, when I saw him in the study the only lamp burning was that reading lamp just beside you, which has a thick, green shade over it, as you see; you don't see much of a man's face when he is standing up and the light is all being thrown on his desk. But if you ask me whether his tone of voice suggested excitement or worry, I'd say, No.'

'Well, Mr Holland, I think I've asked you all that I wanted. Oh, except this – he wasn't wearing an overcoat, was he, by any chance?'

'In his study? On a hot summer night? You might as well ask whether he was wearing chain armour.'

'I know it sounds unlikely, sir. But there it is – he was in a great-coat when he was found. And of course . . . by the way, Mr Holland, when you thought you saw the Admiral outside your window, would he be wearing a great-coat then?'

'Now, what a fool one is about noticing things! I see him as in a great-coat now; but then, I know about the body . . . I feel as if he hadn't had a great-coat on; but then, I may be arguing with myself;

I may be saying to myself that I must have noticed it if it had been worn, on a hot night like that. If only my memory worked by eye! No, Inspector, you may put me in jug, but I should be misleading you if I tried to give you a plain answer to a plain question.'

'Well, thank you for what you *have* told me, sir. Now, about Mrs Holland . . . '

'If you ask me, I expect Mrs Holland will want her dinner. It doesn't seem to occur to you that you're rather spoiling our honeymoon. Look here, we've booked rooms at the Lord Marshall. Elma said she couldn't sleep in this house just yet. I don't dare to think what Mrs Davis's dinner must be like when it gets cold. Can't you leave it till tomorrow and put my wife on the rack then?'

'Well, sir, it's like this. I've got to see the coroner tomorrow morning, and I've got to give him as full an account of the case as I can; and you and Mrs Holland, look at it whatever way you will, are going to be important witnesses. But if you think Mrs Holland would sooner see me first thing tomorrow, why, there's a policeman on duty in the Square, and if I may pass the word to him, I'll feel certain I know where to find you. Perhaps if I was to climb up behind, you wouldn't mind giving me a lift as far as Whynmouth?'

'For fear we might be tempted to take a wrong turning? Well, Inspector, I suppose we've deserved that. All right, come on; we'll play fair this time.'

Rudge sat in darkness at the back of the car, instinctively spying on the two figures whose outlines were blurred against the illuminated patch of road. The impressions he had already formed of the couple were on the whole confirmed; there was little talk between them, and when there was any the initiative seemed to come from Holland; you saw, in the attentive droop of his shoulder sideways, the model of the deferential lover, whereas Elma looked straight in front of her and hardly moved when she answered. But then, she was tired, no doubt; she had much to think of; perhaps she even felt sorrow for the old man whose fortunes she had shared for so many years, now lying under that dust-sheet in the mortuary.

Rudge made an excuse to follow them into the hotel; he was privately concerned to make sure about the locking of that door into the backyard. The Lord Marshall is an old-fashioned hotel, and there is no private entrance for visitors; they have to pass along a narrow passage, with a slight recess in the middle of it which gives you a back view of the gentlemen who are refreshing themselves at the public bar. One of these made a half-turn as they

entered, and Rudge had two simultaneous impressions – that he recognised the man, and that the man did not want to be recognised. At least, he shrank back as they approached, and his face was hidden in the darkness of the space under the stairway. Returning from a mercifully brief interview with Mrs Davis, Rudge found him again and verified his guess. It was Croppedhead, the *Gazette* reporter. By a promise of seeing him next day, Rudge managed to stave off his eager questionings about the progress of the case. Then he had a word with the policeman in the Square, and went back to the seclusion of his own rooms.

Inspector Rudge, we must regretfully admit, was a quite ordinary man. He did not solace himself with the violin, or the cocaine-bottle; he did not tie knots in string, or collect scarabs, or distinguish himself in any way by sidelines. The rooms to which he returned were quite ordinary rooms, from which he had not even troubled to remove the landlady's decorations; the whisky he took out of the cupboard was so well known that the mention of its name would be an unnecessary advertisement; the same may be said of the tobacco with which he filled his pipe. If the full truth must be confessed, Inspector Rudge was so far human that he took off his boots and replaced them with a pair of dressing-slippers. Then he got down to the night's work; and that consisted of selecting from the mass of material he had accumulated during the day the points that seemed most likely to repay investigation. These points he jotted down, in the form of questions; he added no written comment, except an occasional memorandum; but as each question was reduced to verbal shape he looked up at the ceiling and let his mind play around the possibilities which it suggested. The questions are here reproduced, with a summary of the cogitations to which each one led. When he counted them up, his orthodox mind was delighted to find them exactly thirty-nine in number.

1. *Why did Penistone come to Lingham, and why did Sir Wilfrid mind?* Altogether, there was too much of the China Station about this business. On the face of it, there was nothing particularly improbable in the fact that two men well acquainted with China should be living at such close range. But Mrs Davis, representing the local gossip, had seen some significance in it; and, quite unexpectedly, she had volunteered the information that Sir Wilfrid did not seem over-pleased at the neighbourhood. Was it conceivable that there had been a connection between them in the past? A guilty connection? If so, on which side did the guilt lie? On

Sir Wilfrid's surely. Rudge's mind, do what he would, was apt to travel in official grooves; and the notion of blackmail forced itself on him. The more so, because Sir Wilfrid appeared to be in straitened circumstances. *Mem. – Apply to the bank in the hope of getting the Admiral's passbook; hardly possible to have the handling of Sir Wilfrid's.*

2. *Why did Jennie think that Penistone and Elma seemed more like husband and wife than uncle and niece?* Probably mere gossip. Jennie had, after all, seen the couple but a short time; the fact that they managed the household – presumably – in financial partnership would give them, to the girl's mind, the air of equals. Once again Rudge's fancy toyed with the idea of an impersonation; yet it seemed quite impossible that any such impersonation should long persist; Dakers would see through it if nobody else did.

3. *Why was Elma so familiar with the French maid? And why did the French maid leave so suddenly?* The two questions could be treated as one; if there was any significance in the former it would probably provide an explanation for the other. The allegation that Célie had found the place dull was surely a mere excuse; a Frenchwoman who had stood years of Cornish exile would necessarily take more than a week to grow tired of Lingham; Whynmouth, after all, boasted a picture-palace. It might, of course, be some romance or tragedy below stairs which happened to have come to a head at the moment. But it seemed more natural to assume that the move was the cause of the flight – yes, you might almost call it a flight, since there was money owing. Of course, if Célie were not a mere servant, it might be that money was no object to her. But why leave just after a move? Surely it would have been more plausible to give notice when the move took effect. And that meant – that ought to mean that Célie, on coming to Lingham, had found something there which was unexpectedly disconcerting to her; or that circumstances arose at Lingham, which would not have arisen in Cornwall. Too short a time for romance. Had Célie been in Lingham before? *Mem. – Trace, if possible, Célie's present whereabouts and past references.*

4. *Why, again, on Jennie's testimony, was so little love lost between Elma and Holland, on her side at any rate?* Once more, it might be mere gossip. Who was it who was credited with a 'miserably low standard of intoxication'? Perhaps Jennie had an unusually high standard of walking-out. Jennie peered at you; and a couple of shy lovers might have been at pains to disengage their hands at the warning of her heavy-footed entrance. But if there was anything to it, it suggested that the marriage, on one side at

least, was a *mariage de convenance.* On which side? Hers, according to the evidence; and, to be sure, she had had an earlier disappointment; her youth was slipping from her. It might be, too, that she was anxious to deal with her capital, instead of having the interest doled out to her by trustees. But where was the need here? She lived simply; she dressed dowdily. Holland, of course, might be an adventurer; but, if so, he was a clever feigner of love.

5. *What did Elma do with her money?* This question arose naturally out of the last. How simple life would be for the police, if we all audited our accounts, like the public charities! Rundel Croft was not a house of pretensions; its grounds were negligible. Even if Elma paid more than a half-share – and the Admiral must have had *some* money – it was hard to believe that £1,200 a year could be needed for upkeep. Yet the capital was hers; there was no obvious need of saving. Once again the word blackmail suggested itself; but this time it seemed to be the wrong way about. If Sir Wilfrid were the blackmailer, why did his victims settle so close? And why did he manifest annoyance? *Mem. – Once more, consult the Admiral's pass-book.*

6. *What part did Walter play in the background of these lives?* If he was dead, then his influence only persisted in so far as he was keeping Elma out of half of her inheritance; and this, in view of her already comfortable circumstances, seemed a factor that could be neglected. But if he were alive – what would be his influence then? Was he popular with his family, or had the story of his disgrace obliterated all affection? It was odd, when you came to think of it, that a household so connected with a soldier who disappeared in the War should have no photograph of him exposed in study or drawing-room. And yet – there was the scandal of the cheque; awkward, perhaps, to have visitors saying 'Who's that?' If he were alive, what was he doing; what would he be doing? It seemed unlikely that a man of his antecedents would let a fortune pass him by without a struggle. Yet, granted he were alive and were attempting to reinstate himself, what could he stand to gain by committing a crime of this sort, or inducing others to commit it? 'Point is, disappearance of valuable uncle,' Rudge found himself quoting. The corpse of one trustee does not make a legacy.

7. *Why did Ware think the Admiral had altered since he last saw him?* People do change their looks, of course, and a man labouring under a long grievance may be excused for losing something of his old cheerfulness and vitality. But the photographs at Rundel Croft, evidently dating back to the period of Ware's

reminiscences, bore a quite unmistakable resemblance to the man found drowned. Again the wild suggestion of an impersonation flooded across the Inspector's mind; again common sense told him that a long-sustained impersonation is a practical impossibility. Was it conceivable that Ware did recognise the corpse he fished out; then, for some reason, pretended not to; then, by way of explaining his lapse of memory, invented this story of altered looks? But again, why should Ware pretend ignorance? Why not have said, 'I've seen the man before somewhere, but I can't remember the circumstances'? *Mem. – Ask Dakers about this.*

8. *Does Mr Davis's allusion to a runaway wife at the Vicarage lead anywhere?* It seemed a long shot; but so far, apart from Elma, there was no woman in the case except the woman in the car, untraced, and this phantom from Lingham's past, who might surely be expected to give the place a wide berth. It has been suggested that Rudge's mind ran obstinately in grooves of police experience; and the *cherchez la femme* is almost the first item in the policeman's decalogue. But how to make enquiries about Mrs Mount's history since her elopement? The Vicar could supply the name of his guilty rival, but it would be brutality to ask him; and even so the traces of a ten-years-old disappearance would almost certainly have been obliterated by now. No, Rudge decided, he was becoming fantastic. Mrs Mount had never lived at Lingham; presumably her husband had never heard the names of Denny or Penistone at the time of her desertion. There was not even a loose thread to be picked up here.

Rudge drew a line across this page. So far, his questions were all questions which might have been asked, though there would have been no reason for the police to ask them, yesterday afternoon, when the river ran peacefully between the Vicarage and Rundel Croft, the two boys sporting in it with no shadow of tragedy to overawe their high spirits; when the Admiral's brisk walk and sharp voice proclaimed him very much alive, and no pale corpse rested in the Whynmouth mortuary. Now he must get on to the crime itself; its circumstances and the traces it had left. He hitched his chair up a little closer to the table, took a meditative pull out of his glass, emptied out and refilled his pipe, then returned methodically to his self-imposed catechism.

9. *Why did Elma dress up that night to meet the Vicar?* Here again you were dealing with impressions, the impessions of a rather fanciful servant-girl. But one must not despise the testimony of the expert; and a lady's maid, in the little world of her

own limited interests, is an observant critic. Any deviation from the normal, however slight, is worth watching as a possible hint that crime did not come altogether like a bolt from the blue; that somebody was up to something beforehand. But in this case who was up to what? If Elma thought she was going to meet Holland that night, odd that it should have been her uncle, not she, who was in a hurry to get back to Rundel Croft. And if a meeting was projected, it was evidently a secret one, no need, then, to draw attention to it by tricking herself out for the occasion. On the other hand, Mr Mount seemed hardly the man to appreciate a lady's costume; hardly the man whom the most enterprising of adventuresses would have set out to vamp. Old English sports, No. 82, Vamping the Vicar. Was it conceivable that Elma was up to some game which involved leaving Rundel Croft later that night; that she meant to change her clothes for the purpose, and was at pains to put on elaborate evening dress so as to make the later change a more effective disguise? *Mem. – Ask Jennie if any other wardrobe items showed signs of disturbance or hasty folding this morning.*

10. *Why did she hide the dress afterwards?* At least, that was going a little too fast. But she had certainly made a point of packing the dress, and of packing it herself. The conclusion, though not irresistible, was certainly probable, that there was something about that dress which she did not want even a confidential eye to discover. But that meant, unless she was going to tell a quite different story under tomorrow's cross-examination, that Elma had something to conceal, and was giving a false account of her movements. If, after leaving the boat-house, she went straight to bed, it was impossible that any tell-tale evidence – a split or a stain – should have made its appearance since her good night to the Admiral. The trouble was that since Elma had moved to the Lord Marshall, Jennie was no longer in a position to report. *Mem. – If there is a chambermaid at the inn who doesn't talk, ask her to find out whether that dress ever came back from London.*

11. *Was it Penistone who went down to Whynmouth that night?* The evidence came from two sources; both were uncertain, one quite possibly mendacious. Rudge had satisfied himself that the lighting outside the Lord Marshall was particularly inadequate. The direct statement made to the Boots, who could hardly be lying, showed that the man who called at the door was either the Admiral or an imposter who was impersonating him. If Holland's account were true, it confirmed the notion that some deliberate attempt had been made at disguise; Holland did not overhear the visitor's conversation, and yet thought there was a look of the

Admiral about him. But then, was Holland telling the truth? Assume that it was the Admiral; why did he suddenly want to take that late (and bad) train up to London? In the alternative, why did he want to create the impression that he had intended doing so? Either supposition implied that there was some mysterious dealing on the Admiral's own part, which no other evidence, except perhaps his impatience to get away from the Vicarage, suggested. Assume that it was not the Admiral; then what was the point of this elaborate frame-up? To implicate Holland in the crime? But there was no foretelling that Holland would not remain fast asleep at the Lord Marshall; nothing but his own evidence served to connect him with the mysterious caller. To deceive the public about the spot at which the murder was committed? Yes, there was something in that; it might help out an alibi. But would not the bogus Admiral have been at pains to leave other evidence of his visit, besides that of a sleepy and stupid hotel servant?

12. *If it was the Admiral, did he travel by road or by river?* According to the Vicar's evidence, which must be genuine since it could be checked, the Admiral had a game leg, and did not walk if he could help it. It seemed unlikely that he could have taken out the car without waking some of the household. The boat remained as a possibility; and if the Admiral went secretly down the river in a boat, where was he going to put it when he took the London train? Abandoned, it would invite theft; moored among other boats it would bear testimony to his movements. It was hardly to be supposed that he meant to leave Whynmouth for ever. The suggestion seemed to be that all this talk about the train was a blind. Once again, for what purpose? The only thing which seemed certain was that the Admiral's boat had been taken from its moorings that night, and had been restored to the boat-house by somebody who was not the Admiral.

13. *Why did the visitor, whoever it was, ask for Holland and then refuse to see him?* If it was a bogus Admiral, the answer was not in doubt; the man had asked for Holland so as to get an excuse for mentioning the Admiral's name; possibly also to implicate Holland in the trouble which was to follow. He did not actually meet Holland, for fear of detection. If it was the real Admiral, a motive was harder to assign. His behaviour seemed that of a man who wants to make sure that a hotel guest has really arrived, or that he is really in the hotel, and yet does not trouble to conceal those inquisitorial methods from the person against whom they are directed. If Holland's story were true, the Admiral might have contemplated a real visit, so as to reassure him about the consent.

But why, after taking so much trouble, should he go away without leaving any significant message?

14. *Did Holland really see anybody in the street?* Answer: Yes, and it means that Holland's story is true up to a point; he really was in the Lord Marshall, or near it, as late as closing time. But there was that hesitation about the great-coat; was that genuine? Or was the ignorance affected, to avoid possible traps? Answer: No, and it means that Holland still possesses knowledge which he is concealing. Either he knew that the Admiral intended to make that visit, or he was privy to the plans of the fellow who impersonated the Admiral. In either case, his mention of the visitor would be an attempt to prove that he was really in the hotel at closing time; this smelt of an alibi.

15. *Did Holland really go to Rundel Croft that night?* Against the story was its extreme vagueness; the absence of clear motive, the care he took to explain why no witnesses of his journey were likely to be forthcoming, his selection of a fresh pair of shoes, the alleged secrecy of his exits and entrances. On the other hand, if Holland was lying, it was hard to suppose that he was lying to screen himself; bed was his best alibi. The evidence of the Boots and Mrs Davis would be a difficult defence for the police to get over, without some positive clue to implicate Holland – and no such clue existed. Instead of sticking to his first story, that he had slept soundly in his bed, he had gone out of his way to confess himself a liar, had told a story, fantastic in many points, about a visit to Rundel Croft which no witness could attest, and in doing so had deliberately claimed the position of the last man who had seen Penistone alive. He seemed to be running his head deliberately into a noose; why should he do that, unless to divert suspicion from the real criminal? And that meant . . . yes, it would hang together. He had told the truth this morning; since then, fresh knowledge had come to him which induced him to put a halter round his own neck. But then, *was* Holland lying? Would he not, by now, have contrived to make up a more plausible story, accounting for his presence at Rundel Croft?

16. *If he went, did he go by appointment?* Such an appointment might have been made either with the Admiral himself or, more probably, with Elma. If the former were true, nothing could bring the charge home except some record of a message; if it was brought by note, somebody had brought the note; if it was sent by telephone, the call could probably be traced. Also, to be sure, a message sent by telephone to an hotel meant that the receiver would be lifted off by an hotel servant, and the circumstance, at

that hour of the night, would probably be remembered. When you came to think of it, the message (if there was one) must have come from Elma, or Holland must have supposed that it came from Elma. Otherwise, he would have had no reason to conceal it; and he could have made his own story much more plausible by admitting it. *Mem. – See Mrs Davis about the message: enquire if necessary at the telephone exchange.*

17. *Who was the woman who went through Lingham at a quarter to eleven?* At least, that was really the wrong way to put it; you could hardly hope to know who she was, at this stage. But it was worth considering whether her arrival could have had any influence on the situation. Her car, which might or might not have contained another occupant, would reach Whynmouth in time to deposit the mysterious visitor at the Lord Marshall. Alternatively, it would have been possible for the occupants of such a car to be at Rundel Croft in time for the murder, even if you dated the murder early. They might have gone round by Fernton Bridge, the enquiry for the Vicarage being merely a blind; or they might have stopped close to the Vicarage, and ferried themselves across by making free with Mr Mount's boat. This last plan would have the effect of bringing the Vicarage boat on to the scene of action; a point deserving to be considered, from the detective's point of view. But Rudge found himself instinctively recoiling from such an explanation. For it would mean that the criminal or criminals came and went by car, their base presumably London. It was not possible for the Whynmouth police to search for suspicious characters in London; Scotland Yard might have to be involved, and that always meant that the credit went to Scotland Yard.

At this point the Inspector drew a fresh line across his page. He had reached the end of the enquiries which were antecedent, or seemed at first sight antecedent, to the murder itself. It was time now to come on to a fresh set of problems: those created by the circumstances in which the corpse was discovered. The pipe needed to be re-lit; and, for that matter, another tot seemed indicated; the indication was allowed to have full weight. Now for the *facts*. Human testimony was a slippery and uncertain thing to deal with; what you were told was a photograph fogged, as it were, by the shadow of the man who told it you. But Nature did not lie; tides ran, dew formed, blood flowed, doors opened and shut, on uniform and ascertainable principles. The clues pointed you on to the actions which had produced them, and then hinted entrancingly at the motives which lay behind the actions. Well, then . . .

18. *Here is a man murdered; who had a motive, and what motive,*

for murdering him? Ordinarily, one would expect a local quarrel; though the knife, as Mrs Davis acutely noticed, is not the English criminal's weapon. But a month's residence hardly gave time for any supposition of the kind here. A Cornish enemy would have found it difficult to track this man down, would have delayed longer to ascertain the lie of the land. The quarrel, then, which found its satisfaction in that grisly wound, must be a quarrel dating from past history in the Admiral's life. Further, you could assume with some certainty that the murderer either knew the habits, or possessed the confidence, of his victim. A man is found murdered in the Vicar's boat on the very night when he has been dining at the Vicarage; in his pocket is a copy of that very newspaper to which he is in fact a subscriber; the murder is somehow connected with a visit, alleged or real, to a neighbouring hotel where an acquaintance of the victim is in fact staying. All this betrays a knowledge of relevant circumstances; the mysterious Chinaman of the story-books can be ruled out of the list of suspects; he would not have committed the murder just so. That narrowed down the search to people who knew something about the Admiral. Who did? His neighbours: Neddy Ware (not much), the Vicar, the Vicar's sons, Sir Wilfrid Denny, still an unknown quantity. His servants: but they had given, so far, no ground for suspicion. His family and those concerned with its fortunes: Elma, the problematical Walter, Holland, Mr Dakers. Of these, which had a motive – a strong one? Elma had a weak one, the desire to get her money absolutely. Holland had a stronger one, to overcome an obstacle to his marriage; but was it strong enough? Not unless and until it could be proved that the typewritten consent was a forgery. Mr Dakers hardly came into the picture at all; Walter, if he was alive, was a tough customer no doubt; but how exactly did he stand to gain by his uncle's disappearance? This absence of motive was a puzzling feature; was it possible that some guest of Sir Wilfrid Denny's was implicated? *Mem. – Trace Denny as soon as possible.*

19. *Why was a knife chosen as the weapon?* Stabbing usually meant murder in hot blood, or as the result of panic; a thought-out crime would ordinarily depend on safer weapons. Its use suggested that the murder took place at some spot where the report of fire-arms would have been heard, and would have brought rescue; near the house, for instance. Grice had been away all day, and had as yet made no investigation of the wound since the loss of the Norwegian knife had been discovered. If that knife seemed likely to be the weapon, it would look as if the criminal's first plans had

not involved murder, or, at least, murder done in that way.

20. *Why was the body found in a boat?* No use to suggest that the murder had been done in the boat, and the body, from fear or disgust, left where it lay. In the first place, it is very hard to murder a man in a boat; you must be in it yourself, and that means looking at one another all the time – no chance for a sudden attack. And in this case the blood must have flowed, yet there were no marks on the white paint. The body, then, had been deliberately put into the boat; why? For convenience or colportage? That was possible; but granted that your corpse has got to make a journey by boat, it does not follow that it is best left there. Suppose it had been thrown overboard, with a couple of stones tied to it? The Admiral's disappearance would have caused alarm at first; but a report from the Lord Marshall that he had been seen in Whynmouth that night, just *en route* for the late train would have dissipated the rumour of murder until the river gave up its dead; and by that time the murderer might be anywhere – China, for example. The murderer's instinct is always to hide his victim, at least for the moment; this murderer had deliberately put the corpse on show, with the certainty of its discovery next morning. What did that mean? It suggested, at least, that the whole circumstances in which the corpse was found were a deliberate frame-up; the criminal felt certain that suspicion would not fall on him, so long as he left evidence which would fasten the suspicion on other people. Granted that frame of mind, you could just account for the boat. A boat travels with the stream or with the tide at a more or less uniform pace; a floating body, by itself, might get held up by any overhanging branch, any patch of shallows. It might be that the criminal wanted to suggest, by the position in which the body was found, that the murder had taken place at a different hour or at a different spot from the actual hour, the actual spot. Best to ask Neddy Ware to say exactly what combinations of times and places would have brought the boat to the spot at which he found it, e.g., Whynmouth, Fernton Bridge, the Vicarage, as alternative sites; 10.30, 11.30, 12.30 as alternative times. *Mem. – Look up Neddy Ware again.*

21. *Why was the body found in that particular boat?* An easy answer suggested itself, 'To throw suspicion on the Vicar'; for which reason, too, the hat was doubtless thrown in. To suppose that the Vicar, if he were really privy to the murder, would allow his connection with it to be thus blatantly advertised was ridiculous. But then, was it not almost equally ridiculous to suppose that the criminal had chosen the Vicar as his scapegoat? The

frame-up, in that case, was inconceivably clumsy work. The simple bluff of pretending that the Vicar was the criminal seemed too simple; the double bluff of pretending to have pretended that the Vicar was the criminal seemed too complicated. Yet, for what other purpose could the Vicarage boat have been dragged into the story at all? It might indicate that the murderer had started from the other side of the river, and had found that a borrowed boat saved the trouble of going round by the bridge. On the other hand, it might indicate that the murderer had wanted the police to think just that, having in fact started his operations from the Rundel Croft bank. There was not much to be made of this clue, and yet it haunted the imagination.

22. *Why was the Vicar's hat left behind?* Assuming for the moment that Mount was the criminal, the question admitted of no ready answer. On the whole, people are hat-wearers or bare-headers; the former class will notice the absence of the familiar feeling as a kind of discomfort. You would expect the murderer, passing his hand over his forehead, to cry out instinctively, 'Good heavens, where is my hat?' An unconscious exchange of hats between the murderer and his victim seemed just possible; Holland had fancied a clerical appearance about the hat which the Admiral, if it was the Admiral, had worn that night. Again, assuming that the murderer came from the direction of the Vicarage, it was possible that he had found the hat lying derelict in the summer-house, and had borrowed it for his own purpose – to hide his face, for example. *Mem. – Examine the hat on the off-chance of finding lay hairs adhering to it.*

23. *Why was the key to the french window found in the bottom of the Admiral's boat?* This key business was less puzzling. Presumably, when Elma left her uncle to lock up the boat, she took the key with her, and left it in the french window, on the outside, so that he could let himself in later. Did he so let himself in? It looked as if he must have, to find his great-coat. Then, if he ever went out again alive, he would lock the window from the outside and slip the key into his pocket. It might fall out of his pocket, easily enough, when his dead body was put into the boat. Alternatively, if the Admiral was in fact killed in his garden before he had time to re-enter the house, the criminal would no doubt use the key to let himself in, when he was in search of the hidden papers. Once he had got those papers, and the Admiral was dead, it did not matter what he did with the key; indeed, it was necessary to get rid of it somehow.

24. *Why was the Admiral's boat moored, contrary to custom, by*

the bows? Here was a point of genuine significance. It meant that this boat, too, had figured somehow in the movements of that August night. Either the Admiral had been abroad on her, and had been caught in the middle of his travels; or else the criminal, having despatched him in his own garden, had made use of two boats in disposing of the body, or possibly in securing his own escape. And for some reason, a baffling one, surely, he had thought it more important to leave the Admiral's boat moored than the Vicar's. Inexplicably, he must have thought that things looked more natural this way. Another pertinent consideration arose: Elma must surely have known her uncle's little fad about the mooring of boats; and therefore if she or anybody acting under her immediate direction had been guilty of the murder, it was hard to believe that the boat would not have been found in the morning moored as usual.

25. *Why is a whole length of the painter missing?* And such a small length; not as much as you would naturally cut off if you needed the rope for some unusual purpose; to tie a man's hands, for example. No, the Vicar's boat had first been cut loose from its moorings, and then it had been tied up again, either to some other post or to some other boat, and once more it had been necessary to cut it with a knife instead of untying it. This was puzzling, because ordinarily what man has done man can undo, if it is the same man. You had to allow for accidents; e.g., two ropes might have been tied together, and then swelled through being left in the water; or some sudden need for haste might have arisen, so that there was no leisure for untying knots. But following out the indications of the painter for what they were worth, you were led to the conclusion that the painter had been twice cut; that a different person had been responsible for the second cut, and that this new person was shorter than the other. The Vicar, for example, who was tallish, might have cut the rope in the first instance; but if it was he who re-tied the boat, he would naturally do so at a height which would make it possible for him to untie it again without difficulty. This new figure in the story might be called x-n, the original painter cutter being labelled x. Now, it was possible that x-n was simply the Admiral. But the question arose whether you had not to allow for two people besides the Admiral, both concerned in the doings of that night, x and x-n. Holland might be x, but such was his height that he might have been expected to untie the boat even from its first moorings.

26. *Why was the body found in a coat?* It was a pity, when you came to think of it, that that question had not been put down

immediately after No. 20. It would have been a rhyme. Rudge, in his youth, had tried to fill up the last lines of limericks, but he had never claimed to be a poet, and it was a new experience for him to find himself in the position of the young Ovid, writing verse unconsciously. Yes, to be sure, that great-coat. If the Admiral really went into Whynmouth, and really meant to catch the late train, it was conceivable that he would have taken a coat with him to protect him against the chill of the early morning. But Rudge was altogether inclined to discredit that projected railway journey. If the Admiral really went to Whynmouth, or to any other point along the river, in a boat and with the intention of returning in a boat, he would only have encumbered himself with a fairly substantial overcoat for one reason – he must have anticipated having to hang about somewhere waiting for somebody, talking to somebody, in the open air, and was afraid that he would get a chill after taking exercise without this precaution. On the other hand, the great-coat was a loose one; what they call in the shops 'something in the style of a Raglan.' It would have been quite possible, then, for the murderer, unless he were squeamish about handling corpses, to pull the overcoat on to a dead body in a perfectly convincing way. Now, what would that mean? Probably, that the murderer was elaborating a 'frame-up' as before; having disseminated the idea that the Admiral meant to go up to London by the late train, he went on to give that idea corroboration by vesting his victim suitably for such a journey.

27. *And now, why the newspaper in the pocket?* If the Admiral had really intended a train journey, and had gone into the house to get his coat with that in view, was it not humanly certain that his eye would have fallen on the newspaper close by, and that he would have crammed the familiar copy in his great-coat there and then? The train service from Whynmouth to London is not distinguished for speed, and most residents arm themselves with some kind of literature before they set out on it. But this the Admiral had not done; the second copy found in the hall the morning after the murder was the genuine article, for it was marked 'Admiral Pennystone,' with one of Mr Tolwhistle's characteristic mis-spellings. Where did the unmarked copy come from? The shops and the bookstalls at Whynmouth were all shut by nine; and there were no longer any street vendors – Whynmouth is a sleepy place, and the last optimist who had tried peddling alleged 'late editions' had gone out of business some months earlier. The Admiral had not gone into the Lord Marshall; could not, then, have picked up a copy there and walked off with

it. If he was really in possession of it while still alive, it followed that he must have called somewhere else that night. Sir Wilfrid Denny's house suggested itself as a possibility. If, on the other hand, the paper had been thrust into the pocket after his death by the man who murdered him, that could only have been done with the intention of falsifying the evidence. Falsifying it how? In point of time, by suggesting that the murder took place, say, after nine instead of having taken place before nine? But that would bring the real time to an impossibly early hour. In point of place, then; the murder really happened in some place at a distance from Whynmouth; and the murderer, by thrusting the *Gazette* into the dead man's pocket, had tried to create the impression that the murder took place at Whynmouth, or at least while the victim was on his way back from there. Read so, this piece of evidence chimed in with the conclusion which had already suggested itself – that the murderer wanted it to be thought, falsely, that the Admiral was in Whynmouth that evening. If you accepted this argument, a further consideration arose. The murderer was somebody who did not know Whynmouth, or whose knowledge of it was not up-to-date. A resident – the elusive Sir Wilfrid, for example – would not have made the mistake of imagining that the *Gazette* was still on sale at eleven o'clock in the evening.

28. *Of what nature were the documents marked 'X'?* That they were secret, that they were valuable, went without saying. What was much more remarkable, if you came to think of it, was that any reference to 'X' should have been given among the files at all. The Admiral himself, though he was one of the few admirals who had not publicly attested his indebtedness to any system of memory-training, was clearly not absent-minded beyond the average of humanity; why then should he need a reference to remind him where these all-important documents were kept? Yet, if the references were not for the Admiral's own benefit, who else could profit by them? In the event of his desk being broken open, would it not have been safer to leave the very existence of 'X,' as well as its whereabouts, a secret? It looked almost as if the Admiral had expected the fate which ultimately came upon him – after all, there was that loaded revolver in the desk – expected that a police officer sooner or later would rummage in his desk, and would need a pointer to inform him that secret papers were concealed somewhere. It would appear that Sir Wilfrid was somewhat involved, also the nephew, Walter. It seemed probable that the background was Chinese. Was it blackmail? If so, Sir Wilfrid must surely be the victim of it, not Walter; you cannot threaten with exposure a man

who has disappeared from human ken.

29. *Were they destroyed, or stolen? And by whom?* It was just possible that Penistone at some time had got rid of documents which would be damaging to himself or to someone he cared for. It was more natural to assume that the murderer was also a thief. But here was an important point – the person who stole those papers must, almost necessarily, have been an inmate of the house; the desk had shown no traces of being rifled, there were no marks of violence about the secret drawer. If, then, the villain of last night had removed those papers, he had known exactly where to look for them, and had wasted no time over it.

Whew! There was a fresh section of the evidence concluded; that finished the clues which dated from last night. Rudge's left foot had gone to sleep, and he tramped his room for a bit, trying to map out what remained of his task. Yes, he must analyse the behaviour of the various people, against whom suspicion might conceivably lie, since the actual discovery of the corpse. The most noticeable feature, undoubtedly, was what you might call the drain of the rural population – the general dash for London. Very well, then:

30. *Why did Elma Fitzgerald hurry up to London?* The conclusion seemed inevitable that her flight was consequent upon the news of the murder. She was not fond of early rising, and her early rising that morning had been Rudge's own fault. The Whynmouth line assumes, like most railways, that you do not want to travel up to the metropolis much after ten o'clock; after that hour, the speed of the trains sagged noticeably, and day tickets were no longer available. Consequently, if you were going up to London you prepared for an early start. Elma had made an early start, but she had not prepared for it. She had not fled to meet Holland; for she knew, unless his overnight message had remained undelivered, that he was in Whynmouth. She had not been to see Mr Dakers – though, of course, Holland's pursuit might have interrupted that plan. *Better wait to hear what she will say tomorrow.*

31. *Why did Holland ditto?* This was plainer sailing. Innocent or guilty, and whether he believed her to be innocent or guilty, he would naturally want to see Elma and to discuss the situation. But, assuming that Holland was himself innocent, it looked as if he must have believed Elma guilty. Otherwise, he might at least have waited to tell a true story to the police.

32. *Why did Sir Wilfrid ditto?* It was to be observed that Sir Wilfrid, if his movements had been correctly reported, was in the van of the movement. He had gone up to London 'by the first

train,' and that ran, when was it? Soon after seven . . . anyhow, long before Elma was out of bed. Not before the body was discovered, but surely before the rumour of its discovery was likely to have reached him. Either, then, the 'call' which summoned him had been accompanied by news of the tragedy – and that meant Neddy Ware or the Vicar or Rundel Croft as its source; or else he went up to London ignorant that the murder had been committed . . . or at least ignorant that it had been discovered. Well, well, it might be an accident after all; at least he must hear what the man had to say. But what a curious influence Penistone must have had, that his death seemed to scatter his acquaintances in alarm, instead of rallying them in sympathy!

33. *Why did the Vicar ditto?* Once again, mere coincidence was possible; Mount might, quite possibly, have gone up to chat to an archdeacon about dilapidations. But it seemed more natural to connect his behaviour, too, with the general upset. Now, what precise development in the story had led to the Vicar's *Hegira?* The corpse had been discovered, and he remained calm – comparatively calm. The disappearance of Elma and Holland left him still unmoved. What new factor could have arisen in the situation? It looked very much as if the Vicar had made some discovery of his own, a discovery which he had not seen fit to communicate.

34. *Was the Vicar telling all he knew?* Curious how people differed under cross-examination. Elma Fitzgerald had a natural pose of hostility; she so obviously resented being asked any questions about anything, that it was difficult to know whether she was embarrassed at being asked these questions about this. Holland's contemptuous joviality was no doubt a permanent mood with him; it made him a difficult subject for interrogation, because you never knew quite what allowances to make for his fun. But Mr Mount, now, he was evidently a man anxious, as a matter of conscience, to tell the truth. But there was a hesitation in his manner which seemed to suggest that he was not quite sure which part of the truth to tell; not quite sure how he ought to answer one question, for fear the next should trench on ground where he was determined not to tread. He was scrupulous about telling the truth; and the scrupulous in this world are apt to be more of a nuisance than the unscrupulous.

35. *Why did the Vicar water his garden?* It might, of course, be nothing more than a horticulatural *gaffe.* But, if you were prepared to make a long shot, and suppose that the Vicar came into it somehow, you naturally asked, was he trying to hide traces? Indulge the fancy, and where did that lead? Not his own traces,

surely; for he would be conscious of having left them, and would have had the elementary common sense to obliterate them earlier in the day, to obliterate them at some time when the police were unlikely to be about. The same consideration applied, though with slightly less force, if you thought of them as the traces of somebody of whose presence he had been conscious at the time when they were made. And yet he must surely have had some idea whose they were and how they came there, or his meticulous sense of justice would have induced him to point them out to the police. A long shot, but it needed thinking over.

36. *Why was the Admiral's pipe left in the Vicar's study?* Probably because the Admiral forgot it and left it there. He had been in a hurry, it seemed, when he left; and the most punctilious of admirals will have these lapses occasionally. And he was, as Holland had pointed out, a man of many pipes. But Rudge's brain was by now worked up into the state in which it could see significance in everything; and even this pipe – there was the bare possibility that the Admiral had left it there on purpose, in order to have an excuse for going back to the Vicarage (but apparently never went); or that the Vicar himself had found it in some place where it seemed all too likely to tell a story, and had for safety removed it elsewhere. Rudge, perhaps with a theologican's unconscious animus, was already thinking of Mr Mount as the sort of man who would not tell a direct lie, but would be quite willing to let you deceive yourself ('lead you up the garden' was his own less technical phrase).

37. *Why were Holland and Elma in such a hurry to get married?* That the licence had already been procured before the murder took place, seemed evident. But this in itself need not suggest foreknowledge of the murder; Holland's own account – that Elma had encouraged him by her letter to expect the Admiral's consent, and that he had taken out the licence on the strength of that hope – seemed sound enough as it stood. You could understand why there should be haste in their proceedings while the Admiral was still alive, and had given his reluctant consent. Who knew when he might change his mind? But, once he was dead, that motive ceased to operate; you would have thought it common decency to wait a little, and according to Dakers it would have been common prudence too. There must be some reason, but what reason? Rudge admitted that at this point the case defied him.

38. *Why did Holland conceal, at first, his alleged midnight interview?* His own excuse, that he had concealed the whole story of his

midnight journey simply to avoid embarrassing questions when he was in a hurry, seemed strangely inadequate. On the assumption that his first story was true, and his second fake, why should he cast doubt on his own veracity by this curious *volte-face?* On the contrary assumption, why did he not stick to his lie when once he had told it? Having the typewritten consent in his pocket, he could just as easily pretend it had been given to Elma early on the previous evening, before the dinner-party; what motive was there for insisting so strongly that it had only been drafted at midnight? It looked as if some piece of evidence must have cropped up during the day which would make Holland's statement that he had slept soundly at the Lord Marshall inconsistent with the genuineness of the typewritten consent. What could that evidence be? Rudge tortured his imagination vainly over the problem.

39. *Why was the typewritten consent typewritten?*

There was no typewriter in the Admiral's room; the documents in the files which were not holograph had plainly been copied out by a professional. Moreover, the amateur, to whom it is a matter of labour to fit his sheet straight into the machine, does not have recourse to his typewriter unless he has a document of some length, say four or five lines, to deal with. Improbable, then . . . unless the document was a forgery (a signature being much easier to forge, by mere imitation, than a whole line of writing). Or possibly the 'consent' might have been extracted by some threats of violence, in which case it was likely enough that the criminal should have expedited matters by supplying a ready-made formula. *Mem. – Ask Mrs Holland where and by whom she thinks the typewriting was done.*

And so, having got his ideas down on paper, Rudge went off to bed, comforting himself with the old, superstitious hope we all have sometimes, that he would wake up with an inspiration. But the night did not bring counsel. He did, indeed, dream that he saw the actual crime being committed. But as, in his dream, the author of the murder was Mrs Davis, the victim Mr Dakers, the weapon a rolled-up newspaper, and the scene of the whole incident the Charing Cross Hotel, he wisely concluded that oneiromancy has its fallible moments.

9

By Freeman Wills Crofts

THE VISITOR IN THE NIGHT

Inspector Rudge woke next morning with a vaguely troubled mind. He had a subconscious impression that this was no ordinary day and that important duties were awaiting him. Then he remembered. His big chance had come! He sprang out of bed.

During breakfast he laid his plans for the day. First there was a conference with his chiefs. Superintendent Hawkesworth had been on leave when the murder took place, and though Rudge had wired for him directly he had heard of it, he was not expected back till early that morning. The Chief Constable, Major Twyfitt, had also been away, but he had returned last evening, and he also would want to hear the news. Then there was the interview with the coroner about the inquest, after which Rudge supposed he would be at liberty to take up one or more of the lines of investigation he had thought out on the previous evening.

He was a good deal worried that he had not yet been able to arrange for an adequate identification of the remains. Rudge did not himself doubt that the dead man was the Admiral, but this had not been proved, and it was his job to prove it. This question of identity would be the first to be raised by the Super, and it would probably be the only one in which at this stage the coroner would be interested.

Rudge walked round to the Lord Marshall on the chance that Dakers might be about. Dakers should be his man for the identification. By a chance which Rudge took as a good omen for the day, it happened that as he entered the porch he met Dakers coming out.

'Good morning, sir,' Rudge said genially. 'This is a bit of luck for me. I was just wondering if I could see you.'

Dakers was polite, but not genial. He showed no enthusiasm for the meeting. 'What is it?' he asked shortly.

'The identification of the remains, sir. May I ask how long you knew the Admiral?'

'How long?' the solicitor repeated slowly. 'Let's see. Twenty-

one – two – about twenty-two years; possibly twenty-three.'

'Good enough, sir. And during that period you've seen him, I presume, at intervals?'

'Yes, at irregular intervals, I have.'

'Then, sir, I should be obliged if when convenient you would run out with me to Lingham, where the body is lying, and see if you can formally identify it.'

'I should like to have my breakfast first.'

'I said, sir, when convenient. Would ten o'clock suit?'

Dakers agreed and Rudge went on: 'There's another thing I'd like to ask you about while I have the opportunity, and that is the late Admiral's consent to his niece's wedding. Do you happen to have it in your possession?'

'You mean the typewritten statement?'

'Yes, sir.'

Dakers considered. 'How do you come to be interested in that?' he asked.

'In the same way, sir, that I expect you're interested in it,' Rudge returned promptly. 'We both, I take it, want to be sure that it was really given by the Admiral.'

'You mean,' said Dakers frigidly, 'that Mrs Holland is either a liar or a forger or both?'

'No, sir,' Rudge answered imperturbably. 'Mrs Holland didn't say she got it from the Admiral. Mr Holland said that. My question is really in Mrs Holland's own interest. I take it that that document will have to be proved before she can inherit, and I was going to suggest that the sooner its authenticity is established, the better.'

Dakers became if possible even more frigid.

'Thank you, Inspector, but I shall endeavour to look after my client's interests without the help of the police.'

Rudge shrugged. 'As you will, sir. But you must realise that the police will have to examine that document, and I was merely suggesting that if you could see your way to work with us in the matter it would save time and trouble. But of course it's as you like. Till ten o'clock then, sir.'

Superintendent Hawkesworth was waiting for Rudge at the station, and within a few minutes Chief Constable Twyfitt arrived. Rudge at once gave a detailed account of what had happened and what he had done, with the steps he next proposed to take. The two men heard him without interruption, Hawkesworth scribbling copious notes.

'That seems all right, Rudge, as far as you have gone,' the Superintendent said, glancing at his superior.

'Yes,' Major Twyfitt agreed. 'I think Rudge has done quite well. And his proposals for carrying on seem sound.'

'Yes, but there's too much in them for one man,' Hawkesworth decided. 'We'll have to divide them up. Just let's settle what everyone's to do and then you, Rudge, can get along with that identification. Now let's see.' For some moments he scribbled rapidly. 'This'll do, I think,' he went on. 'I'll take on the China affair. I'll get in touch with the Admiralty and the Foreign Office and that newspaper man and any other place or person I can think of. Then I'll follow up Denny: I dare say there's some connection between the two. Sergeant Appleton we'll put on to Holland: Holland's doings in this country, that is: Holland in China will come under me. If necessary, Appleton can go up to the Yard and get some help there. At the same time he can find out if those two were really married in town. Constable Hempstead seems to have done well?'

'He certainly has, sir. He's no fool, is Hempstead.'

'Very well, we'll give him his chance. We'll let him search the river, both banks, over the length along which the boat could have floated. He's to look out for traces of any kind, particularly for footprints on the bank, signs of a struggle, places where the body might have been lifted into the boat, and that missing bit of the painter. That'll keep him busy. You yourself, Rudge, take Rundel Croft and the people in it, excluding the dead man, who I think will come into my department. That covers things meanwhile?'

'Yes, sir, I think that's all right.'

'Well, you get along now. Then you're going to see the coroner? Formal identification and an adjournment of course?'

'Of course, sir.'

Fifteen minutes later Rudge and Dakers reached the public house at Lingham where the body of the deceased was lying. Dakers had recovered his good temper and had chatted pleasantly enough during the drive.

'Well, sir?' Rudge asked, when the solicitor had stared for some moments at the dead features.

Dakers seemed to awake as from a reverie. 'Oh yes,' he said without hesitation, 'it's Admiral Penistone right enough. No doubt whatever.' He appeared somewhat touched. 'Poor old fellow,' he went on, 'I'm sorry to see him like that. We didn't see eye to eye in everything, but still – judging people as you find them, I could say nothing but good about him.' He turned away with a sigh. 'I suppose you want me to give evidence of identity at the inquest?'

'It would save Mrs Holland,' Rudge pointed out.

'Very well. When does it take place?'

'Tomorrow at ten, sir.'

'I shall be there.'

'Thank you, sir. I suppose, sir.' Rudge smiled as if to discount the saying of a stupid thing: 'I suppose Mrs Holland really was the late Admiral's niece? You see, no one here knows the family. As you are aware, they moved here about a month ago.'

'Of course she was,' Dakers answered testily. 'I'm afraid you won't get far on those lines, Inspector.'

'We have to question everything, sir, as you know. Well, sir, I'm obliged to you for doing the identification. Where would you like to be put down?'

They drove back to the Lord Marshall and Dakers got out. Rudge was turning away, but the solicitor stopped him with a gesture.

'About that consent, Inspector. I've been thinking over it and after all I don't see any reason why you shouldn't see it. I haven't got it myself at the moment, but when I get it I'll let you know.'

Rudge thanked him again and the two men parted. Rudge was pleased with his day so far. He was certainly making progress. Already some of his theories had been eliminated and bed-rock fact was beginning to emerge from the mass of speculation in which the case was smothered.

Rudge's business with the coroner was soon settled. It was obviously impossible to complete the inquest, and Mr Skipworth agreed that all that was now necessary was to carry on the proceedings far enough to enable a burial order to be given. This procedure had already been tentatively agreed on by telephone, and the meeting was really to run over the required evidence and make sure that no unforeseen factor had arisen.

For the rest of that day Rudge busied himself in trying to glean information about the Rundel Croft household. He did not learn much, it must be admitted, but he initiated a series of enquiries about each member, the replies to which, when received, should prove valuable. Among the Admiral's papers he found the Cornish address from which the deceased man had moved, and he telephoned to the Superintendent of the district for all available details of the family. He interviewed Elma Holland, though unfortunately without much success. He found out where the servants – the butler and his wife, and Elma's present maid – had been engaged, and wrote to their former employers for further particulars of them. Lastly, he made a general search of the house,

which, however, proved quite fruitless.

At a few minutes before ten next morning Rudge entered the hall where the inquest was to be held. To tell the truth, coroners' enquiries were formalities which completely bored him. A waste of time, he considered them, indeed worse than a waste, for he believed the time could always be used more profitably in carrying on the normal investigation.

As he had foreseen, the proceedings afforded little of interest. The eleven jurors did not elect to view the body, and as soon as they were sworn, evidence was taken.

Neddy Ware first told in detail of his discovery of the body. Then Mr Dakers swore that he had seen the body and that he identified it as that of Rear-Admiral Hugh Lawrence Penistone. He gave a short outline of the Admiral's life, explained how he came to know him, and then stood down. Next Mr Grice stated the cause of death, a wound in the heart from a knife or dagger with a long thin blade. A post-mortem had shown that the Admiral was in reasonably good health for a man of his years.

This brought the proceedings to a close, the coroner stating that in order to enable the police to make further enquiries he would adjourn the inquest till that day three weeks.

Once again Rudge was struck by the keenness of his reporter friend from the *Evening Gazette*. The man simply pestered him for news. A growing shortness in Rudge's manner had no effect whatever, and it was not till he threatened to give anything available to a rival journal, that the man became reasonable.

Another person who developed a surprising curiosity was Mr Mount. Mount was the first man Rudge had seen on reaching the coroner's court. This was not surprising in a way, because Rudge had himself told the Vicar that his presence at the inquest would be required. But owing to the decision only to take evidence of identification that morning, Mount had neither been sent a summons to attend, nor been officially informed of the place and hour. But there the man was, and not only so, but he was evidently in an extremely curious as well as apprehensive condition.

On leaving the room Rudge found himself button-holed by the Vicar. Under the thinly veiled guise of a clergyman's natural interest in his parishioners, Mount made a really blatant attempt to learn the extent of the police knowledge of the case. But Mount was a child in the Inspector's experienced hands. Rudge replied readily and with a convincing air of candour, while warning the Vicar not to repeat his confidences. But Rudge knew that when the Vicar came to think over what he had been told, he would be

hard put to it to find out what those confidences were.

Rudge wondered if he had given enough attention to Mount. Sitting down in his room, he ran through his notes, transcribing anything he had learned about him.

In the first place, Mount was evidently already on intimate terms with the Rundel Croft people. Then it was in his, Mount's, boat that the dead man had been found, and more significant still, Mount's hat had been in the boat. Then there had been Mount's sudden journey to London; there had been his watering of the garden, and now there was this deep anxiety about the case. The more Rudge thought over it, the more he felt impelled to the conclusion that Mount must somehow be implicated.

Rudge considered the above points in turn, but the only one from which he thought fresh light might be obtained was the man's visit to London. He recalled the details.

It was between twelve and one o'clock that Mount had sent his note saying that he was anxious to go up that afternoon to town on an urgent matter connected with his clerical duties. Now that must have been a very sudden decision. He, Rudge, had been speaking to Mount earlier in the morning, and the man had said nothing about this visit then. Rudge did not know much about ecclesiastical matters, but he doubted that business was done at that rate. Most professional visits to London would mean for clergymen meetings arranged a considerable time earlier, or interviews with dignitaries, also arranged some time beforehand. He was inclined to doubt that the clerical duties in question had much to do with the church.

Rudge wondered what he should do. Mount bore a high reputation for probity, and if the matter were put directly to him, he might give the required explanation. Then Rudge saw that he would probably do nothing of the kind. He, Rudge, had nothing to put which would demand an answer.

Mount had hurried up to town. But so had Elma, so had Holland, so had Denny. Was it possible to believe that there was no connection between all these visits? Suddenly it seemed to Rudge that his best plan would be to try to trace Mount's movements in town. It shouldn't take long and it might lead to something vital.

Rudge went in and put his views before Superintendent Hawkesworth. Hawkesworth was impressed, and agreed to release Rudge for a couple of days.

'You'd better advise them at the Yard what you propose to do,' said Hawkesworth. 'I'll ring them up that you'll call.'

The first question was: How had Mount made the journey? Mount had a car, but most persons of moderate income went by train, rail being so much cheaper for the long distance. Mount had been at the Vicarage at one o'clock, and he had rung up Rudge from the Charing Cross Hotel at nine. There were two, and only two, trains he could have used, the 2.5 from Whynmouth, which reached Waterloo at 5.45, and the 4.25 from Whynmouth, arriving at 8.35.

Rudge began by calling at the office of the local newspaper and getting a photograph of Mount. Then he went to the station and began his enquiries. He learned at once that Mount had been seen on the day in question. He had been noticed particularly by both the booking-clerk and the ticket-collector, and for the same reason. He had, it appeared, bought a London ticket, but he had not travelled by a London train. He had gone by the 1.30 which connected at Passfield Junction with the 11.0 a.m. express from Waterloo to the west. He had explained that he wished to break his journey and would go on to London by a later train.

As Rudge jogged along in the next train to Passfield Junction, he reminded himself of the lie of the land. The main line of the Western Division of the Southern Railway ran from Waterloo to Devon, past Whynmouth. It did not, however, go through Whynmouth; it ran at this point some ten miles inland. Whynmouth was the terminus of a branch which left the main line at this Passfield Junction, a small roadside station some fifteen miles away in the London direction. The nearest town to Whynmouth on the main line was Drychester. It lay on the Exeter side of Whynmouth, twelve miles away by road. There was no direct rail connection between the two places, the route being by Passfield Junction.

At each of the small stations between Whynmouth and Passfield Junction Rudge jumped out of the train and enquired if the Vicar had been seen alighting on the day in question. But it was not till he reached the junction that he got any information.

Mr Mount was slightly known to the stationmaster, and he believed he had seen him on that day entering a third-class carriage of the down express. Rudge went at once to the booking-office, and there he learned that only three third-class tickets had been issued by that train – a single to Exeter and two returns to Drychester. From this it seemed pretty clear that Mount had booked to Drychester.

In due course Rudge reached Drychester. But here he had not the same luck. Drychester station was a busy place, very different to the small roadside junction. No one knew Mount and no one

had noticed a clergyman resembling him.

It looked, however, as if Mount had reached Drychester at 2.40. If so, he would have been too late to have caught the earlier of the two trains to town, and must therefore have gone by the second, leaving Drychester at 4.50. That is, he would have had two hours and ten minutes in Drychester. What could he have done in that time?

Rudge could form no idea. He thought first of going down to the cathedral and making enquiries of the vergers, but he wasn't anxious that it should be known that he was making this investigation. At last as a sort of forlorn hope he decided to interrogate the taxi-men at the station, on the off-chance that Mount might have driven to his destination.

Armed with his photograph, Rudge went round the men. He did not expect to get much, and he was therefore agreeably surprised when he suddenly found he had struck oil. But he did not realise, not for a long time after, how deep and how rich was the well he had tapped.

When he showed the photograph to one of the men, a little weazened rat of a fellow, it produced a reaction.

'Aye,' said the man, 'I've seen the gent all right, I 'ave. But not 'ere. I've seen 'im in Lingham.'

'Oh,' said Rudge, 'in Lingham, have you? That's no good to me. I'm looking for traces of him here.'

'I didn't see 'im 'ere, guv'nor. Never seen 'im but the once; in Lingham.'

Rudge's fate, Mount's fate, and the fate of several other persons trembled in the balance. Rudge was about to pass on to the next driver, but fortunately for himself, he didn't. Fortunately for himself, he asked the fateful question: 'When was that?'

'Last Tuesday night,' the taxi-man replied, 'at a 'ouse near Lingham, about a 'arf a mile beyond the village, 'n' down on the river.'

'Beside the church?'

'That's right, guv'nor.'

'And what time was that?'

The man paused in thought. 'About midnight or a bit after.'

Rudge's heart gave a sudden leap. Midnight or later on the night of the crime was a very critical hour in the case. At midnight the terrible drama which led to Admiral Penistone's death must already have been under way. What the Vicar was doing at midnight was something that he would be extraordinarily glad to know.

'Better tell me all about it,' Rudge suggested, carefully keeping the eagerness out of his voice.

But the man's story, instead of clearing up the situation, seemed only to make it still more incomprehensible. It seemed that on that night, the night of the crime, he had been on duty when the last train arrived from town, the 7.0 p.m. from Waterloo. It arrived at 10.20, and he got a fare from it. It was a lady, a small, middle-aged woman with a bright, quick manner. As far as the taxi-man could see in the somewhat poor light of the lamps, she was elegantly dressed and very good-looking. Quite an attractive lady, he evidently thought. She had asked him to drive her to a house in Lingham which she would point out, wait for her for a few minutes, and bring her back to the Anglers' Arms at Drychester.

Except that it was rather late to pay a call, this seemed reasonable to Rudge. He knew the trains from town. The last train having a connection to Whynmouth left Waterloo at 5.30. The 7.0 from town did not stop at Passfield Juntion, and the only way in which a passenger by that train could reach Whynmouth was by driving the twelve miles from Drychester.

'I follow you,' Rudge said. 'Go ahead.'

The man had driven his passenger to Lingham and she had directed him to the house he had mentioned, near the church. She had asked him to wait on the road, so as, she said, not to rouse the children with the sound of the engine. She had said she would not be long. Then she had disappeared in the direction of the house. That must have been a few minutes before eleven.

The taxi-man settled down to wait, and wait he certainly did. The few minutes passed three or four times over, and still there was no sign of her. He began to get impatient, and getting out of the taxi, he walked up the short drive till he got in sight of the house, which had been hidden behind a small plantation. The house was dark and silent and no one seemed to be about. The taxi-man grew anxious about his fare, and he went forward and knocked at the first door he came to. Rudge recognised it as the side-door. For a time no one answered, and the taxi-man knocked louder and louder. At last a window opened upstairs and this parson put his head out. What was it: a sick call? The taxi-man gave him clearly to understand it was not a sick call, and the parson said he'd come down. He came down and asked what was wrong. The taxi-man asked would his passenger soon be out, as he had an early job in the morning and he didn't want to spend the night waiting at the gate. The parson evidently didn't know anything about the lady, but he asked for a description of her. Then sud-

denly he seemed to recognise her. He appeared upset for a moment, then he said it was all right, that he thought the lady was a friend of the housekeeper's, and if the taxi-man would wait a moment longer he would find out when she was leaving. He disappeared for three or four minutes, then he returned to say that the lady had been taken with a fainting fit, and in the excitement the taxi had been forgotten. The lady was not well enough to go back to Drychester that night, but would stay with his housekeeper, and he would pay the taxi. He had done so. The taxi-man had returned to Drychester, and that was all he knew about it.

Here was a fresh complication! Rudge swore. Instead of things straightening themselves out, the tangle was getting worse.

'Tell me,' said Rudge, 'you drove through Lingham, didn't you?'

'Correct, guv'nor.'

'Did you stop there?'

'Not above a minute or two. I stopped and the lady directed me which way to go.'

Here was at least something. This must have been the car Constable Hempstead had seen. So far as it went, Hempstead's report was corroboration of the story.

Rudge postponed consideration of the affair, and walked to the Anglers' Arms, which was near the station. And there he got some news which, he thought, entirely justified his suspicions.

It seemed that about seven o'clock on the evening in question, a telegram had been received from Waterloo, to the effect that the sender, Mrs Marsh, was going to Drychester by the next train and required a room to be reserved for the night. Also, she wished the hotel to be left open, as owing to having to pay a call on arrival, she could not reach it till midnight or later. The room had been duly prepared and the porter had waited up till nearly two, but the lady had not turned up, nor had anything been since heard of her.

This certainly did back up the tale that the lady had intended to return from Lingham Vicarage to Drychester. So far the thing looked *bona fide* enough. It would, however, be easy to get the details at the Vicarage. In the meantime Rudge must not lose sight of his present quest: what was Mount doing at Drychester?

He produced his photograph and asked if the hotel manager had ever seen the original. And then came the information which brought all his suspicions of Mount back with a rush and made him congratulate himself on having followed up this line of the case.

Mount, it appeared, had called at the hotel on the day following that on which the telegram had been received, and Rudge saw that

he must have gone there immediately on arrival in Drychester. He had stated that he was conducting a delicate enquiry on behalf of a member of his church. It concerned an unhappy marriage; he hoped the manager would not ask for details. His parishioner's wife had intended to meet her husband on the previous night with reference to a possible reconciliation, returning afterwards to the Anglers' Arms and there spending the night. But she had not turned up and his friend, wishing to keep his family skeleton hidden, had not himself come to the hotel to make enquiries, but had deputed him, the Vicar, to do so in his stead. Could the manager give him any information about the lady? The Vicar could not say under what name she might have registered.

Though the manager did not personally know Mount, he had seen him at functions at the cathedral, and was satisfied of his *bona fides*. He therefore gave him all the information at his disposal. Mr Mount had thanked him and had at once left.

Rudge imagined that this interview had probably constituted Mount's whole business in Drychester, but to make assurance as sure as possible, he went to the cathedral and in the guise of a former parishioner, asked the head verger if he had ever heard of his old rector, the Rev Philip Mount, who he believed was now in charge of a parish somewhere near. From this beginning it was easy to steer the conversation in the way it should go, and Rudge was soon convinced that the Vicar had not been at the cathedral on the day in question.

Rudge caught the last train to town that night. Next morning he was early at Scotland Yard, where he explained that he wanted to make some enquiries at the Charing Cross Hotel and possibly elsewhere. He was asked if he required help, and on his saying that he did not, he was told to go ahead and ring up if he was stuck.

Assured of a free hand, Rudge went on to the hotel. There with the aid of his photograph he had no difficulty in establishing the fact that Mount had arrived at a few minutes before nine on the evening he rang up, evidently from the train arriving at Waterloo at 8.35. So far as was known he had not gone out that night. Next morning he had paid his bill after breakfast and left.

So far it had been plain sailing for Rudge. Enquiries at the reception office and from waiters and chambermaids had quickly brought him his information. But now he was up against something stiffer. In vain he questioned porters and messenger boys. The head porter remembered seeing the Vicar, but he couldn't remember how he had left. He or one of his staff might have got a taxi for him, but they got so many taxis they couldn't be sure.

Rudge was extremely persistent, but success did not crown his efforts. Mount had gone, but no one knew how.

Rudge went out into the square in front of the station. In all probability Mount had walked to where he had wanted to go, or, if not, had taken a 'bus or gone down to the Underground. If so, Rudge did not see how he could possibly get on his track, and he would be forced to return to Whynmouth and fall back on the chance of getting a statement. Such a statement Mount might, of course, refuse to make, and Rudge didn't see how he could force it from him. No, if he, Rudge, could find out what Mount had done in town, it would be infinitely better.

He wondered whether Mount might not after all have taken a taxi. The porters might have forgotten the circumstance, or Mount might have come out into the square and hailed one himself. Rudge decided to make enquiries of those drivers who used ranks near the hotel.

He began at once, and a long job he found it. To man after man he showed his photograph and asked if he had taken the Vicar up. And man after man shook his head and said he had never seen the gentleman.

But Rudge persevered. These enquiries were his only hope, and he would be quite sure they led nowhere before abandoning them. And then at last his perseverence reaped its just reward. A driver came in from a job and took his place at the tail of the line. Rudge went up to him with his photograph.

The driver was by way of being discreet. He had seen Mount, but he didn't know what business of Rudge's that was. A little judicious backsheesh, however, overcame his scruples, and he told what he knew. Mount, it appeared, had hailed him from the station square and told him to drive to Judd Street, to a private hotel. He didn't just remember the number, but he could find the place again.

'Then find it,' said Rudge, getting in.

Presently they drew up at Friedlander's Private Hotel and in a couple of minutes Rudge was interviewing the manageress. Yes, the clergyman of the photograph had called on the morning in question. He had asked to see Mrs Arkwright, a lady who had been staying with them for some three weeks. But Mrs Arkwright had gone away unexpectedly the evening before and had not yet returned, so the clergyman was disappointed. He had left his name and address: Rev Philip Mount, Lingham Vicarage, Whynmouth, Dorset, and asked that Mrs Arkwright be requested to ring him up when she returned. He had then gone away.

Rudge turned the conversation on to Mrs Arkwright. The manageress was reticent, but still he managed to pick up a good deal. Mrs Arkwright was middle-aged, small, active and vivacious. She was decidedly good-looking and always dressed well. Though evidently not rich, she seemed comfortably off. The manageress was not certain that she might not be French. They had a French girl staying at the hotel, and Mrs Arkwright spoke French to her as fluently as she spoke English to the others.

Rudge felt he was getting on. That this Mrs Arkwright had unexpectedly travelled from London to Drychester on the evening before the crime now seemed clear. Having during the journey mysteriously become Mrs Marsh, she had driven to the Vicarage and there vanished.

Rudge would have liked to search the lady's room and belongings, but he had no warrant and he did not think he could manage it otherwise. However, by judicious pumping he obtained a little more information from the manageress.

Mrs Arkwright was pleasant-mannered and a favourite among the residents. She had not, however, many friends of her own, by which the manageress meant visitors. Indeed the manageress might say she had only one visitor, a man who called at irregular intervals. He was tall and distinguished-looking, and his forehead was bronzed, as if he had lived in some hot country. The manageress indeed had seldom seen so good-looking a man. His name was Mr Jellett.

Rudge was in a reflective frame of mind as he left the hotel and automatically turned his steps to the nearest tube station. There was something very puzzling about this whole business. That this Mrs Arkwright or Marsh had gone to the Vicarage on the night of the murder, there could be no doubt. But it wasn't at all certain that she had seen Mount. From what he had said to the taxi-man it was difficult to believe that Mount knew she was there. At the same time Rudge found it equally difficult to believe the story about her visiting the housekeeper and getting a fainting fit. In either case where had the woman disappeared to? It almost seemed as if Mount himself did not know and that his journeys to Drychester and London were simply an effort to find out.

To Rudge it looked very much as if there had been some secret negotiations in progress between the Vicar and this woman. Whether he had seen her on the night of the crime or not, something had happened to make him want to see her the next day. And there was an element of secrecy about the whole thing which looked anything but well.

Then Rudge remembered something he had been told by the garrulous landlady of the Lord Marshall Hotel at Whynmouth. This man, Mount, had had trouble in his life. His wife had run away from him with some man. Now could it be . . . ?

Rudge whistled softly between his teeth. If Mrs Arkwright-Marsh were really Mrs Mount, it might at least partially account for these mysterious proceedings. Some question, possibly that of a divorce, might have been raised, which would have necessitated an immediate interview. This would account for the visit to the Vicarage and Mount's subsequent journey to town, though it might not explain Mount's denying knowledge of her call. Oh, yes, it might, though. Rudge saw that he had been wrong. In the excitement of discussing a divorce the taxi might well have been forgotten, and when Mount found it waiting he might have invented the story about the housekeeper to allay possible scandal.

On the whole Rudge thought his theory promising enough to justify further enquiry into it. He did not see, it must be admitted, how it was connected with the death of Admiral Penistone, but that connection was suggested by the boat, the hat, and particularly by the Vicar's eagerness at the inquest.

How, Rudge wondered, could he find out about Mount's erring wife? He thought for a while, then, returning to the Yard, borrowed a Crockford. From this he found that Mount had been in his present position for ten years, before which he had been a curate in one of the Hull churches. Rudge immediately put through a call to the Superintendent at Hull, asking him to try to obtain a description and if possible a photograph of Mrs Mount.

In a couple of hours there was a reply to say that a photograph and description had been obtained and were being sent up to the Yard.

On Monday morning they arrived. The photograph had been got from one of the local newspaper offices, and showed the lady in a hospital committee group. The description gave Rudge a thrill of satisfaction. It looked as if he were on the right track.

In half an hour he was back in the hotel in Judd Street. He was sorry to trouble the manageress again, but would she be good enough to tell him if Mrs Arkwright was among this group?

The manageress hesitated a little, but when he explained that the photograph was ten years old she became quite certain. Yes, that fourth lady from the left was undoubtedly Mrs Arkwright.

Full of self-satisfaction, Rudge took the first train from Waterloo. Determined to be thorough, he went to Drychester and saw his friend, the taxi-man. Here he had not such definite con-

firmation, though the man agreed that his passenger might well have been the original of the photo.

It was with the gratifying consciousness of something attempted, something done, that Rudge returned to the police station at Whynmouth that afternoon to report his progress to Superintendent Hawkesworth. Hawkesworth, however, took the disappointingly narrow view of achievement so frequently displayed by Authority.

'Huh,' he said when Rudge had finished, 'it looks to me like a wash-out. This blessed parson is considering making things up with his wife or divorcing her or whatever you like to make it. But that won't help us any with the question of who killed old Penistone. What do you propose to do now?'

'I thought, sir, of going to Mount and asking for an explanation.'

Hawkesworth frowned. 'An explanation of just what?' he asked.

'An explanation of where Mrs Mount went to that night. The boat was gone; it was connected with the murder; who took it? Did Mrs Mount? I think, sir, we could press that question under the circumstances.'

The Superintendent considered, then nodded shortly. 'Very well; try it. You may as well, now you've gone so far.'

Rudge was bitterly indignant as he drove out to Lingham Vicarage. This was always what happened when you took trouble and did anything specially well! What sort of mind had Hawkesworth? Surely to goodness it was clear that this information about Mrs Mount was vital? Her unexpected visit to the Vicarage on the night of the crime; her unexpected disappearance after arrival there; Mount's ignorance or assumed ignorance of the whole affair. The boat; the hat; Mount's sudden attempt to find his wife; Mount's subterfuges to keep his real business from leaking out – ecclesiastical matters, he had said to Rudge; a parishioner's unhappy marriage, he had told the Drychester hotel-keeper; family news, he had explained to the lady in Judd Street . . .

In fact the whole thing was darned fishy, and he would be bound to get some valuable information from Mount. Somewhat cheered, Rudge set out for the Vicarage.

10

By Edgar Jepson

THE BATHROOM BASIN

Police Constable Richard Hempstead had been cherishing his aunt, Mrs Emery. At first when she returned to her native neighbourhood and settled down at Rundel Croft, he had showed himself nephewly, but in moderation, certainly not to the point of cherishing her, and even now the cherishing, it is to be feared, was not a natural effusion of pure nepotic feeling. It was the result of feeling, indeed, of two feelings: a strong feeling, a hunch, in fact, that the secret of the murder of the Admiral was to be found in Rundel Croft, and a scarcely less strong feeling that the society of Jennie Merton was good for him.

So it came about that during the last week he had been often in the house. When he was on his round, all kinds of reasons for just looking in on his aunt occurred to him; the house being empty, except for her and Jennie and Emery, burglars might have broken in, or the chickens might have been stolen; or he had to ask her some questions, connected with the mystery, of no great importance; or he had to give her some information, of no great importance, about the progress of the police towards the solution of it. He was gifted with a quite decent creative imagination, which, doubtless, was often of use to him in the witness-box. When he was off duty he would, in nephewly fashion, drop in to tea or supper.

It is to be doubted that Mrs Emery, who had rather more than her fair share of womanly intelligence, as the wives of the Emerys of this world generally have, ascribed his assiduity to the finer feelings of a nephew. She perceived that Jennie was, as a rule, at hand – she would have a good view of the drive from the windows of the upper part of the house, where most of her work lay – to open the door to him when he called. Also she had once heard her say, as she was bringing him from the back door to the kitchen: 'Oh, go hon, Mr Hempstead!'

Well, as Mrs Emery saw it, Jennie was a good girl, as girls go nowadays, and showed quite a lot of sense in the way she was

picking up cooking, and cooking was what a man really wanted when he was married; and in any case Dick was one of those pig-headed young men, who will go their own way, and he might do worse. Anyhow, who was she to interfere with love's young dream?

So it came about that Hempstead had had the run of Rundel Croft, for Elma Holland and her husband had not been in his way. If sometimes he was not alone, but accompanied by Jennie, when he was having the run of it, it did no one any harm. Also, he was a useful man to have about, for in a big house like Rundel Croft little things were always getting out of order and going wrong, and he was useful with his hands. Mrs Emery soon fell into the way of getting him to set the little things right that the Admiral had been used to set right, putting a spring in a lock that had ceased to work, restoring a patch of paint that had been rubbed off, to maintain in fact the spick and spanness the Admiral had demanded. He was a useful visitor.

He had inspired into Jennie his strong opinion that the solution of the mystery of the murder was to be found in the house, and though she would have helped him in his search, or at any rate superintended it at intervals, in any case, that identity of opinion made her help him with enthusiasm.

Together they searched the house with uncommon thoroughness, every nook and cranny of it, especially the Admiral's study and bedroom and Elma Holland's sitting-room and bedroom, hunting above all for the missing white frock in which Elma had dined at the Vicarage.

'Mind you, Jennie, I don't say as you're wrong in thinking that she packed it up that morning and took it to London with her,' he said. 'But there's a possibility that she rolled it up small and stuffed it away in some hole or corner, and if so be as we could find it, I'll eat my helmet if we don't find it marked in some way or another that would be a useful clue. It might even be blood-stained.'

'It might truly,' said Jennie in thoughtful agreement.

They found several holes and corners in which the frock might have been hidden; but they did not find the frock.

Then on Monday afternoon as they were finishing their tea (and it was just about the time that Inspector Rudge was reporting at Whynmouth police station) Mrs Emery said: 'There's one thing, Dick, as you might have a look at before you go, and that's the basin in the bathroom. Miss Elma complained, when she came back, that the water ran out of it very slowly and now it's quite

choked up and it won't run out of it at all. It's a job for a plumber, I know; but you might be able to do something with it.'

'Well, that's easy, Aunt,' said Hempstead with manly confidence. 'It's just a matter of clearing out the trap.'

He finished his tea – he was always rather longer about it than his uncle and the two women – and having gathered the tools he wanted from the house tool-box, he and Jennie went up to the bathroom, and he got to work. It was an easy job, for, after he had taken up the linoleum, he found the board in the floor above the trap loose, to enable the inevitable plumber to get at the trap easily. He unscrewed the nuts and lifted the cover off the trap. The trap was choked with hair, and he began to pull it out. He was struck by its coarseness and paused to examine it.

Then he said: 'This is rum. If I hadn't seen the beard on the Admiral's chin, I should have said as he'd shaved it off.'

'It is like the Admiral's beard,' said Jennie. 'Only it's not so grey.'

Hempstead picked the rest of the beard out of the trap carefully and put it in the little enamel basin he had brought up with him to hold the debris that was choking the trap, with a very thoughtful air.

Then he said: 'Aunt said that Mrs Holland complained of how slowly the water ran out of the basin when she came back from London after getting married. I don't suppose anybody had used that basin between then and the morning after the Admiral was murdered.'

'I don't suppose they did,' said Jennie.

'So, if anyone was shaving off his beard – ' said Hempstead thoughtfully and stopped short.

He had said enough. It was no good talking about things. Besides, he wanted to think it out.

'I shouldn't say anything about this, not even to my aunt or uncle,' he said. 'It may be important.'

'Of course not,' said Jennie. 'And certainly not to your aunt. It would be all over the place before night.'

'And you might find me a piece of thick brown paper. I can't dry this hair in front of the kitchen fire 'cos my aunt would see it.'

'Of course you can't,' said Jennie, and she went in search of brown paper.

Presently she came back with it. Hempstead squeezed the water out of the shaved-off hairs and wrapped them in the brown paper and put the little packet in his pocket. They went down to the kitchen.

'I suppose nobody used that basin between Mrs Holland's going away to get married and coming back, Aunt?' he said.

'Nobody that I know of,' said Mrs Emery.

'Well, I've cleaned out the trap for you, and the water's running quite free again,' he said and took his leave of them.

He went away thoughtfully, thinking it out, in search of Inspector Rudge.

He found him just outside the Vicarage gates, displayed his find and told him where he had come across it.

'It is,' said the Inspector, 'a rum go – in the trap of the bathroom basin at Rundel Croft? Well, well.'

His eyes brightened as he began to perceive the implications of the discovery.

'Yes, sir. And Mrs Holland complained that the water was running slow out of the basin when she came back after gettin' married, and nobody seems to have used that basin between that and her going away. It looks as if there couldn't have been any hairs in that trap when the Admiral went off to dinner at the Vicarage the night he was murdered. There certainly hasn't been anyone with a beard in the house since Mrs Holland went away the morning after the murder.'

'What you mean is that whoever shaved off that beard shaved it off on the night of the murder?' said the Inspector, frowning thoughtfully.

'That's right, sir.'

'Mr Holland didn't wear a beard by any chance?' said the Inspector.

'No, sir: I saw him about three or four times when he was courting Mrs Holland and he was just the same as now.'

'Ah,' said the Inspector, an he went on frowning.

Then he said: 'But whoever it was called that night at the Lord Marshall and asked for Mr Holland, did have a beard, and it seemed to me pretty clear that it wasn't the Admiral at all, and this seems to settle it. Whoever wore the beard, he went back to Rundel Croft and shaved it off.'

'That's right, sir,' said Hempstead.

'Well, he couldn't have done that, unless he knew someone at Rundel Croft very well, and it could only have been the Admiral himself or Mrs Holland. If the Admiral was alive, it might have been him; but if the Admiral was dead, it could only have been Mrs Holland,' said the Inspector.

'But it could hardly have been the Admiral, sir, because whoever it was shaved off his beard, he shaved it off because he didn't

want anyone to know that he'd been pretending to be the Admiral,' said Hempstead.

'Exactly, and it doesn't seem likely that the Admiral should want anyone to pretend to be him. But it was someone who knew one of them, right enough.'

'But the very last place that anyone who'd committed the murder would want to be seen in, is about here,' protested Hempstead.

'M'm,' said the Inspector. 'If you'd seen the silly things murderers do that I've seen. Besides, there are some people who call themselves criminologists, who say that a murderer always goes back to the scene of his crime.'

'Does he now?'

'No, he doesn't,' said the Inspector.

He was silent, considering the possibilities opened up by Hempstead's discovery.

Then, glowing with quiet cheerfulness, he added: 'Well, what we want is a man with a beard who has shaved it off. Now, where have I seen a man lately who'd shaved off his beard? I fancy I have.'

11

By Clemence Dane

AT THE VICARAGE

Rudge rang, and, getting no answer, rang again. He could hear the bell jangling in the deeps of the house, but he could not hear any sound of footsteps. The peace of summer which lay upon the garden had had its effect, apparently, upon the house itself. All its blinds were down and he could hear the loud ticking of the grandfather clock in the hall. Putting his eye to the key-hole, he observed: (*a*) That there was no key in the lock, and (*b*) that the hall was empty. No guilty Vicar was standing within upon the mat, quaking in his shoes, afraid to ignore the summons yet afraid to open. All was a tea-time quiet, yet there was no pleasant chink of china, no tinkle of spoons. 'Doubtless,' thought Inspector Rudge, 'the maids are taking tea out of doors. Girls often carry out their

sewing to a paddock. I'll go round.'

He went round. The neat, flagged courtyard at the back was, however, equally deserted. The kitchen door was locked, and there was nobody in the sheds at the further side of the yard. On the kitchen door, however, a card was pinned, a white card such as is used at funerals, and on it was inscribed: BACK AT SEVEN-THIRTY.

So that was that! Unwillingly, for in spite of his professional zeal Inspector Rudge would have enjoyed a cup of tea, he tramped out of the little yard. The noisy echoes of his feet breaking the silence, he skirted the garden. He should have gone straight out into the street, and knew it. Unless he were doing his official duty he was a trespasser without rights. But he had two hours to put in before he could return. Virtuously, he resolved to wander about the village, dropping questions casually, as Cockneys drop aitches, and perhaps visit that village sphinx, old Wade, in the hope of gleaning some stray straw of information. Still, it was exceedingly hot. Why hurry? Besides, wasn't that a greengage tree strapped up like a flogged prisoner to the wall at the corner of the garden?

Now, if Inspector Rudge had a weakness, it was for that deceptive fruit, the greengage. The Londoner knows gages only in boxes or barrow-tainted, knows that you have to eat three brackish spheres plucked too early, for the sake of the one sugary perfection plucked too late. But a small boy, Tommy Rudge, had stayed at his grandmother's somewhere up in Norfolk, thirty years earlier, and had eaten Norfolk gages from just such a wall. Memory, the experienced harpist, plucked at the Inspector's heart-strings. There was the tree: there were greengages, each with the golden crack of perfection widening on its jade cheek. The Inspector o'erleaped the years and the three feet of lettuce-bed at the same moment. He plucked, ate, dripped juice from chin and fingers, and dropped the stone at his feet.

As he did so a glint of light caught his eyes and made him peer downwards. The glint explained itself quickly enough, but it was not the bit of broken bottle winking in the sun which held his attention after that first preliminary greengage stones, not of his spitting-out, but not yet dry. By them lay a handkerchief, juice-stained, rolled into a ball, and on the bare ground at the foot of the tree were footprints, small, neat footprints. 'Size three,' thought Rudge, mechanically appraising, 'and French heels at that!'

Stooping without moving in his tracks, he drew the handkerchief to him, shook it out. It unrolled easily, for it was still wet: somebody clearly enough had wiped fingertips messed with juice

upon it. Then, unsteadily rising, still careful not to disturb the neighbouring tracks, he examined his find.

It was stained, it was crumpled; but the linen was fine, the embroidery delicate. 'Two-fifteen a dozen,' estimated the accurate Inspector Rudge, who had a gift for acquiring information of the oddest kind, and whose mother, a lady's maid in her day, had always seen to it that his information was correct. 'Two-fifteen at a guess, unless its sales,' repeated Inspector Rudge thoughtfully, when, fingering the corners, he discovered in one of them, small, detached, not part of the pattern, the initial C.

Very thoughtfully Inspector Rudge smoothed and folded the handkerchief, produced from his note-book a clean envelope, tucked it in, and restored the whole to an inner pocket. Yet more thoughtfully he glanced about him, hesitated over the stones, shook his head, considered the footprints, shook his head again, then, with a precaution entirely unlike his impetuous arrival, high-stepped off the bed on to the path, and began pacing majestically to and fro once more.

The late afternoon sun poured down upon his bowed shoulders till his blue serge suit shone sordidly, as blue serge will on a fine day. An inquisitive robin, mistaking him by his gait for the gardener, kept pace with him in the bushes. So slow was his progress that Michaelmas daisies, swaying over the path and pushed aside as he passed, had time to beat his broad back resentfully. For the Inspector was deep in thought and something more than thought. He was floundering, as once or twice before in his strange life he had floundered, out of the shallow of common sense into the unplumbed deeps of instinct. A mood was on him: that part of his mind which, as he put it, 'felt through his elbows' was in charge. Something was wrong, somewhere, somehow, and Inspector Rudge knew it. There was no one in the house as far as he could tell. He had spied into the hall and found it empty: the placard on the back door was explanation enough. Someone might be hiding in the house, of course. But why should they be? There was no sense in it. And Inspector Rudge had nothing at all to go upon, not even his own shrewd reasoning powers, not even his faculty of putting two and two together and making twenty-two of them. No, he had nothing but the handkerchief with the stained proof that someone had recently been in the garden, and his own feeling in his elbows that something was wrong.

There was no one in the house as far as he could tell, but he had the oddest feeling that there was someone in the garden. So strong a feeling was it that twice he stopped and turned round sharp to

stare down the overgrown glories of the long, straight path. Empty of course. Only an honest blaze of sunshine greeted him. Red, white and yellow heat blazed up again from the mounds of pyrethrum, the early purple daisies, the phloxes. The guardian hollyhocks stood motionless in the heavy, sun-saturated air. What's wrong with honest sunshine and rejoicing flowers? What's wrong with the Vicarage garden, just after teatime on an August afternoon? He turned and resumed his slow pacing. Something was wrong.

If 'C' were Mrs Mount, then within the last quarter of an hour Mrs Mount had been in her former husband's garden, eating her former husband's greengages, perfectly comfortably at home. And now she was – where? In the house? Why should she be? But she might. He had never seen her handwriting, and it was just possible that she had written BACK AT SEVEN-THIRTY on the funeral card. And where did she get such a card unless she had been in the house? It was the sort of card you would find in a parson's study, but hardly in a fashionable handbag. Had she written the message, written it, knowing that the servants were out, in her late husband's study? For whom was the message? For the incomprehensible Vicar? For the handsome unknown who occasionally came to see her at the hotel? Why half-past seven? Suppose she hadn't written the message. Suppose a maidservant had written it? Or the Vicar?

He had an impulse to go to the door and remove that telltale card, then restrained it. The card was a message for someone. Suppose that someone had not yet arrived and read it? Better not disturb the situation.

Unregretfully the Inspector cast aside all thoughts of a hot potter through the drowsy village, of unprofitable conversations with tinker, tailor and candlestick-maker, and another interview with old Neddy Ware. And more regretfully he cast aside also the pleasant, planned finale to that hot potter. No arrival at the local inn for Inspector Rudge, no deep draught of delicious beer, cooled in the well. Instead, instinctively and professionally the Inspector abandoned the open path for the little strip of lawn that ended in a shrubbery, and insinuated himself between the laurels. These began where the kitchen garden ended, and swept round the front garden, thus protecting by a twelve-foot belt of foliage the lawn and the house from the view of passers-by in the road.

The Inspector knew his duty. He glanced at his watch: it was nearing six. If anybody arrived at the Vicarage between that hour

and the seven-thirty of the notice at the back door, Inspector Rudge intended to know of it. The laurels were dirty, as laurels are even in the depths of the country, and the ground below them was dusty. His coign of vantage was airless and intolerably hot. Nevertheless, there Inspector Rudge intended to remain until the writer of the card returned or its destined reader arrived.

He made himself as comfortable as he could, though he did not dare smoke; but he kept chewing-gum for such emergencies and played noughts-and-crosses with himself, patiently; for the loam upon which he lay was dry and loose as sand. As the shadows lengthened the air grew cooler and he suffered less from heat but more from midges. But it was not until the village church had struck seven that his devotion was rewarded. Voices, cheerful and unlowered, struck upon his ear. The hidden gate of the drive creaked and banged again. Footsteps sounded the other side of the impenetrable wall of laurels and holly that divided the lawn from the entrance. Two figures swung round it deep in conversation, reached the porch, dived into its shadows, and the taller figure tugged at the bell.

Inspector Rudge gripped the tough laurel stems in his amazement. The last people in the world he expected at this hour in this place were the Hollands, husband and wife. What were they saying? What were they doing? He could hear the bell jangling, but he could not hear their words: and the porch was so deep in shadow that he could not watch their faces. Should he emerge and cross-question?

While he hesitated they turned in the doorway and Holland's voice rang clear.

'We may as well wait.'

His wife came out on the gravel.

'What's the time now?'

Her husband looked at his watch.

'Just past seven.'

Elma hesitated.

'I'm not coming all this way for nothing.'

'Have you considered,' Holland said uneasily, 'that it may be a trap?'

'A trap? How could it be?'

'Well – ' He hesitated. 'How much does Célie *know*?'

'Oh, don't fuss so, Arthur. It's hot and I won't be harried. Sit down a little.' And, crossing the lawn, she sank into the worn hammock that swung between two boughs of the giant cedar, while her husband flung himself on the grass beside her.

For some ten minutes the two sat there, saying little. Inspector Rudge cursed his luck. Nine out of ten women would have talked a rope about their necks in ten such idle minutes. It was his luck to be suspecting a woman outside his experience, a woman who could sit still and say nothing. Even when she tired of her immobility still she held her tongue, gave neither watcher a reason for her sudden movement. But when she swung her feet to the ground and began to stroll towards the house, her husband instantly rose and joined her. Had she signalled to him? Did she know herself watched? wondered Rudge. But he was sure that he himself had not stirred; nevertheless he remained perfectly still. Elma Holland, Inspector Rudge considered, was quite capable of setting a counter-trap. Meantime the pair had reached the house once more, and Holland's voice came ringing over the grass.

'I say, the door's ajar.'

'She must have come in without our seeing,' the woman's voice answered him. 'Come on! Let's go in! She must be somewhere,' and they disappeared.

Inspector Rudge drew a deep sigh of relief. At last he could move, could yawn, could stretch himself, could lift the weight of his body off one unfortunate foot, which, doubled under him, was almost asleep. It was a very bad attack of pins and needles indeed. He was just beginning gently to massage it when he was nearly startled out of his senses by the sound, faint but unmistakable, of a scream. He stiffened where he sat. Then, pulling himself to his feet, was preparing to grope his way into the open, when nearer, much louder, much more vigorous, came a second scream, a whole series of screams; and there burst out of the dark open entry the figure of Elma Holland.

Once out of the doorway she appeared to have no further power to walk, though she laboured forward a short step or two as if she were thrusting her way through an invisible hedge. Her face was white as the washed walls of the house, and as her husband, who came racing the next moment across the threshold, reached her, she fell back into his arms like a stuffed sack.

The Inspector was not much less swift, but as he broke through the bushes and ran across the lawn to them, his thought ran ahead of him – 'What has she seen to break *her* nerve like that?' Then, as he reached the huddled pair, he noted the condition of Holland's hands and, first crying: 'Here! Out of my way!' – added 'and stay where you are!' pushed past them, leaped up the steps, dashed across the hall and flung open the dining-room door. Empty! So was the drawing-room. But the door of the Vicar's study was

open. In went Rudge and cast a hurried glance about him.

Very still was the study, barred with sun and shadow, very cool, very dark. It was a pleasant coolness and a pleasant darkness after the glare of the lawn. 'Quiet as a tomb,' thought the Inspector to himself. 'So what's she screaming about?' Then, as he moved to the writing-table, which was set at an angle to the window, rampart-wise, he saw what Elma Holland had screamed about.

Slid down upon the floor between the desk and the wall lay the body of a woman. Her eyes were open and glazed like the eyes of a carefully painted waxwork; on her cheeks the make-up stood out in hectic patches on her skin. Her two hands were clasped upon her breast, not peacefully, but in a last gesture of energy. They were clasped about a knife-handle, whose blade was sunk in the stained folds of her flowered summer dress.

12

By Anthony Berkeley

CLEARING UP THE MESS

Rudge plumped down on his knees beside her, heedless of the blood which lay everywhere on the carpet. The woman was still warm, and the blood had scarcely ceased to flow from her breast. But quite certainly she was dead.

A voice from the doorway brought the Inspector to his feet again.

'We were in the hall when she did it. We actually heard her fall.' Holland spoke gravely, but without any traces of panic.

Rudge frowned. 'I thought I told you to stop outside, sir.'

'Oh, damn your rotten little orders, man. Here's a woman stabbed herself; it's no time to stand on ceremony. Is there anything we can do? *Is* she dead? Are you certain?'

Rudge got slowly to his feet. 'She's dead right enough. Must have died just about the time you were in the house.'

'She died in my arms, then,' said Holland sombrely.

Rudge glanced at the blood on the other's hand, and Holland nodded.

'I held her up for a second,' he said. 'I thought she was dead, so

didn't disturb her hands or take the weapon out.'

'That was wise of you, sir.'

'You know who she is, of course? My wife's French maid – Célie.'

'Ah!' said Rudge. 'I shall have a few questions to ask you and Mrs Holland.'

'Later,' Holland said, in his masterful way. 'My wife's very much upset at the moment. Naturally. I can't have her worried till she's had time to recover.'

Rudge lifted his eyebrows slightly, but all he said was: 'I must ask you not to leave these premises for the present, either of you. Where is Mrs Holland now?'

'I put her in a hammock, on the lawn. I must get back to her. We'll wait for you there, Inspector. Anything we can tell you, of course, we will.'

There was the sound of footsteps on the gravel outside, which marched without hesitation into the hall. 'Anyone about?' called a voice. The next moment the figure of the ubiquitous reporter from the *Evening Gazette* appeared in the doorway. With a muttered word Holland slid past him and out of the house.

A shaft of sunlight from the window flashed cheerfully on the reporter's horn-rimmed spectacles. 'Hullo, Inspector. Didn't expect to see you. Is the Vicar about?' He caught sight of what lay at Rudge's feet. 'My God – what's this?'

'I understand it's Mam'selle Célie,' Rudge replied austerely, 'Mrs Holland's late maid. And I must ask you to leave me alone here, *if* you please. I'll see you get your story later. There are – ' Further sounds of footsteps outside caused him to break off short. Both men listened intently. Again the footsteps progressed without hesitation into the house, and along to the study. The Vicar came into the room.

'Why, Inspector,' he said in surprise. 'I didn't know you were to be present too. Has – *oh*!' For a moment he appared too frozen with horror to move. Then he threw himself on his knees beside the body with a little cry. '*Celia*!'

'Don't touch her, please, sir.' Rudge bent down as if to guard the body from the Vicar's ministrations.

The latter turned a ravaged face up to him. 'She's dead?'

'I'm afraid so, sir.'

'She hasn't – killed herself?'

'It looks uncommonly like it, sir.'

Mr Mount dropped his face into his hands and remained motionless for nearly a minute. When he spoke again it was with

more self-possession.

'Inspector, you know who this poor soul is?'

'She's already been identified, sir, as Mrs Holland's late French maid.'

'Yes.' The Vicar paused for a moment, as if to stiffen himself in a resolve. 'Inspector, there are many things connected with this tragedy that I cannot tell you. My lips are sealed by the confessional. But if it will serve the interests of justice this much I can say: this poor woman is my wife. And alas, I fear that it is I who drove her to this terrible deed.'

2

'You, sir?' said the Inspector sharply. 'How is that?' Then catching sight of the newspaper man, he added: 'Here, I told you to clear out.' He was about to seize the fellow by the shoulder and hustle him out of the room, by way of some physical vent for the various emotions that were boiling inside him, when he saw from the other's white face and shaking hands that it was not just callous professional curiosity which had kept him there; the man looked indeed almost incapable of walking. Rudge laid a gentle instead of a ferocious hand on his arm, and led him towards the door. 'In the War, weren't you?'

The reporter mustered up a shaky smile. 'Yes, but we didn't kill – women. I think I'm going to be sick.'

The Vicar pushed past the Inspector and took charge, leading the man into a small lavatory that opened off the hall just inside the front door. 'Stay there till you feel better,' he nodded, and returned with the Inspector to the study.

'Turns some people up, blood does,' commented the latter. 'Now, sir – you were going to tell me?'

They stood side by side, looking down at the dead woman. 'Poor soul, poor soul,' muttered the Vicar. 'The mother of my boys, Inspector. Perhaps I was too harsh with her. Too narrow, perhaps. Yet what else could I have done? My creed expressly forbids divorce. "Those whom God hath joined together let no man put asunder . . . " It's too explicit.'

'She wanted you to divorce her?' Rudge gently dropped the question into the Vicar's musings, which seemed to be addressed more to himself than to the Inspector.

'Yes. I never knew the name of the man who induced her to run away with him; she always refused to tell me; perhaps it was better so. But he seems to have been kind to her, according to his lights.'

It was plain that the Vicar was trying hard to be just. 'At any rate, he was faithful to her; and she to him. They wanted to marry. They always have wanted to marry. But I could not reconcile it with my conscience to divorce her. Then last Tuesday – the night of the murder, in fact . . . '

'Yes?' Rudge almost held his breath. At last something was going to come out about that night's hidden happenings.

'She called upon me here, quite late, and urged me once more to reconsider my decision. She was very upset – agitated – quite distraught, in fact . . . '

'Ah!' breathed Rudge.

'I had the greatest difficulty in soothing her. Especially in view of what I had to say.'

'You repeated your refusal, then?'

'What else could I do?' asked the Vicar piteously. 'I considered that I had no choice. The injuction is too explicit. It distressed me very much to have to say so, but conscience,' added the Vicar, with a wan smile, 'makes brave men of us all.'

'And what time was this, sir, when the lady called?' It distressed the Inspector too to have to continue his cross-examination in these circumstances, but his duty was no less plain.

'I saw her soon after midnight.'

'But we have information that she arrived here at about eleven?' Rudge said gently.

A slight flush appeared on the Vicar's cheekbones. 'I repeat, I saw her soon after midnight. About a quarter past twelve, so far as I can say. I brought her into the study here, and we talked for nearly an hour.'

'But what was she doing between eleven and a quarter past twelve?'

The Vicar's lips stiffened. 'That I cannot tell you, Inspector.'

'Meaning that you won't tell me, sir, or you don't know?'

'I have nothing further to say.'

The two men eyed each other steadily.

Rudge gave up the point. 'And this afternoon? Had she made an appointment with you?'

'She had, for seven o'clock, and with Mr and Mrs Holland too. Unfortunately, most unfortunately I was late. Otherwise,' said the Vicar, with a little break in his voice, 'who knows but what I might not have prevented – this?'

'And you had been – ?'

'At the Ferrers Abbas flower-show. The maids are there still, and my boys. The house was quite empty.'

'Why did Mrs Mount make this appointment?'

'She did not say, in so many words.'

'But you gathered, sir?'

'I think,' said the Vicar, a little uneasily, 'that she had come to some decision regarding certain information she considered she had concerning Admiral Penistone's death.'

'And that information is known to you?'

A look of obstinacy which Rudge in his exasperation characterised privately as mulish, spread over the Vicar's face. 'I told you just now, Inspector, that on some points my lips are sealed. That is one of them.'

Again the two looked at each other.

But this time an interruption came from without. Once more footsteps sounded on the gravel drive, to be followed this time by the jangling in the back regions of an old-fashioned bell.

The Vicar went out into the hall, and Rudge followed him.

Standing in the open front door was a small, elderly man, whose not very spick-and-span suit was set off by a smart grey trilby hat set at a jaunty angle. 'Ah, Mount,' he said. 'Sorry I'm so infernally late. Is the conference over?'

'Conference?' repeated the Vicar stupidly.

'Yes. Seven o'clock I was told to be here. I couldn't quite make out what it was about on the telephone, but the – the lady sounded pretty urgent.'

'She – rang you up?'

'Yes.' The new-comer looked more than a little embarrassed. 'Sounded like a cock-and-bull story to me. Well, she said she was your *wife*.'

'She was,' said the Vicar sombrely. He turned to Rudge. 'Inspector, I don't think you know Sir Wilfrid Denny, do you?'

'By sight well enough, sir. I'm glad to see you've come back, Sir Wilfrid. I've been hoping to have a word with you.'

'About this terrible business at Rundel Croft? Yes, of course. I got back this afternoon. It never occurred to me that you'd want to see me, or I'd have come back sooner. I had to go to Paris.'

'Denny . . . '

The Vicar was obviously going to break the news of the latest tragedy, and, not wishing to intrude on the scene, Rudge turned away. Out of curiosity he opened the door of the lavatory where the sick reporter had been parked, and glanced inside. It was empty. Evidently he had recovered.

Before returning to the study to mount guard over the body and telephone to the Super and Dr Grice, Rudge indulged his curiosity

once more. He took a couple of steps outside the front door and glanced across the lawn. The result gratified him. In the hammock sat Mr and Mrs Holland, side by side; Mr Holland's arm was about his wife, and Mrs Holland's head was on her husband's shoulder. Even as Rudge glanced at them she raised it and spontaneously kissed him.

'So she *is* human after all,' said Rudge to himself as he hurriedly turned away. 'And now she's found out that she loved him all the time. Well, they say it takes a shock to make some of 'em realise it.'

3

Rudge had handed over to Superintendent Hawkesworth.

Major Twyfitt, the Chief Constable, had motored back home, but luckily he had not taken back Hawkesworth to the county town with him. Together the two, as soon as Dr Grice had arrived, had searched the house, but nothing had been discovered to throw any further light on the death. The Superintendent was now making arrangements for the removal of the body, and Rudge found himself at liberty for a few words with Mr and Mrs Holland.

Mrs Holland was still in the hammock. That she had received a severe shock was obvious, but already she was showing such signs of recovery that Rudge, who wished to put his questions while impressions were still strong, thought himself justified in overriding Holland's objections to an immediate interview. He dropped, with a carefully unofficial air, on the grass beside the pair.

'It's unfortunate, sir, I agree. But you'll understand that I must do my duty. Now would you be good enough to tell me first of all what you know about this appointment? When did Mrs Mount make it, and what reason did she give?'

Rudge had addressed his question to Elma, but it was Holland who answered it. 'She rang us up at the Lord Marshall just after lunch today, and asked us to meet her here. She gave no reasons.'

'But you would have inferred one?'

'No.'

'Was it you who spoke to her on the telephone?'

'No,' said Holland – a little reluctantly, Rudge thought. 'It was my wife.'

'I see.' Rudge turned pointedly to Mrs Holland. 'What reason did you infer then, madam?'

'None.' Elma's tone was as curt as ever.

'You did not ask for any?'

'No.'

'But it must have seemed strange to you that your late maid should want to meet you at the Vicarage?'

'I imagined she was upset about something and wanted advice, and did not care to come to the inn, where she might be recognised.'

'But why shouldn't she be recognised?'

Elma shrugged her shoulders. 'That I can't tell you.'

'Did you know that she was Mrs Mount?'

'Certainly not.'

'It surprises you?'

'Very much.'

'Perhaps,' said Rudge tentatively, 'you can see some way in which that fact may throw light on your uncle's death?'

'I'm afraid I can't,' Elma retorted. 'But of course it gives a reason for her having left me – my service so abruptly.'

Rudge nodded. 'Yes, that's true enough. By the way, you say you imagined she was upset about something. Did she sound upset on the telephone?'

'Agitated, perhaps,' Elma said slowly. 'Yes, she did.'

And yet not too agitated, Rudge thought, to eat greengages before the conference she had called.

'It never occurred to you,' he went on, 'that the advice you thought she wanted might be on some matter connected with your uncle's murder, Mrs Holland?'

'Certainly not,' Elma replied sharply. 'Why should it?'

Rudge might have given more than one reason for his question. Instead, he asked, slowly and significantly: 'How much did Célie – *know*?'

His shot got home. Elma paled, then flushed, and sent a glance towards her husband which was a patent appeal for help. Holland supplied it at once.

His words took Rudge by surprise. He did not bluster or attempt to end the interview, merely remarking: 'It's curious you should say that, Inspector; I asked my wife that identical question not an hour ago. I too had considered the possibility that she might be about to give us some information on the Admiral's death. But my wife was positive she could have known nothing.'

'How could she?' asked Elma, in relieved tones.

Rudge glanced from one to the other. He knew very well that Mrs Holland had said nothing of the sort, at any rate just then. He was not sure that he had been wise. In an attempt to frighten

information out of them, he had intimated to the pair that he had overheard their conversation while they were waiting; and Holland, of course, had seen him come out of the bushes. They could not know for certain that he had not been able to hear them too while Elma was in the hammock. And yet Holland had not been in the least frightened. He had taken the thing quietly out of Rudge's hands, reassured his wife, and returned an answer which was admirable in its non-committal quality. Rudge had to console himself with the fact that without doubt Elma had, just for an instant, lost her grip. These two *must* know something – but Rudge recognised that there was not the faintest hope of getting it out of them by direct questioning.

Anxious not to put them too much on their guard, he tried another line. 'Now, will you tell me, sir, exactly what happened when you got into the house? You noticed the front door open, I think, and followed Mrs Holland inside?'

Holland smiled slightly. 'As you saw, Inspector, from your laurel bush, yes. By the way,' he added, more sternly, 'had you some idea that anything like that was going to happen? Because if so . . . '

'I had no idea, sir; no more than yourself. Now, will you kindly give me those facts?'

'Well, I followed my wife into the hall. We thought that Célie – Mrs Mount – must have come, as the door was ajar. We looked into the drawing-room first, then the dining-room. I think it was while we were in the dining-room (which adjoins the study, you know) that we heard a scream – '

'A *terrible* scream,' put in Mrs Holland with a shudder.

'Yes, it was terrible. I've never heard anything so – well, *awful* – producing awe. It was just like an animal. I dashed out of the dining-room and into the study, but before I got there I heard a thud, which must have been made by her fall. And there she was, on the carpet, and the blood streaming out. As I told you, she died in my arms.'

'Oh-h-h-h-h-h,' shuddered Elma.

'I see. Thank you, sir. And you, Mrs Holland? That coincides with your own impressions?'

'Yes. I think so. Perhaps I should have said myself that we heard her fall before my husband moved, but I couldn't be sure.'

'But you think not, sir?'

Holland considered. 'I couldn't say. Perhaps, I suppose we stood still for a few seconds. Sort of frozen, you know. Yes, perhaps we heard the thud before I moved. I'm not sure we didn't,

now I come to think. But in any case there couldn't be more than a second and a half in it either way.'

'And then you followed your husband into the study, madam?'

'Yes,' Elma faltered. 'And saw – and saw . . . ' She covered her face with her hands and her body shook.

Holland leapt up. 'Inspector,' he said, in a low voice, 'get out.'

Rudge got.

In any case he had not expected to learn anything more.

4

'Of course it's suicide,' growled the Superintendent. 'The doctor says her grip on the dagger must have been applied during life; there's only her prints on it; the Hollands were within a few yards of the room when she did it, and actually heard her fall; Rudge had command of the front door, and the back door remained bolted on the inside, and when he searched the house there was no one in it. How could it be anything but suicide?' The Superintendent spoke scornfully.

Rudge said nothing, but his ruddy cheeks grew a shade ruddier still.

'You don't agree, Rudge?' said the Chief Constable.

'No, sir, I'm afraid I don't. The way I look at it is this. Would a woman going to commit suicide fill up the time beforehand by eating greengages? It isn't natural.'

'Then you are saying Holland killed her?' asked the Superintendent sharply. 'Because there's no one else who could.'

'No, sir, I'm not saying that either.'

It was the following morning, and a conference was being held at Whynmouth police station. Already there was tension in the air, and further tension threatened. The possibilities of Mrs Mount's death being due to suicide or murder had been discussed already for at least half an hour, and no decision had yet been reached. The Superintendent was all for suicide, and the Chief Constable had to agree that the logic was on his side; Inspector Rudge obstinately clung to murder, and when challenged to produce his proofs could only mutter puerilities about things being 'natural' or the reverse, and 'feeling things in his bones'; no wonder the Superintendent snorted. Major Twyfitt had persevered nobly in a Chief Constable's first duty, that of holding the balance between two disputing subordinates, but did not know how soon it might not escape from his grasp.

He determined now to shift the ground of discussion. 'Well, of

course, Rudge, if you feel that way you'll do all you can to collect evidence to support your idea. Otherwise I think we can leave it for the time being to the coroner. Now, about the murder of Admiral Penistone. You told us last night of the dead woman's identity with Célie Blanc, the lady's maid, which does definitely connect the Vicarage with the tragedy, as you've felt all along,' said the Chief Constable soothingly. 'And you told us about Hempstead's discovery in the bathroom at Rundel Croft. Now, have you any ideas where all this is going to lead us?'

'I have, sir,' replied the Inspector grimly. 'I've a very good idea indeed.'

'Ah, that's good. What is it?'

'I'd rather not say, sir, if you don't mind, until I've collected a little more *evidence*,' Rudge answered, with a side-glance at the Superintendent.

'Yes, yes, of course. So long as you're working on definite lines. Well, the Superintendent has got the details from the Admiralty now about that episode at Hong Kong, which you'd like to hear. Just let Rudge have the facts, Superintendent.'

Superintendent Hawkesworth drew a folded paper from his breast-pocket, opened it, and in a totally expressionless voice read:

' "Captain Penistone was involved in a disgraceful scene in Hong Kong in 1911. By his own admission he followed a girl, who was being ill-treated by a Chinaman, into a low-class den which was already unfavourably known to the authorities. After that he stated that he remembered nothing further. He was, however, seen, in an advanced state of intoxication, singing and dancing in the company of a number of seamen of both British and other nationalities, and Chinese coolies; and he was carried on board his ship the next morning, still under the influence of drink and opium, by a party of his own men who had recognised him the previous evening. In consideration of his record, Captain Penistone was permitted to send in his papers instead of being tried by court-martial. On the outbreak of hostilities with Germany, Captain Penistone volunteered his services in any capacity, and in view of the emergency he was reinstated temporarily with his rank of Captain. He served with distinction throughout the War, and so far as the Admiralty was concerned, the regrettable incident at Hong Kong was expunged from the records. The Admiral, however, expressed to several of the senior officers here his dissatisfaction with the affair, and his belief that a good deal more lay behind it than had ever appeared, and he used to state his

intention of devoting his leisure on retirement to getting to the bottom of it; but as to whether there were any grounds or evidence for this belief, nothing is known here." '

'I see,' said Rudge. 'Followed a girl in, did he? Well, that clears up one point, sir, doesn't it? File X!'

'You mean, File X contained the evidence he had collected to support his view that the incident was rigged?' nodded the Chief Constable. 'Yes, that's the view we'd come to.'

'And it gives you something else, Rudge,' added Hawkesworth. 'It gives you motive. Those papers had disappeared from the folder, hadn't they? Obviously they were taken after the murder, by the murderer. In other words, the Admiral was right. He'd got his evidence – and it was going to implicate somebody who didn't want to be implicated. So the Admiral was murdered to stop him blowing the gaff. Well, that gives us a pretty strong pointer. The murderer is a man who was in Hong Kong in 1911. Anything wrong with that?'

'Nothing,' Rudge agreed. 'That's right enough, sir. Must be. But there's one thing I can't understand, and that's Mr Holland's story about seeing the Admiral, *in* his study, *with* a lot of papers on his desk, *after* midnight that night. According to what the doctor says, that's just the time the murderer ought to have been looking for File X.'

'And perhaps so he was,' said the Superintendent darkly.

'If you mean Holland, sir,' said Rudge, returning to an old difficulty, 'why did he want to come out with that story at all, when there was no evidence that he wasn't safe in bed and asleep at the Lord Marshall?'

'I don't mean Holland,' snapped the Superintendent. 'I mean the man Holland saw. The man whom he mistook for the Admiral. The man who was impersonating the Admiral – for the third time.'

'The *third* time?'

'Yes. Once in the study, once at the Lord Marshall, and once – in Hong Kong.'

'*Oh*!' Rudge registered such genuine admiration that the Superintendent forgave him his foolishness about Mrs Mount. 'That's a smart bit of work, sir, if I may say so.'

'You can bank on it, that's the murderer,' said the Superintendent complacently, and his tone added that that was not the end of the smart work.

'But wait a bit,' cried the Inspector excitedly. 'That means Mrs Holland's in it. Holland gave it away that she was in the study too.'

'And haven't you thought all the time that Mrs Holland knew a good bit more than she let on?'

'I never thought she was actually mixed up in the murder,' Rudge confessed.

With an air of triumph the Superintendent rose and unlocked a cupboard. From it he produced a package, and from the package a white chiffon frock. His large hands looked absurdly incongruous on the delicate stuff as he draped the dress over the back of a chair before the eyes of the Inspector. His reason for doing so was plain; there was no need for him to point to the rusty-coloured stain that smeared one hip. 'The missing white dress. Got a warrant to search her room at the Lord Marshall, and found it at the bottom of a drawer,' he said briefly.

'I *knew* she knew something!' exclaimed Rudge.

'Why *do* people keep damning evidence against themselves?' Major Twyfitt asked.

'Lucky for us they do, sir,' said Hawkesworth. To Rudge he added: 'Mind you, I don't think she was in it from the start. But she's an accessory after, all right. And that gives us another pointer. See it?'

'Oh, yes,' nodded Rudge. 'The brother, Walter. I've had him in mind from the beginning.'

'You have, eh?' said the Superintendent, somewhat discomfited. 'Why didn't you ever say so, then?'

'No evidence,' replied Rudge smugly.

'Anyhow, it seems clear enough now,' interposed the Chief Constable. 'We can assume, I think, that if anyone has been impersonating the Admiral, either in Hong Kong or here, it must have been this Walter Fitzgerald. There must have been a strong resemblance. We've got evidence of that too, Rudge. Two witnesses who saw a man in Whynmouth on the day of the murder whom they mistook in the distance for the Admiral, and only realised when they were quite close that it was a younger man.'

'Yes, sir? And that gives me another idea. May I put through a telephone call to London?'

'Of course.'

Rudge consulted his note-book, and then gave the number of Friedlander's Hotel and asked for priority. The connection was made in less than two minutes. Rudge explained who he was, and said: 'You remember telling me that Mrs Arkwright only had one regular visitor, a tall man with a bronzed forehead? Did this man wear a beard? He did? Thank you.' He rang off.

The other two looked at him enquiringly.

'That connects up something more.' Rudge was unable to conceal his satisfaction. 'The man who ran off with Mrs Mount, the man whose name the Vicar never knew – that was Walter Fitzgerald, too.'

'Ah!' said two breaths simultaneously.

'It's beginning to work in.'

The Superintendent cleared his throat. 'Now, my theory of what happened that night is this. The man, this Walter Fitzgerald, came down – Yes? What is it? Oh, come in.' A loud knock at the door had broken him off in mid-sentence.

Police Constable Hempstead entered, looking thoroughly pleased with himself. In his hand he held a short length of manilla rope, knotted to another short length. 'Hope I'm not disturbing you, sir,' he said to Major Twyfitt, 'but thought you'd like to know at once. I've searched both banks thoroughly this morning, from Rundel Croft to the sea, and found nothing except this.'

'The missing bit of the painter!' exclaimed Rudge. 'Where was it? Sorry, sir,' he added perfunctorily to the Chief Constable, who nodded good-humouredly.

'Caught up in some bushes, 'bout half-way down, on the Vicarage side.'

'Good man,' said the Chief Constable as he took the rope, and even Hawkesworth grunted approval.

'Did you make any enquiries at the cottages?' asked Rudge.

'Every one, sir. Nobody heard or saw anything. But I've found out something else.'

'You have, eh? What?'

'Well, you remember that set of photos you gave me, sir, of the finger-prints on the oars in the Admiral's boat? Well, I believe I've identified them.' Hempstead produced a piece of paper, which the Superintendent took before anyone else could reach it.

He whipped another set of the photographs out of his pocket and pored over them for a minute. Then he looked up. 'That's the man. Who is it, Hempstead?'

Hempstead beamed with self-importance. 'Neddy Ware, sir.'

5

When Rudge left the police station for a belated lunch he had a good deal to think about. The business was getting altogether too wide-spread for his liking. Half the inhabitants of Lingham seemed now to be implicated in the murder, or at the least accessories after it. The Vicar, Elma Holland, and now Neddy

Ware. There was another point against Neddy Ware too. The plaster casts which had been taken of the footprints on the bank showed a number which had been definitely identified as the Admiral's, several of his niece's, and just a few of a large, coarse sole, studded with nails, which could belong to anybody at Rundel Croft but a gardener; but they might belong to Neddy Ware. The impressions were good, and the Super was going to find out himself, after lunch, whether they were Neddy Ware's or not; but no one had any doubt now on the point.

He had been cunning, had Neddy Ware. The Inspector ruefully acknowledged to himself that he had been completely taken in by the old man. Neddy Ware had given him precisely correct information on all matters concerning the river and its tides which he could have checked from anyone else who was familiar with them; even on points which might have told against himself he had been accurate; but what about his speculations, which the Inspector had unconsciously put on practically the same basis as the rest? It was difficult now to disentangle speculation from fact, even in consultation with his note-book, but there seemed to Rudge two main ideas which Ware had deftly given him and which had lain in his mind ever since as a basis on which any theory of the crime must be founded: that if the Admiral had taken his boat out at all that night he must have taken it down-stream, and that it would have taken him an hour to row to Whynmouth. How did these two ideas look now?

For the first there really seemed no reason at all. Why must the Admiral have gone down-stream? So that the abandoned boat could have drifted to where it was found at the time it was found. But was it found at that time? And at that place? The whole of Ware's first story must now be viewed with the deepest suspicion.

What about the second point, then? From Rundel Croft to Whynmouth, by water, was about two and three-quarter miles. The Admiral must have started at between a quarter-past and half-past ten. At that time the tide was, even according to Ware's own information, at its strongest ebb. Could a lusty man not row a boat, with a swiftly flowing tide to help him, at faster than a slow walking pace? Nonsense; of course he could. Twice as fast. Very well, then. Neddy Ware had wanted to deceive the police as to the time the Admiral could have reached Whynmouth that night (assuming for the moment that on the other point he had been speaking the truth, and it was down-stream the Admiral had gone). Now why the deuce had he wanted to do that?

At this point the Inspector mechanically pushed his full plate of

gooseberry pie away from him and allowed one of his landlady's best efforts to get stone cold.

There were only two possible reasons that Rudge could see; one, that somebody had an alibi for half-past eleven, but not for eleven o'clock; and the other, to make the police think that the man who called at the Lord Marshall just after eleven was an imposter – which was exactly what they did think. But in that case the man really was the Admiral . . .

This was getting altogether too difficult. Rudge noted the point for future reference, and followed another line.

There was another advantage too in shifting forward the time of events by half an hour or so. Just after midnight the brother, Walter Fitzgerald, had been in the Admiral's study. This extra half-hour gave him plenty of time to get there, break the news to his sister, and begin his search for File X, by midnight. Without it, Rudge had found the time-table exceedingly cramped.

Well, there already were the answers to any number of his thirty-nine articles of doubt. Rudge turned them up in his note-book and glanced through them, to see whether this intervention of Neddy Ware's cleared up any more puzzles.

It did, at once. 26: Why was the Admiral wearing a coat? Rudge remembered the difficulty. If it was the Admiral who had taken out his boat that night, and a fairly warm night at that, why wear a coat for hard rowing? But suppose it was not the Admiral who had been doing the rowing. Suppose it was Neddy Ware, who had not only brought the boat back but had taken it out too, with the Admiral as passenger. There was a profitable line of enquiry. If only that were true, Neddy Ware must know not only where the Admiral had gone, but who had killed him. But how on earth to find out if it were true? Because quite certainly Neddy Ware would not give himself away on that point.

Well, there was only one possibility. The Vicar had been sitting in his summer-house. He might have seen. Rudge had had a suspicion already that the Vicar had seen something from that summer-house. Well, the Vicar had got to be made to speak, that was all.

Falling at last on his gooseberry pie, Rudge swept the plate clean in half a dozen gargantuan mouthfuls, followed them with a couple of bites of bread and cheese, and ran down to the street and his car.

Mr Mount was in, and had just finished his own lunch. He received the Inspector in his study.

Rudge came to the point at once. 'Sorry to bother you again, sir,

but we've information that Admiral Penistone left Rundel Croft in his boat, at about ten-fifteen. You were sitting in your summer-house at that time, overlooking the river. Did you see him leave?'

The Vicar answered at once. 'Since you ask me the direct question, Inspector: yes, I did.'

'Thank you, sir. Is it any good my asking why you didn't let me have this information sooner? Although I never actually asked you, you must have known it would be very valuable.'

'Certainly, I will tell you. It was because I feared that my knowledge might lead you to suspect an innocent man.'

'I see, sir. Then you know who murdered Admiral Penistone?'

'No,' the Vicar retorted, 'I don't. But I'm pretty sure who didn't.'

'Well, we'll leave that. Which way did the Admiral head, sir? Up-stream or down?'

'Down.'

'And Neddy Ware was rowing him?'

The Vicar looked first startled, and then distressed. 'Inspector, if you suspect old Ware of – '

'I don't, sir. Not of the murder.'

'I have your word?'

'You have, Mr Mount.'

'Very well. Then I will admit to you that Ware *was* rowing the Admiral that night; and extremely surprised I was to see it. I had no idea they were even acquainted. But that is the reason why I said nothing of what I saw. We parsons have to rely a good deal on our estimate of people's natures, you know, and I would stake everything I have on the fact that old Ware is totally incapable of anything of that kind. I've known him ever since he came to Lingham, you see, so I feared that this information of mine would put you on an entirely wrong scent. I therefore determined to volunteer nothing myself, but to use what influence I may have with Ware to induce him to come to you of his own accord and give you a full account of his own knowledge of that night's happenings, whatever it may be. I may say I have quite failed.'

'He told you he wouldn't come to us?'

'More than that. He denies that he was in the boat at all; he says that I was mistaken.'

'We have quite definite evidence that he was, sir; his finger-prints on the oars.'

'Yes, I was quite sure I was right.'

'Well, we must tackle Ware ourselves.'

'I doubt whether you'll get much out of him.'

'We shall see, sir. In the meantime, are you sure there isn't anything else you'd like to tell us yourself, sir, about that night – without necessarily incriminating anyone?'

'Nothing,' said the Vicar firmly.

6

Rudge left the Vicarage in some elation. Not only had his surmise been confirmed that Ware was rowing the boat, but definite evidence was at last forthcoming that it had headed down-stream. Curious that old Ware had been so insistent on that point too. Except for the single suggestion about the length of time needed for the journey, it seemed as if Ware had not been trying to deceive him at all – almost as if he had been attempting to put him on the right track. Was it possible that Neddy Ware's guilty knowledge sat heavily upon him, that he thoroughly wanted the Admiral's murderer to be caught, but that at the same time, like a schoolboy, he would not directly give him away? When one came to think of it, that really was the only explanation of his behaviour. But if so it was a pity in a way; for Rudge knew Neddy Ware well enough to be quite certain that if the old man had made up his mind not to give the murderer away, no possible means could be found of making him do so.

Anyhow, one could but try. Hastily obtaining permission from Major Twyfitt for the interview, and learning at the same time that the theory of the footprints had been proved correct, Rudge drove out to Ware's cottage.

The old man was sunning himself in the garden, and seemed thoroughly pleased to see his visitor.

'Well, Mr Rudge, still puzzled about them tides?'

Rudge sat down on the same bench. 'No, Ware; it's not the tides this time; it's something more serious. I want you to tell me what you were doing in the Admiral's company last Tuesday night – the night he was murdered?'

Old Ware looked the picture of innocent astonishment. 'Me? I wasn't in his company. Whatever put that idea in your head, Mr Rudge? I didn't even know him by sight. Didn't I tell you the next day I hadn't recognised him?'

'You did, and I'm afraid I can't believe you. Especially as you were in Hong Kong when there was that scandal about him, so you must have known all about that though you never let on a word. Now look here, Ware, I'm not threatening you, mind; I wouldn't do anything like that; but at the same time I'm ready to tell you

that we've got evidence that you called for Admiral Penistone at Rundel Croft last Tuesday evening and rowed him down-stream at a quarter past ten. And what's more, I'll tell you what the evidence is: you were seen starting, there's your fingerprints on the oars, and there's your footprints on the bank. So you see there's no getting away from it. Now I needn't tell you this puts you in a nasty position. Mind you, I don't think you had anything to do with the murder, but there's others who might.'

'I'm glad *you* don't think I had anything to do with the murder, Mr Rudge,' said Ware dryly.

'But there's others who might,' repeated Rudge, 'and will, too, unless you tell us all you know about that evening. Now come, Ware.'

Neddy Ware drew a moment or two at his pipe before he spoke. 'You're pretty sure it *was* murder, eh, Mr Rudge?'

'Well, you don't imagine it's suicide, do you? And I'm afraid I can't see how that knife could have got into his chest by accident. Accident, suicide, or murder, it's got to be one of those three.'

'Oh, no, it hasn't,' retorted Ware. 'Not by a long chalk it hasn't.'

'What do you mean? Are you saying that the Admiral's death wasn't due to either accident, suicide, or murder?'

'Me? I'm not saying anything. That's your job, to find out what the Admiral died from. All I'm saying is that every death isn't due to one of those three. What about hanging a man, eh? What's that, Mr Rudge – accident, suicide, or murder?'

'Well, never mind that,' said Rudge impatiently. 'What I want to know is, what did you do last Tuesday evening, and where did you take the Admiral? And I needn't repeat what I said about it being in your own interests to tell me.'

Again Ware paused before replying, so long that the Inspector began to think that he was never going to reply at all; but at crucial moments such as these he had learnt that silent patience was the best policy.

At last the old man took the pipe out of his mouth. 'This woman, now. What's all this about her? They're saying she's Mr Mount's wife, and there's others saying she was the Frenchy maid that the Admiral's niece had.'

'She's both,' said Rudge, shortly, annoyed at this sidetrack but thinking it best to bustle the old man. Rudge was something of a fisherman himself.

'Is she? That's queer now. And killed herself, they say.'

Ware turned round suddenly and looked full at the Inspector. 'Is that true, Mr Rudge? Did she kill herself? What is it this time,

eh? Accident, suicide, or murder?'

'The Super and Major Twyfitt are satisfied it's suicide,' said Rudge, and did not add that he was not.

'Ah!' said Ware, and returned to his pipe again.

Once more the Inspector reminded himself that patience is a virtue.

And then Neddy Ware did a thing which surprised his listener. He voluntarily returned to the subject of his own doings. 'So you want to know about me, Mr Rudge? Well, seeing you know so much, perhaps I'd better tell you. I would have told you before, but it seemed better to say nothing about it, in case you might get foolish ideas into your head about me. That's why I said the next morning I didn't know him. Well, I *did* call for the Admiral, like you said. He'd offered me five shillings that afternoon, seeing me fishing near his place, to row him down to Whynmouth after late dinner, him not wanting to do any hard work with the oars just after eating a lot, you understand.'

'And where did you take him?' Rudge asked eagerly.

'Why, where he wanted to go – Whynmouth. I put him ashore at the steps, and he asked me the quickest way to reach the Lord Marshall. And that's the last I see of him.'

'You didn't wait for him?' Rudge said, disappointed.

'I did not. He said he'd be late, and come back likely by motor.'

'You left the boat, and walked back?'

'I did not. I rowed it back, and put it in the boat-house for him all ship shape.'

'Which end first?'

'I can't say that. Probably bow. That comes easier. Why, Mr Rudge?'

'Oh, nothing. Do anything else?'

'I give her a bit of a swab out before I left her, that's all.'

'What time did you get to Whynmouth?'

'Couldn't say for certain. 'Bout eleven, I suppose.'

'And you rowed the boat back nearly three miles against the tide. How long did that take you?'

'Not much under two hours. Must have been – yes, nigh on one o'clock (*your* time) before I berthed her.'

'And then you walked straight back to your cottage?'

'I did, Mr Rudge. And that's all I know. So I'm glad *you* don't suspect me of murdering the Admiral, whatever others may think.'

Rudge persevered for some little time longer, but could get no further information. As he returned to his car he was not al-

together satisfied with what he had got. How far could Neddy Ware be trusted? If one accepted his story it seemed proved that the man who visited the Lord Marshall that night really was the Admiral: and that might well be the case. But the rest of the story did not seem to ring quite so true. Would it be likely, for instance, that the Admiral would saddle Ware with that two-hour pull back against the tide for the sake of the forty-minute run down with it? It was possible, of course, but somehow the Inspector had a strong feeling that it was here that Ware's story left the rails of truth. He was pretty sure that the old man had not told all he knew. Why, for instance, after getting to bed so late, was he up and fishing at such an early hour the next morning? It almost looked as if he knew what he was going to catch.

But for the present at any rate there was nothing to be done about it: and at least Rudge thought he might now take it as established that it was to Whynmouth that the Admiral had gone that night. But whom to see?

Whom but – his murderer?

Walter Fitzgerald had been in Whymouth. With any luck he had been staying there, and could thus be traced. It was to Whynmouth that every signpost seemed not to be pointing: and it was towards Whynmouth accordingly that Inspector Rudge now headed his shabby little two-seater.

7

Nevertheless his journey thither was occupied by reflections of a matter alien to his errand. The more he thought about it the less satisfied he was that Mrs Mount's death was due to suicide, as the Super and Major Twyfitt were so comfortably convinced. The matter of the freshly eaten greengages was only one of a dozen indications, slight enough in themselves but in the aggregate formidable, that suicide had never been intended. It was quite obvious that Mrs Mount had been mixed up somehow in the Admiral's murder. At any rate she must have known a good deal about it – too much, Rudge fancied, for its perpetrator. Her suicide was really too fortunate, for him, to be true. And especially just before that conference which she herself had summoned, and at which without the smallest doubt she intended to shift at any rate some of the burden of knowledge from her own shoulders. Would it be likely that after summoning her husband, the Hollands and Sir Wilfrid Denny, Mrs Mount should intend to confront them with nothing less than her own corpse? That would

have been a grim joke indeed: but Mrs Mount had not been a grim lady.

No, it was altogether too lucky for Walter Fitzgerald that she should have died when she did.

But how had he managed it? There the Inspector had to admit himself completely at a loss. As soon as his telephone messages had brought relief, he and the Superintendent had searched the house from attic to cellar, and had found nothing. Moreover, he was satisfied that nobody had escaped while he was still confined to the neighbourhood of the study. He had had both the front door and the kitchen regions continuously under his eye, to say nothing of the drive. If Walter Fitzgerald really had done the thing, he had done it exceedingly cleverly.

All the way to Whynmouth the Inspector beat his brains against this stone wall.

Nor did he have any better luck on his other errand. Though he spent the entire afternoon calling personally at every hotel, inn, public-house, and apartment-house in the place, no trace could he find of his bearded quarry. It seemed that the man had not been staying in Whynmouth at all.

Well, it did not really matter. The Admiral must have arranged to meet him there: but that did not necessarily mean that he would be staying there. It was quite possible to understand why the rendezvous had not been arranged for Rundel Croft; no doubt the Admiral would not have him in the place.

Rudge began to regret his lack of information about this nephew. It seemed impossible to get a line on the fellow from any angle. It was worse than useless to apply to the only person who could give any really valuable information, Mrs Holland. Besides, in her present rôle of accessory after the fact Mrs Holland herself was once more in the limelight of suspicion. The only possible hope was Sir Wilfrid Denny.

Rudge put his car up in Whynmouth and had himself ferried across the river to West End.

Sir Wilfrid was in his garden, spraying his roses for green fly with tobacco juice. A rose lover himself, Rudge was interested to notice now that the little rose-garden was the only part of the grounds which did not wear the same air of neglect.

Sir Wilfrid greeted him with a nod. 'Afternoon, Inspector. I was rather expecting you today. Look – did you ever see anything more lovely?' He cupped a half-opened Emma Wright in two fingers and turned it towards the Inspector.

'Beautiful, sir,' agreed the latter wholeheartedly.

'But she loses her colour almost as soon as she opens,' mourned Sir Wilfrid. 'That's the worst of these modern roses – at least, I class her with the moderns. They don't keep their colour. Give me the old-fashioned ones. That pink over there now. There's no modern variety to come anywhere near it, in the pinks.'

'Madam Abel always has been a favourite of mine,' Rudge nodded.

Sir Wilfrid beamed up at him. 'You're not a rose enthusiast too, Inspector? That's magnificent. I'll take you round. This is my latest importation. Mrs G.A. van Rossem. Know her? I can't say I'm altogether satisfied. The usual mix-up of colours they seem to like so much nowadays. I must say I prefer my roses self-coloured. Mabel Morse, now . . . Eh? Don't you agree?'

'Yes, I do, sir. Entirely. I think you're quite right. But to tell you the truth, I came to see you about something rather different.'

'Ah, yes,' Sir Wilfrid nodded, descending to earth. 'Poor Admiral Penistone. I remember; you said you wanted to ask me something. Yes?'

'It's about his nephew. Walter Fitzgerald. Can you give me any information about him?'

'Walter Fitzgerald?' Sir Wilfrid looked puzzled. 'No, I don't really think I can. Of course, Inspector, I never knew the Admiral really well. We'd been acquaintances for a very long time, but I can't say that we ever got much beyond that stage. I imagine,' Sir Wilfrid added with a slight smile, 'that few people did, with Admiral Penistone.'

'You were in Hong Kong when he was stationed there, sir, weren't you?'

Sir Wilfrid nodded gravely. 'Yes, I was. And when a certain incident took place. But no doubt you know all about that already?'

'Yes, we've heard about that. Did the Admiral ever refer to that incident to you, sir?'

'He did. Frequently,' replied Sir Wilfrid dryly.

'Yes, I understand it was a bit of a bee in his bonnet. Do you agree with his idea, sir, that there was a good deal more behind it than ever came out?'

'I wish I could,' said Sir Wilfrid, looking a little distressed. 'But the facts were too plain. And I happen to know the authorities made a very searching investigation. It was always my belief that this idea of Admiral Penistone's was due to a kind of obstinate pride. It was his one lapse, you see, in a thoroughly honourable life; and he simply refused to face it.'

'Then you don't fancy there was any possibility of the Admiral's having been impersonated on that occasion?'

'None. To anyone with even as little acquaintance as myself of service conditions, the notion's simply moonshine. Why, there were some of his own men there. How could they have been mistaken? No, I'm sorry to have to say so, Inspector, but Captain Penistone had no one else to thank but himself for the affair. That was the opinion of everyone on the spot. But in any case, this is all old history. It can't have anything to do with his death.'

'No, of course not,' said the Inspector tactfully. 'Then you can't give me any information about the nephew, which is what I really came to see you about? You knew he was in Hong Kong at about that time too?'

'By Jove, I remember now. Yes, he did come to dine with us once. A tall, good-looking fellow. I remember. Pleasant chap, too. I heard he'd rather gone to the dogs, afterwards. Pity.'

'Had a beard, sir?'

'A beard?' repeated Sir Wilfrid, puzzled. 'I don't think so. I don't really remember. Why?'

'Oh, just a small point. Then you never saw him again?'

'No, I think he only came once. But I wouldn't swear. We used to entertain such a lot in those days,' said Sir Wilfrid, rather ruefully. 'He might have come again, but I don't remember it.'

'I see, sir. Thank you. Now there's one other point. Were you by any chance in the garden here late Tuesday evening?'

'The night of Admiral Penistone's death? Yes, almost certainly; though again I couldn't swear to it. But unless it's raining, I always have a stroll round the roses after dinner. So far as I remember it wan't raining that night, so I expect I did. Why do you ask?'

'Because we have information that the Admiral landed from his boat at Whynmouth steps at about eleven o'clock that night, and as you know, they're almost opposite this garden. I was wondering if by any lucky chance you'd seen him and could confirm that?'

'No,' said Sir Wilfrid decidedly. 'Not so late as that, I'm afraid. And I'm pretty sure I had a couple of friends in that night. (Funny, isn't it, how hard it is to say for certain what one was doing only a week ago?) But what's all this about the Admiral being seen in Whynmouth that night? I'd gathered he was killed up-stream somewhere.'

'Why did you think that, sir?'

'Well, I don't know. Wasn't the boat floating down-stream at four in the morning? I took it for granted that must have meant it had been up-stream.'

With a slightly superior air the Inspector explained the tidal vagaries of the River Whyn, and pointed his remarks by accompanying Sir Wilfrid over his own rather dishevelled lawn to the water's edge and illustrating his meaning on the spot. Sir Wilfrid, a somewhat mild little man, had the air of promising to know better next time.

Having delivered his lesson, the Inspector took his leave, with the unhappy reflection that he had really learned nothing at all from his visit. Sir Wilfrid's private opinion regarding the Superintendent's 'smart piece of work' could hardly be called information.

Having walked, in full view of his host, out through the main entrance, Inspector Rudge doubled round to the back one. There he learned, after judicious and veiled questioning, that so far as was known Sir Wilfrid had not left the house at all last Tuesday evening, but had had two friends in to see him. 'Leastways, the decanter had gone down by a tidy bit, it had, and there was three glasses to wash up the next morning, to say nothing of more cigarette-ends in the ash-trays than any one man could smoke, so it looks as if there was, don't it?' Rudge agreed that it did.

As has been said before, Inspector Rudge left nothing to chance.

8

Rudge called in at the police station in Whynmouth before going back to his lodgings, and found that Sergeant Appleton had telephoned through his report from London. He had had no difficulty in obtaining information about Holland. Holland, it seemed, was thoroughly well known in his own line. Several important men had spoken of him to Appleton apparently, not only all over the East but in London too as the very best type of trading Englishman – energetic, determined, dead honest and reliable, the sort of man whose word it was never necessary to obtain in writing; what he promised, he performed, and what he performed he performed just a shade better than anyone else. Appleton had been impressed, and said so frankly.

About the marriage too there was no room for doubt. It had been performed at a registry office in the West End, and Appleton had inspected the register and spoken with the registrar, who had described husband and wife exactly; he had taken particular notice of them, he said, because they were both so out of the ordinary type.

'Humph!' said Rudge to himself. 'And yet according to the Super he's an accessory after. At least his wife is, which almost always means the same thing. Something funny somewhere.'

He went back to his supper.

As usual he ruminated during the solitary meal. On the whole he was not dissatisfied with his day's work. It had not been true that he had learned nothing from Sir Wilfrid Denny. Going over the conversation again in his mind Rudge fancied that he had learned one thing of real value, which might lead to quite remarkable results – so remarkable, indeed, that when Rudge first began to realise their possibilities he feared that his imagination, goaded by the events of last week, was running hopelessly away with him. And yet . . .

But it was useless to speculate. He must shelve that line of enquiry until there was evidence to support it. In the meantime he would turn his thoughts to the death of Mrs Mount.

There was one point which told badly against murder, and Superintendent Hawkesworth had, of course, made the most of it. According to the doctor, if Mrs Mount had been stabbed by some other person, her murderer could not have escaped being spattered, and liberally, too, with blood; her clothing had been of the flimsiest; it would have interposed only a feeble barrier against the stream of blood that must have spurted from a wound in such a position – as indeed the condition of the carpet plainly showed. And yet not a single person so stained had been seen by anyone. Therefore, argued the Superintendent, contemptuously logical, no such person existed.

Rudge, still obstinately fixed in his idea of murder, thought now that he saw a way round this difficulty; and it was a way, too, which might be made to carry several other of the peculiar circumstances of the death. Perfectly simple too: Mrs Mount had been stabbed from behind, not from in front at all. And that argued that her murderer must be a man. But of this the Inspector was already convinced. If he was right and Mrs Mount really had been murdered, the man who had killed her was the same as the murderer of Admiral Penistone. Rudge had no doubt at all about that. And he had killed her to close her mouth, which she was just about to open against him.

From the weapon, that usually hopeful source of enquiry, nothing could be learned. Mr Mount had identified at once the knife that had been drawn from his wife's breast as his own, a steel paper-knife with a pointed end which lay habitually on the desk in his study. The only argument from that fact was that murder had

not been intended from the first; circumstances had arisen in the course of the interview that must have taken place, which had made murder imperative. But it was not an argument on which one could really rely.

As to the Superintendent's chief objection to the theory of murder, namely, that murder was impossible since no murderer could have got away and yet no murderer had been found, Rudge was not disposed to bother too much about that. He already had a theory to account for that. Rudge did not believe that the murderer had got away at all.

His meal finished, he got up from the table and began to wander aimlessly about the room. He felt restless. Something must be done, and he did not know quite what. Finally he went down to his car and drove out to Rundel Croft. He would smoke a quiet pipe in the boat-house, looking out over the river, and see if that would help matters.

It did, but the pipe was hardly needed. Quite automatically the Inspector, as soon as he arrived in the boathouse, cast an official eye over the Admiral's skiff, and something took that same eye immediately. Caught in between two of the planks in the bow was something of a vivid red colour. Rudge bent over it. It was a head of valerian, dropping and sad, but not withered.

'Humph!' said Rudge.

This was extremely interesting. He knew where he had seen valerian last: that very afternoon, in Sir Wilfrid Denny's garden. There was a big clump of it growing close to the water, at one end of the landing-stage. And, so far as Rudge knew, there was no other on the river. But the really interesting thing was that this head had not been there when the boat was examined on the morning after the murder (Appleton would never have missed it in any case), as indeed its comparatively fresh condition showed. There were only two possible inferences: one, that the boat had been taken out today and had picked up the flower by accident, and the other that the latter had been deliberately placed there.

Rudge considered these for a moment; then he picked the flower out. The stem came out in a straight line from the little crevice in which it had been lodged; by no possible chance could it have got in there just like that as the boat brushed past the clump. The second inference was the correct one: somebody was trying to throw suspicion upon Sir Wilfrid Denny.

Rudge became very active. He knew perfectly well who had put that piece of valerian in the boat. He went up to the house. Constable Hempstead was there, cherishing busily as usual.

Rudge asked one question of the company assembled in the kitchen, and it was Constable Hempstead who was able to answer it.

'Has that reporter from the *Evening Gazette* been up here today?'

'Yes, sir. I saw him from the other bank this morning. Near the boat-house, he was.'

Rudge took his car, drove as fast as he dared to the nearest magistrate, and obtained a search-warrant. Then he headed for the Lord Marshall.

'Is that reporter from the *Evening Gazette* in?' he asked the porter.

'Mr Graham? No, Mr Rudge. He went out after dinner.'

'What's the number of his room?'

'Seventeen.'

'Thanks. No, don't come up. And say nothing about this to anyone.'

The porter nodded importantly.

Rudge was busy for over half an hour, undisturbed. When he left, however, he had in his pocket nothing but a piece of paper on which he had laboriously typed a few sentences from a portable typewriter which stood on a table near the window.

As he passed unobtrusively out into the street he looked about him. On the other side of the road a man was lounging. Rudge nodded to him, and the other followed him round a corner.

'They're both in,' he said in a low tone, as he reached the Inspector. 'Had their dinner there, and haven't been out since.' Since the discovery of the blood-stained frock, Mr and Mrs Holland had been placed by Superintendent Hawkesworth under close observation.

Rudge nodded. 'Never mind about them. I want you to look after somebody else. That reporter chap from the *Evening Gazete*. Know him?'

'Him with the short hair and the spectacles?'

'Yes. Calls himself Graham.'

'Isn't that his real name, then, Mr Rudge?'

'It is not. His real name,' said Rudge, 'is Walter Fitzgerald.'

9

'You should have rung me up last night, Rudge,' said Major Twyfitt severely. 'Or at least you should have got in touch with the Superintendent. The fellow might have got away.'

'I had a man at the back of the Lord Marshall as well as the front all night, sir,' pleaded Rudge.

The Superintendent said nothing, but his look was voluble.

'How long have you known this man Graham was Fitzgerald?'

'Not definitely till I identified that specimen of typing I took in his room as coming from the same machine that typed the Admiral's consent to Mrs Holland's marriage. Of course, I suspected it before,' said Rudge, with a side-glance at the Superintendent, 'as soon as I heard about Hempstead finding those remains of a beard in the wash-basin trap at Rundel Croft; because I remembered that this reporter's face was a good deal lighter round the chin than on the forehead. I thought at first that he'd been dosing himself with some kind of sunburn application.'

'And you say you rang up the *Evening Gazette* last night?'

'Yes, sir; and he's their man all right. *And* he had a beard when they saw him last. The editor told me he's not their real crime expert. He's ill as it happens, so when Fitzgerald rang them up on the morning after the murder to tell them he was on the spot and ask if he could cover it, they said he could, though I gather he wasn't on their salary-list before. Sort of free-lance contributor, but they liked his stuff. "Graham" was the name he wrote under.'

'Ye; that gave him an excuse to be on the spot and keep in touch with developments of course. Very handy, from his point of view. He doesn't know you suspect him? You're sure of that?'

'I've got no reason to think he does, sir.'

'Well, let's hope he doesn't,' said the Superintendent with energy. 'Because if he's got wind of it and gets away – well, you'll be for it, Rudge.'

'I didn't think there was enough evidence for an arrest,' pleaded Rudge. 'Not then.'

'But you do now?'

'Well, that's for you and the Major to say,' replied Rudge smugly. 'But I haven't wasted the extra time, sir, I can assure you.' This was no less than the truth. Rudge had not got to bed at all the previous night.

'Tell us what you've done, then, man,' said the Superintendent impatiently.

Rudge cleared his throat. 'Perhaps I'd better run through the case as I saw it before last night, more or less. I don't mean the facts. We know those. I mean, the ideas that the facts gave me.'

The silence of the other two encouraged him to do so.

'Well, first of all, of course, there was the question, *why* was the Admiral's body in a boat at all? So much easier, if you've got a

boat handy, to have taken it out to sea and sunk it with a few weights. The only reason I could see was to create a misleading impression; and the only misleading impression I could see was that the body had floated down-stream instead of up – in other words, that the murder had been committed some way above Lingham. That gave me a pointer towards a theory that it had actually been committed at Whynmouth, or at any rate between Whynmouth and Lingham. Anyhow, I concentrated on that area.'

'Even then,' observed Major Twyfitt, 'it seems a pretty poor reason for not sinking the body and hiding the fact of murder altogether.'

'That also occurred to me, sir,' Rudge replied, a trifle complacently. 'I was sure there was another reason, and I believe I know now what it is. Old Ware put me on to it. I'm as certain as I am of anything that he knows more than he's let on; and I'm pretty certain he knows who killed the Admiral. Anyhow, he dropped me a hint. He said, how did I know it *was* murder?'

'What's that?' demanded the Superintendent.

'Not murder!' exclaimed the Major.

'I didn't say that, sir,' Rudge replied quickly. 'What I do say is that old Ware doesn't think it was murder. Whether it was or not, of course we can't know yet, but I'll take my oath that's what Ware thinks.'

'What's your evidence?' snapped the Superintendent.

'None, sir. An impression only. But I know Neddy Ware pretty well; and though he may not be above a bit of trout-poaching and so on, I'd bet all I've got that he wouldn't stand for murder. And my inference is that whatever the others wanted to do, he wouldn't stand for the body being sunk or any hanky-panky. I believe the boat was his idea altogether.'

'You believe this and believe that,' growled the Superintendent. 'Let's have a bit of proof.'

'There isn't any,' Rudge returned, unabashed. 'And in any case I only put it forward as my own idea. But I do suggest, sir, that there may be something in it; and if there is – why, it alters the case considerably.'

'It is a possibility,' Major Twyfitt agreed.

The Superintendent, seeing his murder slipping away from him, only looked sulky.

'Still, we must proceed as if there was no question of it being anything but murder,' pointed out the Chief Constable.

'Of course, sir. So I'll get on with my reconstruction. Well, we had the Admiral being rowed down to Whynmouth by Neddy

Ware, and this reporter fellow, the nephew, rowing the Vicarage boat after him about an hour later, with Mrs Mount as his passenger.'

'Eh?' said the startled Chief Constable, who did not remember having heard anything of the sort. 'What's this?'

'I think it's obvious, sir. I mean,' said Rudge, with a naughty glance at his Superintendent, 'there's evidence to that effect. We know Mrs Mount got to the Vicarage about eleven; we know the Vicar didn't see her till well past twelve; we know the Vicarage boat was taken out that night; we're pretty sure Fitzgerald had a hand in the business; we know Fitzgerald was Mrs Mount's lover. What's the result? Why, that Fitzgerald, knowing she's coming down that night to see the Vicar about the divorce, intercepts her in the garden, takes her to the summerhouse for a talk, decides they'd better go down to Whynmouth after the Admiral (it's more than possible there was some sort of appointment between the two men), takes the Vicar's hat to put on in case anyone sees them going off in the boat (nothing like a hat to establish identity), takes the Norwegian knife the boys left there, to cut the painter with – no!' said Rudge thoughtfully. 'She ran back for the knife when they found they couldn't untie the knot.'

'How the devil do you know that?'

'I don't know it, sir. But if she did it would explain a lot. It's always puzzled me that the Vicar was watering his garden so hard the next day in the blazing sun. Mr Mount can't be such a bad gardener as all that. But suppose she'd left footprints on the beds when she ran back for the knife. A nice strong jet of water would destroy them, and so much less obvious than a fork or a trowel, the garden being under observation all the time by our men in the Admiral's boat-house. And he even gave the inside of the summer-house a bit of a splashing. Suppose she left powder scattered about there, like they do?'

'It's a possibility,' the Chief Constable agreed with interest. 'More than a possibility.'

The Superintendent said nothing.

'Well, anyhow, as I said, we have Fitzgerald chasing after the Admiral. It would take him half an hour to forty minutes, I suppose, to get down to Whynmouth. Then there's a gap of, say, fifteen or twenty minutes, during which the Admiral is killed and arrangements made about the two boats. The body is dumped in the Vicarage one, the two painters tied together, and someone rows them up-stream. Who? Not Fitzgerald. He wouldn't have time; we've got him at Rundel Croft soon after twelve. Not Mrs

Mount; she's at the Vicarage at about the same time.'

'Ware,' nodded the Chief Constable. 'Yes, that seems clear.'

The Superintendent said nothing.

'Neddy Ware, sir, yes,' said Rudge, who was now very much enjoying himself. 'And cuts the two painters again when he arrives at Rundel Croft a couple of hours later, with his own knife which isn't so sharp as the Norwegian one.'

'That doesn't sound like a naval man,' demurred the Major, 'to cut a painter instead of untying it.'

'But supposing it wasn't a naval man who tied it, sir? Suppose it was a landsman, with a ridiculous knot, which the dragging in the water had made tighter still. Besides, it's my opinion that old Ware was in the sort of mood then when one does cut instead of untying, even a naval man.'

'All right,' assented the Chief Constable. 'Go on.'

The Superintendent said nothing.

'Fitzgerald must have come back by car, on the Whynmouth side of the river to drop Mrs Mount at the Vicarage for her interview. And he parked the car while he was over at Rundel Croft. I made a bit of a bloomer over that, sir. I'd suspected he must have a car, but seeing he himself was at Rundel Croft I'd only had enquiries made that side of the river. As soon as Sergeant Appleton got back last night I sent him off to work the other side. He's found two witnesses who saw a car, with the lights out, standing just inside the Vicarage gate, behind the laurels, out of sight of the road, one at twelve-fifteen and one at twelve-forty.'

'How could they have seen it if it was out of sight of the road?'

'How do people in the country see so much, sir? They'll have some plausible explanation you can be sure. But you know as well as I do that if it had been parked in the Vicar's cellar with a tarpaulin over it, someone would have seen it there. And very handy for us, too.'

Major Twyfitt laughed. 'All right. How did Fitzgerald get across the river, then?'

'He must have swum it. No other way. I suggest he stripped quickly, rolled his clothes up in his coat, tossed the bundle across the stream (it's not more than forty feet wide there), and swum after it. And there he was, looking for File X as comfortable as you like, and his sister helping him, when along comes Holland and taps at the french windows. That must have given both of them a nasty shock. But he rose to it. Muttered to her to get rid of him at once, kept himself in the shadow and handed over the typed consent to their marriage. That was quite enough to send Holland

half off his head with pleasure – far too much to have any room in his mind for noticing how young the Admiral was looking nowadays. Then Fitzgerald gets the papers, destroys them, goes upstairs and shaves off his beard, crosses the river again, picks up Mrs Mount, and goes off with her in the car. I haven't been able to trace where they went, but I expect they made for London – as far away as they could.'

'Then you think Holland was genuine in his identification of the Admiral that night?'

'I do, sir. Mind you, I think he knows the truth now all right; but he didn't then.'

'That makes him an accessory after, too.'

'Yes, sir. Though it seems likely that he's been told the same tale as Neddy Ware was – that it wasn't murder. And Mrs Holland, too. That would explain why she didn't seem surprised, the first time I saw her, to hear that her uncle was dead, but she did jump when I said he'd been murdered.'

'That fits very well, Rudge,' commented Major Twyfitt.

The Superintendent said at last: 'Have you found the weapon?'

'No, sir,' said Rudge.

'Ah,' said the Superintendent.

'But I found this.' Rudge produced from his breast-pocket a strip of brown paper. Unwrapping it, he brought to light a long slender Norwegian knife, rather rusty.

The Superintendent took it eagerly.

'Then you have found the weapon.'

'No, sir.'

'Where did you find it, Rudge?' interposed Major Twyfitt.

'In a clump of antirrhinums in the Vicar's garden, sir.'

'Were you looking for it there?'

'Yes, sir. There was a nice bright moon last night.'

'Why, Rudge,' asked the Chief Constable patiently, 'were you looking for this knife in a clump of antirrhinums last night in the Vicar's garden?'

'Well, sir, you see, I'd worked it out this way. Was the crime premeditated or was it not? Somehow, what with Ware's remarks and the rest, I didn't think it was. Anyhow, I could soon test it. If Fitzgerald had intended to murder the Admiral that night, he would have taken this knife along with him, because he'd have known as soon as he saw it that nothing would serve him better. If he hadn't the intention, I thought he might most probably have thrown it back into the garden as soon as he'd used it on the painter. So I had a look round Mr Mount's ground last night within

an easy throw of his mooring-post.' Rudge by this time was so pleased with himself that he could not resist sending a highly unofficial beam at his superior officer.

Major Twyfitt smiled back. 'Smart bit of work, Rudge.'

'What I want,' observed the Superintendent, unappeased, 'is the *weapon*.'

'I found this too, sir.'

Rudge produced another piece of brown paper from his pocket, and from it another knife, an ordinary jack-knife such as sailors and navvies use. 'There are no prints on it,' he said, as he laid it on the table.'

'And where did you find that?'

'In a clump of valerian, sir, at the bottom of Sir Wilfrid Denny's garden, overhanging the river.'

'Sir Wilfrid Denny's garden!'

'Yes, sir. It's like this.' Rudge gave an account of his finding of the sprig of valerian stuck into the Admiral's boat, which had not been there when Sergeant Appleton overhauled it. 'It's like those treasure-hunts,' he added, 'where you go from one clue to another. That valerian was a clue, so I followed it up, and that's what I found. It's a plant. There's not even any blood on the knife, only rust. Of course, the real weapon's at the bottom of the sea.'

'You think so?'

'Rivers,' said Rudge, 'can be dragged.'

'And you think that Fitzgerald planted these two clues?'

'I'm certain of it, sir.'

'It's about time,' remarked the Superintendent, 'that we got our hooks on Master Fitzgerald.'

Rudge glanced at the clock. 'I'm expecting him at eleven-thirty. Another fifteen minutes to go. I told him I'd have an exclusive piece of information for him if he came along then.'

'He'll come?' said the Chief Constable doubtfully. 'You don't think you're taking a risk?'

'Sergeant Appleton's tailing him in any case, sir.'

'If Fitzgerald gets away, Rudge,' growled Superintendent Hawkesworth.

'He won't, sir. Is there anything else you want me to report on before he comes?'

'Have you traced that copy of the evening paper in his pocket?'

'No, sir. He must have picked it up in Whynmouth, perhaps at the Lord Marshall. I don't think there's much importance to be attached to it.'

'You think now, then, that it was the Admiral who went to the

Lord Marshall?' asked Major Twyfitt.

'I do, sir. I know the Superintendent thought differently, but we've proved he was in Whynmouth, so why shouldn't it have been him? It's my notion that he anticipated danger at the interview ahead of him, and wanted to take Holland along to stand by; but when the porter told him Holland was in bed he didn't bother to have him roused and just gave the first excuse that came into his head. Of course, he never intended to catch a train at all, but he had to say something.'

'Humph!' said the Superintendent, not too pleased at having his bright idea snatched from him by a mere inspector.

'And the door-key in the Admiral's boat?' asked the Major.

'Why shouldn't the Admiral have dropped it there himself, sir? It seems a pity,' said Rudge, 'to bother to find complicated explanations when there's a simple one handy. I felt that,' he added with a look of great innocence, 'about the Admiral's visit to the Lord Marshall; though I know Mr Hawkesworth didn't agree with me.'

Mr Hawkesworth's large face looked for a moment so suffused with honest emotion that the Chief Constable hurriedly led the conversation into quite a different track.

'And Mrs Mount's death, Rudge? Have you got any further with your theory of murder there?'

'Not so far as evidence goes, sir,' Rudge said slowly, 'but I could put a case of murder for you, if you'd care to hear it; though I know well enough we could never put it before a jury as it stands.'

'Let's hear it.'

'If it was murder, sir, it was done this way. Mrs Mount makes this appointment. She's lost her nerve, and she's going to give things away. The Hollands know a good deal already; she's going to tell them more. I don't know how much the Reverend knows, but he's going to know a good deal more by the time she's finished. Naturally, this doesn't suit a certain person's book. He gets wind of it, and goes there to stop her. He must have reached the house just before I got there myself. She lets him in, and they start arguing. Suddenly they see me coming up the drive. He snatches up the steel paper-knife from the desk, and threatens her with it if she utters a sound. She keeps quiet. They watch me hide in the laurels. Then an hour or so later along comes the Hollands, and he does the same thing. They sit on the lawn, and the situation's saved for another few minutes. But he's getting badly rattled, and she's probably nearing hysteria. He doesn't trust her one inch. All the time, while the three of us are out there, he's got to keep the knife

at her breast to make sure of her silence. And what does he do? He makes her hold it there herself, both hands on the hilt, and the point right on her heart; with one hand over hers he can control her more easily like that, and use his eyes elsewhere. She's half-dead with fright of him – sees he means murder – does whatever he tells her. Then the Hollands come up to the house again. From their conversation he learns that the front door, which he can't have shut properly, has blown ajar. They're coming in. He hears them go into the drawing-room, and then into the dining-room; he knows they're bound to come into the study. It's his life or hers now. What does he do? He's behind Mrs Mount now, both his hands over hers on the hilt of the dagger. With a convulsive pull he forces the thing into her heart. She screams once. He drops her and darts behind the door, wiping his hands on his handkerchief. In come the Hollands; Mrs runs out, Holland stays a moment, then follows her out of the house. I'm on my way across the lawn. The murderer's got a couple of seconds to get inside the lavatory just by the front door. He does it. But he can't leave the grounds in case he's seen. So then,' concluded Rudge, somewhat breathlessly, 'all he's got to do is wait till the coast's clear, creep out of the house, hide round the angle of it, scuffle on the gravel, and walk in again. And that, sir, is just what I suggest he did do.'

There was a silence after Rudge had finished.

Superintendent Hawkesworth broke it, by remarking quite mildly: 'Can you prove he didn't come up the drive? What about those two on the lawn?'

'They couldn't see from where they were. The angle of the house is in the way.'

'Besides, they wouldn't say.'

There was another silence.

'Mr Hawkesworth,' said Rudge, a little diffidently, 'who is to make the arrest, you or I?'

'You'd better. You've put in some very good work on this case,' said the Superintendent, who after all was a fair man, 'and I think you ought to have the credit of it. The one who makes the arrest always gets the credit. That is,' he added rather perfunctorily, 'if Major Twyfitt agrees.'

'Certainly, certainly,' said that gentleman. 'I quite agree. Rudge has done very well. Saved us a lot of trouble, to say nothing of Scotland Yard.'

'Thank you, sir,' said Rudge modestly, and looked at the clock. The time was close on half-past eleven.

'Well, I suppose we can only wait,' said the Chief Constable. All

three were beginning to feel uneasy.

They did not have to wait long. Before the hands of the clock had reached the appointed time a constable put his head round the door to announce, in a stentorian whisper, that Mr Graham was there, to see Mr Rudge by appointment.

'Show him in,' nodded the Major.

The cropped-headed reporter entered with no less than his usual assurance, greeting the three heartily and receiving three very curt nods in exchange. 'What's this, Inspector?' he said. 'Something rather special for me? That's very decent of you.'

'Something very special,' replied Rudge dryly. 'I'm going to make an arrest.'

'An arrest!' Fitzgerald stared at him. 'Oh! For Admiral Penistone's death?'

'For Admiral Penistone's murder,' returned Rudge grimly. 'And something else.'

'I see. Er – very good of you to let me in on it.' The reporter's assurance was not so pronounced now. Without being asked he sat down in a chair as if his legs had suddenly gone weak. The three others eyed him in silence.

Again the constable put his head round the door. 'Sir Wilfrid Denny, to see Mr Rudge by appointment.'

'Show him in, Gravestock,' said Rudge. To his superiors he said briefly, as he rose from his chair: 'I asked Sir Wilfrid to be good enough to come down here himself, so that we could ask him about – certain things.'

The others nodded.

Rudge went to the door to meet Sir Wilfrid. Sir Wilfrid, however, was already in the doorway, as Rudge reached it. Rudge was a large man, Sir Wilfrid a small one. It was Sir Wilfrid who sprawled on the floor. With every sign of embarrassment, and apologising heartily, Rudge helped him up and brushed him down.

'I'm sorry, sir. Most sorry. Very careless of me. Do you know Major Twyfitt? And Superintendent Hawkesworth? I'm so sorry to have brought you down here, sir, but there were just one or two questions we wanted to ask you, to clear up a doubtful point. It's about a sprig of valerian that was found wedged between two of the boards of Admiral Penistone's boat. Now, I've searched up and down the river, and the only clump of valerian growing close to the water is in your garden. We were wondering if you could account for the sprig in any way?'

Sir Wilfrid thrust his hands into his jacket pockets and stared at

Rudge with perplexity. 'No, I can't.'

'Nor for this knife, found in the same clump of valerian, with traces of blood on it?'

Sir Wilfrid looked at Major Twyfitt, he looked at Superintendent Hawkesworth, he looked at Walter Fitzgerald. Then he coughed. 'I never saw it before,' he said.

'Thank you, sir. Tht's all I had to ask you. And now I have a very painful duty to perform.'

Rudge paused, and looked hard at Sir Wilfrid. Sir Wilfrid coughed again, more rackingly.

'Sir Wilfrid Denny,' said Rudge, 'I arrest you for the murders of Hugh Lawrence Penistone and Celia Mount, and I warn you that anything you say may be used in evidence against you.'

10

'Hardly, I think,' replied Sir Wilfrid, dryly. 'Well, I congratulate you, Inspector. How did you find out?' He sat, with an air of jauntiness, on the edge of the table.

'Look here, Denny,' interposed Major Twyfitt awkwardly, as he and Superintendent Hawkesworth emerged slowly from the stupor into which they seemed to have fallen. 'Look here, I don't know whether . . . I mean, better not say anything. Your solicitor . . . '

'I know perfectly well what I'm doing,' returned Sir Wilfrid. '*He* gave me away, I suppose?' He nodded towards Fitzgerald, who had not moved from his chair.

'Am I to understand that you wish to make a statement, Sir Wilfrid?' put in Rudge suavely, though there seemed little ground for such an understanding.

'Yes, I'll make a statement, certainly. I killed both of them, I'll tell you that at once. I don't know whether it's any good adding it, but I didn't mean to kill the Admiral; at least, I suppose I did, but it was in self-defence. He went for me with a poker.'

At the table the Superintendent had grabbed a piece of paper and was writing furiously.

'Then why did you kill Mrs Mount, when you thought she was going to give you away?' asked Rudge.

'Really, Rudge,' said the Chief Constable unhappily. 'I don't think we should ask . . . Sir Wilfrid really should see his solicitor.'

'Oh, I'll answer any questions. Why did I kill her? Because I didn't want to be arrested, of course. How could I have proved self-defence? When the circumstances came out, it would look as

if I had every motive for murder.'

'You mean your share in the Hong Kong business?'

'I see you know all about it. Yes. But I'm sorry about Mrs Mount. I – I suppose I lost my head. Gave way to panic. Horrible thing to do – I suppose,' he added in a low voice to Walter Fitzgerald, 'it's not good telling you that I'm ready to make amends with my own life?'

Fitzgerald got up without answering and, crossing to the mantelpiece, leaned his head on his hands.

'Better get this down quickly,' said Sir Wilfrid to the Superintendent. 'We haven't much time. The Admiral had suspected for some time my share in the Hong Kong business. Somehow or other I managed to stave him off. Then Ware ratted on me.'

'Ware?'

'Yes. He'd known all along – though how the devil he found out I never discovered. That's why he settled here when he retired.'

'He'd been blackmailing you?'

'Well, I suppose you'd call it that; but only a matter of a present of a pound or two now and then, and he never used any threats. He just *knew*, and I gave him a few pounds occasionally to keep his knowledge to himself. That's all. But the Admiral got hold of him; and whether he paid more, or appealed to "duty" and "honour" and the rest, I can't say, but Ware must have ratted. Then the Admiral came down to see me, breathing, as you may imagine, flames and death. He got me in a corner, till I couldn't persist in my denials any longer. Then he must have seen red, because he simply went for me, cold blind, with the poker. I snatched up the first thing I could (as a matter of fact it was a trench dagger one of my nephews once gave me as a War souvenir), dodged under the poker, and got in first. Then I went down to where Ware was waiting, with the Admiral's boat, and found that Fitzgerald with Mrs Mount had just arrived in another boat.'

'One minute, Sir Wilfrid,' interrupted the Superintendent. 'What time was that?'

'Oh, I suppose about twenty minutes to twelve. I told them what I'd done and that we must get rid of the body. I'm afraid I'd lost my head a bit, because I wouldn't listen to them when Ware and Fitzgerald both urged me to come out in the open and ring up the police. It was justifiable homicide, they said, and nothing could happen to me. But I knew that if I did, all that Hong Kong business would come out, and I should lose my pension in any case; and I thought it almost inevitable that I should have to face a charge of murder. In the end Fitzgerald agreed to stand by me, but we had a

lot more trouble before we could persuade Ware. Finally he agreed that if he wasn't to be expected to tell any direct lies except to conceal the fact of his having been out with the Admiral that night at all, he wouldn't give me away; he would just know nothing. I was too upset to make any arrangements at all; as no doubt he's told you, Fitzgerald saw to our plans. Ware insisted that the body should not be concealed, everything was to be as plain and above board as it could be; so we went up to the house, had a stiff drink apiece, and put the body in the Vicar's boat, covered with a bit of tarpaulin. Ware undertook to tow it upstream and set it adrift before returning the Admiral's boat to its boat-house. In the meantime Fitzgerald promised to go at once to Rundel Croft and look through the Admiral's papers, to destroy anything he might have in writing against me, which I understand he did. The next day, feeling unable to stay and face it, I frankly took to my heels and escaped to Paris. Fitzgerald sent me word there that no suspicion seemed to be directed against me, so I came back.'

'And Mrs Mount?'

In a low voice Sir Wilfrid gave the details. They turned out to be almost exactly as Rudge had surmised, except that he maintained that there again he had never really intended murder. Mrs Mount, hearing the Hollands actually in the next room, had made a desperate attempt to escape, and in the struggle Sir Wilfrid had mechanically tightened his grasp on her and so driven the knife in. There had been no set plan in his subsequent movements. He had just run in sheer panic from one hiding place to another as opportunity offered.

He had nothing else to say.

Major Twyfitt shook his head. 'I shouldn't have let you say anything, until you'd seen your solicitor.'

'My dear fellow,' returned Sir Wilfrid, almost happily, 'don't bother. I shall never face a judge. You heard me cough just before your man arrested me? Under cover of the second one I slipped something into my mouth which I bought for just such an emergency in Paris. I've got about ten minutes more to live, I reckon.'

Major Twyfitt sprang forward in consternation, as did the Superintendent. It is a bad thing for the police when a prisoner succeeds in committing suicide under their noses.

Rudge, however, got there first. 'Well,' he said, 'we'll put you in safety for that ten minutes anyhow. Will you come with me, please?' Taking the other by the arm he led him from the room.

When he returned the Superintendent was telephoning

frantically for a doctor, who was out. 'Put him in a cell,' he said briefly. 'Don't worry, sir. We don't need a doctor. I knew what he'd got in his left-hand coat pocket. I expected it. So I made up another similar packet, and changed them during that collision. Here's his.' Rudge produced a small twist of white paper.

'But how did you know what his packet looked like?' asked the Chief Constable.

'I did a bit of spying on Sir Wilfrid last night, sir, through the blinds of his sitting-room. I saw him making it up, and I guessed what it was, and I knew it was his left-hand pocket because he had his hand in it when he came in. Sir Wilfrid's just swallowed three tablets of bicarbonate of soda; that's all.'

11

Major Twyfitt dropped back into his chair. Everyone seemed to have forgotten Walter Fitzgerald, who still stood by the mantelpiece in a dejected attitude.

'You knew last night it was Denny?'

'Not to say knew, sir. I'd suspected it for some time, ever since I interviewed him in his rose-garden. He seemed very eager to volunteer that he hardly knew the Admiral at all, and then, for a gentleman who lived right on the river, he seemed to know very little about the tides; I couldn't quite swallow that. Then there were those rumours about bad blood between him and the Admiral, and what with him having been in Hong Kong at the time I thought he might possibly be mixed up in that business on the wrong side; besides, he was a bit too strong against the Admiral having been an innocent party. And though he remembered that Mr Fitzgerald was handsome, he couldn't remember whether he had a beard or not.'

'Then you were pulling our legs this morning, when you told us all your suspicions were directed against – someone else?'

'Sir, I never told you. I didn't mention any name. I was quite sure in my own mind that it was Denny, but what was the good of saying so? I hadn't any real evidence. At first I thought of arresting – someone else in Sir Wilfrid's presence, with the idea that if he had done it he'd say so there and then. But that mightn't have come off. Then last night, when I saw him making up that packet, I knew for certain it was him; so I thought I'd take a chance and arrest him. If it came off, well and good. If it didn't . . . '

'You'd have been broken,' said the Superintendent with severity.

'But it did, sir. I thought somehow it would,' admitted Rudge, 'if Sir Wilfrid thought he'd got the contents of that packet safe inside him.'

'Very unofficial, Rudge,' pronounced the Chief Constable. 'Most unprofessional. But dam' smart.'

'Thank you, sir.'

'So now what about Mr Fitzgerald here? I think we'd like to ask him a few questions.'

'Fire away,' said Walter, turning round. 'I'll tell you anything you want to know. Thank God it's all over. It's been a nightmare, I can tell you. I knew you were after me.'

'Now . . . ' said Superintendent Hawkesworth, and began to put his questions.

Fitzgerald's tale of the night's happenings exactly bore out Rudge's reconstruction, except that he and Mrs Mount had not returned to London that night. They had driven about forty miles and then turned the car into a wood and slept in it – so far as either of them could sleep. Mrs Mount, as the days went by, had been more and more vehement that Denny should give himself up, and had even divulged some of the facts to her husband under the seal of confession; he had promised to join her in urging both Sir Wilfrid and Ware to go frankly to the police and tell them the truth.

Holland had been an innocent party all the time. Elma had known the truth, but Holland did not yet know who had killed the Admiral; he had, quite simply, taken Fitzgerald's word that he had not done so. The matter of the typewritten consent to the marriage had arisen in this way. Holland had met Fitzgerald in the East, seen that he was drifting, and liked him enough to try to pull him together. Walter, without telling him about the Hong Kong affair, had divulged that there was a charge hanging over him –

'The warrant out against you for forgery?' interposed the Superintendent.

'You know about that? Well, then, yes.'

This charge prevented him from making himself known in England, and consequently from obtaining his inheritance. Holland promised to see what he could do. He interviewed the firm in Hong Kong, who undertook, in view of the time that had elapsed, to withdraw the charge if Walter prepaid the money. This he could not do until he had received his inheritance, and he refused to allow Holland to lend him the money, a considerable sum. Holland had therefore undertaken to get in touch with the Admiral in England and try and bring about a reconciliation, so

that the money could be advanced by the family; at the same time he promised to see Elma and assure her that everything was coming right at last.

While abroad Walter had always kept in touch with Elma, and when the Admiral tried to stop her communicating with him, Mrs Mount had gone to the house as Elma's maid, both to keep a roof over her head and to act as a liaison.

The Admiral received Holland with suspicion, as a friend of Walter's, and at first would have nothing to do with him. Holland saw that it would take time to make him change his attitude, and settled down to play him as patiently as he could. In the meantime, having seen Elma, he promptly fell in love with her.

It was now Walter's turn to do Holland a favour. He had arrived in England, and taken lodgings in London. Mrs Mount hurried up too, and he installed her near him, under the name of Arkwright. Walter was delighted to hear of Holland's feelings for Elma, for knowing himself, he had always feared that Elma, unless she became attached to somebody of strong character, might become a drifter too. He had strongly urged Elma, who was by no means in love herself, to accept Holland. Finally, seeing how much her brother wished it, Elma consented to do so. The Admiral, however, still proved an obstacle. He would not give his consent to Elma's marriage with any friend of Walter's. Holland had already improved his standing, but the Admiral was by no means won over.

In the meantime Elma too was trying to do something for Walter. He and Mrs Mount had always wanted to get married, but the Vicar would not divorce her. Elma had fancied that Mr Mount had shown signs of being interested in herself. She deliberately set about strengthening this interest in order to be able to use her influence with him to persuade him to agree to the divorce. It was for this reason that she always took particular trouble with her appearance whenever she was to meet him. Walter did not know of this at the time, but Holland observed with pain his fiancée's decided set at the Vicar, the reason for which she did not give him. He therefore told Walter that he had come to the end of his patience; he was going up to London to get a special licence, and he was going to use it, consent from the Admiral or no consent. He went.

Walter knew that this would put the Admiral's back up more than ever, and Elma would certainly lose the control of her money. He was aware, from his sister, of his uncle's obsession with regard to the Hong Kong incident, and resolved to use this in order

to obtain consent to the marriage. He therefore typed out the form of consent and, taking his courage in his hands, went to see his uncle shortly after tea on the day of his death, lying in wait for him in the garden, so as to keep their meeting secret.

It was the first time he had seen the Admiral for many years, and at first the latter refused to have anything to do with him. When Walter said, however, that he could tell him the exact truth about the Hong Kong episode, the Admiral changed his tune. Walter then put his proposition: the truth in exchange for the consent. The Admiral did not hesitate; he signed on the spot. Thereupon Walter told him everything. He had to sacrifice Denny to do so, but after all Denny was a criminal; he had grossly tricked Walter; and Elma's marriage, to say nothing of Holland's happiness, could no longer be jeopardised to save Denny's face.

The Admiral was beside himself with rage. He raved, he swore, he thundered, he stamped. With the very greatest difficulty Walter calmed him down and made him promise to behave at the Vicar's as if nothing had happened at all. In the end, however, the Admiral had given this promise and had departed to dress, breathing fiery vengeance for the morrow.

Walter had intended to go across first thing the next morning to West End to warn Denny; it never occurred to him that the Admiral would do anything that night. Concealed, however, in the Vicar's garden, where he had an appointment with Mrs Mount, he had seen the Admiral set out with Ware, whom doubtless he had intended to pump on the way, and was perturbed. He felt he must wait till Mrs Mount came and then, talking it over, decided that they should both go down the river and put off the interview with the Vicar till they got back; this did not matter as there was no appointment, a surprise assault having been intended on the Vicar's conscience. The details of their departure had been exactly as Rudge had said.

The rest they had heard from Denny himself. When Walter got back to Rundel Croft he had broken the news to his sister that their uncle had been accidentally killed. She was shocked, but pulled herself together and helped him look for the papers.

'There was blood on her dress,' said the Superintendent.

'So she told me afterwards. It must have come from my hand. Anything else?'

'The valerian?' asked Rudge.

Walter nodded. 'I put it there. Whether my uncle's death was justifiable homicide or not (I believe it was) when it came to Celia . . . I wanted,' said Walter simply, 'to put you on the right

track. I wanted Denny to hang.'

'Then why didn't you come and tell us all you knew?' asked Rudge, reasonably enough.

'I could hardly give the fellow away,' retorted Walter.

'Oh!' said Rudge. It was a distinction he could not appreciate.

'Look here,' said the Superintendent suddenly. 'What was behind that Hong Kong incident? It was you impersonating your uncle, I suppose?'

Walter flushed. 'Yes. This is what happened. Denny had me to dinner one night and made me rather drunk. He suggested it would be a rag if I put on a naval uniform, which he happened to have handy, and went down to some dive and did a song-and-dance; somebody might mistake me for my uncle, and it would be a glorious joke. He knew my uncle hated me, and I hated him – at least, we didn't love each other. I was tickled to death, being a silly young ass, and agreed like a shot. Denny lent me the uniform and took me down there himself. I didn't have to act much; I was as drunk as a lord.

'The next day I was to go on a trek into the interior for my firm, miles away from newspapers or anything like that. Denny knew, and that's why that particular night was chosen. I didn't get back for some months, and by that time the whole thing was over. Denny put the wind up me. He said it was a fool thing to have done, that I had laid myself open to a criminal prosecution, and that he wouldn't back me up; the damage was done; I had better lie low and say nothing about it. I thought it was fishy, but I was frightened and agreed to keep quiet.

'I didn't come on the truth for years afterwards, and then only by chance. This was what lay behind it. There was a big ring of opium-smugglers operating in Hong Kong at that time. Denny was in charge of the customs, and he was in with the ring; they'd either blackmailed or bought him. My uncle had got wind of the ring and was getting close on their track. They had to get rid of him, or beat it; and they hit on that plan. My uncle was lured somehow into that street; a girl decoy, whom a Chinaman was pretending to maltreat, got him into the dive, he was sandbagged and then drugged, and his clothes saturated with whisky and opium. In the meantime I had fallen into it as well, like a child of two. I had a beard in those days too, and a little powder on it and a line or two on my face had made me so much like my uncle that nobody ever suspected that it might not be him – and even he himself had his doubts! Altogether, it was a very pretty little plot.

'Anything else?' He sauntered towards the door.

'We can't let him go,' whispered the Superintendent urgently.

'But what can we hold him on?' Major Twyfitt whispered back.

'He's an accessory after.'

'Not to a crime,' smiled Walter, whose ears must have been particularly sharp. 'You can't be an accessory after to justifiable homicide.'

'That hasn't been proved yet,' said the Superintendent sternly.

'No? Well, you can't detain me till it has been.' With a quick movement Walter was through the door.

'We must hold him,' muttered Hawkesworth, jumping up. 'I don't know what on, but we must. Get him, Rudge, man! There's that Hong Kong warrant still out against him anyhow.'

But Walter was already through the charge-room and at the street door. By the pavement stood a car, its engine ticking over. On seeing Walter, the driver thrust in the gear. The car jumped forward, and Walter leapt into the back.

'Walter Fitzgerald,' enunciated the Superintendent, charging through the doorway, 'I – '

'Don't want to lose you, but I think you ought to go,' chanted Walter mockingly as the car gathered speed. 'Goodbye, Superintendent. You can send any message through my sister.'

Elma, sitting in front beside Holland, turned round and waved enthusiastic confirmation.

The Superintendent darted for the telephone. 'I'll have that car stopped before it's gone three miles,' he said grimly.

Major Twyfitt touched him on the shoulder. 'Why bother? We don't really want him, you know. We've got the right man. We'll let him go. It's my belief that he's in better hands than ours.'

With an air of disgust the Superintendent relinquished the telephone. 'As you say, sir, of course. But we ought to have held him. Yes, Gravestock?'

The burly constable looked scared. 'Could you come to the cells, please, sir? I think there's something wrong with the prisoner Denny.'

The three officers tramped there in silence.

'There's certainly something wrong with him,' said the Superintendent a minute later. 'He's dead. That's what's wrong with him. Rudge!'

In consternation Rudge drew from his pocket the swisp of paper and hurriedly opened it. 'No,' he said with relief, 'these are his. He had my soda bics – nothing else.'

'Then what did he die of?'

'He just died,' said Major Twyfitt, looking down on the still

figure. 'He's old. He knew he was going to die – so he did die.'

There was a moment's rather awed silence.

'And he never signed his confession,' said the Superintendent disgustedly.

Appendix I

SOLUTIONS

1

By Canon Victor L. Whitechurch

No Solution

2

By G.D.H. and M. Cole

No Solution

3

By Henry Wade

In 1919, soon afer the War, Admiral Penistone (young, rapid promotion for brilliant active service exploits) becomes involved in a disreputable brawl in a house of ill-repute in Hong Kong. Owing to his war services the Admiralty allow him to send in his papers, instead of court-martialling him. There were also involved in this brawl three other Englishmen: (1) Walter Fitzgerald, young and weak-charactered, struggling with drink and drugs; (2) his friend, and partner in a trading concern, Vanyke, an older man; (3) another trader, Holland. During the course of the brawl Fitzgerald is killed by Chinamen, but this is not known to the naval authorities when they deal with Penistone.

Holland, learning of old Fitzgerald's will, blackmails Penistone, his price being 'the hand of your niece, Elma.' Elma, a woman of spasmodically passionate nature, does for a time fall wildly in love with Holland, but cools off and (when the story begins) is backing out of the engagement. This is the real cause of the Admiral's annoyance with his niece.

Elma is now setting her cap at the Vicar, a handsome and vigorous man, though fifty. On the night in question she persuades him to a romantic trip up the river after she is supposed to have returned home. The Vicar's 'shock' at the news is largely due to his fear that this 'adventure' will 'come out.'

Penistone, after locking up the boat-house and finishing his cigar out of doors, returns to his study, where he is murdered by the butler, Emery. Emery is in fact Vanyke, who believes Penistone to be morally, if not actually, responsible for the death of his 'poor young friend, Walter.' 'Emery' puts Penistone's overcoat back on to the body, to suggest that he was killed out of doors. The newspaper (the one delivered at the house at 9 p.m.) was splashed with blood, so he thrust it in the pocket for the same reason. At 2.30 a.m. he carries the body to the boat-house, unlocks it with the Admiral's key, rows across to the Vicarage wharf, dumps the body in the boat (in which the Vicar had left his hat on his romantic voyage) and cuts it adrift. (This to suggest murder at the Vicarage – or at least to lay a false trail.) As suggested by P.C. Hempstead, the boat is stranded at slack tide and comes back on the flow. Emery swabs out the Rundel Croft boat for fear of blood-stains.

Elma probably went to London to see her solicitors, and her dress and shoes may have been hidden by Emery, further to confuse the issue.

Probably Neddy Ware knew something about the Hong Kong incident.

4

By Agatha Christie

The real Elma Fitzgerald is dead and her brother Walter is masquerading as her, being unable to claim his inheritance under his own name as he is wanted by the police. Holland has been a friend of his in remote parts of the world. Walter finds it hard to get any definite statement as to money out of the Admiral and, to force his hand, pretends to be engaged to Holland. The Admiral will then be forced to hand over the money. Unknown to Walter, however, the Admiral has speculated with it and lost it.

Walter, who has been an actor at one time, has had no difficulty in deceiving the Admiral, who has not seen his niece since she was a child. He takes no great pains with Holland, but reserves his best

effects of make-up when asked out in the neighbourhood, when he takes an artistic pleasure in playing the vamp.

The Admiral, however, has received an anonymous letter from 'Célie,' stating that 'Elma' is a man. He slips this into his pocket unopened just before starting for the Vicarage and opens it when waiting for 'Elma' to say goodbye to the Vicar.

He immediately taxes Walter with the truth as they go over in the boat, and says he will give him up to the police. Walter, who knows the Admiral's uncompromising character, stabs him as the boat glides into the boat-house.

He then goes up to the house and waits till all is quiet. Then he makes up as the Admiral, dons an overcoat, puts the newspaper in the pocket and shows himself at the Lord Marshall, which is badly lighted and where the Boots is a rustic who is nearly half-witted. He asks for Holland, then says he can't wait.

He returns. Later goes down to the boat-house, takes the boat across the river, puts the body in the other boat and cuts the painter. He thinks the boat will go out to sea, and as the Admiral's boat will be in the boat-house, the Admiral will be supposed to have left on foot and gone to town by train. The boat, however, drifts down and drifts into the bank, to be sent up-stream later.

The murder discovered, 'Elma' hastens away with the white dress on which are blood-stains. He intends to return with a good excuse, secure in the *alibi* he has created.

The Vicar *did* take his boat out again. He met his former wife at Fernton Bridge. He was terribly anxious to have no 'talk,' hence his peculiar manner.

5

By John Rhode

The so-called Admiral Penistone was an imposter. He was, I think, by profession a blackmailer (hence the files of newspaper cuttings) who had contrived to get several people into his power, among them Sir Wilfrid Denny, who had been impoverished by 'Penistone's' constant demands.

Denny decides to commit the murder. He learns that 'Penistone' has arranged to meet Holland on the night of the ninth, and lies in wait for him at Fernton Bridge. As he passes, Denny hails him, saying that he has urgent business to discuss – perhaps that he has money which 'Penistone' had demanded. He gets back into

the boat, sitting in the stern with 'Penistone' facing him as he rows. When they reach the railway bridge (see Map) he suddenly rises and plunges the dagger into 'Penistone' as he leans forward to take a stroke.

He leaves the boat under the bridge, among the piles, where it is safe from observation in the dark. He then calls at an hotel in Whynmouth, in order to establish his presence there at a particular hour (11 p.m.). He slips out from here, and goes to the Lord Marshall, where he impersonates 'Penistone,' not a very difficult matter owing to the darkness of the hall, with the object of suggesting that 'Penistone' was then alive. Then he returned to the first hotel, where he remains till after midnight. He had thus established as good an alibi as he could.

The body, being under the cover of the bridge, remains dry. As soon as the tide slackens, he rows up the river, transfers the body to the Vicar's boat, swings the stern in to shore, and lands. Seeing the Vicar's hat, he puts that in the boat, by way of confusing the trail. Then he proceeds according to Ware's speculation.

He replaces the Admiral's boat in the Rundel Croft boat-house, making the mistake of doing so bow first. This done, he walks home to West End. His sudden departure for London is concerned with the will of John Martin Fitzgerald, a subject at present somewhat obscure.

6

By Milward Kennedy

1. Four men are engaged in the supply of arms to Chinese armies: they are Mr X (main financial element), Admiral Penistone (Gunnery Expert: acquainted with China: retired under a cloud from the Navy: the Admiral has a smaller financial interest), Sir Wilfrid Denny (formerly of the Chinese Customs Service) and Holland (who does the 'transactions on the spot'). Holland is naturally unready to discuss the business with the police.

2. The Admiral wants to increase his financial holding – in other words to oust Mr X. He is in negotiations with Sir Wilfrid and Holland to that end.

3. Sir Wilfrid is reluctant; he refuses to move openly and warns Mr X secretly.

4. Mr X, already suspicious of the Admiral and wishing to keep an eye on his doings, has persuaded his mistress to go as French

maid to Elma Fitzgerald.

5. When the Admiral moves to Rundel Croft: (a) Sir Wilfred is afraid that Mr X will think he too is letting him down; (*b*) the 'French maid' discovers that just across the river lives the husband whom she deserted ten years ago. She clears out, and tells Mr X why.

6. Sir Wilfrid reports to Mr X that the Admiral is trying to arrange a meeting of the three partners. Holland apparently has agreed. Sir Wilfrid is told to agree also and to get the meeting held at some 'neutral' place, say near (not on) Fernton Bridge. He is told, moreover, not to let it be known that he has any dealings with Holland and the Admiral.

7. The Admiral will not give his assent to Elma marrying Holland unless Holland falls in with his 'commercial' plans, and further agrees to put into the new concern which he hopes to form some of the capital which Elma will acquire. Perhaps he also wants to help in 'manipulating' her brother's money. Her brother, always a rolling stone, has disappeared, but has been heard of too recently for his death to be 'presumed.'

8. Mr X, informed by Sir Wilfrid of the time and place fixed for the 'secret meeting,' drives down dressed as a chauffeur and wearing gauntlets. He insists that the 'French maid' is to go to the Vicarage and to arrange matters with the Vicar that she can resume her place at Rundel Croft if necessary. He hopes, himself, whilst she is with the Vicar, to get into Rundel Croft (with which he is perfectly familiar, thanks to the 'French maid's' account of it) and to extract various documents relating to 'Chinese Contracts.'

9. While the 'French maid' is with the Vicar Mr X walks down through the garden, intending to cross the river in the Vicar's boat. He meets the Admiral, who has just returned in his boat.

10. The Admiral hustles away after dinner at the Vicarage, because he wants to get Elma home, and then go to his 'secret meeting.' He tidies up his boat as usual, but finds he has left his pipe at the Vicarage and his cigar-case is empty. He goes and gets his coat, meaning to *walk* to the bridge; but it is practically as quick to cross to the Vicarage, get his pipe and walk on from there. (According to the Map, the distances are practically identical.)

11. Mr X and the Admiral talk. Mr X produces the evening paper with its Chinese news. The Admiral, conscious of the 'secret meeting,' is somewhat uncomfortable. They retire to the summer-house. There, there is not only the Vicar's hat but also the knife. The talk ends in a quarrel and Mr X stabs the Admiral. The time is about 11 p.m.

12. Mr X reflects that his arrangements hold good for a murder as much as for anything else. He has even told Sir Wilfrid, as it happens, to use the Admiral's name when he asks for Holland at his hotel – which may make it appear that the Admiral was alive and in Whynmouth at 11 p.m.

13. He finds the key of the french window, crosses in the Admiral's boat (leaving the body in the summer-house), collects the papers from the study, locks up again and re-crosses in the Admiral's boat – by mistake dropping the key. He assumes that he has dropped it in the river, he dares not strike a light to make sure.

14. He waits in the car. When the 'French maid' reappears (and he is, of course, quite satisfied that neither she nor the Vicar will talk about the meeting) he tells her to drive gently on alone to Fernton Bridge and thence towards Rundel Croft. When he is sure that the Vicarage is asleep, he carries the dead body down to the Vicar's boat, leaving the knife with (not in) the body and adding the Vicar's hat to the cargo. His original intention is to set the boat adrift, but then he realises that the river is probably tidal and that the boat might not drift out to sea. So he decides to leave things as they are. (The body therefore has been 'under cover' until nearly one o'clock; and the blood has ceased to flow before the body is put in the boat.) Mr X crosses again in the Admiral's boat (which he fastens up wrongly), makes his way through the grounds of Rundel Croft to the car, and so departs with the 'French maid.'

15. The non-appearance of the Admiral perturbs both Holland and Sir Wilfrid. They wait a considerable time, and then Sir Wilfrid goes home (next morning, when Mr X telephones to 'enquire' about the meeting, he hurries up to London). Holland decides to have it out with the Admiral then and there. He starts to walk to Rundel Croft, sees a car standing near the entrance and decides to go round *via* the Vicarage. For the whole business is somewhat fishy and he has no wish to be seen. His anxiety not to attract notice retards his progress. To his horror he finds the body in the Vicar's boat; it is by now about two o'clock. He realises his danger – he has no alibi; the Admiral may have said he was going to see him by the bridge; there is the question of the will and the marriage. He thinks things out deliberately. The tide will turn, he supposes, fairly soon and start to run up the river – 'away from the bridge,' as it were. He must wait for the turn. The waiting is anxious work; he gets more and more jumpy, and more and more anxious to clear off. At about three o'clock the tide is slackening. He cuts the painter – not because he cannot reach to untie the

knot, but because to cut it suits his state of mind – it *seems* quicker than untying a knot. Then he thinks of finger-prints and throws the knife into the river.

16. Holland's plan is now to try and make it appear that he spent the night at his hotel. He must see Elma as soon as he can reasonably appear at Rundel Croft. He is there before the Inspector. Emery has to be 'drilled' a bit; also Jennie Merton. The delay when the Inspector calls is thus explained. Elma and Holland agree that there is no evidence but theirs that the Admiral hesitated to consent to their marriage; Holland was accepted as her fiancé. So the 'will' motive will not be so serious; anyhow it can be argued that Elma is likely soon to inherit her brother's money. If they get married she cannot be made to give evidence against her husband – and only she can say what the Admiral meant to do after dinner at the Vicarage. They have already got a licence – for the circumstances (the gun-running, the Admiral's 'negotiations,' etc.) have suggested the need to be ready to marry at short notice. They go off to London.

17. The 'favourite frock' was never hidden. But it was a favourite, and therefore suitable for the occasion in London: and for the same reason Elma hesitated to let her new and untried maid pack it for her in the suit-case. She folded it herself, put it on a shelf and packed it on top after seeing the Inspector. As to her regard for her appearance – she (like some others) took more trouble before strangers than before intimates (she had no time in the Inspector's case, of course). Her 'acting' during the interview was what one would expect – partly good and partly bad.

18. As for the Vicar: when first the police come, the thing uppermost in his mind is that nothing must come out of his wife's visit. He has his sons to think of, above all (almost his first thought). His hat can have nothing to do with it; he will stick to his story; he knows nothing about the murder and cannot be connected with it – and if the visit of the 'French maid' comes out, there might be an added complication. And then, after he has maintained the 'all quiet after ten-fifteen' story, comes the loss of the knife, and his discovery of ominous stains in his summer-house. He will water the garden, and if he misdirects the hose-pipe, it will merely be a sign of his wordly incompetence.

7

By Dorothy L. Sayers

John Martin Fitzgerald of Winchester, solicitor, married, in 1888, Mary Penistone, and had by her two surviving children, Walter, born in 1889 and Elma, born in 1898.

In 1909, Walter, aged twenty, got into some kind of trouble with his father and left the country. He went to China and got a job as a clerk with a tobacco company in Hong Kong, where, being idle and vicious, though handsome and attractive, he got into the opium-smuggling business.

The assistant-commissioner in the Chinese customs was a man called Wilfrid Denny, who had got into difficulties through having an extravagant wife, and was heavily in debt to a big Chinese money-lender. Denny soon found that the price of this 'accommodation' was to be the turning of a blind eye to the passage of opium through the customs. This brought him into contact with Walter, who soon saw himself in a position to blackmail the weak and foolish Denny. Denny was then about forty years of age.

In 1911, the Captain in command of the cruiser *Huntingdonshire*, stationed at Hong Kong, was Captain Penistone, young Fitzgerald's uncle, and to get the opium through meant getting it past Penistone. The previous Captain had been fairly easy to diddle, but Penistone was alert and incorruptible. He was then forty-three, a vigorous, jovial man, well liked by his crew, and a smart officer. As it was impossible to square him, it was necessary to get rid of him. Walter, in collusion with Denny, used his knowledge of his uncle's character to involve him in some discreditable affair (e.g. with a woman, or in connection with the ill-treatment of natives). Penistone, though really innocent, is made to appear at the very least extremely indiscreet, and is advised to send in his papers.

Penistone never knew who was at the bottom of his trouble – and did not even know that Walter was in Hong Kong, but he became a changed and soured man. During the War he is permitted to rejoin and retires finally with the rank of Admiral in recognition of his services, but he still broods on what he might have done but for 'the trouble,' and when the War is over he determines to get to the bottom of the business. He energetically

collects information about everything and everybody who might possibly have been concerned in the plot against him – a job made more difficult by the post-war confusion in China. The thing has become almost a monomania.

Meanwhile, Walter continues his illicit activities, and in 1914 commits himself to a forgery. The War breaks out just in time to rescue him from arrest. He manages to get away and joins up. But the warrant is still out against him, and if he survives it seems likely that he will be haled up and sent to a long term of penal servitude. He therefore makes arrangements to disappear. He sends home a letter of the 'Dear Father-I-have-neglected-you-all-but-hope-I-am-now-forgiven-and-have-turned-over-a-new-leaf-and-am-doing-my-duty' type, enclosing, in case of accident, a will drawn in favour of Elma.

After the Loos show in September, 1915, Walter deserts and disappears. He is 'missing, supposed killed.' Old Fitzgerald, who has long repented of his harshness to 'dear Walter, poor boy,' is now getting very doddery and ill. Having come into money, he redrafts his will, but retains the dispositions made some years previously in favour of Walter and Elma, for Walter has turned up once and he may turn up again. (See Chapter 7.)

Meanwhile, Walter has contrived to turn up somewhere else with somebody else's papers. He keeps secretly in touch with Elma, to whom he is still the wonderful and beloved 'big brother' – a radiant memory of childhood. If Walter is in trouble, it must be the fault of some wicked person who got him into it. Walter takes Elma into his confidence. The idea is to prove his death, when Elma will come into his share of the money and hand it over to him in his new name.

Old Fitzgerald dies in 1916. Nothing much can be done till 1918–19, when the British prisoners of war are released and the 'presumption' of the death of missing combatants is recognised by the courts.

Everything is put in trim for 'presuming' the death of Walter, when an inconvenient person turns up who knew Walter when he first joined the Army and states positively that he saw him alive in Buda-Pesth in 1918. He does not know the name under which Walter was then passing, but insists that he cannot be mistaken in the man. Under the circumstances, the court refuses to presume death. Note: It is only *now* that it becomes necessary for Elma to marry in order to provide Walter with money. See Chapter 7 as regards her present opportunities. This is when the forgery business comes to light (see Chapter 7).

Time goes on. Walter, now known as Mr X, is living rapidly and expensively abroad – chiefly on his wits and by exploiting his charm of manner. In 1920 he seduces a Mrs Mount, who is staying at Monte Carlo with some friends, and has some money of her own. Walter is at a low ebb, or he would not be bothered with the parson's wife. Having sucked her dry, he abandons her to get on as best she can. She takes a post as a maid in Paris.

Life becomes increasingly sordid and difficult for Walter. Then one day he hears that Denny has retired to England with a knighthood and a pension. Splendid idea! He will blackmail Denny! He does so – knowing that Denny dare not expose him for fear that the old Chinese story will come out, when pop goes Denny's pension.

Walter's line is: pay me, and I keep quiet. Stop the payments and I blow the gaff. I am so damned hard up that I don't really care a curse whether I go to prison or not, but you will be for it, my lad! The miserable Denny pays up: all his savings go – the proceeds of the smuggling business, and he has to go on paying Walter out of his modest pension.

Meanwhile the Admiral (now living in Cornwall), in the course of his energetic enquiries, has at last got upon the track of the old Hong Kong business. A man called Arthur Holland, who, under cover of a vague export business, does a certain amount of secret enquiry in China (he is probably mixed up with Chinese post-war politics), gives him some useful information. The Admiral is beginning to suspect that (*a*) Walter is alive, (*b*) Walter was concerned in his disgrace, (*c*) Denny had something to do with it also.

Walter is now becoming bolder. He has grown a beard and changed his appearance, and one day he turns up on Denny's doorstep. Denny must now keep him and establish him firmly in his new personality as Mr X. If not – up goes the monkey!

Denny is harried from pillar to post. He *knows* (from what Walter has told him in moments of expansiveness), however, that there is one person in England whom 'Mr X' does not want to meet, and that is Mr Mount. Mr Mount knows enough about 'Mr X' *as* Mr X to make any place too hot to hold him. Denny consults Crockford, discovers that Mount has taken a living at Lingham and takes a house in the same neighbourhood. Walter, returning from a trip abroad, finds that Denny has fled to sanctuary. He tries to dislodge Denny, but Denny sits tight.

But now a new source of trouble begins. Denny writes in agitation to Walter. He has heard from the Admiral. The Admiral

– after all these years! – is most tiresomely starting to ask questions about that dead-and-buried business in Hong Kong. He looks as though he really suspected something. Denny is doing his best to be amiable and noncommittal, but it is all dreadfully difficult.

Walter feels that a little spying ought to be done. He hunts up his former mistress, Mrs Mount, over whom he still exerts great influence, and makes her go as French maid to his sister, under the name of Célie Blanc. She is to find out what she can about who comes to the house and what the Admiral is doing, and to act as liaison between Walter and Elma. For the Admiral, suspecting that Elma knows where Walter is, is beginning to keep her under strict control and supervise her correspondence.

To Elma, of course, Walter is the poor, wronged boy who never gets a chance. She is anxious to get him his money, by fair means or foul. As the scheme to prove the death was a failure, she now wants to make over her own share of the money to him. Fortunately, Holland has fallen desperately in love with her sulky beauty. Though temperamentally disinclined to marriage, she is keen to marry Holland to get the money. The Admiral has a pretty shrewd idea of this, and therefore tries to oppose the marriage. Elma, of course, does not confide in Holland – he is a tool of the Admiral's. Everybody is in a conspiracy to keep dear Walter out of his own. She therefore breaks off open correspondence with Walter, and treats the Admiral with the contempt he deserves.

Holland has been told by the Admiral that if he marries Elma, she will probably send all her money to this scamp of a brother. But Holland, being in love, says he wants Elma, not her money. The Admiral says: 'You won't get my consent.' Holland replies: 'I don't care.' But Elma *does* care. The control of the money is what she is marrying him for. The situation drags on. Elma alternates between encouraging Holland and rebuffing him. If she seems too affectionate he will urge marriage without the Admiral's consent; if she appears too mercenary he may get put off altogether. As he is the only man whom she has much opportunity of meeting nowadays, and no other suitor seems forthcoming, she must keep him on the lead if possible.

Mrs Mount is a weak sort of woman, still infatuated by Walter. I think she knows him to be Fitzgerald all right, but supposes, like Elma, that he has been deeply wronged. Walter is quite cocksure that she is completely under his thumb, and as a bait, has promised to marry her if she succeeds in helping him to get the money.

Very well, then. The Admiral comes to the conclusion that the

one person who really can help him to find Walter and disentangle the Chinese business is Denny. Making one of his lightning decisions, he takes Rundel Croft, and carries the whole family off there, bag and baggage.

This is dreadfully disconcerting to Walter, and Mrs Mount is appalled when she finds herself – not only in the same village as, but actually next door to, her former husband. (I don't think Walter mentioned to Mrs Mount where her husband was living – why should he? – and by the time Mrs Mount has been able to tell Walter where they are going, the move has taken place. Or it is just possible that Mrs Mount *did* know, but deliberately didn't tell Walter at first, because she was bitten with the idea of getting a sight of her two boys. Perhaps this latter idea makes the thing more credible and more suitable to Mrs Mount's weakly emotional character.)

The Vicar, of course, sees and recognises his wife, and is greatly shocked. He has an interview with her in private, in which he regains a good deal of his old influence over her, as a priest, at least, if not as a man. He asks her kindly about Walter (whom he, of course, knows only as X) – is she still living with him? She has never asked for a divorce and he, the Vicar, would never think of divorcing her on his own account, as it is against his principles. To him, she is always his wife; if she *asks* for a divorce, he will not let his religious convictions stand in her way. She is touched by his real consideration for her, and admits that X has behaved badly to her, but that she now has hopes that he may marry her after all, if his 'affairs' can be put right. Mrs Mount (always readily accessible to the latest influence) becomes very much troubled after this interview. Moreover, from what she hears at the Admiral's, she begins to fear that she is being mixed up in something much more wicked and dangerous than the restitution of a persecuted man to his 'rights.' After all, she can by this time have few illusions as to Walter's personal character. She works herself up to going to the Vicar again, and telling him what she knows of the story, under the seal of confession.

The Vicar is stern with her. It is absurd to suppose that he can give her absolution. She is not repentant – she is merely frightened. She is deceiving her employer and engaging in a conspiracy to defeat the ends of justice. Her duty is to break with Walter and make a clean breast of everything to the Admiral.

Mrs Mount characteristically does neither one thing nor the other. She won't go on with it and she daren't tell the Admiral – she simply leaves Rundel Croft, merely telling Walter that her

husband has recognised her and that the situation is impossible. Walter is annoyed, but recognises that she is no longer to be trusted. He tells her not to be a fool. Why shouldn't Elma marry Holland? Nothing more is contemplated. He gets out of her an exact description of the Admiral's house and the Vicarage, etc.

Two weeks later, Walter hears from Denny. The Admiral is getting dangerously near to the truth. 'Old friends' have been visiting him: something has been discovered. The Admiral must be silenced.

Walter agrees. His plan is to:

(*a*) Kill the Admiral.
(*b*) Manufacture proof of his (Walter's) death at some period *subsequent* to old Fitzgerald's death.
(*c*) Let Elma inherit *Walter's* share of the money under *Walter's* will of 1915.

He and Denny will then be safe, and *all* the money will be, to all intents and purposes, in Walter's hands. If Denny is good, he shall get a share of it. Walter then gets Denny to convey a letter to Elma. He says he has found means to obtain a hold over the Admiral and force him into giving consent to Elma's marriage with Holland. She is to say nothing of this to Holland (who might high-mindedly object to these methods), but she is to tell Holland that she is ready to marry him, Admiral or no Admiral. Holland is to get a special licence, and she will come up to town to marry him on the morning of August 10th.

The plan is then laid to murder the Admiral, steal the compromising papers, and thus leave everything happy and comfortable all round.

The Murder

1. Holland comes down unexpectedly by the eight-fifty to see the Admiral. He is worried by the idea that he will injure Elma's prospects by marrying her, and wants to give the Admiral a final chance of consenting before it is too late. He rings up from the Lord Marshall and is answered by Mr Emery. He hears that Elma and the Admiral are out to dinner and will probably not be back till pretty late. This is tiresome, but he must do what he can. He will stay the night and make one more effort to see the Admiral but, if not, he will simply go up to town next morning and carry out his plan. He dines at the Lord Marshall and then goes out for a walk;

while doing so he is seen by Denny.

2. Denny has told the Admiral that he has found out something the Admiral would like to know about Walter and the Chinese business. He has got hold of a man who knows something. This man is 'in trouble' and cannot appear openly, but if the Admiral will come down after dinner to an old deserted boat-house near Fernton Bridge, Denny and 'the man' will meet him there. The rendezvous is fixed for 11.15 sharp. The Admiral swallows the bait eagerly. Walter (through Denny) has told Elma about all this, though to her, of course, 'the man' is the mysterious person who has got 'the hold' over the Admiral and is going to squeeze the consent to the marriage out of him. The Admiral, equally of course, thinks Elma is quite in the dark about it all.

3. The plan for the murder is this: Denny is to go on foot to the old boat-house, meet the Admiral at 11.15 and hold him in talk. Meantime, Walter goes to the Lord Marshall, arriving about 11.15. There, with his beard and family resemblance to his uncle the Admiral, he will easily be mistaken for him in the dim light. He is to leave some sort of message. (When Walter hears from Denny that Holland is in Whynmouth, they seize on this circumstance. Walter is to ask for *him*, suggesting that Holland may be involved in the business if anything goes wrong with their plans.) Thus they will establish the fact that the Admiral intended to travel by the 11.25 train. Walter will then take Denny's car to Fernton Bridge (about three minutes by car) and, while Denny holds up the Admiral, Walter will bash him savagely about the head with a blunt instrument. The body is then to be taken to the level crossing, which is the kind worked by a lever from the signal-box. All this should not take more than about seven minutes (say, one minute for the bashing, three minutes from boat-house to car, three minutes to level crossing – this allows him to drive at only thirty-five miles an hour over one and a quarter of a mile or thereabouts – he could really go much faster for that brief distance). At about 11.22 they will carry the body on to the *down* line, through the side wickets, trusting to the darkness. At 11.24 the down express is due to pass through, not stopping at Whynmouth. With any luck it will smash up the Admiral and the conclusion will be drawn that he met his death by accident, through passing the level crossing through the wickets as a short cut from the Lord Marshall up the UP platform (see Map).

Walter will then go on to Rundel Croft to see Elma, who is expecting him. He will explain that the meeting has taken place, and that, in consequence of what has transpired, the Admiral has

gone up to town, but that, before going, the Admiral has given consent to the marriage. Walter will then hand Elma the typewritten consent, which he has forged for the purpose. Elma is to carry on and marry Holland at once, since Walter needs money desperately and there is no time to be lost.

4. This beautiful plan goes wrong. What actually happens is this. Mrs Mount, who, what with the Vicar and one thing and another, has begun to suspect Walter of worse things than she ever thought him capable of, has started to do a little detecting on her own account. I think she probably intercepts some communication from Denny referring to the date and time of the meeting of the Admiral. She is living in London either with Walter or in some place selected by him. She discovers (*a*) that Walter has no genuine intention of ever marrying her, having made other arrangements, and (*b*) that there is a plan to do away with the Admiral that same night. She determines to warn the Admiral. There is no train she can catch (the 8.50 has gone and the express doesn't stop at Whynmouth), so she hires a car and starts out for Lingham.

She does not go straight to Rundel Croft, preferring not to face Walter, who may be there (she does not know *details* of the plot). She will try to get hold of the Vicar and warn *him*. In the village she directs the chauffeur to stop at the Vicarage gate and wait for her. She will not be many minutes. She reaches the Vicarage at 10.40.(N.B. – This is earlier than the constable said in Chapter 6, but he only said *about* 10.45.) She does not like to ring the bell (the boys! the servants!) – perhaps the Vicar is down the garden having his bed-time pipe (she remembers his habits). She creeps down to the summer-house. Nobody there – only the Vicar's hat and Peter's knife on the table. She wonders what to do. Shall she throw stones at the Vicar's bedroom window? (But which is it?) Or shall she take the boat and go boldly across to Rundel Croft? She is playing with the open knife, and it occurs to her that if she has to face Walter on her own it may be a useful weapon. Suddenly she hears the unmistakable noise of oars in the rowlocks. She hurries down to the boat-house and in the summer dusk sees the Admiral starting off down the river. He must be going to the fatal rendezvous! In the summerhouse she has snatched up what she thinks is her black calf-skin bag, but is really the Vicar's hat. She pulls the Vicar's boat in by the rope at the stern, but, owing to the strong stream and the stiffness of the new painter, has some difficulty in unhitching the painter from the mooring-post. She therefore cuts the painter with Peter's knife, and I think that at this

point she drops the knife into the river, to be subsequently found. She gets the rowlocks into place and starts off in pursuit of the Admiral, who by this time is well away down the river. (She may try to hail him, but the Admiral will probably pay no attention – or she may be afraid of causing a disturbance. The boys! the servants!)

5. *The Coat.* The Admiral has decided to go by river to the meeting. To get the car out means making a racket, and he does not walk because he has a game leg as a result of the War. (This will make it OK about his not being supposed capable of walking to Whynmouth in the time, by the way.) He waits in the boat-house till Elma is well out of the way and reflects that he had better take a coat with him, since he will get hot rowing and the interview in the old boat-house may be a long one. He goes up to the house and fetches the coat, and returning re-locks the french window. He then gets the boat out. He reckons that with the tide setting strongly down the river, he will make Fernton Bridge well within the half-hour, being a vigorous old boy at the oars.

6. Mrs Mount is not able to make such good time down the river as he does. She used to boat in the old days with the Vicar, but she is out of practice. Actually, the Admiral makes Fernton Bridge in twenty-five minutes, arriving at 11.10, to find Denny waiting for him. Mrs Mount arrives five minutes later. She sees the boat but no Admiral. She moors at the rotten old raft and creeping round the boat-house, which is derelict and water-logged, sees Denny and the Admiral behind it. Now, Denny has the grimmest doubts about Walter. He thinks it quite likely that Walter may do *him* in, as well as the Admiral. He has therefore come armed with a knife – a relic of Chinese days, no doubt. Mrs Mount calls out to the Admiral: 'Take care, Admiral! They mean to murder you.' The Admiral (who has the grimmest doubts about Denny!) turns menacingly on Denny. Denny loses his silly head, whips out the knife and stabs the Admiral. Mrs Mount shrieks and collapses.

7. At this distressing moment, enter Walter, having carried out his part of the programme. He is aghast to find the Admiral dead, with a wound in him which by no stretch of imagination could be inflicted by a railway engine – and Mrs Mount having hysterics in the background! He is furious with both Mrs Mount and Denny. They wrangle in angry whispers. Denny says he couldn't help it. Walter says he is a blasted idiot. Denny says, couldn't they go on and carry out the plan – perhaps the dagger-wound won't be noticed in the general mess-up. While they waste time in recriminations and in subduing Mrs Mount – who is showing

every disposition to scream and attract people on the road – a distant roar and rumble is heard, and the 11.24 thunders over the railway bridge. It is too late. The only other train that night is the 11.25 and there is no time to do anything about that.

8. Now what are they to do? Here they are with two boats, a car, a woman and a corpse. The easiest thing would be to let the Admiral float peacefully out to sea, but, with the tide running as it is, he would be down at the harbour in half an hour. Somebody would find him – and then there would be enquiries at Rundel Croft, and it is urgently necessary that Walter should go up there and collect the papers. Then, too, the search would at once be made upriver; blood and footprints would be discovered at Fernton Bridge. Much better to suggest that the crime was committed elsewhere. The Vicar's boat – the Vicar's hat – why not take the whole caboodle back to Rundel Croft and leave the Vicar to explain things as best he can? Walter will take the car to the house and get the papers and leave the forged permit-to-marry. Mrs Mount and the miserable Denny must get the boats back as best they can, stream or no stream.

9. 'By the way,' says Walter, 'how did Mrs Mount get here?' After a certain amount of harrying and bullying he gets the story out of her. Damn it! That chauffeur must be got rid of! Here they are – it is already twelve o'clock (for there has been a good deal of argument). No time to lose. Walter returns to the car and drives along to the Vicarage. The car has gone! This is puzzling and tiresome, but it is all the more imperative to make haste. He returns over Fernton Bridge and drives to Rundel Croft, concealing the car somewhere off the road. Here he gets in through the french window with Elma's key, goes into the study and starts hunting for the papers.

10. *The Car.* Meanwhile the hired chauffeur has been getting impatient. His fare said she would only be a few minues and here it is getting on for an hour. Nobody seems to have opened the door to her. The Vicarage is as dark as a tomb. He gets a strong impression that he has been bilked. He hoots violently several times and then walks up to the side-door, which is the first he comes to, and hammers on it. The Vicar, who sleeps over the side-door (servants and boys on the river side of house) looks out. What is the matter? Some parishioner dying? The chauffeur's reply is unintelligible – to him – but he thinks he had better come down and see what it is all about. Chauffeur says, Will the lady be long, because he has got to get back to his garage, he has, for another job? Vicar says, What lady? – Lady what came in here.

Describes lady. Is he going to get his money? Because, if not – shows every intention of making a disturbance. The Vicar, who with extreme uneasiness has recognised the description of the lady, does some quick thinking. At all costs a disturbance must be prevented. He makes some sort of explanation and pays the man off, after taking his name and the address of the garage. Then he returns and ponders. Where did his wife go? Why did she come? Perhaps she is over at Rundel Croft. He goes down to the boat-house. His boat is out. She must have gone across in it. He shakes his head over this. Obviously the poor woman is still under that scoundrel's thumb. What will she do when she returns and finds the car gone? Obviously he must wait and explain what has happened. He will drive her himself if necessary. He returns and dresses; then sits in his bedroom to watch the road. (Why does not he watch the boat-house? Because, if Walter returns with her there may be trouble and possibly a noise – and then, the boys! the servants! – In any case she *must* return to where she left the car, so he will wait at the high-road side of the house.)

11. Denny and Mrs Mount are now left to bring the boats back. They swab up the blood behind the old boathouse as best they can. Mrs Mount, threatened by Denny whom she has just seen kill a man, helps without protest. Denny puts the Admiral's coat on him – (or he put it on himself when he arrived) – and stuffs in the pocket the evening paper which Walter or Denny brought to the meeting. (It was purchased in Whynmouth that night or Walter brought it from town.) At about one o'clock they start with the slack of the tide. They put the body in the Vicar's boat, unshipping the rowlocks, and putting Denny's coat over it to hide the face. This explaines why the body is not wet with the dew. The Vicar's boat with the body in it is tied by the painter to the stern of the Admiral's boat and towed along. The incompetent Denny naturally ties it in one of those landsman's knots which nothing but a marlin-spike will ever undo, especially as the painter has got wet and the new rope has swollen with the water. With a boat to tow and two incompetent oarsmen, they do not make very good time, and the ghastly dawn is breaking before they get up to Rundel Croft. Walter is there, chafing at the delay. He has locked the window and brought the key, but in helping the idiotic Denny alongside he drops the key. It falls, as he thinks, into the mud, but actually into the Admiral's boat and is kicked under the boards by Denny. Anyway, they can't search now. It is getting light. Damn Denny and his inextricable knot! They hew the rope off with Denny's knife and push the boat with the body adrift. It

dawdles out into the river and fetches up against the opposite bank. Later, the tide frees it and carries it on up the river. They hack and tear away the remains of the rope from the Admiral's boat, having taken it into the boat-house wrong end first. Then they return to Whynmouth in Denny's car, dropping Walter and Mrs Mount. Walter retrieves his own car from wherever he left it when he came from London and takes Mrs Mount away in it – and if that poor woman comes out of this business alive I shall be very much surprised. (N.B. – Or Walter's car can be used throughout. Or Walter and Mrs Mount may return to town by the milk-train. In any case these movements of cars should be traceable.)

12. *Holland.* What has he been doing? He *may*, of course, have been innocently in bed and asleep, but I think it would be more fun if he wasn't. I think that, after putting out his boots to be cleaned, he thought he would have another shot at the Admiral. He went out, unseen by the Boots, sometime between ten and eleven (not too early, or the family will not have returned from the Vicarage). He strolls two and a half miles leisurely in his rubber-soled canvas shoes. He reaches Rundel Croft say at 11.15 (Admiral at boat-house, Elma upstairs). House dark. They are not in yet. He goes down to the boat-house. No boat. They are still at the Vicarage. Good. He goes for a stroll down the road, keeping an eye on the house. No lights yet. Very odd. He muses on love and marriage and recites the Ode to the Nightingale to fill up time. House still dark. Can he have missed them? He goes down to the boat-house again. Boat still out. No lights anywhere. Past midnight. Well, he can hardly knock them up at this time of night. Hullo! Somebody has gone in by the drawing-room window! Light in the study. He distinctly sees the Admiral's bearded profile (really Walter's, of course, with the family resemblance) in the study. Curiouser and curiouser. Where is the boat? He goes up to the house. The curtains have now been drawn in the study, but there is a light in the drawing-room now. He taps. Elma opens the window. She seems very much startled at seeing him. Can he see the Admiral? No – Oh, no – but there is no need. The Admiral has consented to the marriage. Look! Here is the written consent. Then, says Holland, there is no need to go to London tomorrow. Oh, yes – let them do it now, as it is all settled. In fact, the Admiral has only given his consent on the understanding that she never darkens his french windows again. Has he, by Jove! He'll tell the blighter what he thinks of him. Please, *no*! that will only make things worse. *Please* do as she tells him. Of course, darling – and she does love him, doesn't she? – Oh, of course, but please go now. Very well –

but she is looking so beautiful tonight. Very well. Good night, sweetheart.

Exit Holland to ramble round in a dream of ecstasy till he is ashamed to knock up the Lord Marshall. Instead, he drifts round the harbour (where he may be seen if necessary) till six, when he goes in, unseen by Boots who is occupied in the bar. (Observe that Holland will now be ready to swear that he saw the Admiral alive after midnight.)

When the news of the Admiral's death comes along, he is worried. He must see Elma. He goes to Rundel Croft, thinking that, as things are, she won't want to go through with the marriage. He is delayed by Inspector Rudge, and when he gets free learns that Elma has gone to town as per schedule. He hastens after her, and, feeling that there is going to be a lot of trouble about this business, marries her. As his wife he can protect her. He sees, naturally, that it is impossible for them to stay in town as she suggests – they will have to go back for the inquest and funeral – but she is upset, and for the moment he humours her. (Note: He says nothing to Rudge about his midnight excursion, fearing to be detained. He will get hold of Elma first. Indeed, he may possibly at this point suspect Elma himself.)

13. *Elma*. The emphasis laid on the time spent in calling Elma and in dressing seems to me a little exaggerated. When she hears of the death, she is horrified. She can hardly help suspecting Walter of some guilty knowledge, but hopes, naturally, that the crime was committed by the other unknown man after Walter left them. She feels faint and sick – but will Emery bring her a cup of tea and she will try to pull herself together. Emery does so. Yes – she is better now – tell the Inspector she will be down in a quarter of an hour. She thinks over what she had better say. Nobody knows about Walter. Holland evidently thinks it was the Admiral who came in at midnight. She had better say nothing. She hopes Holland will say nothing without consulting her – in fact, he is probably already in town. She must tell Jennie to pack. Her white frock will do to be married in – she looks at it! Heavens! A smear of blood on the waist. Walter's hand or coat must have made the mark when he greeted her.

Then Walter – ! Horrible. She hastily hides the dress, gets into her clothes and comes down.

Time to break news	5 minutes
Time to prepare tea	5
Time to drink tea	5

Time to examine dress and prepare story	5
Time to dress	5
	25

Elma will, of course, leave Holland to suppose that it *was* the Admiral he saw in the study, since otherwise she will have to explain about Walter. But she will have difficulty in explaining why she let Rudge suppose that she last saw the Admiral at ten o'clock.

14. *The Vicar.* Goes out early in the morning. No one has come to the car. What has happened? Finds his wife's bag in summer-house and marks of high heels on path leading from house to summer-house, also on flower-bed near summer-houes. (Note: It is the path between the summer-house and boat-house that is of brick. The other garden paths will be of gravel.) Anxious to avoid scandal, he takes a rake and fork and digs these over.

The weather has been hot and dry, but there has been rain on and off for a week or so before. (Note: There has been no *prolonged* drought, or Neddy Ware would have had something to say about its effect on the height of the river, which appears to be at least normal.) Therefore the earth, when turned up, looks suspiciously black and moist. After hearing of the murder the Vicar cannot help suspecting his wife of complicity or guilty knowledge at least. He learns the difference between preaching and practising the religious man's duty to the State. He conceals the bag and waters the dug-up patches.

He *must* now find his wife. He *must* know whether she is guilty or not (his boys' mother hanged for murder!!!). He hopes that she is not guilty and that by proving to her that he is aware of her presence that night in his summer-house, he may induce her to reveal what she knows about Walter. He cannot, of course, supply this information himself, since it is impossible for him to reveal what he heard in confession. He knows the address of the garage from which she hired the car. As soon as he possibly can, without arousing the suspicions of the police, he must get upon her track.

15. The Admiral's pipe was left on the Vicar's table during his visit. It has no significance in the plot except that, when coupled with Holland's story of having seen the Admiral at Rundel Croft after midnight, it may serve to throw fresh suspicion on the Vicar.

8

By Ronald A. Knox

Chapter 1. The sailent feature of the situation – none of the later contributors have dealt with it – seems to me the fact that the body is in a boat at all. A murder in a boat is very unlikely; but why put a body into a boat, when it would be simpler to throw it into the stream? Unless, indeed, a very elaborate frame-up is intended, the position of the boat on the river having been artificially engineered so as to cast suspicion of murder upon some innocent person.

If Canon Whitechurch has any murderer in view at all, Ware should be the man – we must assume that Canon Whitechurch respects the honour of the cloth. *Ceteris paribus*, in a modern detective story the first person named is likely to be the criminal.

In favour of Ware's guilt, it must be observed that he claims not to recognise Penistone's corpse, though he had met him long before on the China station. It does not seem probable that Ware would not know Penistone by sight after even a month's residence, in the height of the summer, since Ware was always fishing, and Penistone kept a boat. Against Ware's guilt, the fact that Penistone has come to settle next door to him forms an improbable coincidence, if we are to suppose that Ware harboured an old grudge against him.

I once laid it down that no Chinaman should appear in a detective story. I feel inclined to extend the rule so as to apply to residents in China. It appears that Admiral Penistone, Sir W. Denny, Walter Fitzgerald, Ware, and Holland are all intimate with China, which seems overdoing it.

Chapter 2. I imagine that the Coles meant to incriminate Elma, though they may have had their eye on Denny.

Chapter 3. Wade seems to suspect Elma; the packing up or concealing of her evening things points this way. (Why *did* she dress up to meet the Vicar? This must be considered.) The words 'And if it was . . . ' on p.40 seem more designed to incriminate Ware; so does Appleton's theory of the murder having taken place up-stream.

Does dew form on boats floating in rivers? The encyclopaedia gives me no help.

Chapter 4. Mrs Christie seems suspicious of Denny; he is hard

up, Penistone's change of residence is attributed to a desire to be near him, and, according to Mrs Davis, Denny was none too pleased over it. On the ordinary principles of a mystery story, this should mean that Penistone is blackmailing Denny. I cannot find out what is the importance, if any, of the Vicar's runaway wife. She left her husband in 1920, well after the War, so it seems difficult to identify her with Elma, who was with her uncle at that time. How far is Whynmouth from London?

Chapter 5. Rhode seems to be fixing it on Holland. Penistone might have gone to Whynmouth to interview Holland, who met and murdered him, and conveyed him up-stream; afterwards transferring the corpse into the Vicar's boat, and running the other boat in head first. But of course Denny is under suspicion, from the position of his house. And again, Ware's insistence that the murder was committed down-stream might be an effort to exculpate the real criminal, himself. How far up was the river tidal?

Chapter 6. Kennedy seems to point to the Vicar. If not, why was the weapon taken from the Vicarage summer-house? (Unless caught up at random.) And why does the Vicar water the garden so thoroughly, if he is not obliterating footprints? (I take it we are not to fix a juvenile crime on the sons.) I do not understand the woman in the car. If she was Elma, I do not see how she got there. If anybody else, she is a new character, not mentioned in the first five chapters, and therefore on my own principles not the criminal. She might be the Vicar's runaway wife; but it seems a coincidence that she should have happened to pay a call on a night so *accidentée* already.

Chapter 7. I suppose Miss Sayers thinks the Vicar knew something about it all. The length of the rope ought to indicate that the Vicarage boat was twice moored that night, and loosed each time by a cutting of the painter from a position of disadvantage; hence the missing two feet of rope, which should be hanging up somewhere, unless deliberately removed since the murder. The double loosing of the boat suggests either that there were two separate plots afoot, or else that there has been a very elaborate frame-up.

The return of the Hollands, with their story of having seen Penistone alive after midnight, seems to put a wholly new complexion on the story; I wish I could discover what. If the permission to marry was genuine, their motive for murder ceases, and their motive for hurry is difficult to see. If they were the murderers, why throw suspicion on themselves by their haste to marry? It all beats me, and I wish she had not left me to conduct the interview.

Anyhow, this is my solution:

Walter Fitzgerald took strongly after his mother and could, with make-up, pass as the Admiral, his uncle. It was probably thus that he managed to shift a peccadillo of his own in Shanghai on to his uncle's shoulders. The Admiral suspected this; which is why he collected papers in his desk calculated to blast Walter's reputation if he reappeared in Europe. Almost more important, the Admiral held and was suppressing papers which would have proved Walter's innocence in the matter of forgery, and would have made it possible for him to reappear in Society. Walter survived the War, and ran away with Celia Mount, the Vicar's wife, in 1920. Celia, to further his interests, went to act as (French) maid to Elma, the sister. Elma knew that her brother meant to recover the papers, but not that he intended to murder, and thus silence, his uncle. The Admiral came to Lingham so as to be near Denny, whom he was blackmailing. Celia, finding her husband so close, went to see him and urged him to divorce her. He refused on conscientious grounds. She left, having taken a wax impression of the key of the Admiral's desk.

Holland had somehow become an enemy of Walter's in China. Walter therefore decided to saddle him with whatever suspicion attached to the murder. Elma was not in love with Holland, but wanted to marry him so as to get the full control of her own money. Penistone refused his consent, because he suspected Holland, whom he had met in Denny's house, of acting in Denny's interests.

Walter and Celia, on the fatal night, motored down to Lingham. They knew from Elma the plans of the Rundel Croft household. Celia was put down at the Vicarage, where she found the Vicar in the garden, and persuaded him to ferry her across in his boat and detain the Admiral in conversation, while she went into the study and secured the papers 'needed to save an innocent man.' The Vicar had to cut his painter, owing to the state of the tide. Celia secured the papers, about 10.30; and sent a telephone message as from Elma (who was upstairs, ignorant of her presence) asking Holland to come round at midnight. Meanwhile (the Vicar still talking to the Admiral) Walter has gone to the inn and posed as Penistone, hoping thus to implicate Holland. (It would be found that he had not taken the trian, and that Holland had gone out at night; it would be assumed that the murder had taken place, and the body set adrift, at or near Whynmouth. Perhaps the plotters made a mistake about the tides.) Then Walter returned to Rundel Croft, where he either murdered Penistone, or found him murdered by Celia (caught in her act of theft). The Vicar, who was

scheduled to keep the Admiral in talk till (say) eleven, was waiting at the boat-house, and ferried Celia across; she told him to go to bed, the chauffeur would pick her up. Actually she returned, stumbling over flower-beds, to the river, cut the painter a second time (she was much shorter than Mount) and rejoined Walter. He, meanwhile, had put Penistone's body into its greatcoat, and thrust a paper into the pocket to suggest that Penistone had really gone to Whynmouth. He meant to put the body into the Admiral's boat, but imagined that this would be the one moored by its bows; hence actually he put the body in the Vicar's boat (where the hat had been left by accident) and, using the Admiral's boat, towed boat and body out to midstream; then cut adrift. Celia pointed out the mistake when he landed, but it was too late to do anything; Holland's steps were heard on the gravel. Walter rushed into the study and personated the Admiral, showing Holland the forged consent. He left this in an envelope for Elma (who knew it was a forgery); Holland went home, letting himself in by a door he had left unlocked: Walter and Celia got off in their car.

On the discovery of the body, Elma hastened to marry Holland, thinking that Walter was the murderer and she would lose another chance of marrying; Holland hastened to marry Elma, chivalrously, because he thought she would be under suspicion. Denny, hearing (from Emery) that documents had been taken from the desk, dashed up to London to know what was being done with those which compromised him. Mount found the extra coil hanging to the mooring-post, did not understand it, but destroyed it to screen his wife, which was also why he obliterated her footmarks on the bed. The white dress (which had been worn by Elma because she wanted to attract the Vicar, hoping to persuade him to divorce Celia) was taken up to London because it was the nearest thing she had got to a wedding-dress.

The precise time of the murder and the precise distance to which the corpse was towed by Walker are to be settled by the tide experts. Walter wanted to make it look as if the boat had been drifted up with the tide all, or most of, the way from Whynmouth. The key was left in the Admiral's boat by Celia. This was meant to suggest that Penistone had left all locked when he (supposedly) went to Whynmouth; and would have done so but for Walter's confusion of the two boats. Celia had a false key to the french window, as well as to the desk.

The plotters assumed that Holland's story would be believed, and that he would be thought to have murdered Penistone at or near Whynmouth round about eleven o'clock.

9

By Freeman Wills Crofts

On the afternoon before the crime, Walter calls on Celia, whom he has fixed up at the Judd Street hotel. After he leaves, she somehow suspects what is going to be done that night. She is horror-struck and resolves at all costs to save Penistone. She will enlist Mount's help, who, through her confession, knows the circumstances. The five-thirty train has gone, so she travels by the seven to Drychester and motors to the Vicarage. The house seems shut up and before knocking she goes to see if Mount is in the summer-house. While making up her mind to knock, she sees Penistone starting. She grasps the knife and what she thinks is her bag and rushes to the river, shouting as loud as she can. But the Admiral doesn't hear her. She thinks it may be too late if she goes for Mount, so she follows Penistone herself. If desirable, she can have seen (or felt?)the knife in the summer-house. She cannot untie the painter, so runs back for the knife.

She comes on Peniston's boat about half a mile down the river. (If it was at the bridge, there would not be time for Walter to get back to personate Penistone.) There she finds Walter and Denny, and the Admiral already murdered. Denny seems almost out of his mind with fear. She is horrified. She fears Walter is guilty, but she doesn't *know*. They tell her Penistone committed suicide. She doesn't believe it, but she doesn't *know*. Weakly, she takes no step. Walter sends her to his car, which is hidden close by. He and Denny row the boats back and shove both into the Rundel Croft boat-house. Denny waits while Walter goes up and steals the papers – which clear Penistone's character, incidentally revealing the trick Walter and Denny have played on him in China. Walter tells Elma what has happened. She is aghast, but cannot do anything without destroying Walter, of whom she is so fond. She decides to know nothing about what has happened.

Walter has prepared the consent, and this he gives to Holland. When Holland goes, Walter and Denny put the body into the Vicar's boat, as the best thing they can think of, and send the boat adrift. They had intended to throw it into the river, but the Vicar's boat seems a better idea. This putting the boats into the boat-house accounts for the boat's tidal movements, as also the

clothing on the body being dry.

Denny then walks home, letting himself in unseen. Walter takes Celia to London, but because he is afraid of her giving the show away he takes her on to Paris till the storm blows over.

It should be explained that Celia took the Vicar's hat by mistake, and therefore left her bag behind. In this bag Mount found the Drychester and London addresses.

Chronology

The dates appear to be as follows:

Monday, 8th August. – New moon.
Tuesday, 9th August. – Penistone dines with Mount. The murder in the evening.
Wednesday, 10th August. – Discovery of body. Rudge investigates up to end of 39 Articles.
Thursday, 11th August. – Rudge reports to his superiors and investigates lives of Rundel Croft household.
Friday, 12th August. – The inquest. Rudge goes to Drychester and London.
Saturday, 13th August. – Rudge finds Judd Street hotel.
Monday, 15th August. – Rudge goes to Drychester and reports to Super.

10

By Edgar Jepson

Walter is the murderer. He has a beard and strongly resembles his uncle the Admiral, whom he impersonated at the Lord Marshall. After the crime he returns to Rundel Croft, sees his sister, whose help he enlists by means of some explanation that does not give the real facts, is mistaken by Holland for the Admiral, while he is searching for File X, which contains the truth about the Hong Kong incident and Walter's share in it, and then goes upstairs to shave off his dangerous beard in the bathroom. By this means he is able to go unrecognised, and keep in touch with the situation, by posing as the reporter for the *Evening Gazette*.

11

By Clemence Dane

Here, roughly, are the points I have made. Célie, the French maid, and the Vicar's wife are one person. She has been living with Walter, the murderer, or at any rate, there is a tie of some sort between them, and she knows enough to make her dangerous. He knows that she has gone down to consult her former husband (or for any purpose anybody likes to invent) and desires to divert suspicion from himself, and on to the Vicar by a second murder; or, alternately thinks that she intends to give him away. Anyway, he follows her down.

She has gone to the Vicarage, found her husband is out, and the maids also. (A genuine accident this: they had been given a day's holiday by the Vicar. He and they have gone to a local flower-show at some distance, or a village outing of some sort.) She has also written to the Hollands to meet her there, for purposes of consultation.

Célie, not knowing that the Vicar's absence is more than temporary, wanders into the garden, and there picks the greengages, then comes back to the house and encounters Walter. There is some sort of an argument. At any rate he murders her, arranging it to look like suicide, and leaves only a few minutes before the Inspector arrives. Walter thinks himself unseen, but later it must transpire that one of the villagers has seen him. He has a perfectly good excuse: he has called to see the Vicar in pursuit of his reporter's duties, and, like everyone else, has found the house empty. The Inspector, however, knows that Célie has been in the garden within ten minutes of his own arrival – the wet greengage stones and the handkerchief – and that therefore she must have encountered Walter, who would have just had time to murder her and leave without running into Rudge.

If more time is needed, the handkerchief and greengage stones can be found lying in the shade and would thus take longer to dry. The other importance of the greengage clue is Rudge's deduction from it, before Walter's recognition by a villager happens, that a woman who strolls cheerfully into a garden and eats greengages is not likely to commit suicide three minutes later. The funeral card is a false clue: it is really written by one of the servants or by the

Vicar himself, and is a genuine message to any possible caller. Or it might be a fake message written in the Vicar's hand-writing by Walter in order to avoid the discovery of the murder for several hours. I don't know how to explain Elma and Holland's share or non-share in the business. It's quite inexplicable to me. So I have gone on the ground that they are two perfectly innocent people, and that all the evidence that points to them is purely accidental. I am, frankly, in a complete muddle as to what has happened, and have tried to write a chapter that anybody can use to prove anything they like.

APPENDIX II

NOTES ON MOORING OF BOAT

(Extract from letter from John Rhode)

I, too, wanted it to be necesary to get into the boat in order to cast it off or make it fast again. Now, as it happens, in a river with a considerable rise and fall of tide (as this river must have had, to account for the swiftness of the ebb and flow of the tidal stream), this is nearly always necessary, if it is desired to keep the boat afloat at all states of the tide. One method of mooring a boat under these circumstances is as I visualised it.

The mooring-post is driven into the bed of the stream, beyond low-water mark, in water deep enough to float the boat at all times. A hard, made of a few loads of stone, is run from the bank to low-water mark, to save ploughing through the mud. A ring-bolt is fixed at the shore end of this hard.

Now, having been out in the boat, you want to come ashore. Right. Make fast the painter to the mooring-post. Pole the boat round till her stern touches the hard. Jump ashore, taking with you the end of a light line, made fast at the other end to the ring in the stern of the boat. Then push the boat off again, and make fast your end of the line to the ring-bolt on shore, adjusting the length of the line so that the boat lies parallel, during the ebb, with the bank.

Having had your drink, you want to put off again. Cast off the line, and haul the stern of the boat in till it touches the hard. Jump in with the line up in the stern. Go forward, haul in on painter till

you are near enough to the post, then cast off.

I gather that you want someone to get into the boat and cast off the painter. As you will see, unless the boat is approached by water, this is necessary in any case. In describing the incident, remember how the boat swings. During the ebb the boat lies as described. But during the flood the stern will swing in on itself, and will remain touching the shore throughout the flood. This, of course, does not matter since the water is rising.

Remember, too, that any particular point in the tidal phase occurs (near enough for this purpose) about three-quarters of an hour later on successive days. Don't make it high-water at 10.a.m. one day and low-water at 11 a.m. the next. Also, in a river like this, the tide ebbs longer than it flows. I laid down rules for this particular river, though I don't remember them exactly now, for the guidance of those who followed.

As for the distance of the pole from high-water mark, you can, within limits, make this to suit yourself. If you allow twelve feet or more, measuring horizontally, between H.W.O.S.T. and L.W.O.S.T., and six feet or more between L.W.O.S.T. and the post, you wont be far wrong. These distances can be increased almost indefinitely, but I shouldn't decrease them much, or you will make your bank awkwardly steep.

COUNSEL'S OPINION ON FITZGERALD'S WILL

Have looked up your point in the library this afternoon and the result of my researches, for what they are worth, is that it certainly has been held again and again, where a certain person's consent to marriage was required and that person had died by act of God, or at least by no fault of the beneficiary, the condition requiring a particular consent is void.

None of the cases run the thing so fine that there is only twenty-four hours between the death of the person whose consent is required and the wedding of the beneficiary who wants an absolute title to the property, and I think it would be necessary, where the death is within twenty-four hours of the ceremony, for the beneficiary, in order to get her absolute right, if there were any contest, to show:

Either (1) That she intended to ask the necessary consent before the marriage ceremony;

(2) That she was prevented by death, and would have had time to ask consent but for the death;

and (3) If suggested that the death was any fault of hers, to defend herself against the allegation;

or else That the ceremony was not arranged until after death had made it impossible to obtain the necessary consent. Provided this last is true, it matters not how soon after the death the beneficiary claims to treat the condition as void.

As to the last possibility, I am no authority on marriage licences, but from the books it appears that provided one party has resided *fifteen* days *in the locality in which it is intended the marriage should take place*, notice may be given to the registrar by that party and a marriage licence obtained from the registrar after the lapse of one full week-day – in law language in forty-two to forty-eight hours, provided Sunday does not intervene.

This procedure is applicable to marriages in any other place than the established church, i.e., registrar's office, or Nonconformist place of worship licensed for marriages.

Without the fifteen days of previous residence the business takes longer.

Once obtained a marriage licence is available for quite a long time: three months I think, but you might verify this. It is possible that one of your parties had got a licence and was waiting for a favourable opportunity for the beneficiary to ask the necessary consent. This sort of licence is only granted for marriage in a particular place. See Whitaker.

In the case of conditions, subsequent, if the condition is impossible through the act of God, the gift remains, tho' there may be a gift over on non-performance of the condition. *For instance, if the person whose consent to a marriage is required dies before the marriage.*

Collett v. Collett. 35. B. 312.

In this case the widowed mother's consent to marriage was required. The mother died in 1856.

In July, 1865, her daughter Helena married.

Master of the Rolls held 'that the gift over (i.e., to remainder man in case of life tenancy only) will not take effect, if the performance of the condition has become impossible thro' the act of God, and *no default of the person who had to perform it.*

'Here it is reasonably certain that the mother, if she had lived, would have given her consent to this marriage, one eligible in all respects.'

The principle is the presumption of the testator not requiring the performance of impossibilities, and that his intention will be substantially carried into effect by permitting it to be executed as far as can be done.

'The condition having become impossible by act of God, her estate for life is become absolute.' *Aislabie v. Rice*. 3 Mad. 25 C.

MYSTERIOUS PRESS—

the exciting new crime imprint from Arrow Books

☐ A CAST OF KILLERS	Sidney Kirkpatrick	£2.95
☐ ROUGH CIDER	Peter Lovesey	£2.50
☐ WEXFORD: AN OMNIBUS	Ruth Rendell	£5.95
☐ WOLF TO THE SLAUGHTER	Ruth Rendell	£2.50
☐ KILL ZONE	Loren Estleman	£2.50
☐ MOONSPENDER	Jonathan Gash	£2.50
☐ HARE SITTING UP	Michael Innes	£2.50
☐ THE JUNKYARD DOG	Robert Campbell	£2.50
☐ THE COST OF SILENCE	Margaret Yorke	£2.50
☐ THE GONDOLA SCAM	Jonathan Gash	£2.50
☐ PEARLHANGER	Jonathan Gash	£2.50

ARROW BOOKS, BOOKSERVICE BY POST, PO BOX 29, DOUGLAS, ISLE OF MAN, BRITISH ISLES

NAME ....

ADDRESS ....

....

....

Please enclose a cheque or postal order made out to Arrow Books Ltd. for the amount due and allow the following for postage and packing.

U.K. CUSTOMERS: Please allow 22p per book to a maximum of £3.00.

B.F.P.O. & EIRE: Please allow 22p per book to a maximum of £3.00.
OVERSEAS CUSTOMERS: Please allow 22p per book.

Whilst every effort is made to keep prices low it is sometimes necessary to increase cover prices at short notice. Arrow Books reserve the right to show new retail prices on covers which may differ from those previously advertised in the text or elsewhere.